CRYSTAL HOPE

CRYSTAL DRAGON SAGA, BOOK 2

KATIE CHERRY

BOOKS BY KATIE CHERRY

The Crystal Dragon Saga

Rising from Dust: Companion novella

* * *

Crystal Dragon
Crystal Hope
Crystal Lies
Crystal Curse - June 24, 2020
Crystal Allegiance - July 29, 2020
Crystal Fate - August 26, 2020
Crystal War - September 24, 2020

* * *

Crystal Dragon Saga Boxed Set: Books 1-3

The Dragon Blood Trilogy

Dragon Blood
Dragon Soul
Dragon Heart

PROLOGUE

As the tears drip from Janet's eyes, the skies above open in their downpour as well, seeming to join in the couple's sorrow. The rain begins to soak Janet's' long hair, but she remains seated on the old bench in the park, sniffling. Her husband, Dave, doesn't bother attempting to console her, knowing she wouldn't respond to it well. Instead, he simply removes his coat, draping it over her shaking shoulders. His vest is thick and warm, but isn't waterproof. Soon the soggy article of clothing clings to him, but still he patiently waits.

Finally, she turns to him, teary-eyed. "Dave?" she begins, her voice quivering.

"Yes, dear?"

"Do… do you think that the obstetrician could have been wrong?"

He hesitates, knowing that no matter what he says, it will be the wrong response. "Well…"

"I mean, I know we haven't been able to have a child yet, but surely… surely I'm not infertile?"

"I don't know, darling," he sighs. "I know that you want children, but…"

She continues as if she hadn't heard him. "I mean, we've been married for five years… maybe she was right… maybe I just can't get pregnant…" she sobs. "Dave, what are we going to do?!"

"Janet, if you really want children that bad, we can always adopt…"

She stands abruptly, Dave's coat sliding off her back and splashing back onto the bench. He sighs and patiently retrieves the coat. "No! I don't want to adopt! Those are all *other* people's children! They would never really be *mine!*"

"Sweetheart, you know that's the only other option."

"No!" she cries, desperation in her voice as she stares at his face. "No, I can't be infertile! I can have kids! We just... we just have to try again..."

Dave sighs and turns his face to the heavens, growing exasperated. "Janet..."

"No! Don't *Janet* me! There has to be another option! I don't want to adopt some random child!"

"Janet, just give it a shot... if you look at all of them and you don't receive any... *signs* that you should adopt them, I'll let it go."

She pauses, looking at him with glittering brown eyes. "Fine. I'll adopt a baby if I have a sign that I should do so."

He lets out his breath in relief. "Good. Now then, can we go home?"

"Of course," she agrees, and they hurry to walk the last block to their apartment complex.

Dave slips the key into the lock and ushers his wife into the room, shutting the door behind him. They both freeze at the sight of a baby on their table.

"What the..." Dave hurries over and scoops up the small child. "Where did she come from?"

"How should I know?" Janet asks, coming over to peer at the baby. "Maybe she was... a gift?"

He looks at her like she's insane. "A gift. From who?"

"How should I know? Maybe it's a practical joke."

"Who would want to prank us?" He wonders.

"Maybe they just got the wrong room, and it was meant for someone else!" she groans wearily. "Either way, you should just take it to the manager's office. Maybe he knows."

The baby stirs in his arms, stretching and yawning. "Alright, fine. I'll be right back." he sighs, opening the door. He carefully makes his way down the old wooden stairs to the manager's office. He knocks.

"It's open," comes the call from within. He eases the door open. "Why Mr. Shay...is there something wrong?" The manager asks, eyeing the child in his arms through his thick glasses. "Why did you bring a baby down here?"

"That's exactly what's wrong," he sighs, sinking into the chair on the other side of the old manager's desk. "I just got home, and someone apparently left this baby in my apartment... Janet and I were wondering if you know who it was."

The manager leans towards him, his arms resting on his potbelly as he inspects the baby. As he does so, she reaches out and grabs his large nose, giggling. Grunting, he pulls back. "I've never seen her before."

"Well did you see anyone go up to the second floor in the past hour or so?"

"No. You are the only one on the second floor to arrive since you left. No one has been up there."

Dave freezes. "What? What do you mean... no one's been up there since we left?" He pulls the baby's hand back as she reaches for some crystals on the manager's desk.

The manager sighs and leans back in his office chair. It creaks as more weight is put on the back of the chair. "Yes, that's what I said, isn't it? Now go on. I'll alert the authorities. I'm sure you two can take care of her until they locate the parents," he says as he yawns, then scratches his bald spot on the crown of his head.

"But..."

"I said, get!"

Dave sighs, gets to his feet, and tugs open the door, letting it swing shut behind him. He lifts the child in his arms up to his face. "What am I going to do with you now?" She pokes his nose and coos. He smiles a little, then sighs and returns to his apartment.

"Why is she still here?" Janet demands when he walks into the room.

"He didn't know where she came from either. He says no one's been up here since we left."

She groans and plops into her chair at the table, letting her head rest on her hand. "Of course, he doesn't. Now we have no idea where to return this baby. What are we going to do with her?"

Dave hesitates. "We could always keep her."

"No. No way. We have no idea where she came from! What if we got in trouble with the police or something?"

"Janet, I'm sure it will be fine. If anything like that happens, we'll deal with it then. For now, this poor girl has nowhere to go, and we can't exactly throw her out on the streets!"

"Well... I suppose..."

"Besides, if her just showing up in our apartment isn't a sign, I don't know what is."

"Fine," she submits.

"Now then... what are we going to call her?" he wonders.

"I think it should be a pretty name," Janet declares, standing beside him and peering at the baby, who stares inquisitively back.

"Hmm... what about Crystal?" he suggests. "I noticed she seemed to like the crystals in the manager's office," he explains.

"Oh, that's a gorgeous name!" she gushes. "It's perfect." She gently takes the baby from Dave and smiles down at her.

"Welcome to the family, Crystal Shay."

1

The bus jolts as it goes over another pothole in the road, throwing Nathan Anderson straight into the back of the worn-out seat in front of him. He groans, rubbing his nose with his hand to try and get the pain to go away. A girl sitting behind him giggles and puts a gentle hand on his shoulder. He turns to see who it is and comes face to face with one of the prettiest girls he'd ever seen. He takes in a deep breath as his eyes discern her curled honey-brown hair and her sparkling hazel eyes that are made even more stunning by the subtle purple eyeshadow on her eyelids. She blinks, and Nathan realizes that her eyelashes sparkle a little in the faint morning light as the sun creeps slowly upward in the sky.

"Oh... I... Hi," he stammers, unsure of what to say.

She laughs again, then bites her lower lip gently and lowers her eyes. "I'm sorry, I didn't mean to laugh," she says apologetically, slowly looking back up at Nathan with a soft smile.

"Oh, I... N-no problem," he manages to get out, trying not to stare at her red lips as she talks. He clears his throat. "Was... was there something you wanted to say to me?"

She smiles. "Yes... I was just going to ask if you were new here. You don't seem to be used to the bus, plus I hadn't seen you last year."

"Oh... yeah, I am. I just moved in a few weeks ago."

"Oh, you moved in? Where from?"

"Tanguay, Sicillago," he replies, watching warily for her response.

"Really?" Her eyes light up with excitement, and she tilts her head to one side as if inspecting him. "That's really cool! So you lived with the rich people? I bet you had all kinds of technology that we don't have here... that's why you're not used to the bus, right? Because you had flying cars there?" She continues before he can reply. "Where do you live now?"

"Walnut Creek Drive, here in Pargunma," he replies. The girl's smile grows even wider.

"I only live a street away from there!" she exclaims. "You should come over to my house some time!"

"Yeah, sure," Nathan replies, surprised at her forwardness. "Maybe sometime this week... I'll have to check with my mom to make sure it's okay first, though."

"Oh, of course! My name's Angela, by the way. Angela Dove."

"Nathan Anderson," he says as the bus stops at a red light.

"So what did you..." she starts to say until a scaly red hand punches through the window next to her, sending shards of glass cascading over her. Screaming, she raises her arms above her head and scoots away from the window. The bus driver doesn't seem to notice what's going on as he waits for the light to turn green, humming to himself.

Nathan watches as an ugly red face appears in the window, sneering at him. Its eyes are yellow with pupils that are slits, like a cat's. Its nose is very small and is raised only slightly from its face. Its nostrils are just small slits in the skin, but they flare open as it breathes in deep, leaning closer to Nathan. Without thinking, he punches it right in the middle of its face. It doesn't flinch, but his hand is now searing with pain and his knuckles are bloody. The scaly beast laughs at him and reaches its hand in through the window. Nathan scoots back.

What does this thing want? And where did it come from? He wonders as it gropes around. He tries to kick the hand, but the creature is faster and grabs his ankle. He attempts to pull free, but its grip is too tight. With another wicked cackle, it pulls him out of the window, breaking more glass. He hears Angela scream again and the other kids shouting, but it all fades into the background as he focuses on figuring out how to get away from the creature.

It starts dragging him away from the bus as it pulls through the intersection. He distantly hears Angela screaming his name and shouting at the bus driver to stop. "Let... me... go!" Nathan shouts at the creature. It doesn't respond except to tighten its grip and haul him away a little faster.

He's lost as to what to do for a moment, but then he smiles as he remembers the ring in his pocket. Nathan pulls out the gold and silver band and slips it on, instantly becoming intangible and sliding through the creature's grasp. He stands and laughs as the creature turns and rushes at him, arms outstretched. It races right through him, its head passing through Nathan's heart, then spins around, looking confused and angry. It charges again, with the same results. It narrows its eyes at Nathan as if hoping to see what kind of trick he's pulling.

Nathan glares back at it, his arms crossed. "Tell me, creature, who sent you?"

The creature glares at him and bares its pointed yellow teeth. "...No one sent."

"Tell the truth. I know someone had to send you." The thing shakes its head. Frustrated, Nathan then notices another one, more pink than red, emerge from a bush nearby.

It peers up at him inquisitively. "Yep, we was sent by someone. We too stupid to think up this wonderful plan by just us!"

Nathan looks at the creature in astonishment. The red one looks at the pink one, shocked as well. "You no tell human that! We was told to lie to him, remember?"

"Oh, yeah! Sorry, Gorldf."

Gorldf snarls at the pink one. "Rosulkip, you so dumb!"

"Yep!" she agrees, peeling back her lips in what must be an attempt at a smile. Shaking his head in confusion, Nathan decides to try and get some answers from the pink one since it seems to be more willing to talk.

"Rosulkip, you aren't dumb!" he begins, hoping to flatter the beast. "You are a very, very smart... thing... person."

Rosulkip looks confused. "Is... is smart good thing?"

"Oh, yes! It's a very good thing!" he assures it. Rosulkip beams.

"Rosulkip very, very smart!" It grins and starts dancing around in a circle. "Smart, smart, smart..." Nathan can't help but crack a smile. *It's like a little kid*, he thinks.

"Rosulkip, who sent you to find me? ...Um... because I want to tell them how very, very smart you are," he tells her.

"Don't tell him!" Gorldf snarls at the pink creature. It ignores him, thankfully.

"Zarafa, of course!"

"Zarafa? Who is that?"

This time, Gorldf tackles Rosulkip before it could say anything else. "It is no one," it growls at Nathan.

"It? Is… it… human?"

"Yep, yep! Well… not exactly…" Rosulkip peeps before Gorldf stops her.

Gorldf scowls at Rosulkip. "Shut up, Rosulkip, or I'll kill you." Rosulkip's thin, pale grey lips snap shut at the threat, although it doesn't look happy about it. Gorldf turns back to Nathan, undisguised hatred on its face. "We be back," it sneers, snapping its clawed fingers. With a puff of smoke that smells to Nathan a lot like rotten eggs, the creatures disappear.

Nathan sighs and pulls off the Matter Ring. He has no clue who this 'Zarafa' is or why they seem to be out to get him, but he has other concerns at the moment. He missed the bus, and that meant he had to run in order to get to school on time. He didn't want to be late on the first day.

Twenty minutes later, Nathan arrives at the school, panting and sweating. He looks around through the crowd of teenagers, hoping to find the bus so he could get his backpack. Finally spotting the worn number eighty-five, he jogs over. He knocks on the doors and the bus driver lets him on. The old man smiles at him with his twinkling blue-grey eyes. "Yes, sonny?" he asks him, acting like nothing out of the ordinary happened just a few minutes before.

Nathan clears his throat uncertainly. The bus driver seemed nice enough… but you never can tell who wants to help and who wants you dead. And since the bus driver hadn't even stopped when Nathan was snatched, it seemed more likely that he wasn't a good guy.

"I think I left my backpack in here."

"Hmm, I seem to recall that the girl you were talking to took it so she could get it back to you. I would go find her."

"Oh… thanks," Nathan says, confused, as he turns to leave. He feels a heavy hand on his shoulder before he steps off. His breath catches in fear.

"Be careful."

"Of… of course…"

"T. Call me T."

"Okay… thanks, T."

"No problem, kiddo. I'll see you later. You might want to hurry to class now," he suggests, removing his hand from Nathan's shoulder. Nathan jumps off the bus, relieved to get away from the weird bus driver. He glances at his watch. His first class was going to start in two minutes.

~

He bursts through the door about ten seconds after the tardy bell rang, drawing the attention of everyone in the classroom. Nathan lowers his head and starts to slink to the back of the room, but is stopped by his teacher, Mrs. Sternile. Her shrill voice freezes him in his tracks. "Stop right there!" she demands. Gulping, he turns around to face her. Only one inch taller than him in her two-inch heels, she's quite intimidating. Her brunette hair pinned up in a tight bun, her business-like attire and her thin lips, pinched tight together with disappointment, reflect her no-nonsense attitude. Nathan takes a tiny step back.

"Name?" she demands.

"N… Nathan Anderson," he stammers.

She repeats this into the tablet in her hand, then turns back to face the class. "I do not tolerate tardiness in my class, Mr. Anderson," she scolds. "Starting today, every time one of you is tardy to my class, your name will be recorded in my tablet. For every tardy after that, I will put a tally mark by your name. For every mark I put, ten points will be deducted from your grade. After the first three, each mark will take twenty-five, fifty, seventy-five, and finally, one hundred. Mr. Anderson, I am giving you one tally for being late on the first day and taking so much time from the class."

He bites back a complaint and just nods. "Now then, please find a seat so we can begin." She walks back to her desk, her heels clicking on the hard floor. Nathan saunters slowly over the shiny black floor to a desk in the corner of the room, aware that every pair of eyes in the room followed him there. He sighs. *This is going to be a long year,* he decides, leaning back in his chair and closing his eyes.

The teacher starts her lecture, but Nathan isn't listening. His mind is far away, in a land where trees sing, and grass dances with a girl who saved his life countless times, although she would never admit it. He smiles a little as he watches as she dances in the snow, laughing, her blue-gold eyes shining with mirth as she teases him and laughs... He sighs, feeling a pang in his chest.

It had been almost four months since he last saw Crystal Dragon, and he was starting to really miss her. She was his first thought when he awoke in the morning and the last thing he sees before he falls asleep at night; she was a part of him that was missing. She was his best friend.

"Mr. Anderson!"

Nathan bolts upright, flinging his eyes open to find the teacher standing in front of him and everyone in the class watching him and laughing. He swallows hard. "Y... yes, Mrs. Sternile?"

"Pay attention, Mr. Anderson. I am deducting another ten points from your participation grade. Unless you can tell me what I was just talking about?" He shakes his head ashamedly. Nodding, the teacher walks briskly back to the front of the classroom and resumes her lecture.

Nathan sighs and rests his head on his hand and pretends to pay attention, but he sees something in the corner of his vision. Turning, he sees Angela a few desks away from him, waving to get his attention. He blushes, wondering how long she had been doing that before he noticed. He raises his eyebrows at her, asking what she wanted. She bites her lip, thinking, then pulls out her trans-tablet and the e-pen that goes with it and starts writing. He watches as she does so, confused and curious. She puts it on the floor once she's finished and it turns into a mouse and scurries over to him. He picks it up, and it returns to normal. *Oh, she wants to talk to me... I guess passing notes would be the best thing to do with this teacher. As long as we don't get caught.*

Nathan,

Oh my goodness! Are you okay? What happened with that ugly creature? Why did it take you? How did you get away? Is your hand okay? It's bleeding a lot! Oh, and I have your backpack. I guess I can't get it to you until after class, is that okay?

He smiles a little at her concern. He picks up the e-pen and writes a reply.

Angela,

I'm okay. I don't know what that creature wanted from me, but it wasn't too diffi-cult to get away from it. It was really stupid. All I had to do was tell it that I was the wrong person and it left... my hand is fine, it's just a little blood. I can still move it without much pain. And thank you for grabbing my backpack! I'm glad it wasn't lost somewhere on the bus with that weird bus driver. ...By the way, can I sit with

10

you at lunch? I don't know anyone else in this school yet… if you don't want me to, though, that's fine too.

Putting the trans-tablet on the ground, he pushes the mouse button, and it quickly scurries back to Angela with his reply. It comes back to him a minute later.

I'm so relieved you're okay! That was really lucky… and I think you should go to the nurse for your hand, still. Just to be safe. And of course you can sit with me at lunch! I should warn you, though… my friends are major flirts, so if you think you can take it, you're welcome to join us! :) …The teacher's watching. Talk to you later!

Thanks, Angela! See you then, he replies, then quickly sends the trans-tablet back while the teacher's back is turned.

The rest of the class is uneventful, and Nathan can't even try to concentrate on the lecture about Quazek history, so he daydreams and waits anxiously for the bell to ring. When it finally does, he quickly stands and heads toward Angela, feeling the teacher's eyes on him the entire time. Angela smiles at him and hands him his backpack, then starts heading towards the door. He follows her.

"What's your next class?" Nathan asks her.

She smiles. "Gym."

"Me too!"

"Really? Awesome! Now I may have some competition!"

"What do you mean by that?" he asks, curious.

She laughs. "No one can keep up with me when I run. I beat them all so easily it makes me feel like I'm alone. But you got here really quickly—not too long after the bus did, in fact—so I assume that you can run pretty fast."

He grins. "Yeah, you could say that. Although I haven't run full-out for a few months…"

"Mmhmm," she murmurs teasingly. "That's just your excuses so it won't look so bad when you get shown up by a girl!"

"What? No, it's true!" Nathan replies, laughing as well. "I just jogged here this morning, I wasn't sprinting. I just used some shortcuts."

"Uh huh."

"Whatever. I guess I'll just have to show you in person."

Angela smiles charmingly at him. "I would love that," she replies, her eyes sparkling. He suddenly gets butterflies in his stomach. *Why… why does she make me feel like this? I don't get it… I was less nervous visiting dragons in Zilferia!* He shakes it off. *First thing's first. This girl needs to get humbled!*

~

"Ready?"

"I was born ready," he replies to Angela's taunt.

She laughs. "Then don't cry when the inevitable happens, and I win. … After all, you were born ready to be defeated!"

Nathan laughs in reply. "Good one, but I'm not going down."

"We'll see…"

The gym teacher and cross-country coach, Jim Hefferson, walks up to the group of kids with a hearty smile. "Angela has pulled me aside to request another race." Half the class groans, but Nathan grins. "After the race, you may play basketball or tennis." The kids cheer up at this. Nathan's smile deepens. He had spent a majority of the summer running and playing sports such as tennis to spend some time out of his head and had become rather skilled at tennis. "Alright, everyone line up! We're going for a mile today. Four laps, then you're done."

Nathan crouches next to Angela in the front of the class. She smiles at him. "Good luck."

"Won't need it," he replies, turning back to the track. He takes a few deep breaths to prepare himself.

"Alright, on 'go,'" Jim says, standing next to them, his hands on his hips. "One… two… three… go!"

Nathan and Angela take off. Nathan quickly starts pulling ahead of her. Two minutes later, however, she pulls up beside him, smiling. He gets flustered and stumbles. She pulls ahead, laughing as she runs. Growling, he picks up the pace and catches back up to her. He stays on her tail for a while, then pulls up even with her again. He taps her on the shoulder. "Hey," he says, then laughs and pushes even harder toward the finish line. He's almost there when Angela overtakes him and crosses first, with him just a split second behind. The teacher jogs over, laughing.

"Well done, son! I've never seen anyone so close to Angela in a race! You're amazing, kid."

"Thanks," Nathan pants, his hands on his knees. He then looks up and glares at Angela. "But I… should have… won."

She giggles and shakes her head, panting as well. "I warned… him, coach, I really… did!"

He laughs. "I'm sure you did, Angela, but a guy like him doesn't back down from a challenge like that! ...What's your name, kid?" He asks.

"Nathan Anderson."

"Well, you're welcome to join cross-country, Nathan. We could use someone like you."

"Well, I did... Track and Field at my last school... but I don't know about... cross-country."

The coach winks at him. "I'm sure you'd do great, Nathan. I'll let you think about it. If you want to come, there's a meeting in my room on Monday right after school for those interested in joining. Just think about it, alright?" He says, patting Nathan on the back. The coach then starts to walk away. "Oh," he adds. "And Angela is the queen at tennis... just so you know. In case you wanted to get her back," he adds, chortling.

Nathan glances at Angela. "Well? Feel up to a game of tennis?"

She chuckles. "I'll take you on any time, anywhere, Monster Slayer!"

"Monster Slayer? I told you, all I did was talk to it!"

"Sure, but Monster Slayer sounds better, doesn't it?" she winks. "Well, come on, then! Looks like you still need some humbling!"

"We'll see who gets humbled this time!" he retorts, following her onto the court.

"You want to serve?"

"Nah, ladies first."

She grins. "Alright, then—but you asked for it." She tosses the ball in the air. It seems to fall in slow-motion. Nathan tightens his grip on the racket. She hits the ball. It soars down the court so quickly Nathan can hardly see it. Gritting his teeth, he whacks the ball back to her. It flies past her right leg, barely missing it.

The class goes quiet, staring at him. Everyone stops what they're doing and rush over to watch the game. Angela's smile disappears. Narrowing her eyes at him, she prepares to serve again. Nathan watches her eyes. They flick over to his right once, briefly, but it's enough—he now knows where she's aiming. He crouches, preparing for the serve. The ball screams down the court. Everyone gasps, thinking that he'll miss it for sure. He quickly whacks the ball back over the net. This time, Angela is ready for his return. She hits it back, sending it to the far side of the court. Nathan takes three large bounds and manages to hit the ball. It buries itself in the net. A small smile starts to creep back onto Angela's face as she prepares to serve again.

The game goes on for another half an hour. Nathan is a little ahead- one more point, and he wins the game. Taking a deep breath, he tosses the ball in the air, watching it fall in slow motion before sending it into the corner of the box. Angela dives for it, but misses. The crowd erupts into cheers as Angela crashes to her knees, exhausted. She had been defeated for the first time in almost five years. She looks up at Nathan, disbelief in her eyes. He walks over to her and helps her up.

"Good game," she says, not sounding happy about it.

He laughs. "You were amazing, Angela. I was lucky. You are the best tennis player I think I have ever seen."

"Besides you," he sighs, but she's starting to smile again as well.

"Well done!" the coach says as he walks over to them. "You are an astounding tennis player! Even better than the tennis coach... not that I'm going to tell him that," he adds to the laughter of the class. "If you don't come to cross-country, then you should definitely join the tennis team." Their classmates all agree.

Angela pipes up. "I'm in both. You should join at least one of them so I can keep kicking your butt!" she says, drawing more laughter from the crowd. Nathan smiles.

"Maybe."

"Come on, it will be fun!" Angela says.

"Alright. I'll have to tell my mom when they meet, though."

"Cross-country meets on Tuesdays and Thursdays, right after school," Jim Hefferson announces. "Until about five o'clock."

"And tennis is on Wednesdays and Fridays," Angela adds. "Also from five until seven o'clock. And both start next week."

Nathan smiles, feeling included and accepted already. "I'll be there."

After filling his tray with food, Nathan looks around the crowded lunch-room, searching for Angela. He finally spots her at a large table. Every chair is filled, except for the one to her left. What stands out to Nathan the most, however, is that the table is full of cheerleaders, all dressed up in their uniforms for the assembly after lunch. He swallows. *So this is what she meant,* he realizes as he walks toward them. The girls look up as he approaches.

"So, this is Nathan?" A girl with short brunette hair says, tilting her head to the side and examining him. After a few seconds, she nods, satisfied. He sighs with relief and sits down. The girls all start talking at once, leaning towards him, their eyes bright with curiosity.

After a few minutes, Angela is able to quiet them down. "One at a time, girls!" she exclaims. She turns to Nathan apologetically. "I'm so sorry. I should have warned them first."

"Oh… no, it's okay…"

"They just want to get to know you," she explains.

"Tell us what happened on the bus!" One of them squeals. Her hair is short and white, with pink highlights.

"I… I think Angela can tell you about that," he says.

"She did," another one sighs. "We want to hear it from *you.*"

"Oh… I suppose…" So he tells them his own version of what happened like he had with Angela, enjoying the rapt attention from his audience.

"Wow," the one with the short white and pink hair whispers. "You were so brave!"

"Yeah, I can't believe you punched it in the face!"

"You were so smart!"

"I would have been so freaked out!"

"That thing sounds so gross!"

Nathan laughs. "It was nothing, really. I was just lucky, plus it was really dumb."

"You were still really brave and smart," the girls insist.

The bell rings. Nathan looks down at his uneaten burger and sighs. He stands up. "I need to go to class," he says, grabbing his burger and dumping the rest in the trash.

"Bye, Nathan!" the girls squeal, waving to him. Smiling, he waves back, then starts walking to class, wolfing down his burger at the same time.

Come on, come on, come on… yes! Finally! Nathan thinks as the final bell rings at long last, releasing them from school. He grabs his backpack and heads to the bus. Partway there, though, he gets attacked. Again. This time, it's a group of guys rather than a strange creature, although that doesn't make them any less dangerous.

The biggest one shoves Nathan against a wall. His head smacks against it. He can feel blood start trickling down his neck. "What… what do you want?" he asks, his eyes darting back and forth, sizing them up. There are six of them, and they don't look happy. They all look like football players, big and strong.

The one holding him against the wall then punches him in the gut, causing him to double over in pain, eyes watering. "I don't know what you did to get those girls to like you, but you need to cut it out. Angela's mine, got it?" Confused, Nathan nods anyway. The six sneer at him. "Good. Now hurry and go catch your bus—looks like it's leaving."

Nathan turns quickly to see that what the big guy said was true. He takes off running, the six bullies laughing at him. He catches up to the bus just before it pulls into the road. He knocks on the door and the driver opens it, winking at him. Confused, Nathan gives him a small smile and collapses into an empty seat. The bus pulls out, rumbling and shaking as it chugs slowly along down the road, nearly the only vehicle doing so. Glancing up at the vehicles soaring quietly overhead, Nathan sighs a little to himself, already feeling envy well in his chest. *This bus is ancient. How did I get stuck in one of the only cities to still function while clinging to the past?*

Angela plops down beside him, breaking him from his thoughts. "What happened?" she asks, concern dancing in her eyes as she notices him wincing in pain. He tells her, and she frowns in response. "That was Jake and his posse… I'm so sorry. He's such a jerk. Oh! You're bleeding!" She gently touches the back of his head. He winces. "Sorry!" she gasps, looking at the blood on her hand. "Hey, it's a good thing mom got me a medi-bot, right?"

Relieved, Nathan nods. "Mine's at home, still packed away." She smiles and pulls the tiny robot out of her backpack and pokes its chest. It wakes up and immediately gets to work, climbing all over Nathan's body. It drips something from a tiny green vial onto his knuckles, which are instantly healed and the blood washed away. It does the same thing to his head. When it gets to his stomach, however, it tilts its head and makes a whirring sound as if it's thinking. Then it just shrugs and climbs back into Angela's backpack and shuts off.

"Hmm. I guess we can't do anything for your stomach... but that shouldn't last too long, right?"

He nods. "Yeah, hopefully. Thanks, Angela."

She shrugs. "It's no big deal."

They sit quietly for a while. "Are you still going to come over to my house sometime this week?" she asks.

He chuckles. "Sure, if you want me to."

"Even with Jake being—"

"A jerk? Sure. I could take him if I wanted to anyway." She looks at him with disbelief and admiration. Then she laughs.

"You're crazy."

He smiles at her. "Maybe. We'll have to see... this is my stop. I'll see you later."

"I sure hope so," she says, grinning as he gets off the bus. He stands on the sidewalk watching the bus until he couldn't see it anymore. He sighs, then heads into his house.

"Mom, I'm home!" he calls.

"Nathan!" his grandma exclaims, hobbling up the stairs. "You're finally home!"

He laughs. "Yeah, it's been a pretty long day."

"Oh?" she says, raising a grey eyebrow. "Was it that bad? It looks like you had an adventure to me! Look at all that blood in your hair and on your sleeve and pants!" she says sarcastically, touching her own curly, silvery-grey hair. Nathan laughs and tells her about his day while she makes him a snack. His grandma Beryl is the only one in his family who would believe him about the red and pink creatures, so she's the only one he tells about them— and what they told him.

"Hmm... sounds like you're in for a new adventure here at home!" she laughs, handing him the snack.

"As if being a Junior at High School wasn't bad enough!" Nathan complains jokingly, wolfing down the food.

"Oh, come now! You thought that the Games were going to be worse than they actually were, now didn't you?" Nathan frowns, remembering his trip to Zilferia. As far as he's concerned, the only good thing that happened because of that was meeting Crystal, Ham, and Sierra.

"I... suppose. The merfolk weren't as bad as we thought, and neither were the dragons, but that's just because of Crystal. Now it's just me..."

"So? Don't you have two Gifts that can help you now? As well as that Matter Ring and the Lightning shoes... and let's not forget about Greg!"

"Oh! Greg! Where is he?"

Beryl laughs. "Probably out terrorizing the neighborhood cats again. You know him. He'll be back for dinner, I'm sure." Nathan laughs as well, picturing the rat chasing cats down the street, howling and screeching.

"Yeah, you can always count on him to be on time for dinner," he chuckles. "So where's mom?"

"Picking your father up from his interview."

"And Anna?"

"Your mother picked her up from preschool first. They'll be home soon..." As she says this, he hears the garage door open. She smiles. "See? What did I say? Now then, let's go see if your father got the job!"

The door opens, and the tall frame of John Parker Anderson fills the doorway. He catches sight of his son and rushes forward, grabbing him and giving him a noogie before he can get away. He's laughing... until he notices the blood on his hand. He releases Nathan and inspects his head. "What happened?" he asks, his deep voice booming with concern.

"Oh... just a bully at school," Nathan replies. "It's nothing to worry about. ...So did you get the job?"

"Yes, sir! You're looking at the newest engineer at Theriosk, starting tomorrow!"

"Daddy's an end-in-ear?" A small voice squeals, confused.

His mom laughs and picks little Anna up, tucking her long brown hair behind her ear. "No, daddy makes those little robots you play with. Can you say engineer, Anna?"

"En... gin... eer?"

Nathan smiles. "Good job, Anna! That's right!"

The little five-year-old beams with pride. "I can say Engineer! Daddy's a Engineer!"

"Alright," Nathan's mom sighs, setting Anna down and heading into the kitchen. "I guess I should start on dinner. Nathan, how was your day, dear?"

"It was... great, mom."

"Did you make a lot of friends?"

"Yeah.."

"And how many of them were girls?" she asks teasingly.

"All of them. Unless you count the gym teacher."

She laughs. "That's fine… but you should try to make some *guy* friends tomorrow, okay?"

"Sure mom. One of my new friends lives near here... She invited me over to her house. Is that okay?"

"You're going to study, right?" She glances at him as she ties on an apron, one eyebrow raised.

Nathan drops his gaze to his hands, fighting a knowing smile. *I highly doubt we'll be studying. Especially on the second day of school.* "Yeah, sure, of course, mom."

"That should be fine. Are you going tomorrow?"

"Yeah, right after school."

"Were you going to stay for dinner? I won't be home until late."

"Uh, yeah, I'm sure that will be fine. Thanks, mom!"

"Mmhmm… now go do your homework, okay? Dinner will be ready in a bit."

"Okay," he says, running up to his room, feeling better than he had in days. *Tomorrow's going to be great,* Nathan thinks, a smile settling on his face.

2

My alarm goes off, startling me. I leap out of bed and slam my hand down on it, turning the loud, annoying noise off. I breathe. Sitting back down on my bed, I let the breath I just took in escape in a rush. *Great. School's starting again... this is going to be horrible. Much worse than talking to vicious merfolk and hoping they won't actually eat me. Teenagers... can be just as vicious- if not more so.* With another sigh, I make my tired body stand and start getting dressed. Grabbing my backpack, I head to the kitchen to grab some food before I catch the bus.

I munch on an English muffin and stand at my bus stop, alone. A soft, cool breeze slips through the air, and the grey sky overhead seems to match my sullen mood. I am anything but excited to start school again. School has never been a great experience for me, and with my self-esteem at an all-time low, the bullying will only be more difficult to put up with. The bus then rolls up and I climb on, sliding into the seat directly behind the bus driver. I stare out the window and ignore everything around me.

When we get to the next bus stop, I'm startled when someone sits down in the seat with me. I look up to find a cute guy about my age, probably a senior, with blond hair, bright blue eyes, and a charming smile. My heart skips a beat.

"I'm sorry... should I sit somewhere else? You just seemed... lonely, I guess, so I thought..."

"You're fine," I say, turning and looking out the window again, ignoring him. *Keep your emotions under control, Crystal,* I order myself. *Remember what happened last time? Or what almost happened... Brandon was Hunter in disguise, and he would have kidnapped me had Vlad not gotten to me first... and things would have turned out very differently. I can't trust this guy. In fact, simply because he's being kind to me proves he's probably undercover for the Dragon Hunters. ...And I'm so not ready to go back there yet... I'm even more powerless now than before, since they took my Gifts... No. Stop it. Just stop thinking about it,* I order myself once I realize where my thoughts had been wandering.

I return my attention to the views outside of the bus. I can feel the guy's eyes on me. He's fishing for something to say. I roll my eyes. *Sometimes they try just a little too hard,* I laugh to myself. *This imposter is pretty good. Acting nervous. ...As if he actually... no, stop it. Stop trying to like him. He's obviously with the enemy.*

He clears his throat. "I... I'm Justin."

"Crystal," I grunt, not turning around or acknowledging him in any other way.

"So... are you a senior?"

"Junior."

"Oh. Okay, that's cool... Are you new here?"

"No."

I can tell my short answers and lack of cooperation are throwing him off track. He gets more flustered and confused. "I... um... are you happy about school starting again?"

"Nope."

"Why not?" I hesitate. I want a friend, I want one so badly... I almost decide to tell him. But no... I can't. I can't let him get inside my head. He's faking. He doesn't actually want to help me or get to know me, he just wants to kidnap me or something. So I eventually shrug and avoid the question. "Come on. You can tell me. I won't tell anyone else if it's a secret and you don't want me to. ...Everyone needs a friend, Crystal. Let me be your friend."

I swallow hard. *Surely... surely telling him won't hurt anything. They say to keep your enemies close, right? So maybe it's okay to at least pretend to give in...* Comforted by the thought, I decide to confide in him. "I... that's actually just it. I don't... have any friends. Everyone... everyone hates me or at least avoids me, and I don't really even know why..."

He cautiously lays a hand on my shoulder. "Well... you have a friend now, Crystal." I slowly turn and look up at him, hope fluttering in my heart despite my best efforts to refuse it entrance. *He's just playing with your emotions...* a small voice in the back of my head whispers. I smile a little to myself. *Then maybe let's play with his...* I lay my head on his shoulder. He stiffens, then relaxes. After about a minute, he slowly puts one of his hands on my head and starts smoothing down my hair, tucking strays behind my ear. Butterflies erupt in my stomach. I try to ignore them, but it's nearly impossible. I haven't been this close to a guy since Lloyd and I fell under the Hausdorff tree's spell back in Zilferia.

Before long, our journey is ended as the bus pulls up in front of the school. I find myself sad to have to leave my new friend, Justin; not to mention all the bullying. Sighing, I slowly get off the bus, stopping in the long, green grass to look up at the sky. There aren't many clouds today, but one of them looks a little like... a person... riding a dragon, with fire flying out of its mouth...

I shake my head, banishing the image. *That can't be good... I'm starting to see things with dragons... I really need to stop thinking about Zilferia. ...But my friends are in trouble,* I argue with myself, lowering my gaze from the sky to the building before me. *With the Dragon Hunters on the loose... with the Gift Stealer that I- stupidly- helped them fix... No. I need to go back to school. I can't help them anyway- I'm more powerless than they are.* I take a deep breath and walk into the school, pushing all thoughts of Zilferia from my head.

Heading to my first class, I have to squeeze between large groups of friends that always tend to form in the hallways and lobby. Someone shoves me. I keep walking. Something hits me in the back of the head- probably an eraser. I keep walking. Someone- one of the football players, I think- steps in front of me. "Where're you going, Blondie?" he mocks.

"To class," I mutter, trying to edge past him.

"Hear that?" he calls to his friends, who join him, blocking my way. "The dumb blonde wants to go to class!"

"Let me through," I snarl.

He laughs. "What's wrong, Blondie? Don't you *like* me?"

"Let me through," I repeat.

"Why? You gonna pay me to go through? There's a price to go through this hallway, ya know."

"No, there's not," I bite back. "I'm not a freshman, I know how things work around here. You can't haze me. Now let… me… go."

He laughs again. "Oh? Not a freshman? Just a dumb blonde, then… it's the same thing. Challenging a senior football player… it's not too smart," he says, to the appreciation of his friends. "Now pay up, or I guess you'll just be late to class…"

I frown, rage boiling up inside of me. I struggle to contain it. A fight won't be a good way to start the new school year. …But it's difficult to control, just as it has been ever since I got back from Zilferia. "Dude… back away. Now. Before I… hurt you."

"Hurt me? This little blonde chick thinks she can hurt me? Did you guys hear that?" he guffaws. His laughter is the last straw. I quickly kick him in a few choice weak spots, swing around behind him, and jam my finger into a nerve in his neck before pushing him to the ground. I turn away, leaving him momentarily crumpled behind me. As I resume walking, I can feel the weight of the stares of everyone in the lobby. I walk faster and duck into the math classroom.

I have never been so glad to be there in my entire life.

I eat alone at lunch again. Justin is eating with his friends and doesn't notice me, which makes me second-guess myself again. *Surely if he was working for the bad guys, he would be with me as much as possible… right? Since he's not, it makes it seem like he's an average guy- forgetting about me within a few hours… he'll probably talk to me on the bus again, though. If he really is an average guy, that is… which there's still no proof of.* I sigh and munch on the flavorless pizza slice, thinking about how much I just want to go home.

I watch as the football player from that morning walks into the room and scowls, searching the room for something. Me. He finally spots me and stomps over. I calmly sip my chocolate milk and wait for him. He slams his hands down on the table, hoping to startle or intimidate me. I slowly set down the milk and look up and him with a sly smile. "Yes?"

He gets flustered, suddenly unsure of himself from my lack of response. "I… I need to talk to you."

"Then talk," I invite, tilting my head to the side as if interested in what he has to say.

"You... you've got a lot of nerve, you know that?"

"Yeah, sure."

He shifts his feet, uncomfortable with my utter lack of concern. "I'm gonna make you pay for what you did this morning," he finally threatens.

I raise an eyebrow. "Really? And how will you do that? By initiating a fight- right in front of the principal?" He turns to see if he's really there. He is. The football player turns back around, scowling.

"I'll get you, Blondie, you can count on it," he says before stomping off to rejoin his friends. I sigh and dump the rest of my lunch in the trash and head to my next class. *Might as well get this over with,* I decide, again longing to go home.

Dragons are flying in the sky; so many that they block out the sun. One of them, a black one, is leading them. A person is riding it. The dragon flies unevenly, suddenly swinging to the right or the left once in a while before continuing on as it had before. The cluster swoops down above a small part of the Village, flames arcing from their mouths, setting buildings on fire. One of the dragons suddenly gets hit by lightning, and everything erupts into chaos; people flying around amid fire, water, and lightning. Dragons falling from the sky. People running, screaming... Dragons roaring, diving, and tearing with their mighty claws. Blood... blood is everywhere. Huge groups of people try to flee while others arrive to help. A voice booms amid the chaos, but it barely cuts through the noise. The dragons turn to escape the chaos with only one remaining- the leader. It spins in a circle, eyes searching the skies. It and the person riding it suddenly plummet toward the ground, but it pulls up at the last second. It fights an invisible foe. Its rider shouts and the man is revealed. The King looks up, panic written on his face as the dragon's snarling head comes closer.

"Crystal Shay!"

I gasp and look up from my notebook. "Y... yes, Mr. Quiler?"

"Pay attention, please."

"Y... yes, of course. Sorry. I was just... daydreaming. It won't happen again, sir."

"I trust that it will not," he warns before turning back to the board.

I sigh and slouch back into my chair, shaking my head to try and clear it. These 'daydreams' have been getting more and more frequent as well as clear and realistic. I take a deep breath and look down at my notebook. As I feared, I had written something that I was not aware of writing.

Return. The same message as the last time I had been caught off-guard by a vivid daydream of Zilferia. But what did it mean? Why... How did I write that- without even knowing what I was doing? Was someone trying to tell me something? Was it Gale? But how was that possible when Patrick had taken away my dragon part as well as my Gifts? Especially when I'm in a different realm?

Even if I could return to Zilferia, I had no way of getting there besides using my watch to ask Thaddeus or Vlad to make a portal for me. Although I couldn't do that anymore either.

My watch had been stolen.

~

"So, how was your day?"

I turn and find Justin walking up beside me in the hallway as I head to the bus. I can't help but be a little surprised. "I... uh... well, I don't know, it was a normal day, I suppose," I lie, avoiding telling him the truth.

"And what's a normal day like for Crystal?"

"Oh... you don't want to hear about it, I'm sure..."

"Oh, come on. I told you I would be here for you to talk to, so I expect you to take me up on it!" he says jokingly.

I chuckle. "Well..." I stop when I see the football player coming down the hallway. He spots me and walks faster, followed by his buddies. I gulp and turn a corner. Justin picks up his pace to keep up with me, looking surprised.

"What's wrong? The bus is the other way..."

"I know," I say, trying to act normal. "I just... um, forgot something in one of my classes. You can go ahead and get on the bus, don't wait for me."

He looks confused and unsure. I glance behind me and see the football players gaining. I walk faster. Justin has to nearly jog to keep up. "Are you sure you don't need help with anything? ...Why are we walking so fast?"

"No reason. I just... like walking fast." We come to a dead-end. I had been too preoccupied with getting away to realize that I had accidentally come down the hallway that leads to the janitor's closet. My breath catches with worry and I spin around. The football player sneers as he strolls down the corridor towards us.

"Dumb little blondie… trying to get away from me, eh? Too bad you weren't smart enough to pick a hallway that didn't have a dead end. Time to pay, girl."

"What's going on?" Justin asks, looking utterly lost.

I grimace. "I kinda… beat him up earlier today."

"Wait… you did *what?*"

"Time to pay for your mistake, Blondie," my foe announces, walking closer and cracking his knuckles menacingly. I frown, thinking quickly. Should I fight him, or try and run? I lost my Gift for fighting… but that doesn't mean that I can't stand up to a bully. I've been taking self-defense lessons since I was seven. As powerful or scary as this guy looked, I was someone that shouldn't be underestimated either. Dropping my things in the corner, I step forward to meet him as his friends make a loose circle around us, boxing Justin out. The football player grins and leans closer to me.

"I have your watch, by the way." His voice sends shivers racing down my spine. "I may not have any Gifts, but you don't anymore either… now I can show Patrick my worth and get into his inner circle and get my own insignia on my-" He stops suddenly and leans back, clearing his throat. "Uh, I didn't mean to say that much… Not that it will matter much for you anyway, Crystal… not after I take you back to him…"

I try to swallow back the painful memories of Patrick, but it's difficult… I duck as his fist flies through the air above my head as I duck. In my mind, I see the memories of Zilferia play though in fast forward, so vivid it is difficult to distinguish the past from the present. So I'm too slow to move aside as his fist connects with my jaw, sending me spinning backwards into the circle of boys, who shove me back into the center. They all begin cheering for him to hit me again. I move my tongue around my mouth and taste blood. I swallow and return my attention to the situation at hand.

Not a moment too soon, either. I pivot on one foot, and his fist glances off my shoulder. It burns a little. He's stronger than he looks. I crouch and prepare to fight back when I'm again caught off-guard by one of my vivid daydreams. *Not now!!* I plead. *ANY time but now!*

My vision becomes a mix of what's happening right now and my 'daydream.' The Dragon Hunter smirking at me. I crowd of people crying amid ashes and unmoving bodies. Justin's worried face as he reaches out to me. Flaming arrows screaming through the air, leaving a trail of burning black cloaks. A big pair of hands coming towards me menacingly. Someone sprinting away from the group of screaming people, face black with soot. A fist speeding toward my stomach. A huge explosion and maniacal laughter. Justin stepping toward me as I'm on my knees, holding my stomach with my hands. A group of dragons circling in the air. The dirty floor of the school. A black dragon flying towards the Dragon Hunters' castle with Hunter Dragon upon his back.

Finally, I see, hear, and feel nothing.

3

Feet pounding, Nathan tears down a dark hallway. He's alone in the cold, dark place. He runs into a wall and blood starts to pour from his nose. He continues to run, cradling a box in his arms. His wrists hurt, his nose hurts, his leg hurts, and his Familiar, Greg, is still nowhere to be found. Yet he continues onward anyway. Then he's forced to stop. He's come to a dead end. He turns as the noise of people running towards him echoes through the hallway. They've found him. And he has nowhere else to run.

Nathan sits upright in bed, gasping for air. He's dripping with sweat. He looks around the room, slowly realizing that it was just a dream. He falls back into bed and closes his eyes, trying to return his breathing to normal. He slowly falls back asleep.

The instant he does, however, his alarm-bot jumps onto his stomach and begins bouncing to wake him up. He groans. "I'm up, I'm up…"

The alarm-bot beeps once to warn him not to sleep in, then climbs back up to its spot on the dresser. His light turns on. Squinting against the harsh light, he asks it to dim. Sighing, Nathan stumbles past the dimmed lamp towards the shower, trying to shake the feeling of despair lingering from the dream.

"How are you this morning, Nathan?" the voice installed into the shower asks. Nathan sighs, wondering once again why his father had made his shower intelligent.

"I'm fine. Medium hot water and light rose soap today, please."

"Of course, Nathan."

Nathan's muscles slowly relax as the hot water cascades over him. He closes his eyes and enjoys the feeling of the shower cleaning the sweat and grime off him. His mind clears as he wakes up a little more. He smiles as he recalls the previous day. *I get to go to Angela's house today too, and hang out with her! Today will probably be even better than yesterday... especially if I don't get attacked this time,* he thinks to himself, recollecting the ugly monster that had grabbed him and hauled him off the bus.

He quickly finishes getting ready for school and hurries to the bus stop. As the bus rolls to a stop in front of him, he can't help but reflect on what had happened just twenty-four hours previous. As the bus doors open, he looks up at the bus driver, 'T,' and frowns. Why had he just ignored what was going on? Was it on purpose, or was he just seriously out of it?

T smiles at him as if nothing had happened. "Good morning," he greets.

"Uh... good morning," Nathan replies before hurrying past the strange old man. He notices as he sits that the broken window had been replaced. Angela gets on at the next stop. She spots him almost immediately and quickly heads toward him. He scoots over to give her a place to sit.

"Hey, Nathan," she greets, smiling widely.

"Hey," he replies, returning the smile.

"You talked to your mom about coming to my house today, right?"

"Yep," he replies, watching as she melts with relief. "She said that I can go if I can stay for dinner."

Angela beams. "We were planning on it! My parents are really excited you're coming. They can't wait to meet you."

He laughs a little. "Really? What did you tell them about me?"

She looks a little surprised. "The truth, of course. I told them how awesome you are at fending off ugly creatures, running, tennis... they're really impressed," she says, looking into Nathan's eyes and smiling.

He blushes a little and looks down at his hands. "I told you, I just told the monster it had the wrong person and it left... I'm not as awesome as you make it sound." She laughs, causing Nathan to lift his head and look at her again. "What?"

"I also told them about how humble you are," she winks. Nathan can't help but feel a small smile creep across his lips.

Angela's eyes suddenly shift from his to something behind him. She frowns in confusion. "What is that?" Turning, Nathan notices what looks like a fairy. He blinks and looks closer. No, he was mistaken. The thing flying beside them was simply a dragonfly. He shakes his head sheepishly, laughing at himself. *I can't believe I thought I saw a fairy... how childish and ridiculous is that?* "I wonder why that dragonfly is following the bus," Angela muses, watching him carefully.

He shrugs. "I have no idea."

"Hmm. Weird. ...So did you talk to your mom about doing cross-country and tennis?"

"Yeah," Nathan replies, turning from the window as the dragonfly seems to stop following the bus. "She said it was fine as long as I still get good grades and get my homework done."

"Awesome! So you can do both then?" she asks to clarify.

"Yep, I can do both!"

"Sweet! Now I can kick your butt again!"

They both laugh at this as the bus comes to a stop outside of the school. Nathan finally relaxes and realizes just how tense he had been throughout the ride, worrying that the day would be a repeat of the one before.

They walk to their first class together, talking and laughing. Nathan suddenly stops in the middle of his sentence. "What's wrong?" Angela asks, concerned.

"Jake," he growls, glaring at the guy who punched him the day before.

She frowns. "I thought you said you could take him on?"

"Oh, I can," Nathan assures.

"Then why..."

"I can't take on him *and* his friends at the same time," he explains.

Angela's mouth hardens into a thin line. "He won't attack you like that... if he really wants to fight you, it won't be in a public place like this. Plus he'd prefer to fight one-on-one if he can."

"Well, that sure makes me feel better," Nathan remarks sarcastically. Angela smiles and takes his hand in hers. She starts walking past Jake and his friends, hauling an unhappy Nathan behind her. "Angela..." he starts.

"Shh," she warns, continuing to smile, although it doesn't look heartfelt anymore. "Just go with it. We have to pass them eventually anyway. Act like you didn't even notice them." He warily obeys, and they get past them without any problems, although Nathan can feel Jake's eyes on them as they pass by. He shivers, concerned by the malice he could feel radiating from him; cold as ice. Nathan sighs with relief as they leave him behind. They quickly continue to their first class, not wanting to be marked tardy. They sit together at the back of the room.

They survive Mrs. Sternile's lecture and escape to their gym class together. The gym teacher, Mr. Hefferson, seems ecstatic to see Nathan again. "Nathan!" he greets, slapping a hand down on his shoulder, grinning. "I trust you talked to your mother about coming to cross country?"

Nathan smiles. "Seems like my mom's trying to get me out of the house-she let me sign up for both cross country *and* tennis!" The three of them laugh. *This is going to be a great school year,* he thinks, grinning from ear to ear as he watches Angela laugh at his little joke, mirth dancing in her pretty hazel eyes.

~

"You beat her at basketball too?!" Rachael, one of Angela's friends, exclaims at lunch. Nathan laughs at the bewildered stares from all the girls.

"Yes, but only because I got lucky."

"I'll say," Angela remarks. "That three-point shot should NOT have gone in- your form was so sloppy!"

The group laughs. "What else do you do, Nathan?" Another of Angela's friends, the pretty girl with white-blonde hair and pink highlights asks.

"Um... well, I think you'd be surprised at how well I can swim," he says, subconsciously fingering the black speck at the base of his throat, remembering how the tiny device had helped him breathe underwater in the ocean at Zilferia. Memories of Crystal Dragon and the realm flash through his brain. He takes a moment to slowly come back to himself and pull his thoughts away.

"...Wouldn't stand a chance," one of the girls says. They all turn and look at Nathan, expecting him to say something.

He blinks. "Uh... I'm sorry, what were we talking about?" he asks sheepishly. The girls laugh.

The one who was talking smiles and calmly repeats herself. "I was just saying that Angela's *amazing* at swimming. She was on the swim team in her other school last year and got first place! If you were to race her, you wouldn't stand a chance." She watches him carefully. The other girls stare at him as well. He smiles a little and takes another bite of his food.

Angela finally breaks the silence. "Well?"

"Well, what?" Nathan asks, casually continuing to eat his lunch.

She looks confused. "Well... that sounded to me like a challenge. Are you going to turn down a challenge?"

He struggles to keep from laughing as he slowly replies. "Haven't you challenged me enough already? Do you really want me to take your crown, oh Princess of Fitness?" he asks sarcastically. Angela's mouth falls open in shock, followed by her friends. Nathan stills the chuckles wanting to burst from him and smiles kindly at Angela instead. "If you really want to challenge me and lose your title of being the best, then so be it." His eyes lock onto hers. "I would rather just be friends and *not* have everything be a competition; although that's fine now and again. Can't we just have fun doing things together rather than trying to be better than the other?"

Angela's mouth opens and closes a few times before she regains her composure. "Y... yes, of course!" she finally manages to say.

The bell rings. Smiling, Nathan stands and heads toward the door, calling back over his shoulder, "See you on the bus, Angela!" He laughs as he hears the girls erupt into conversation again as soon as he's almost out of sight. All of them but Angela, that is. He can feel the weight of her stare on him as he leaves, studying him. Trying not to feel nervous, he hurries to his next class.

On his way to the bus after school, Nathan keeps a sharp eye out for Jake and his friends. He quickly spots them heading towards him, but rather than try and run, he stops and waits for them. *Might as well confront them now,* he reasons. He realizes that may not be the best idea when he sees the look on Jake's face. He stands in front of Nathan, a wild look in his eyes, as his friends surround Nathan. Nathan tries to keep calm, although he feels like an animal in a hunter's trap, staring down the barrel of a gun. He swallows dryly. "Can I help you gentlemen?" he asks politely, hoping to avoid a conflict.

Jake's face reddens and his hands clench into fists. "I told you... to stay away from her!" he finally spits out. The circle around Nathan gets a little tighter. He starts to sweat nervously. "Last warning," Jake continues, a wicked gleam in his eyes. "Stay away from her. ...That is, if you ever want to be able to walk again."

"I… uh…" Nathan hesitates, cowering back. He couldn't use any of his Gifts, not in public. He then remembers how strong Crystal was, even without her Gifts, and suddenly his fear vanishes. Straightening, he continues, "No. I won't stay away from Angela unless *she* asks me to. She can hang out with whomever she wants to! And if that person is me, then deal with it!" he declares with growing confidence, glaring back at Jake.

The first fist flies at Nathan too quickly for him to avoid. The punch lands squarely on his nose, breaking it. Blood instantly gushes from it. He quickly recovers, however, and delivers a nasty blow directly to the bully's right eye. Just as he feared, as soon as he does, Jake's friends join in the fight.

He had no chance.

"Oh my—Nathan!!" Angela shrieks, covering her mouth as tears fill her eyes. She turns her head away as he carefully sits down beside her with a wince.

"Surely I'm not that bad," he jokes. He knows he must look awful—he sure felt terrible. One of his eyes was swelling shut, his face and the front of his shirt were still covered in blood, and his jaw, gut, arms, wrist, and legs are hurt. Heck, *everything* hurt.

"What… what happened?!" she exclaims, managing to look at him again. "Was it Jake? And his friends?" He quickly fills her in, skipping the details of his severe beating. Her eyes fill with tears again. One escapes and races down her cheek. He instinctively reaches up and softly wipes it away. "I'm so sorry, Nathan…"

"Why? It wasn't your…"

"Yes, it is my fault. Jake is… my… ex. I guess he's just out for revenge or something. I'm so sorry. You should have—*I* should have heeded his warning. You would be better off staying away from me," she says as another tear runs down her face. She shifts her gaze to her knees, unable to look him in the eye.

He frowns and lifts her head with his good hand and looks into her pretty eyes with his one good eye. "Angela, I don't care what Jake says- or does- to me. I don't *want* to stay away from you. …But I will if *you* really want me to go. Just say the word, and I'll be out of your hair," he assures her.

Two more tears escape her eyes. She looks down at her hands. After a couple of minutes, she whispers, "No... I don't want you to leave." He smiles. "But," she adds, "I *really* hate seeing you so beat up."

"Well then it's a good thing I thought to bring this," he remarks, holding up a vial about the size of his pinky finger.

She looks at it with mild confusion. "What's that?"

"It's medicine from Tanguay. It heals injuries, like your medi-bot... but it's more potent," he explains, then dumps it down his throat. He gasps as it spreads like wildfire throughout his body, burning and cleansing. His wrist snaps back into place, his eye's swelling goes down, and his nose, jaw, and everything else gets fixed. Except one of his legs. He frowns. "I guess I didn't bring enough," he says as she looks at him worriedly. "It ran out before it could fix my left leg."

The bus pulls up to Angela's stop. She looks at him with a worried frown. "Can you walk?"

He stands, grimacing. "I made it to the bus after being beaten up, and I'm better now. I should be able to make it," he points out, walking carefully down the stairs out of the bus.

"Take care now," T calls. Nathan looks back at the old bus driver and just shakes his head. He's not in the mood to try and figure him out. He turns to Angela.

"So... Where's your house?" he asks.

"It's just a little way down the street," she replies, pointing to a cute, old-fashioned house about five doors down from where they're standing. The house, a warm chocolate brown on the outside, is very inviting. They start walking toward it as the bus pulls away, but they don't get far before Nathan starts to limp. The limp gets more and more pronounced as they continue on. Angela finally speaks up.

"Do you need some help?" she asks. He shakes his head stubbornly, sweat shining on his face. His hands are shaking and his knees wobble with each step. She moves closer to Nathan and slides his arm about her shoulders anyway. He doesn't complain and leans on her a bit for support. They go the rest of the way together, but Nathan still barely makes it.

Immediately after entering through the front door, he collapses onto one of the couches- careful not to let the bloody parts of his clothes touch it. Although it should wash off of the leather pretty easily, he does his best to be courteous to the Doves' home. Angela runs to find her parents, promising to return quickly. He waits patiently on the couch, trying to get his breathing back under control. It slows almost back down to normal, along with his heartbeat. He relaxes and finally notices the inside of her house.

Although a little old-fashioned, it's a beautiful and loving home. The walls, unlike most he had seen, weren't electronic. Rather than having a screen on the wall, it was solid and unmoving. The room seemed quiet with the warm golden color on the walls with no movement or sound coming from them. It was still. The room was clean and tidy, yet still also had the happy, loving feeling of a home about it. The window behind him is open a little. A cooling, peaceful breeze plays with the hair on the back of his neck.

He's examining a shelf full of awards that Angela had won when she and her parents burst into the room. The dad takes one look at him and runs to grab their medi-bot while the mom grabs a washcloth and quickly wets it. She starts to gently clean the blood off of his face while Angela sits down next to him. Angela looks a lot like her mom, whose green eyes are soft with concern as she cleans him up, her short blonde hair falling into her face. She absent-mindedly bushes it back behind her ear. "Angela told us all about it," she informs him while she works. "We're so impressed with you! You know, Walter did something like that for me once..."

"Now don't go making me sound like a hero," the dad laughs as he enters the room, medi-bot in hand. "I'm not nearly as impressive as you try and make it sound." He hands the little robot to Nathan. "Here you are, son. Fix yourself right up."

Nathan smiles in return. "Yes, sir." The little robot zooms to his left leg and starts working. Nathan sighs a bit with relief as the pain in his leg diminishes and disappears. Angela and her family also smile and relax.

"You probably want to shower now don't you, son?" Angela's father, Walter says, accepting the medi-bot when Nathan hands it back to him.

"Yes, sir," he replies, standing. Angela stands up with him.

The dad smiles. "Please, call me Walter."

"Okay, Walter," he grins.

"Meet me out back when you're done," Angela instructs.

"Alright."

Walter leads the way out of the front room, which is joined to the kitchen. The black tile gleams under his shoes as he enters the kitchen, which is a little larger than the front room. The sunlight streams through the large glass doors, reflecting off of the black marble countertops and shining through the glass coffee table. He notices how the bright flowers on the small table lighten the atmosphere. The walls are painted the same light color as Angela's hair, reminding him of honey. Angela opens the sliding glass door and steps outside, her mom following. The soft breeze brings Nathan back to alertness. He notices Walter watching him and smiling.

"Uh... I... like your house," he says lamely, trying to play off the awkwardness of him staring at the house so obviously.

Walter's smile widens. "Do you, now? I like it too. I'm thrilled Ramona didn't listen to me when I told her I wanted a high-tech house like everyone else. This feels so much more..."

"Peaceful and warm?" Nathan suggests.

"Yes! Just what a home *should* feel like. It certainly doesn't need to be overly complicated and distracting."

"I agree, sir... Walter," Nathan corrects himself.

Walter laughs and turns, waving for him to follow. "Come on and get cleaned up," he says as he starts up the stairs. "I'm sure you'll want a nice hot shower after such a long day."

Nathan's relieved to see that their shower is old fashioned as well. It doesn't say a word to him when he turns it on. He relaxes and stands in the cascading hot water for a couple of minutes before moving to scrub off all the dried blood and sweat coating his body. He gets out of the shower to find his clothes folded on the white marble counter, already cleaned and dried. *They must have a launder-bot too,* he figures as he pulls the clothes back on.

Once he's done, he walks into the hallway and doesn't see anyone, so he heads back to the kitchen to join Angela outside. He pauses just outside the door and closes his eyes, enjoying the last of the fading warmth of summer. A small smile creeps onto his lips as he feels the warm, gentle breeze play with his damp hair. He opens his eyes to see Angela staring at him. He meets her eyes and grins. She blushes and looks away from him, clearing her throat, obviously embarrassed to be caught staring at him. "So... um... do you feel better?" she asks, mumbling a little and staring at the ground to avoid eye contact.

He smiles. "Yep, pretty much as good as new."

"Good," she replies. She bites her lip and takes a deep breath, letting her shoulders relax. She suddenly looks up at him, no longer looking embarrassed. "So, what do you want to do?" she asks, gesturing to all the things around them. He shrugs and glances around her spacious backyard and finds a trampoline, a large pool, and a ping-pong table. He's standing on the back porch, which has a grill and a few tables in the shade.

Angela's mom walks over and hands him a glass of ice-cold lemonade. "I figured you would be thirsty," she explains with a kind smile.

"Thank you," he says, taking a sip. At first the lemonade is sweet, but then he can taste the familiar tang of lemon. He smiles. "This is delicious, Mrs. Dove."

"Oh, please dear, call me Ramona!"

"Okay. Thanks, Ramona."

"No problem, dear!" she beams, heading over to sit by Walter in the shade. He quickly gulps down the rest of the lemonade and sets the empty glass down on the nearest table. He glances up to see Angela watching him again, biting her bottom lip. She blushes again as she sees him watching her in return. She shakes her head and murmurs something to herself before looking back up at him with a smile.

"So, what do you want to do?" she repeats.

"Well… I didn't bring my swimming suit," he laughs. "So swimming is out…"

"That's okay," Angela interrupts. "We have something that might fit you…" she stops for a moment, sorrow crossing over her gaze. "…So you could try those on if you want."

Nathan hesitates, wondering about the reluctance and buried sadness in her voice. Finally, he just smiles and accepts her offer. She smiles back and heads back inside to grab them. After she returns, he accepts the swimming trunks from her and quickly changes into them in the bathroom. When he gets back, he sees that she isn't there yet. Smiling mischievously, he dives into the water then settles to the bottom, calmly breathing the water while he waits for Angela to emerge.

<<<Angela>>>

Angela walks out of the door, but doesn't see Nathan yet. *He'll probably be out soon,* she figures, heading toward the water. She lowers herself in gently, continuing to face the door, expecting Nathan to emerge any minute. Nathan, moving slowly, breaches the surface of the water behind her. He grins to himself in anticipation.

"Ahh!" she cries out as he grabs her waist. Her hands fly up to her face and she closes her eyes as he dunks her under the water. He gently helps her regain her footing and stand back up. Eyes still clenched shut, she laughs, wiping water out of her eyes before opening them. "Hey!" she exclaims, trying to sound angry. Nathan grins, knowing she wasn't mad by her laughter. "That's not very nice!" she continues, smiling despite herself.

"Sure it is," he replies, winking at her. She blushes a little before diving into the water, sitting at the bottom of the pool and looking up at him. He grins and joins her, slowly breathing water through his nose so she wouldn't be able to tell that he can breathe underwater, thanks to a small device he had acquired in Zilferia. This thought causes another small pang to his heart. He missed Zilferia and all his friends there- especially Crystal. At that, Nathan heads back up to the surface, wanting to clear his head. Angela follows, breathing hard after breaking the surface of the water.

"I... win," she pants, grinning. Nathan nods distractedly, but she notices. "What's wrong?" she asks. He hesitates, then just shakes his head, and smiles at her.

"Nothing," he replies before grabbing her again and falling backward into the water, pulling her with him.

4

"Crystal? …Crystal! Crystal Dragon! Are you alright? Talk to me! Say something!" The worried tone carried in the voice helps rouse me. I groan and open my eyes, confused about where I am. It looks like the school… but why would I be just outside the school building- especially laying on the ground?

"What…" I start to ask, then stop as a sudden rush of pain hits me. My body, bruised and bloody, reminds me of what just happened and I struggle not to cry. I close my eyes and lose consciousness once again.

This time I wake up slowly and gradually. The pain is still there, but it's diminished enough that it doesn't hurt to breathe anymore. I take a shaky breath and open my eyes. It's dark and I can't see anything until my eyes adjust, so I wait patiently. I slowly sit up, realizing that I was lying down on a small pile of blankets—a homemade bed.

Where am I? How did I get here? What happened after I passed out? Who healed me? The questions threaten to overwhelm me, so I stop asking them until I can find someone who can tell me what I need to know.

Grimacing, I lurch to my feet, swaying unsteadily. I lean against a wall and wait for my head to stop spinning. That's when I notice a familiar smell.

I breathe in a little deeper. I was right- the smell of dust and rotting wood permeated the air. I knew where I was, but I wasn't so sure I wanted to be there again.

"Crystal! You're up!" A light flashes on, temporarily blinding me so I can't make out the figure coming towards me. But I don't need a light to know to whom that voice belonged.

"Vlad," I sigh, relaxing and sitting back down on the blankets. "What are you doing here?" I ask. *Funny how this is where I met him the first time as well... I suppose it's only fitting that we meet again in the same dusty old theater.*

"What, no 'I missed you, Vlad,' or 'Welcome back,' or 'I'm so glad to see you here, Vlad!'? I'm disappointed," he says, winking at me. I choke back a laugh, knowing it will hurt since I'm not fully healed from my recent beating. I smile instead.

"Good to see you, Vlad. Sorry if I'm not more enthusiastic... I've just been a little distracted lately," I remark with a touch of sarcasm. "Plus, you don't exactly come bringing happy news very often, now do you?"

He laughs. "Okay, you've got me there. However, you should still be glad to see me- I just saved you from being hauled off back to Patrick!"

I look at him, a little confused. "You did? But... how..."

"How did I know you were in trouble? I didn't know before I got here and found out you weren't at home. How did I get there so fast? Well, I find flying to be an excellent way of getting around quickly," he winks, referring to his shapeshifting abilities. "How did I manage to rescue you from that Hunter in disguise? I've been fighting for a while, my dear. And his form was quite sloppy, might I add."

I start to laugh, then quickly stop, grimacing. After a second, I smile up at him again. "You always know what I'm going to ask," I say.

He laughs. "Well it's not hard since you ask about everything! Must you know every little detail?" he teases.

I grin. "Yes, actually, I do. ...Speaking of which..."

"Where's Justin? I sent him home, assuring him that you will come back to school tomorrow and that you'll be fine."

"And..."

"If I wasn't here to save you, why did I come to Second Earth?"

I laugh a little. "Get out of my head!"

He smiles and sits next to me on the blankets. "You're an open book, my dear. One doesn't need to have the Gift of mind reading to know what you're going to ask next."

"Okay, fair enough," I concede. "So why are you here, then?"

His smile falters. "How about we get to that in a moment? Care for a sandwich?" he asks, pulling a wrapped sandwich from his jacket pocket. I smile. It's the same kind that he gave me the day I first met him. I accept the sandwich, knowing that any food from Zilferia would help me heal and clear my mind from the haze of pain in which it is now trapped. Sure enough, the delicious sandwich helps me recover a little more and helps me feel fresh and completely awake and alert. I'm not entirely healed, but the food sends a wave of relief through my body.

I sigh contentedly. "Man, I've missed Zilferian food!" I say, laughing a little. Vlad just smiles and hands me a water bottle and watches me finish it off.

"Ready?" he asks.

"Sure, I guess," I respond, a little confused. What would I have to prepare myself to hear? Surely not...

"Your parents are fine," Vlad says, watching me with his heavy gaze.

I sigh. "You knowing what I'm about to say is already getting old," I remark, exasperated.

He laughs a little. "Sorry."

"So, what did you have to tell me, then? ...How's Nathan?"

"Fine," he replies. "Absolutely nothing interesting seems to have happened to him at all over the summer or at school the past couple of days."

I breathe a sigh of relief. "Well, that's good. So what is it? Tell me already! I can take it!"

Just as Vlad opens his mouth to reply, a light but persistent tapping sound comes from the front door of the theater. Vlad and I share a look and he gets up and walks cautiously to the door, pulling a knife out of his boot before cautiously opening the door. It swings open and he jumps back, holding the knife out in front of him. His back is to me so I can't see what's happening until he steps aside to let the visitor in.

"Nora!" I exclaim, standing and rushing towards the door to greet my Familiar.

"*What happened?!*" she demands, flying in circles around me, inspecting

41

my bloodstained clothes. *"Why weren't you on the bus? Why is Vladimir here? Is it even the real Vlad? Why are you hurt? Are you okay? What happened?!"* I quickly fill her in with my mind as Vlad and I walk back to the blankets set up on the stage. *"Oh dear, oh dear, oh dear... this is why I insisted I come to school with you!"* she cries, pacing on my legs and flapping her wings agitatedly. *"If I was there, I could have warned you that they were approaching early enough that you could have easily avoided them! Not only that, but I would have pecked his eyes out!"*

"Yes, but birds aren't exactly allowed at school, Nora. You would have been taken away or I would have been sent home and not allowed back until you weren't with me..."

"I know I wouldn't exactly fit in, Crystal," she replies, indignant. *"That's why I've been practicing some magic. I can turn invisible now. They wouldn't send you home for having an invisible bird, now would they?"*

I blink in surprise. *"You can do* what *now? Since when? When were you going to tell me?"*

"Whenever it was necessary for you to know," she calmly retorts, staring me in the eye.

I sigh. *"Okay, fine. Whatever. Can we talk about this later? Vlad still has some explaining to do."*

"Of course," she replies, turning to stare at Vlad instead. He squirms uncomfortably under her intense gaze.

"Um, ready now?" he asks, eyeing the bird of prey nervously.

"Yes. I'm always ready for answers, Vlad, as you should know by now," I hint.

He chuckles. "Okay, okay, I guess I've kept you waiting long enough." He takes a deep breath and his tone grows serious again. "I... we... need your help," he simply states.

I sit there for a few seconds, waiting for him to continue. He simply watches me, waiting for my reaction. "Okay... three things," I begin. "One, I can't help anyone—as you well know; two, who needs my help exactly; and three, what do you need help with? I'm powerless!"

Vlad takes one of my hands and holds it gently in his while he looks me in the eyes. "Crystal, you are our Princess. You are useful- Gifts or not- and we need you. All of Zilferia is in trouble. The Dragon Hunters have taken over everything, and we are losing people—and Gifts—at an alarming rate. The Dragon Hunters are getting more and more powerful with each passing day. We need your help to talk with the dragons, the Sohos, the merfolk, and maybe even some Hunters themselves. You won't seem like a threat anymore, so they shouldn't attack you. They might listen to you and fight with us. ...If you are up for the job, of course. I understand if you don't want to go since it's so dangerous there, but I figured it would be worth a shot to ask you, at least."

I stare at him. "Are you crazy? I can't do anything! I would probably be killed the instant I walked through the portal! I don't have my dragon powers or my Gifts anymore. Why would anyone listen to me?"

"Oh, I don't know... you were a pretty fierce opponent even before you knew about dragons or Gifts. And the Sohos don't let not having any Gifts get them down. ...Your parents and I truly believe that you can do this, Crystal. But it's up to you. You have to believe in yourself first, or else this wouldn't work anyway." He sighs and stands up, releasing my hand. "Just contact me with your watch if you ever decide to come back, then. It's not exactly safe here either, though. The Dragon Hunters are after you, and now they know exactly where you are. ...And where Justin is, too. Either way, there's danger. But, I won't try to influence you either way. Stay or go, it's your choice."

"Um... yeah... I won't be able to contact you with the watch," I say sheepishly.

"Why not?" he says, then notices that I'm not wearing it. "Where's the watch?"

"...That Dragon Hunter you beat up said he stole it."

He stares at me in disbelief. "You're kidding me." I shake my head. Vlad puts his face in his hands and sighs. "Well, then you're going to have to decide now. Zilferia is your home, and it's about to be destroyed. So if you choose to stay now, it's choosing to let go of Zilferia forever since it will no longer exist in the state you once knew it to be in. This is your only chance to take back your life- your true life- or just muddle along and try to be a normal person on Second Earth, always feeling unfulfilled."

"I thought you said you weren't going to try and influence my decision," I remark teasingly.

"That was before it became necessary for me to try and persuade you."

I bite my lip and turn to face Nora. *What do you think?* I ask her. She stares at me like it should be obvious. I laugh. I suppose it is pretty clear what my choice will be.

~

It's not dark yet, but I can tell by the sun setting in the west that night is fast approaching on Zilferia. "It's so quiet," I whisper. No living thing could be heard moving and not even the trees were singing, although there was a light breeze rushing past the leaves. Vlad nods, then quickly leads the way to the castle where my mom, dad, and the newly formed Village Council are waiting.

He knocks on the door. Three knocks, pause, eight knocks, pause, one knock. The door opens and the next thing I know, I'm trapped in Pearl Dragon's loving hug. I'm released only to be caught in Alexander Dragon's warm embrace as he lifts me off the floor in his strong arms. He sets me down, chuckling, then lets us in, closing the door behind us. "We missed you so much," Pearl says, again giving me a quick hug.

"And we're glad you're here," Alexander adds, "Although I wish it were at a happier time. Unfortunately, I fear Zilferia will never be the same again. Especially not if we can't vanquish these Dragon Hunters from among us. And to think, this all started because of one man. A crazy, now very powerful man, but just one man nonetheless."

Thaddeus comes up to me and offers a hand for me to shake, but I give him a hug instead. He laughs in surprise and gently pats me on the back. "Welcome back, Princess."

I release him and stick my tongue out at the name. "Don't suddenly start calling me Princess, Thaddeus! I'm still Crystal and always will be."

He grins. "Of course. But you are our princess, too. So don't get overly surprised when people start calling you Princess."

I frown. "Fine. But I don't want you or any of my other friends calling me anything but Crystal! Okay?"

"Very well, Crystal," he laughs, then gestures to the people behind him, still seated at the table. "This is the new Village Council."

"Greetings," an old man says, hobbling over to me with the aid of his cane. He takes off his hat and tips it to me with a small bow. "Pleased to meet you at last, Princess Crystal. I look forward to working with you for the good of the Village- and all of Zilferia." I swallow nervously. This is a huge and daunting task, and it only just hit me just how much I have to do- and the fact that none of it may affect the war here at all. If I can even do the tasks before me in the first place, that is. I knew that I might fail before I came, however. So I'm not going to chicken out now. I will do my part to save this place and everyone living here.

Thaddeus introduces me to the other eight villagers making up the council before we all sit down at the table with them. Something suddenly strikes me as odd. I lean over to Vlad. "If you and Thaddeus are here… why aren't Zelda and Y'vette? Shouldn't they be a part of this council too?" Vlad and Thaddeus share a glance before he answers me.

"They were both part of the council. But they… were recently captured by Patrick. We aren't sure what he's going to do to them. He could be holding them hostage for something, or he could have taken their Gifts by now. However, he's probably at least torturing them for information about our plans. They are strong, but I fear they won't last more than a couple more days in there."

"Exactly. We need to get them out. Now," the King states, his voice a growl as his eyebrows pinch together. "Which is where you come in," he reluctantly finishes, looking at me.

"Me? How am I going to rescue them?"

"You have been there before, haven't you? You can lead a group of people in there and hopefully also lead them all back out, with the addition of Zelda and Y'vette. Two of the group will be assigned specifically to protect you, no matter the cost. The people can't lose their Princess again."

"And we can't lose our daughter again," Pearl finishes, looking at me with tears in her beautiful green eyes.

I take a deep breath, trying to make myself feel braver. "Okay. I'll do it. What's the plan? Who's going with me?"

I pull on the black leather boots, completing the midnight black outfit that Taylor gave me. The silky soft form-fitting clothes allow me to move without making a sound and appear to blend into the shadows. I pull up the hood and look into the mirror. Lowering my head, I can't see any distinguishing features on my face. It's unlikely that I will be seen, but if I am, no one should be able to easily recognize me. I grin. As a little girl watching spy movies, I had always wanted to be one. Now I'm about to finally be a proper secret agent. I may not have all the gadgets from the movies, but I have enough to help me out if I happen to get caught. The black belt fastened loosely about my waist and hips hides a small dagger, a vial of poison, a grenade, pepper spray that causes permanent blindness, and a spray that can eat through metal. At the last second, I remember to grab a small bell- the only thing that will deter Patrick's porcupine-tiger from mauling us to death.

Practicing my stealth, I slink down the stairs and lurk in the shadows. The rest of the group that will be on the rescue mission with me enters the room. Sierra Davis walks in first, followed by Ham Jacobson. These two are my main 'guards,' although everyone in the group will be looking out for me. Vlad and Thaddeus aren't coming, since if they get captured as well, Patrick will have all four of the advisors- and the main leaders, besides the King and Queen, of not only the council, but also the main Village.

A tall, slender woman with short brown hair enters behind Ham. I spot a sword at her waist, a knife in her boot, tiny poisonous darts in the cuffs of her gloves, and I'm sure there are other various weapons hidden elsewhere on her person as well. This must be Susan Parker- the weaponry master, in her early twenties. Obviously, her main Gift is Fighting. Her other Gift is reading minds, according to Thaddeus. The next member of our group, Josh Papke, enters next. He's an average height with brown hair that looked like he never styled it; also in his early twenties. His Gifts are flying and logic.

The last two members of the group walk in at about the same time. Reed Agee and Brent Alder. Both in their late twenties, Reed has the Gifts of speed and memory, and Brent has strength and telepathy. All of them are dressed in black as well, although made of a different material than mine.

I wait for someone to notice me, but no one seems to see me at all. After about a minute, Josh growls, frustrated. "How long is it going to take that girl to get dressed? I mean, I know girls like clothes, but still..." he stops suddenly, seeing a knife appear about an inch away from his eye.

Susan, still smiling amiably, calmly says, "She'll be down soon, I'm sure. Oh, and that teddy bear you sleep with? That's real cute. Do you play dress-up with it too?"

Josh's mouth falls open and his face turns crimson. "How did... hey, that's not fair! You read my mind?"

Susan continues smiling as she slowly puts the knife away. "Yes, and it wasn't hard either, kitten."

He looks confused. "Kitten?" He sighs. "Alright, listen, I'm sorry, okay? I didn't mean what I said about girls."

"I take it you won't make the same mistake again though, now will you?"

"No ma'am," he responds ashamedly. Sierra, Ham, Reed, and Brent all laugh while Susan smiles, satisfied with her work.

Again, I wait for someone to notice me in the shadow by the stairs, but still no one does. I grin. I'm a better spy than I thought, then. I take a small step out of the shadow and walk towards them stealthily, watching their faces to see who spots me first. As I suspected, it's Susan. Her eyes pass over me a couple of times before she narrows her eyes and a look of surprise crosses her face. "Crystal? Were you here the whole time?"

I pull off the hood and nod. The others jump as though I appeared out of nowhere. "What... Crystal? Where did you come from?" Ham exclaims.

"She... she appeared out of nowhere!" Reed says, pointing out what the others already noticed. "She must have gotten another Gift! How else would she have been able to disappear like that?"

Susan's brow furrows in thought. "No. I still would have sensed her thoughts loud and clear... plus, she wasn't completely invisible. ...Crystal, do you know what your outfit is made out of?"

Josh coughs, thinly veiling his words, "Girls and clothes... what did I say..." I can tell Susan heard it too, but she chooses to ignore it this time.

I shrug. "I have no idea. I just know that it's super comfortable and light, that's all."

She narrows her eyes at me, then extends a hand. "May I?"

"Sure," I say, taking off a glove and handing it to her. She takes off her own to feel the silkiness of the fabric. She then pulls out a knife and gently drags it across the surface, gradually adding pressure. Confused, I move to stand beside her to see what she's doing. She removes the knife and holds up the glove for me to see. There isn't a cut on it anywhere.

She looks at me seriously. "I believe that this is made from the underwater monster, Glaoud. His skin, dark as obsidian, was sometimes seen as a dark blue for better camouflage beneath the water. He is the only one of his kind, and he was a giant. He's bigger than this room... approximately the size of a dragon. They say he's a sea dragon, from Quagon. His skin is nearly impervious to anything sharp- even immune to most poisons. It's said... he could turn nearly invisible if he moved slowly or not at all."

Brent takes the glove, turning it over in his hands. "And you think that Crystal's clothes are made from his skin?"

"I don't see how it's possible, but that's the only explanation I can think of. I could hardly feel Crystal's thoughts and barely see her movements when that hood was up. I've never encountered anything like that before, although the closest I've come to feeling that kind of block on her mind is when I talked with a dragon." She pauses and takes the glove back from Brent and hands it to me, looking me in the eye as she does so. "This is a treasure beyond comprehension, Crystal. Protect it, and it will protect you. Never let anyone else wear this or take any part of it off. It only works as a complete set."

I nod and slip the glove back on, feeling self-conscious with everyone looking at me, wide-eyed. "Thanks," I croak. She nods and straightens back up, turning to the door just as it opens again. Thaddeus, Vlad, Pearl, and Alexander enter the room.

"Everyone ready?" Pearl asks the group, looking only at me. We nod.

"Then good luck," Alexander says, opening the door for us to go outside. The group slides past him into the night. As I pass him, I give him a quick hug.

"Don't worry, we'll be okay," I reassure him before hurrying after the others. I look back once and see my parents standing at the door with tears in their eyes. I vow to come back to them, no matter what it takes. I won't break their hearts again.

5

Nathan's eyes pop open as he's yanked out of sleep. The bus! He's going to miss it! He scrambles out of bed and throws on some clothes, skipping the shower. He grabs his shoes and backpack and races out the door, getting to the bus stop at the same time as the bus. Panting, he climbs on and sits down. He quickly gets his shoes on before the bus gets to Angela's stop.

"Almost miss the bus?"

"Yeah," he replies, turning around and finding himself just a few inches away from Angela's face. They both scoot back a little, diffusing the tension and awkwardness immediately.

She laughs. "I can tell," she says, rubbing his head like a dog. "Your hair's a mess!"

He mockingly sticks his tongue out at her. "And your hair is perfect, as I'm sure it always is."

She frowns and reaches back to fiddle with her high ponytail. "But I didn't do anything with it. I just stuck it in a ponytail! I was running late too," she laughs.

"It doesn't matter that it's in a ponytail, it still looks great," Nathan murmurs with a shy smile.

She flushes. "Well, thank you."

He smiles back. "So, did you do the history homework?"

They then talk about the assignments from various classes on the way to school. When he gets off the bus he's still talking to her, but suddenly stops dead, staring at something in the distance. "What is it?" Angela asks, following his gaze. "I don't see anything…"

He blinks and shakes his head. "It's nothing. I'm just tired, that's all." He smiles reassuringly at her and guides her into the school. He stops and glances back before following her through the door, but there's nothing there. *I could have sworn there was, though…* he wonders as he enters the building. *And not just anything… I thought I saw Rosulkip.* But the little pink monster was nowhere in sight, so he brushes it off as being tired and seeing things, then heads to class.

"Hey Angela, can we come watch your tennis match today?" One of her friends asks at lunch, glancing at Nathan.

She laughs. "Sure…but I'm not playing against Nathan," she adds, smiling with a knowing look on her face.

The girls are crestfallen. "Oh. Okay then." They continue eating their lunch silently, heads down. Angela shares an amused look with Nathan before she continues to eat her own lunch. After a few minutes, one of the girls' head pops up. She has a determined look on her face as she glares at Angela. "Why not?" she demands, arms folded. "Why aren't you playing against Nathan anymore?" The other girls glance from the one who spoke to Angela and back again, obviously waiting for the answer just as expectantly as the one who asked.

Nathan answers her before Angela can. "I'm not going to the meet today."

"Oh. Why not?" Another girl inquires.

Because I keep seeing Rosulkip everywhere and I want to find her to prove I'm not going insane, he thinks to himself. But all he says is, "I'm busy. I forgot about other plans I had that I can't skip. …Family stuff." Their faces all fall and they stare sadly at their trays.

"Oh. Okay," the first girl sighs, her disappointment clear. Nathan hesitates and almost changes his mind.

"Well, you could all come and watch the game on Monday. Friday's just practice anyway, the real fun happens on Monday." Angela glances at him, a little surprised, as the other girls brighten up considerably.

"Okay!" they readily agree, happily returning to their food.

Angela stares at Nathan, trying to figure him out. Confused, Nathan mouths, "What?" but she just blinks and turns back to her lunch, ignoring him. He shrugs, figuring it was nothing and returns to his own food. He finishes his lasagna just as the bell rings, ending the lunch period. Gulping down the rest of his milk, he dumps his tray in the trash, then turns the corner to go to his next class. He passes the men's bathroom and catches sight of a blur of pink dashing inside. Glancing around, he quickly follows it into the bathroom.

The door slowly swings shut behind him. The bathroom is silent. Nathan slowly takes another step into the dimly lit room. The one working light flickers, threatening to plunge the windowless room into complete darkness. He holds his breath until it stops flickering, then slowly lets it out. He stands under the lone light and peers into the semi-lit darkness of the rarely used bathroom. He catches another dim sight of pink, followed by a wet, nasally laugh that was definitely not human.

"Hello?" he calls out hesitantly. He's answered by another hacking giggle, but nothing more. "Who's there?" he asks, although he already knows. "Rosulkip?" Another giggle. This one was closer. Goosebumps suddenly erupt across Nathan's skin. Not just from the cold, damp breeze. His hand slowly slips into his pocket and clutches his ring, eyes darting around the room.

The light starts flickering again. *Oh no... Please don't. Don't go out...* he prays. Despite his pleading, the bulb fizzles out, leaving him blind in the darkness. Quickly slipping on the Matter Ring, he blinks rapidly, trying to get his eyes to adjust enough that he can see with just the light emitting from beneath the door.

He suddenly feels something go through his intangible wrist and hears a hiss of disappointment. "Nasty boy! Horrible, treacherous boy! Why I can't grab him?" the pink creature moans to itself.

He swallows. "Um, why are you here?"

The light from the hallway is finally enough to see the glower on her face. "To grab boy Nathan," she simply states.

"Well... how do you that I'm *that* Nathan?" he asks, hoping to confuse her.

Her reply is swift, however. "You smell of Dragons," she states, swiping a hand through his arm once again in a futile attempt to grab him. The bell for the next class to begin rings, and he hears it in what seems to be a faraway place as he contemplates what Rosulkip said.

"What does that mean? Dragons? Why would I smell like dragons?"

Rosulkip snarls at him, backing towards the door. "Not that kind. Yous smell of Dragon girl." She opens the door, causing the sudden light to blind him. "I be back," she growls before speeding away. The door slowly swings shut behind her, leaving Nathan dazed and confused.

"Nathan? Are you sick?"

He gazes back at the teacher with glazed eyes before blinking and trying to focus on what he said and how he should reply. "I... um..." He glances down at his shaking hands and wipes the sweaty palms on his jeans.

"He sure looks sick," one of the girls in the class comments.

"Why were you late to class, Nathan?" the teacher inquires.

"I... um... well, I was in the bathroom," he finally replies. He lifts a trembling hand to his face, his thoughts still far away. *I 'smell of the Dragon girl?' That can only be Crystal... but why would Rosulkip mention her? How would she know what Crystal smells like? Is she in danger?! I have to find Rosulkip again and get some real answers out of her...*

"Can I just go home?" he suddenly asks, cutting the teacher off as he starts to say something. He's surprised, but he agrees and sends Nathan to the office with a checkout sheet. After gathering his things and leaving the front office, he starts walking home. Although he keeps a sharp eye out for Rosulkip, he doesn't see her the entire way. When he turns onto his street, he notices that there are no cars on the driveway or in the open garage. He breathes a sigh of relief. At least he won't have to deal with trying to sneak in unseen.

Going up to the front door, he tells it his name and it opens, accepting his voice signature. Peeking his head in, he confirms that no one's home. Leaving the lights off and the blinds closed, he climbs quickly up to his room, dumping his backpack onto the bed. *"Hey!"* An indignant voice squeaks.

Nathan tries to suppress a smile. *"Sorry, Greg,"* he apologizes to his small

Familiar as he inches out from under the bag. The rat yawns, whiskers wiggling.

"Why are you home so early today, Nathan?" Nathan quickly runs through his encounter with Rosulkip while slipping on his Lightning Shoes and filling another backpack with things that he surmises might help with the hunt. *"So you're going to chase after the thing that's trying to capture you?!"* Greg exclaims in horror, racing onto his backpack as he finishes zipping it up.

"Well, yes. I would rather not be caught off-guard later when I'm unprepared. Plus, I need answers, and Rosulkip isn't too hard to manipulate. I can get her to tell me anything I want to know."

"Yes, but what if the other one is there?"

He hesitates, remembering the other monster that had attacked him on the bus and pulled him out. *"No one can grab me while I'm wearing the Matter Ring,"* he finally says, closing the matter.

The Familiar sighs. *"Fine, but I'm coming with you."*

Nathan smiles. *"I wouldn't have it any other way."*

Greg follows behind him as he walks down the stairs to the door. As he opens it, the sound of someone walking towards them reaches his ears. It's coming from right behind him—in the house he thought was empty. Tensing, he spins around, ready to fight, but relaxes when he sees who it is.

"Grandma," he sighs in relief.

She raises a curly gray eyebrow at him. "And just what are you up to?" He quickly explains the situation to her, once again grateful that he has someone he can tell the truth to. After all, who else would believe him if he told them he was kidnapped, taken to another realm called Zilferia, and fought for his life there with a girl he'd just met? Even if he showed off his new Gifts of Shapeshifting and Controlling the Weather, he's doubtful anyone would respond the way his grandma had. She smiles slowly once he's finished relaying the details of his most recent adventure. "I'll tell your mom you're at a friend's house until Monday."

Nathan grins and gives her a huge hug. "Thanks, Grandma! You're the best!"

"You just do what you have to do and come back safe and sound, okay?" she says, patting him on the back.

"Of course," he assures her, shouldering his backpack and setting Greg on his shoulder.

"Good luck," she says, shutting the door behind him.

"Ready?" he asks Greg.

The rat's tail curls with anxiety. *"No,"* he answers honestly. *"Do we have to do this today? I mean, there's this one cat that's really mean to me... we could go bug him instead..."* he continues, trying in vain to dissuade Nathan.

He smiles grimly. *"Nope. I'm doing this now, and you can come with me, or you can stay home and feel tremendous guilt if I never return..."*

"Oh, come on now, that's not fair! Now you're trying to manipulate me! I'm coming, but that doesn't mean I have to be happy about it."

"Fair enough. I'm not happy about this either—we're not exactly going for a walk in the park," Nathan states as he steps out into the street, shouldering his backpack full of supplies.

"I think you're just having withdrawals from Zilferia," the Familiar contemplates. *"You miss having all those near-death experiences, don't you? What's wrong with you?"*

Nathan turns and looks at the rat seriously. *"No, I don't miss nearly dying. However, that* was *the highlight of my life..."*

"See?" Greg says triumphantly.

"But nearly dying is not *the reason."*

"Then what is?"

"You know who," he replies, walking back up the street. Greg is silent for a while, then, thankfully, changes the subject.

"Do you even know where we're going?"

"Not exactly. I was kind of just hoping Rosulkip will find us."

"And what if she doesn't?"

"I don't know. We'll see."

"And if the other creature comes? What then?"

"I can make him take me to his leader just as easily," he replies confidently. *"That's all he was concerned about when he ripped me out of the bus the other day."*

"Fine. We better be home for dinner, though," Greg adds.

Nathan laughs. *"I packed food, don't worry."*

"Oh, good. At least you remembered the most essential part of this whole trip. If you hadn't packed food, Nathan, I would be quite worried about you."

"I'm sure you would be," he chuckles, shaking his head.

He wanders around for a few hours, keeping a sharp eye out for Rosulkip, but doesn't see the pink creature anywhere. They stop for dinner in a park. After eating, Nathan lays back on the grass and gazes up at the trees, hearing the song of the Zilferian trees in his mind. Sighing, he closes his eyes. Unbidden, images of Crystal come to him once more. Her eyes closed and face peaceful as she sleeps. He feels a pang in his chest. Oh, how he missed her. Even now, he can still hear the sound of her voice in his mind, still remember her fierce, unwavering determination and stubbornness. The memory lifts the corner of his mouth into a small smile. *She was never afraid of anything,* he recalls. *She excelled at the challenges put before her... I just wish I could do as great of things as she could,* he sighs, sitting up.

Sitting there in front of him, just watching him, is Rosulkip. They stare at each other for a moment, then Nathan scrambles to get his Matter Ring on, but he's too slow as small, scaly red arms reach around him from behind, pinning his arms to his sides. He's surprisingly strong. "We got him!" Rosulkip cheers, jumping up.

"Yes, but now we got to get him to Zarafa," Gorldf, the red monster, growls.

"Who *is* Zarafa?" The frustrated Nathan demands to know. The two ignore him.

"Oh, right," Rosulkip contemplates. "How we gonna do that, Gorldf?"

"...I don't know," he growls, frustrated. His breath is hot and wet on the back of Nathan's neck.

"Um, I can help with that," Nathan pipes up. They continue to ignore him.

"We could steal a car and fly him there!" Rosulkip suggests.

"No... we not know how to drive."

"Oh... right. We could... drag him!"

"Zarafa said not to hurt him," Gorldf replies, clearly disappointed.

"Oh."

"I'll come willingly!" Nathan shouts.

They both turn to him. "We no listening to you," Rosulkip states. "You a liar. You tricky."

"No, seriously," Nathan pleads, not wanting to be dragged painfully to their leader. "I'll come with you! I want to meet... Zarafa! Just show me the way!"

Gorldf narrows his eyes at the boy. "No, Zarafa said no talk to boy. We not going to listen to you."

Rosulkip sighs. "Wish we could just teleport back."

Gorldf growls. "Did Zarafa gives you anything, Rosulkip?"

"Yep!" she yips happily, pulling a small silver device out of a sash around her small waist. "This thing. What is it, Gorldf?"

He sighs impatiently. "That a teleporter. Give to me," he demands. She hands it over.

Gorldf pushes the object into Nathan's hand and pushes the button. His vision instantly fades, then there are bright, swirling colors all around them, hurting his eyes. Rosulkip and Gorldf fade away, replaced by a white wall. He can't seem to move the entire time, but when the wall flashes into focus, he finally can. Dropping the handheld teleporter, he jumps up and spins around.

"Hello, Nathan Anderson." The sweet voice somehow soothes his nerves and slows his racing heart. The person before him is a woman who looked to be in her twenties. Her long, straight red hair accents her piercing green eyes, which lock onto his. He can't seem to form a reply, her eyes holding him captive. "My name is Zarafa. I'm pleased to meet you at last. I'm so sorry about those two Dorff. I couldn't come to you personally, I'm afraid. While the Dorff have their uses, they are terribly dumb. Welcome to my home."

"Z... Zarafa?" Nathan stammers in confusion.

She smiles kindly at him, her perfect red lips curling upwards to reveal her straight white teeth. "I can see you are confused. We will talk later, I suppose. For now, this is your room. Please make yourself at home. Feel free to join me for dessert in an hour," she invites, exiting the room and shutting the door behind her.

Nathan stares after her, confounded. *Now what do I do?* He hadn't thought this far ahead in his plan. He had no idea what to do now that he had finally found Zarafa.

6

The forest is silent and dark, lit only from the small amount of light provided by the large crescent moon and the stars above. The smaller moon hidden behind the larger one. Nothing is moving, and there isn't even a wind to cause the leaves in the trees to stir. The night is peaceful and still. Everything seems to be sleeping—everything except the seven of us, creeping quickly and quietly through the shadows. I glance at Ham and Sierra. To think, I missed them so much over the summer, and now that we're back together, we're immediately thrown into yet another life-or-death situation.

While the fear is written clearly on my two friends' faces, the other members of our team have faces of stone. I can't read any of their emotions. They are focused on the task at hand—deadly, silent, and powerful. Once again, I wonder why I was even included in this mission at all. Not only do I not have any Gifts, but I am also sadly inexperienced compared to these veterans. I can tell Ham and Sierra feel the same way. I'm just a seventeen-year-old girl. What can I do to help Zelda and Y'vette?

I reach a line where the trees are suddenly sickly looking and stop. My gut clenches in fear and I can hardly breathe. Memories flash before my eyes while I stand frozen in place. A small, cold room with no windows. Men in black everywhere, keeping me under watchful eye. A massive, ferocious porcupine-tiger. A young man named Chet. The memories halt on his hopeful face. Blinking, I return to the present to see Susan watching me carefully. "Crystal? Are you alright?" she whispers hesitantly.

"Where's Chet?" I demand. "He could have shown you the way here. He knows the inside of the castle better than I do, as well. I didn't exactly roam the halls of their secret building during my captivity. Why didn't you ask *him* to come?"

She frowns. "We don't need to address this now. We need to move on."

"No," I insist. "Tell me now."

She glances back at the other members of the group, then shrugs. "He was recaptured by Patrick. We have no idea what happened to him. ...He may be dead," she finally warns, her voice devoid of emotion. Clearly, she has dealt with death before and remains strong as others fall around her.

I stare at her in disbelief. "Then we'll rescue him too," I finally declare.

"That's not such a good—" Josh begins before Reed punches him in the arm, silencing him.

"That's just fine, if we find him," Reed says, watching me as he cautiously continues. "But if we don't come across him, we can come back for him another time, alright? We aren't going to go looking for him tonight. We have a mission to fulfill, and that's our priority."

I nod, accepting this. I notice the others breathe a sigh of relief. I don't bother to wonder why. "Then let's go," I say, continuing over the brown line. The protective spells surrounding the building have been lowered for a short time by Thaddeus. He told me before we left that he would be keeping an eye on us using magic and drop the shields around the building as we walk through, but he won't be able to see us once we get past the last one. We'll be on our own on the way out.

My soft leather boots prevent the dry leaves from crackling when I step on them, and the others move as quietly as they can without such aid. Susan is amazingly light on her feet and doesn't cause even a whisper of a sound. I can tell she's the most experienced of the group. The warrior. Ham and Sierra follow me closely as we get closer to the stone building up ahead. I slow down and whisper to the others that the porcupine-tiger should be near and to watch out for it. They nod and we continue, peering into the darkness, alert for any sign of movement. We start to spread out a little. After a few minutes, I begin to get confused. *Where is it? I thought it was around here somewhere…*

I freeze as I suddenly feel hot, wet breath on the back of my neck. I don't dare move or breathe. I remain frozen as the head lowers toward me and I can hear it sniffing me like a curious dog. I close my eyes, praying that someone will notice and help me. I slowly inch my hand toward my belt where my bell is tucked. Just as I grasp it, the presence of the beast at my back abruptly disappears. My heart leaps into my throat and I spin around, my eyes sweeping the area.

"Chet?!" I exclaim, shocked. Standing before me, bloodied sword in his left hand, is the boy that I rescued from the Dragon Hunters mere months before. And lying before him is the sprawled form of the porcupine-tiger. The rest of the group comes running, having heard me. "Chet, how did you... what..." He strides toward me and puts a gentle finger on my lips, silencing me. I obey this command for silence, but beg him with my eyes to explain.

"Later," he whispers, his face mere inches from mine. He pulls back a little to include the rest of the group. "Why are you here?!"

"I... um..."

"We came to rescue two of our own. Would you happen to know where they are?" Susan asks. I jump. She was so quiet, I had no idea that she was at my side, blade half-drawn. However, I can hear the rest of the group come up and join us.

Chet's eyes flicker from Susan and back to me. I'm surprised by the new intensity of his gaze. "Yes," he finally confides. "Follow me," he says, quietly leading the way to the stone castle. I remain frozen in place for a moment from shock before I turn and see him waiting for me, hand outstretched. "Come on," he urges. I hesitantly take his hand, and he pulls me to the front of the group before releasing it. I can't help but stare at him as we continue onward. He's become so strong and self-assured I barely recognize the gentle, hopeful boy I met not so long ago. I also can't help but touch my lips, remembering his finger on them... I shake it off. *What's wrong with me? I have a mission to finish. I can't be sidetracked by other things!*

I take a deep breath as we stop beside a back door to the building. *This is it... but am I ready? Am I really prepared to face this dark place again? After everything that happened...* I glance around at the determined faces of my companions and decide that I am. This time, I won't be alone.

This time, I will show Patrick no mercy if I encounter him again.

Chet glances back to me. I nod to show that I'm ready. He slowly nods back, then carefully eases the door open. I take a deep breath, and follow him inside. The others follow behind me. Ham and Sierra are especially hesitant. They remember this place almost as distinctly as I do. But they never had to live through the horrors this place had to offer, I shudder and force myself to stop thinking about it. I can't be distracted from this mission.

Chet turns to us once the door is quietly shut behind the last person inside. "There are two possible places I can think where they might be kept," he whispers. "However, we don't have much time until someone combs through the hallways and rooms checking for intruders. We'll have to split into two groups. Who's going to come with Crystal and me?" I glance at him. He had never asked my opinion. I would have chosen to go with him, but still, he should have at least asked me first.

He glances at me as if he knew what I was thinking. "Provided she wants to go with me, of course," he adds. I nod, feeling even more confused now. Sierra and Susan opt to come with us while the four boys go in the other direction. Chet points them to the dungeon where Vlad was being kept. I feel a rush of gratitude. I don't have to go down in the dark where I can feel things watching me- while I feel I am powerless. I feel a shiver run down my spine at the thought. I don't know how Chet knew about my fear of the dark, but I'm even more glad that I am going to go with him now. "Follow me," he whispers, creeping silently down the hallway. I follow him closely with Sierra right behind and Susan bringing up the rear.

We head towards the section of the building where I had been held. The higher we climb, the tighter the knot in my stomach gets. By the time we reach the all-too-familiar hallway, I can hardly breathe. I swallow and forge on anyway, not giving voice to my complaints for what this place is doing to me. Chet stops in front of a door only a few steps from the room I was held in for so long. He turns to us and whispers, "I heard this is where Patrick keeps most of the things that he doesn't want intruders to discover. I don't know if that means prisoners or information, but I figure either could be beneficial." We nod. "There may be a guard inside," he continues. "Since there wasn't a Dragon Hunter outside. Or I suppose we could have just gotten lucky and arrived just as they were switching guards. Either way, we should be quick and quiet."

We nod again and he crouches, pulling a key out from between two stones in the wall where the mortar had been chipped away. He slowly inserts the key into the doorknob, then gestures for us to back up. Once we do, he flings the door open and rushes into the room, sword in hand. After a few seconds, he steps out and waves us in.

No one is in the room, but like Chet guessed, it's packed full of books, diagrams, and other things that look important. "Since this will probably be our only chance to infiltrate this building for a while, we should gain as much information on his plans as we can. But we have to make it fast. We still need to help the others with the rescue," Susan states. We all agree and focus on the bounty of information before us. Susan and Sierra head to the shelves around the perimeter of the room while Chet heads to one of the tables in the center and I head to the other. Papers and books are scattered all over the table in a disorganized mess as though someone had been in a hurry to find something. I rummage through diagrams of dragons, buildings, and fortifications before stopping on a familiar drawing.

The Gift Stealer; my biggest mistake and Patrick's greatest achievement and most effective weapon. Something that made not only my life more difficult, but also tons of innocent Villagers lives worse as well. I had helped Patrick forge a weapon, and had accidentally completely turned the tables in the war that is now raging.

Everyone who has died, been captured, or otherwise hurt in some way… was all because of me.

A tear falls unbidden from my eye, splashing onto the diagram. I suddenly notice Chet by my side and quickly wipe at my eyes, setting the paper back onto the table. "It's not your fault," he says comfortingly, laying a hand on my shoulder.

I shake my head. "But it is. I was the one that figured out how to fix his stupid machine… so now everyone that he's used it on… their pain and… everything… is all because of me…"

"How do you know that Patrick hadn't been on the verge of figuring it out himself? Maybe asking you actually slowed him down. You didn't do anything immediately—you waited as long as you could before you told him, right? So don't blame yourself, okay?" His voice soothes me and I nod, sniffling.

"Okay," I whisper. "…Thanks."

He nods. "I… um, found something I think you might want to see," he says, handing me a small book with a soft leather cover.

"What is it?" I inquire.

"Open it," he urges.

Hesitantly, I obey and read, *'Today was another success. All of Zilferia is cowering before my might. As soon as I finish off the dragons and Sohos, I will concentrate my efforts on the Village. They still believe that they have hope. I must show them that they are wrong."* I glance back up at Chet. "Is this… Patrick's journal?" I ask incredulously.

"I'm pretty sure," he confirms. "Let me know if you find anything interesting," he says, heading back to the other table to continue searching. I gaze at the black leather book clutched in my hand, unable to believe what I have in my possession. This might have his plans for whatever he's going to do next. We can be ready for him! I stuff down my excitement, setting it down carefully on the corner of the table. I'm taking this one with me.

I catch sight of another diagram on the table and reach for it. Most of it is buried under some other papers, so I can't tell what it is until I pull it out. I freeze, unable to breathe. The hand holding the paper trembles and it falls to the ground. I stoop down and retrieve it. Holding it closer to the light, I trace the letters on the page with a shaking finger. *Dragon Slayer.* The huge contraption must be the weapon that Tatiana told me about when I went to Dragon Mountain a few months before. The weapon that is impervious to fire and strong enough to endure the strength of their claws… the device that is slaying dragons at an alarming rate.

I suddenly hear a commotion just outside the closed door. Thankfully, Chet had thought to relock it before closing it behind us, so no one would immediately notice we're in here, but there's still every possibility that we'll be discovered regardless. Scrambling, I stuff the paper into the journal, which I clutch tightly to my chest. With my other hand, I pull out my dagger. Chet steps towards the door, and we follow him silently. He listens for a few seconds before grabbing the door handle and ripping it open. In a flash, the handle of his sword hits the man in the back of the head, sending him to the ground. I watch Chet carefully. He just doesn't seem quite the same as when I first met him… he wasn't ever this skilled with a sword, or this swift. He was just a boy…

Once again, I shake off these distracting thoughts. Now is not the time for them. I can puzzle over it all later. "Come on, let's find the others," Chet whispers. "We're bound to be found out soon. Let's just hope the two you were looking for were in the dungeon." We run as quickly as we can down the hallway while still keeping our footsteps light and soundless. We're almost there when we run into trouble.

We turn a corner and stop dead. Standing there are six Dragon Hunters, armed and waiting. Susan, the fastest to react to this new threat, takes down two of them with throwing knives before anyone else even really knows what's going on. Chet helps her take down the remaining four. They finish before I even take a step forward to try and help. "Hurry!" Chet calls, racing down the steps into the dungeon. He quickly opens the door. Standing there is the rest of our group, their faces crestfallen.

"Where are Zelda and Y'vette?" I ask frantically.

Reed just shakes his head sadly. "They weren't down there."

Susan doesn't let us stew on this for long. "Well, we have to go now before *we* are captured. Come on, come on!" she calls, hastening us toward the door.

We burst outside, only to find ourselves surrounded by more than twenty men covered in black cloaks. Standing directly in front of us is Patrick, grinning triumphantly. "Hello again, Crystal Dragon," he greets calmly.

Fury suddenly builds in me so rapidly and without warning everything around me disappears in a haze. The only thing I can see clearly is Patrick's smug face. His scar, for once not hidden, doesn't throw me off at all. I focus on the proud look in his eyes and act without thinking. Moving faster than I ever have before, I charge at him while screaming at my friends to run—run away as fast as they can. Before I reach Patrick, however, I suddenly freeze mid-step. I quickly find the source of my block, a man standing close to Patrick has his hand outstretched and his eyes narrowed in concentration. Without hesitation, I throw my dagger hard. It flies straight and true, burying itself in the man's fleshy neck. He goes down in a gush of blood.

I continue racing at Patrick, watching as the proud, power-hungry look on his face turns into surprise, shock, and even a little fear. Reaching in my belt as I continue forward, I pull out the small grenade and remove the pin. I throw it hard at Patrick, who somehow dodges it at the last second. It flies past him and explodes with a deafening retort, ripping a massive hole in the circle of men caging us in.

With the debris thick in the air, Patrick is suddenly veiled from my sight. I stop and spin around but am unable to see much in the murky air. The smoke and dirt particles are thick and hang in the air. I feel like I'm being smothered. I start to pull up my hood when a strong hand suddenly grabs my arm.

A face appears through the dim surroundings, his gruesome features curled into a sneer. "Get away from me!" I scream, whacking Patrick's hand with his journal. He curses and lets go. I see his eyes widen at the journal in my hand. His mouth opens to say something and his hand extends toward me again.

Quickly backing away, I pull up my hood and race away as fast as I can. With the cloth over my mouth and nose, breathing is easier and I'm able to escape. I don't stop running until I'm well past the line where the trees become healthier. Letting go of the hood and allowing the wind flying past to fling it onto my back, I run faster.

When I finally do stop, I collapse and slide down to the ground beside a tree and start sobbing. The tears come fast and hard, and I'm still gasping for breath from my run. My heart is racing, and I feel overwhelmed by every-thing that happened. After a while, my crying slows, along with my heart rate and breathing. Exhausted, I let my head rest between my knees.

And fall asleep.

A sudden rustling nearby jolts me back to alertness. I swing up my head and find two green, glowing feline eyes staring back at me. I'm too surprised to scream, or even move at all. I simply stare back at it, watching its every move even as it does the same to me. It takes a step toward me and is too close for comfort. I swallow nervously and am about to scream for help when more rustling reaches my ears.

"Crystal?" I hear a worried voice call. The large cat backs away, finally breaking its gaze and racing off into the trees at the exact same moment that Sierra bursts out from the trees. Relief spreads quickly over her face. "Oh, Crystal... I found her!" she shouts. Immediately the sound of many footsteps come racing towards us as Sierra kneels in front of me. "Are you alright?" she asks, holding my face between her hands. Her touch is cool and helps bring me back to my senses.

"Sierra? How long—" I glance at my watch.

"You've been missing for almost an hour," she informs me. "We've been searching like crazy. We didn't realize you got so far! We were mostly looking closer to the explosion, then spreading out. We thought... we thought maybe..."

I feel a pang in my chest. I keep accidentally hurting those nearest to me.

"I'm so sorry, Sierra," I say, feeling a tear fall unbidden from my eye. "I should have tried to find you—you thought that Patrick had captured me again..." She nods, sniffling, before regaining control of her emotions just as the others arrive.

"Crystal! Thank goodness you're okay!" Ham cries, rushing to me and giving me a hug as I rise to my feet, surprising me. He pulls back and holds me at arm's length, eyes going up and down my body. "You *are* okay, right? I mean, I don't see anything wrong..."

"She's fine," Susan assures, amusement making her eyes shine in the faint moonlight. "Come on, we'll talk about it later. We need to get out of here before Patrick sends a search party after us."

Josh snorts back laughter. "Do you really think he'd dare? Crystal just blew up about twenty of his men! And—"

Reed cuts in impatiently. "You're an idiot to think that he won't. He didn't know that Crystal was back before now. He would rather grab her from a few of us now while we're in the woods—in his territory—before he would have to face the entire Village in order to get her."

Susan starts, a flash of fear spreading across her face and disappearing again so quickly I almost think I imagined it. "They're coming," she states. "I can hear their thoughts... they're looking for us. Run," she calmly finishes, racing off into the darkness.

I glance at Sierra, who grabs my hand and tears off with me in tow. She isn't going as fast as I know she can with her Gift of speed, but she's going plenty fast enough for me to barely keep my footing and prevent her from dragging me along the ground.

We quickly catch up to Susan, who waves us onward. "Get Crystal home, Sierra. Don't come looking for the rest of us, and don't stop. Keep the Princess safe."

She nods and speeds up, racing around trees and leaping over fallen ones, dragging me behind her. I grimace. Not only does no one ever let me make my own decisions, but my arm feels like it's being pulled out of its socket. "Sierra... wait..." I start.

"No," she responds, not even breathing hard. "I was on this mission with the sole order to protect you at all costs. That's what I'm doing, and you can't stop me."

"Okay, but..." I gasp as she leaps over a boulder and yet another wave of pain races from my shoulder down to my hand. "You're... hurting me... slow down, at least... please."

She immediately slows down and releases my hand before stopping and turning around. "What? How did I hurt you?"

"My... shoulder," I gasp, clenching it between my fingers. It's not dislocated, thankfully, although it had gotten close. The entire area aches, but I roughly try to massage it out. It helps a little. "I can run... on my own now," I say. "You don't need to drag me. We got a really good head start."

She looks at me a little despairingly, then merely shrugs. "Alright, fine. For now. If anyone comes up too close, though, I'm grabbing you again and high-tailing it out of here. If your shoulder gets hurt, we can fix it at the hospital which we can't do if you are dead or captured. Okay?"

I stare at her. *Way to think of the positive,* I think, a grim smile sliding onto my face before disappearing in a flash. "Fine. ...Whatever you say, oh guardian angel," I add sarcastically.

She frowns. "You know I'm just doing my—"

"I know, I know. I'm sorry," I sigh. "I just..."

She shakes her head. "Forget about it, alright? This mission is putting a strain on everyone. ...Come on, we should go before they catch up."

I nod, but am only able to take a single step forward before there's movement in the bushes behind us. "Run!" Sierra screams. But I don't run. Instead, I turn, pulling a small knife from my belt. I *hate* running. Especially when I can fight. My curiosity builds to a crescendo when someone races out of the bush.

I lower my arm with a sigh, sheathing the knife. "Chet," I say, relieved. "How did you find..."

"No time," he pants, stopping in front of me. He grabs my hand. "We have to go! Now! They're right behind me!" Then he takes off, hauling me behind him. I race along with him, my heart pounding with fear that seems to have only just set in from when I woke up. He grabbed the same hand that Sierra had, but it doesn't hurt since he's going slowly enough for me to keep up. Sierra runs behind us, but I can feel her impatience as I stumble. Chet, however, patiently helps me back up and continues running. It's easier to run without holding hands, but somehow the contact comforts me and keeps me from panicking. I don't let go of his hand, and he doesn't release his grip on mine either. I almost feel as though he's linking me to the real world, keeping me from slipping into a land of hysteria that had been creeping in on me ever since we returned to that cursed castle.

When we went inside, I didn't just feel the memories of pain. I felt as though the walls themselves were emanating evil. The place made me feel sick, almost... in physical pain. I've secretly been on the edge of delirium ever since. I never mentioned this to the others, of course. Not only would they think I'm insane, but they would also send me back to the Village immediately. I would be of no use to anyone if they sent me to the hospital for insanity.

"The edge of the forest!" Sierra exclaims behind me, relief and excitement in her voice. "We're almost—" her voice is cut off as a knife flies from behind her and buries itself in her leg. She goes down immediately.

Chet instantly lets go of my hand and drops to his knee to help her. I stare back as the blood squirting from the wound gets all over his shirt as he picks her up. Her face is bathed in tears, but she hardly made a sound. *Brave Sierra...*

"Go!" Chet yells at me. "I'll be right behind you. I promise!" Nodding, tears streaming down *my* face now as well, I turn and run even faster than before, holding the journal tight to my chest with both hands. Each breath rattles in my lungs. My vision seems to all but disappear. The only thing I can see is my destination. My thoughts have narrowed to simply *get out as fast as possible!* I can't worry about Sierra. I just can't. There's nothing I can do, and Chet promised to be right behind me as I escape this nightmare forest.

I close my eyes and keep running. My tears made everything almost too blurry to see very well anyway. My mind, unbidden, replays what just happened. The look of shock on her face as the knife pierced her flesh... Chet, so heroic, saving her; picking her up easily in those big strong arms... When did he get so strong anyway? He wasn't nearly that strong when we first met...

Smack!

My eyes fly open in surprise. It takes me a moment to realize what the thing in front of my face is. When it finally registers in my tired mind, I breathe a sigh of relief and sink to the ground, my back to it. *I made it... to the Village...* I lean back against the house and close my eyes, trying to slow my heart back down to normal, as well as my breathing, which comes out harsh between my dry, cracked lips. I can feel my heartbeat in my stomach, as well as in my throat and head. It's slowly giving me a headache, but I don't have the luxury to care about it.

My eyes are only closed for a few seconds before they fling open again. Chet! And Sierra! They're still in there! I leap to my feet and take a few steps back into the forest. I see something charging at me and instantly recognize Chet; Sierra in his arms. He's covered in blood from her leg.

As they come closer, I notice that Sierra's face is ashen. *She's lost a lot of blood...* Chet stops beside me and gently lays Sierra on her back. Her eyes are closed. "Is she..."

"She's unconscious," Chet quickly answers. He takes off his shirt, then looks up at me a little sheepishly. "Can I borrow that knife of yours?"

"Oh, of course," I say, trying in vain to keep the blood from rising to my cheeks. *Hopefully it's dark enough that he can't see it,* I think, handing over the knife. He swiftly slices a strip of the silvery fabric, followed by another. Handing back the knife, he then quickly covers and ties the wound before picking the poor girl back up.

"She needs to go to the hospital," he states as he sets off toward the building. I stand there and watch him walk away, silhouetted by the large moon on the horizon. My heart skips a beat and I can't help but think of a prince rescuing his princess. Then I turn and peer into the dark, menacing woods, malice seeping like a poison from among the trees. I shiver. As much as I'm itching to plunge back in there and rescue my friends, I can't. Not only would I not be able to find my way back, but once I get there, I would just be sent away immediately.

Taking a deep breath, I spin on my heel and follow Chet to the hospital. *I guess they will all just have to fend for themselves...* I feel guilty, however, as my back turns to them and every step I take feels like I'm abandoning them.

7

Nathan collapses heavily onto the bed in the corner of the room. He absentmindedly runs his fingers along the lines of the white and blue quilt, feeling the silkiness between his fingers. For the first few minutes after Zarafa had left, he had stood stock-still in the same place, mind racing, trying to figure out how to get out of this new predicament until he had finally exhausted his mind and his fear. Once his panic had faded, he turned and examined 'his' new room.

The walls were mostly white, with little creatures painted in light blue along the bottom of the walls. The ceiling was white and had strange, interesting shapes and designs that he wasn't sure were meant to be there or not. He had stared at that ceiling for a few minutes before tearing himself away. He could probably gaze up at it all day and not get bored, his imagination causing him to see different things every time he shifted his gaze.

Other than the bed, there wasn't much in the room. There was a small table beside the bed with a simple alarm clock, a lamp, a pad of paper with a pen on it, a chest at the foot of the bed filled with clothes, and a chair in front of a small table in the corner opposite the bed. The wooden door was simple, but sturdy. The golden handle gleamed in the light. The handle seemed normal, but when Nathan had grabbed it, hoping to get out of the room and sneak away from the house, it had zapped him, throwing him backward until he hit the wall behind him. That was when he discovered that there was no escape from this strange place. He had picked up the device that brought him here, but it didn't do anything. It seemed to be a one-way teleporter. Meant to bring him here, but not allow him to escape.

He sighs and checks his watch. It was still another ten minutes until Zarafa had told him to join her in the kitchen. He didn't know where the kitchen was, but he figured he could find it without much trouble when the time came—assuming he could even get out of the room. He lies back on the bed and gazes up at the ceiling again, looking at it without really seeing it. *How am I supposed to do this? I don't have Greg, I don't have my backpack with my stuff in it, and my plan didn't go how I wanted it to at all! I'm trapped in an enemy's house with no plan and no way out...* He sits up quickly. He could smack himself for being so thoughtless. *My Gifts! I'm so stupid! How did I forget about my Gifts? I mean, I haven't had the opportunity to use them for a while, but still...* He shakes his head at himself. *I can still shapeshift... or control the weather. That should be enough to get out of here. I may even be able to get some answers out of her before I go...*

He's just about to shift into a small snake to slip under the door when it abruptly opens, surprising him. He stumbles back and falls onto the bed. Looking up, he finds Zarafa at the doorway, smiling amiably. "Dessert is ready," she proclaims, her voice sweet as honey. "Would you care to join me?" Her sparkling, unnaturally bright green eyes seem to make his brain freeze up. He struggles to make it work again. But when her smile grows, he seems to lose all ability to speak.

"I... uh..."

She holds out a hand to him, a look of understanding on her face. "Come, then. I can't wait to speak with you, Nathan. I've heard so much about you," she continues, her soft voice compelling him to stumble forward the few steps to take her hand. *She... she's heard about me?* He can't help but feel a rush of pleasure that this beautiful—*gorgeous*—lady would want to talk to him so badly. He forgets how he got here, lost in the bliss of being wanted. He's suddenly just as anxious to talk to her as she seems to be to talk to him.

She leads him into a large room. Her heels click as she leads him across the tile floor towards the large table. She pulls out a chair for him, and he sits. He's still stunned and dazed as she seats herself across from him. Ringing a little silver bell that rests beside her plate, a couple of servants enter the room, bearing silver platters. The chime of the small bell helps to pull Nathan out of his trance. When the servants set down their burdens, they both bow to Zarafa and leave. She smiles at Nathan and gestures to the food before them. "Go on," she encourages. "Try it."

He tears his eyes away from her and looks down at the dessert. It looks like a small cake but with a different consistency, more like that of cheesecake. "It's strawberry," she continues, picking up her fork with her long, delicate fingers. "My favorite. This came straight from Zilferia, you know," she continues slyly, taking a small bite of the cake.

Nathan hesitantly picks up his fork as well. The texture of the food is moist, but not wet; the flavor sweet, and unlike any strawberry he'd ever had before. However, just like Zarafa said, it did taste like it was from Zilferia. It had the same calming and mind-clearing qualities as the rest of the food he had partaken of in the other realm. The small, delicate desert is gone in a few more bites. After finishing the treat, Nathan feels refreshed and calm. He's in control of his thoughts once more. Setting his fork down on the white tablecloth, he clasps his hands in front of him and leans forward a little. Locking his eyes onto Zarafa's, he's unaffected by her charm, too focused on what he's about to say.

Clearing his throat, he glares at her. "Okay, now it's time to answer my questions." He pauses to see if she'll object, but she just leans back in her seat and nods slightly. "How do you know who I am? What have you heard about me? How do you know about Zilferia? Why did you kidnap me with those... things... if you wanted to talk to me? What do you want to talk about? Does it have to do with Crystal—"

She holds up a hand to stop him, a smile tugging at her blood-red lips. "Hold on there. If you want me to answer any of your questions, you're going to have to give me some time to talk," she says, mirth in her voice. "I know who you are because of Alexander and Pearl Dragon. They told me all about you, and sent me to find you and speak with you. I regret that I had to use others to get to you, but unfortunately I cannot go into the sunlight in this realm without pain."

Nathan just stares at her, not comprehending. "Why not?" he asks.

She smiles teasingly. "Oh, come now. You aren't even going to venture a guess?" He continues to stare at her blankly. She sighs as if disappointed. "I'm a vampire. Ever heard of us, Nathan? I'm fairly sure Thaddeus mentioned them, as did Vladimir when you first met him, I believe."

He scoffs in disbelief. "A vampire? Seriously? You expect me to believe that? Vampires aren't real. They're only in movies and really bad books."

She laughs. "Nathan, you've met werewolves and dragons—even a girl who could turn *into* a dragon— and you don't believe in vampires?" Nathan's mouth snaps shut. *Well, when you put it like that...* He groans. *With everything I've seen... I doubt the existence of a vampire? Just the fact that she knows about Zilferia, has been there, and claims to be one, should be enough proof that she probably is one.* He shakes his head.

Taking this as a sign of continued disbelief, Zarafa sighs. "Alright, I'll prove it to you." She opens her mouth. Held captive by the sight, Nathan can't seem to tear his eyes away. Her teeth had become long and sharp, just like in the vampire movies. Her pupils had gone into slits like a cat's. After a few seconds, the teeth shrink back to normal, and her pupils do as well. "Believe me now?" she says.

He nods dumbly. To think, he's sitting with a real vampire... who could probably easily tear out his throat. Swallowing, he pushes this thought away. If she wanted to eat him, she would have already. "The King and Queen sent you?" he confirms.

"Yes."

"To talk to me. Why did they do that? Thaddeus could have just contacted me with my watch," he says. Her eyes immediately flick to his wrist.

"I see. Well, they wanted me to come in person, I suppose. Besides, I am also not here just to talk to you. I'm here to accomplish a task I've been assigned."

"And what would that be?" he inquires, curious.

Zarafa smiles. "That's actually why I need to talk to you. I need your help, Nathan."

He frowns. Something just isn't right about this vampire lady. "...Where's Crystal?" he asks.

Now she frowns. "What? She's in Second Earth. Why would you ask me that? Do you really think I would do anything to the Princess?" She sounds hurt, but Nathan is unaffected.

He stands. "I wouldn't put it past you. After all, you just kidnapped me. And Crystal's been kidnapped and tortured a lot. Besides, I don't trust you. I have a feeling you're just trying to say what I want to hear. You know that I trust Alexander and Pearl, and you're using that against me." He starts walking away. "I'm leaving. After I contact Thaddeus, I will ask him to confirm your story. If he doesn't, I'll know you're lying."

He turns to see her standing, a look of panic flashing across her face so quickly he almost misses it. "No! Wait... I... I can prove it!"

"How?" he asks incredulously. She closes her mouth and thinks. He folds his arms. "You have ten minutes before I leave. Convince me, or I know you're just lying to me."

Her mouth tightens into a firm line. "Can I have a little longer? I'll see if I can contact Pearl or Alexander for you. They can back me up."

"Very well." He goes back to the table and sits down, arms still folded. Zarafa leaves. He can hear talking in another room for a few minutes, then silence. After a few more minutes, there's more talking.

Zarafa comes back into the kitchen, hands on her hips. "I got Alexander for you. You're just lucky he was there."

Nathan nods and follows her into the next room. In the center of the small room is a raised square emitting blue light. Standing in that light is a hologram of Alexander Dragon. "Nathan," he says, relieved. "I'm so glad Zarafa found you! Nathan, I need you to trust her. I really did ask her to help me with something. Something that I'm hoping you'd be willing to also lend a hand with."

"Where's Crystal?" he asks. "Why don't you ask her to help?"

He frowns, a sad look in his eyes. "She's still on Second Earth. I was going to ask her to help as well, but she is having a hard time without her dragon part or her Gifts. She's still trying to get used to the loss. She can't help."

"Well, how can I?"

A tear falls from the King's eye. "Nathan, you know about me and my family. You know about Crystal and Hunter... and you've heard the sad news about Rex."

"Yeah..."

"Nathan, I need you to help me find Rex. Crystal would try to help if she knew about this, but she can't. Not in her condition. Please don't tell her about this. It's far too dangerous for her at the moment."

"Dangerous? Why is it dangerous?"

"It's nothing like what you had to go through in the Games," he assures. "It would only be dangerous for her because she's in such a weakened state. You, however, have both of your Gifts, do you not?"

"Yes..."

"Good. Nathan, I need your help to find Rex before Patrick does. He would either kill him or take him just as he has Hunter, and I can't take that. ...Crystal deserves to have at least one of her brothers, don't you agree?" Nathan's heart softens at this. It was true, Hunter was brainwashed by Patrick, leaving her alone. Crystal did deserve to have a brother who didn't betray and hurt her.

"What do I have to do?"

<<<Zarafa>>>

Zarafa smiles triumphantly as she leads the boy back to his room. He had been completely won over by the hologram and no longer suspected anything. He may not have been blind and dumb enough to trust her at first, but he trusts her now. Her grin widens as she recalls her quick thinking that saved the almost ruined plan.

Patrick would be proud of her now.

After shutting the door behind the boy, she quickly heads back to the Projection Room. Lightly touching the square in the middle of the floor, another hologram rises into the air. Patrick smiles at her. "Quick thinking, having me pretend to be Alexander," he praises. "I knew the boy would be cautious, but I figured that your Charm would win him over."

"As did I," she agrees. "He's a strong one. I think he felt the magic being worked on him and fought back. Whether consciously or not, he knew what I was doing."

Patrick looks thoughtful. "He would be a great ally."

"I'll see what I can do," she replies, white teeth flashing in the light of the sunset streaming from the window.

"I trust that you shall," he says with a small smile in return. "Just remember, don't feed on him and *don't* change him. I need him as a human, not another vampire."

Zarafa frowns. "My self-control is better than that."

"I know, I know," he assures, "I can never be too careful, however."

"That is how you survived for so long, after all," she praises, flashing a cunning smile. "It's always brains over brawn that wins the war."

"Speaking of which, my plans for this war have changed," Patrick announces.

"What?" she replies, surprised.

"Crystal Dragon is back."

<<<Nathan>>>

After Zarafa left, Nathan wandered over to the window and peered out. The building is surrounded by trees, and on the horizon, mountains rise into the sky, their sharp tops seeming to slice into the sun as it sets behind them. The clouds near the mountains turn a brilliant purple, orange, and pink. And for a moment… it seemed like they were on fire.

Nathan steps away from the window, shaking his head to clear it. *You're imagining things again,* he scolds himself. *Although why I was imagining trees burning around a stone building is the real question…* He stops himself before he notes that the building looked just like the evil place where he had rescued Crystal back in Zilferia. Patrick's castle. He takes a deep breath. *I'm just paranoid… probably because of Zarafa. I thought that she was working for Patrick, so now that I was thinking about him, my mind immediately jumped back to when that happened. …Yes, that must be it.* Feeling better now that he had come up with a theory to the strange vision, he sits down on the soft bed.

After a few minutes, he realized that he's hungry again. He hadn't really had much for dinner. So he heads to the door with the intent of finding Zarafa so he can get some food. He grabs the door handle, forgetting that it will shock him. But this time, it doesn't. Deciding to ponder this later, he closes the door behind him and heads up the stairs. When he reaches the kitchen, he finds that she isn't there. However, he can hear voices down the hall from the room he had just talked to Alexander in. Figuring it's Zarafa, he heads toward the sound.

As he gets closer, he hears her say, "It shouldn't be that hard. Children are so easy to…" her voice suddenly cuts off. Gulping, Nathan backs away. He has a feeling he heard part of a conversation that he shouldn't have heard. He creeps quickly and quietly back down the stairs. He reaches his room just as Zarafa opens the door. He slips quietly into his room, hoping that she hadn't seen him.

<<<Zarafa>>>

75

"What was that about?" Patrick asks as Zarafa closes the door again.

"I thought I heard someone."

"You mean Nathan? Why didn't you put the spell back on his door?"

"I must have forgotten. I'll do it now," she says, narrowing her eyes, her lips moving as she goes through the spell in her mind, no words actually spoken. After a few moments, her mouth closes and she opens her eyes again, fixing them on Patrick. "There. He won't be bothering us now."

"Good. Now then, you were saying?"

"I was saying that it shouldn't be difficult to influence the boy. It's quite obvious that he has a thing for the Dragon girl. We can use her against him. He will do anything we ask if he thinks that his actions will keep her safe. Although, if he thinks that we have her, he will fight us with all his might."

He nods thoughtfully. "Yes, that's very true. He risked his life a few months back to rescue the girl from me. He knows that I could have killed him or taken him captive as well, but he didn't falter. ...Yes, I do believe that she is the key to using him. I can even shapeshift into *her* if we need."

"Speaking of the girl, what do you plan to do with her? She's powerless without her Gifts or dragon abilities. Plus, you already have Hunter to use against the King and Queen. I just don't understand why you don't just kill her. I would if I were you..."

"Yes, but you are *not* me. You were also not here to see her fight so vigorously against me. She's a force to be reckoned with, even without her Gifts. If we had her on our side, we would win control of Zilferia without question."

There's a pause in the conversation as Zarafa mulls over what he told her had happened with Crystal. "So Hunter is with them now? Posing as a friend?"

Patrick grins. "Yes. Chet is in my grasp, and Hunter is undercover as him. The girl came almost too quickly, however," he comments, gazing into the distance. "Had she come but an hour earlier, all may have been lost. Thankfully, my inside source alerted us to their impending mission. Hunter and I had come up with a plan."

Zarafa's face creases in confusion. "Then... he gave her the journal on purpose?"

He smiles, full of pride. "Yes. The things written in there will convince her to turn herself into me, I am sure of it."

"Why is that?"

"That is not my real journal. I made that one specifically to get her to come to me willingly." He grins gleefully. "There's nothing better than defeating someone's spirit. Getting to them mentally... You know, for a long while, I considered physical pain to be victory. However, I eventually discovered that there is nothing quite like watching someone go through a mental breakdown. And Crystal seems to be strong on the outside, but really, her emotions are all over the place since she lost her Gifts and dragon part. She will be an easy target," he says, his grin widening in anticipation.

<<<Nathan>>>

Nathan sighs. The door had electrocuted him when he tried to leave again, so now he's stuck in the room with nothing to do. He glances at his watch. *I suppose I could just get some sleep...* He then remembers the other things the watch can do. *...Or I could contact Thaddeus! It would be nice just to double check that I can trust Zarafa... besides, I'm out of the loop of what's going on in Zilferia. I haven't heard anything all summer, but when I left, it sounded like the Dragon Hunters were probably about to wage war. They have the Gift Stealer- which we know works now; the machine that kills dragons; and a ruthless leader. They seemed all set to start laying waste to anything in their path.*

He twists the raised circle around the circumference of the face of the watch. He doesn't really know how it works, but it should show either Crystal or Thaddeus in a small hologram when he lifts the circle.

Nothing happens. *Hmm. Is it broken? I haven't really tried to use it since I got home from Zilferia... maybe it doesn't really work across different realms.* He sighs. So much for that idea. *I suppose I'll just go to bed. There's nothing else I can do today anyway. Tomorrow, however, there will be lots to do.*

Tomorrow, I'll start helping Zarafa find Rex.

<<<Zarafa>>>

"You're sure the boy won't suspect anything anymore? I made sure to encase his watch with magic so he can't contact Thaddeus and ask questions, but..."

Patrick sighs. "He thinks that the King himself just told him to go for it. I seriously doubt he thought that I was anyone other than that buffoon."

"True, you were quite convincing," Zarafa concedes.

"Plus, it makes perfect sense for Alexander to want to find the boy before I do," he says. He grins, almost laughing. "He probably *would* be sending out a search party for him if I wasn't occupying his time..."

"You really have him worried, don't you?" she comments, laughing herself.

"Well he should be worried," Patrick snaps, suddenly serious. "Because although I'm saving *him* for last, I'm slowly picking away at his villagers, claiming their Gifts for my own. I already have multiple Gifts myself now- as does Hunter. Most of my men now have at least one Gift as well, thanks to the King's people."

"How are you doing against the dragons?"

"I believe I have already conquered or slain half of them," he brags with a malicious smirk. "Once they are eradicated, I will direct my men and the dragons we have under our control to attack the Sohos. They will not take long to destroy. Then we'll finish off the merfolk. Finally, I will destroy the Village. Alexander Dragon will beg for his life after seeing my might. And after enjoying that for a while, I will slay him."

"And what of Pearl?"

He looks thoughtful. "She shall either be my Queen, or she will die. ... That all depends on her."

8

"Crystal." A soft voice behind me causes me to turn from the window I had been anxiously staring out of. Chet is there, leaning against the door frame, eying me with worry. "Crystal, you need to get some rest. Being here isn't going to change anything for Sierra, plus, you need your sleep. I can keep an eye on her during the night if you need, though," he adds, walking around Sierra's bed. He crouches in front of me and takes one of my hands in his, holding it tenderly. A blush creeps onto my cheeks at his nearness.

"It's not just that," I say, pulling my hand away and turning to gaze back at the forest. "It's been an hour, and only Ham and Josh are back... I'm worried about the others."

He nods and stands. "Well, get some sleep if you can. Don't worry about the others- I'm sure they'll be fine. They are very experienced fighters, and they have their Gifts to aid them." I wince at this, yet another reminder that I no longer have my own and am therefore useless. Chet notices and immediately begins to apologize. "Oh, I'm so sorry, I forgot. I'm so sorry..."

My head down, I stare at my knees, fighting back tears. I shrug and manage to choke out, "It's okay. I'm okay. I'm fine..." I don't even believe my own words, so I'm a little surprised when it seems like he does.

"...Alright. But, Crystal, if you're that worried about the others, I can go and find them myself." He holds up a hand to stop me as I start to protest.

"I'll be fine, I promise. I'll go and get them all back for you," he announces, leaving before I can say anything else. I stare after him, wide-eyed. Great. Now there's just one more person to worry about.

<<<Hunter>>>

Hurrying towards the woods, Hunter, in the disguise of Chet, pulls out his sword. It's all for show, of course, in case Crystal is watching out a window. His plan is not to kill anyone. Not any of his Dragon Hunters or Crystal's friends. He's out to save them so he can earn her trust. He's just relieved that Nathan Anderson, the boy who took his sister from Patrick, isn't around. He wouldn't trust him, which would only make everything more difficult. Without him here, Hunter could, in the guise of Chet, sneak closer to Crystal's heart, using his mind 'reading' Gift to put specific thoughts in her head and prevent other ones, such as ones of Nathan. He needed to get her to trust him- that was also part of the reason for the journal. Not only would it aid her in learning to trust him, but Patrick had assured him that the things he had written would show her the truth about their family, as well as the Dragon Hunters, so she would come back to them willingly.

Hunter, never one to doubt Patrick's plans, feels quite sure that it will work. He just needed to do his part and earn her trust, sneak into her heart, then slowly feed her the words that Patrick had instructed him to tell her. He smiles. He will be glad when his sister is no longer led blindly along by the lies the Villagers had weaved to ensnare her with. He wants her to know the truth, like he does.

Patrick had warned him that she would argue and put up a good fight, but no matter what she said and looked like on the outside, the words would pierce her and slowly she would come to recognize them as the truth. He was not to listen to the things that she told him, for they were just lies that were fed to her. She didn't know that they are lies, and would assure him that they are the truth. But he will not be led astray from his mission to show her the truth and get her on his side.

He knew how to get her dragon powers back, and he wanted her to have them so she wasn't so broken. He hadn't realized just how damaged she was until the mere mention of Gifts had nearly set her to tears. He wanted her to be happy.

But Patrick had told him explicitly not to tell her what to do to get them back, so he wouldn't. He sighs heavily as he stomps through the dark forest towards the sounds of battle raging. *As soon as she realizes the truth and joins us, I will tell her,* he decides. *She should be happy. I know that I can give her that happiness... I just have to get her to see things my way. I'm happy, because I'm not clouded with conflicting lies. But there is a lingering sadness and restlessness I sense in her. She needs Patrick and I. We can help her.*

He stops, finding himself standing before a scene of blood and carnage. He frowns. There wasn't supposed to be this many deaths. He quickly changes back into himself, then rushes into the clearing. Only one person notices him, and before he can even blink, he has a knife buried in his forearm. He winces and glances down at it, then locks eyes with the woman named Susan. She grins wickedly at him, finishes cutting down the man before her, then starts toward him.

Grimacing, he pulls out the knife, holding it in his other hand. Ignoring the blood pouring out of the wound, he shouts loud enough for everyone nearby to hear. "Dragon Hunters, cease your attack!" The fighting stops as everyone turns to look at him. He tosses back his hood. "Retreat," he orders, glaring around at his men. They look utterly confused, but they obey and back away from the Villagers. "Go now, and tell Patrick of your failure. I shall be right behind you."

The knife woman arches an eyebrow at him. He hears her thoughts with his mind. *"You lowlife scum... I don't know why you did that, but I will kill you regardless... and should I find that you took Crystal again, I will feed your corpse to the wild animals in this forest personally."* She pulls out another knife, the intensity behind her eyes causing his insides to wither. *"The King and Queen don't need to know that I killed their traitorous son, and neither does Crystal. Should anyone find out, I'll just tell them that it was a creature in the forest..."*

Then, out loud, she growls, "Prepare to die, boy," and throws the knife. He avoids it, but she is already charging at him with a sword, knocking him to the ground. The breath rushes out of his lungs. He gazes up at the woman, who holds the sword to his neck. Narrowing his eyes, he causes a bolt of lightning to strike the ground immediately behind her. She goes flying over his head from the force. Standing, he rushes off into the night after his men, leaving the group that Crystal was so worried about behind him.

He catches up to one of his men and stops him. "Tell Patrick that it was something I had to do to gain her trust. Everything is still under control."

The man nods, and Hunter changes back into Chet, races past the group with the knife woman, then comes running forward, panting as if he were tired. "Crystal was worried… about you… where are all the Dragon Hunters?" he asks. He feels a warm glow at his acting skills. None of them suspect a thing.

The knife woman, Susan, is picking up her sword, which she dropped when she went flying from the lightning burst. "Hunter came and shooed them off. I don't know why, but I have a bad feeling about it. …Wait, what's that on your right arm?" she suddenly asks suspiciously. "And why do you have my knife?" Her eyes narrow and she takes a menacing step toward him.

Thinking quickly, he gasps, "Hunter… found me… and stabbed me with it," he says, holding out the knife handle first for her to take. She snatches it from his hand.

"That's the same spot that I hit him…" she notices.

He grimaces. "I bet he thought that was real funny then. Does anybody have something to stop the bleeding?"

Reed steps up with a piece of his shirt that was cut off during the battle. "Here. One of the Dragon Hunters nearly got me, but ended up with just this instead. It should work until we get to the hospital."

"Thanks," he says, fumbling with it until he managed to tie it around his arm. He tightens the knot with his teeth, then looks back up. "Crystal wanted me to help you guys, but it seems you didn't need any."

Reed nods. "Lucky for us Hunter came when he did. We were just about to drop," he comments.

Susan laughs. "Speak for yourself. I was about to finish the rest of them off when he waltzed in here. Question is, though, why did he send them away?"

"Maybe he was scared of you," Reed laughs. "I would be if I was in his place. I mean, you almost killed him in ten seconds flat!"

"He would have been dead before he could blink if it weren't for that weather trick," she complains, but Hunter can see the pleased glint in her eye. The group then stumbles back to the hospital. As they walk, Hunter makes sure that Reed is between him and Susan. Just in case.

<<<Crystal>>>

Chet comes back in the door, followed by the other members of the rescue group. I jump up and so relieved, I rush to Chet and hug him tight before suddenly letting go and backing up, blushing a little. "Sorry," I apologize. "I'm just so glad you're okay- and the rest of you are too!"

Chet chuckles. "Well, as much as I would love to claim that it was all because of me, they were actually just fine when I got there. They seemed to have scared the rest of them off... although one of them got me with a knife as he was fleeing," he winces. I glance down and notice the blood-soaked sleeve of his shirt.

I gasp. "Oh, my goodness! We need to get that taken care of. Now!"

Chet smiles a little nervously. "Um, no, it's okay, actually... see, I bandaged it up..." I don't listen, grabbing his elbow and hauling him with me to find a doctor. I locate one quickly and show him Chet's wounded arm. He takes Chet into another room to fix him up. I head back to join the others. I peek in and see that they are all fine, so I then go back to Chet to make sure he's really going to be okay. There was a lot of blood...

He's sitting on a chair with the doctor wrapping a clean white bandage around his forearm. He glances up at me and smiles. "See? I told you it was fine," he says.

The doctor shakes his head. "No, it's not. The knife scraped your bone. I gave you something to help it heal faster, but it's not 'nothing' like you claim. Not only that, but there seems to be a poison in your bloodstream. The knife was probably coated with it." Chet goes pale, and so do I.

"What kind of poison?" I ask hesitantly.

The doctor frowns. "I'm not sure yet. I gave him something that should slow its progress enough that I can hopefully figure out what it is and how to prevent it from harming him, though," he assures once he sees the panicked look on my face. I nod, only slightly relieved. The doctor leaves, and I turn to Chet again. His face is a sickly white, but he pretends what the doctor said didn't unnerve him- though obviously it did.

"I'm sure he'll figure it out," he soothes, standing and guiding me toward the door. "Let's just go check on the others, alright?"

"Yes... of course," I reply, following him down the hallway.

<<<Hunter>>>

Curse that woman... of course, she just HAD to poison that knife she threw at me...

and now no one knows what the poison is exactly or what the cure is… I'm willing to bet that she knows. I will wring it out of that blasted woman, I don't care if she gets hurt or not… Crystal would get over it, even if she died. First, though, I suppose I'll just ask nicely to give her a sporting chance. Although if she doesn't tell me, or insists that she doesn't know, then I'll just have to pry it out of her mind with my new Gift of 'reading minds'… I will enjoy making it hurt for what she did to me… He grimaces as his arm throbs with pain, as if responding to his thoughts. Crystal glances at him, worry written on her face.

"Is there anything I can do, Chet?" she asks. He almost laughs at the thought. *No, not unless you know the cure for this poison that's slowly creeping up my arm,* he thinks sarcastically. *Why does she think she can help anyway? She's completely powerless. I have all of her Gifts, and then some! I do not need help.* His heart softens as the thinks about her offer. *Although it's kind of her to be concerned, I suppose. I don't need her help, but it's a nice gesture.*

Out loud, he merely says, "I don't think so. Thanks, though."

She nods, trying to hide the worry on her face. She isn't very good at it. *Not nearly as good of an actor as I am,* he brags to himself. *No one has any clue who I really am… the one who came closest was Susan, and that wasn't because of any fault of mine—in fact, it was my quick thinking that saved my own skin… although she's likely still suspicious of me. She seems like one that is slow to buy anything that anyone says to her. Which is probably why she's lasted so long, fighting against our group for so many years. Most of the Dragon Hunters have no idea of her reputation, but I know differently. I've heard tales from Patrick of how deep this woman was able to burrow into our secret operations… which is another reason I should just kill her… after discovering the location of the cure, of course.*

He follows Crystal into the room and acts casual, managing to not glare at Susan. Crystal sits down, following his lead. Susan glances at Hunter. "What's wrong with him? He doesn't look so good," she comments. He barely contains a sneer. *You know why, you evil little conniving woman,* he thinks angrily. However, Hunter just offers a tight-lipped smile in return, hiding his true feelings.

Crystal frowns. "There was poison on the knife that stabbed him, I guess. That's what the doctor said. Although he also said… he doesn't know what the poison is, so he doesn't know the cure either. And he has no idea what the symptoms will be. He slowed down the spread of the venom, though, so he can have time to research the poison he found in Chet."

Reed's eyebrows knit together. "Wasn't it Susan's knife that cut him?" He turns to her. "You know what the poison is, don't you?"

She ignores him, examining her fingernails nonchalantly, picking out dried blood. "I don't know. Maybe Hunter poisoned the knife before stabbing Chet." *You know that's not true, woman! This is all your doing! ...She's testing me,* he realizes. *Crafty woman... well, I'm smarter than she is. I'm not falling into her little trap. I'll never give away my true identity.*

"I saw him right after he left the clearing," he says, matter-of-factly. "I don't think he had the time- or the foresight- to poison it himself." Crystal nods, agreeing with him. He can't help but smile a little. *She has no idea what she's doing, backing me up,* he thinks. *I really am Hunter... she's so trusting,* he smirks on the inside. *She almost makes it too easy.*

Reed joins in, also coming to his defense. "Come on now, Susan. Why are you trying to hide it? We all know that you are the master hunter. It's only logical to assume that you have some nifty tricks up your sleeve. If you're worried about your secret poison getting out, I'm sure everyone here will promise not to tell anyone about it," he coaxes. Everyone nods, including Hunter. He doesn't intend to hold to the promise, but no one can know about that. Not even Miss 'I-read-minds-and-throw-knives' since he figured out how to manipulate the Gift of mind reading so he can also divert or even block another mind reader's mental ray as they send it to him. He can make her see whatever he wants her to see in his head. At the moment, he's displaying a feeling of truthfulness and innocence. He's just an unlucky, injured boy- as far as she knows.

Everyone's eyes are on Susan, waiting for her to say what her decision is. Finally, she sighs. "Alright. I'll go and get the cure—stay right here and don't move," she tells him. He nods solemnly while silently gloating inside. He had tricked her- and everyone else in the room as well.

Crystal sighs in relief. "Well, I sure am glad she has the cure!" He nods. *Although really, she should be glad she decided to give it to me, or else I would have had to extract it from her. Painfully.*

<<<Crystal>>>

Once Susan comes back with a murky green liquid in a needle, Chet insists that I leave the building while she applies it. She says she has to put it in where the poison started- meaning directly into his cut. Chet asked me to leave so I didn't have to watch- or hear- anything. I step outside, enjoying the fresh spring air and the beautiful sky as the sun rises. Then I remember that I should go and tell the council of what came of our mission... and how we failed. I sigh and start heading over to Thaddeus's house to break the news to him. He opens the door on the first knock, immediately sighing with relief. "Oh good, you're okay."

I nod. "Can I come in?"

"Of course," he replies, a look of understanding in his eyes. He closes the door behind me, then quietly mutters a spell to make it so no one can eaves-drop on us. Then he sits me down at his table and encourages me to tell him everything- and that's just what I do. When I finish, he stares down at the table, a frown on his face.

"I'm sorry," I finally say. "I thought we could do it—"

"No," he interrupts, holding up a hand to stop me. "It's alright. I wasn't so sure you would be able to find them anyway. I'm just relieved you got away safely," he says. I nod in response. He stands and sighs. "I suppose we should go inform the King and Queen of the fate of your mission."

"This is terrible," Alexander sighs, running a nervous hand through his hair. "Now, how are we ever going to get Zelda and Y'vette out of there?"

"I'm sure we'll find a way," Pearl soothes, putting a comforting hand on her husband's arm. "...A way that will *not* include putting our daughter in danger once again," she adds, glancing at me.

I immediately start to argue, but Thaddeus cuts in. "Yes, I believe that would be wise. We have Chet with us once again, and he knows the castle's inner workings. There is no further need to endanger Zilferia's only Princess." He turns to me. "There will be no arguing about it, Crystal. You are overruled." I frown, but don't say anything. They've made up their minds, and there's no way I will be able to change them. Of course, that doesn't mean that I will stay behind every time my friends go out and risk their own lives to clean up a mess that *I* had worsened. I won't always stay back and entertain my parents' hopes to keep me out of danger. That's never been an option for me. I have to do my part to keep Zilferia from falling under Patrick's crushing grip. I cannot do it alone... but with the help of all the friends I have made here, we can beat the Dragon Hunters, I know it.

We just have to stand united.

~

"So, where are we going?"

I turn to see Chet, dressed in his armor with a bandage wrapped about the still-healing wound from the knife, a backpack slung over one shoulder. He has a hand on one hip as he watches me, waiting for my answer. I turn from the door, releasing the handle. The backpack on my back swishes quietly through the air as I turn around and peer at him. "*We* aren't going anywhere," I reply in a hushed voice. It's not that I don't want the company —the things I'm about to do just aren't safe for others to accompany me to.

He raises an eyebrow. "You mean to tell me that you don't want someone with the Gift of Fighting to have your back wherever you're going?" I wince. I hate it when someone mentions Gifts... ever since that dreadful day that Patrick... I take a deep breath, pushing back the tide of sorrow. I really need to get over this. I can't react this way whenever someone mentions Gifts. I cannot wallow in depression and self-loathing when there are things to be done.

"It's not that..." I start, then stop, unsure of how to word this. "It's just... what I have to do... I have to do alone."

He strides forward, coming close to me. He's so close I can see the light from the morning sun cause his green eyes to sparkle. "And why is that, Crystal? What on earth do you have to do that requires you to do it alone? You may deny that you need protection... but I can't help but feel I should be protecting you nonetheless. Not just because you are the Princess, either..." His voice fades out uncertainly.

My heart softens. "I... I suppose you could come... it's just..."

"What?" he asks intently. "What is it? I want to help you."

I swallow. "Um... it's just... I don't know how my friends will react to you," I meekly attempt to explain.

He looks confused. "Well, if they're your friends, then why would they harm me? I'm your friend too," he adds.

I sigh. "...Because my friends are the Sohos, Dragons, and merfolk that sometimes eat people," I simply state.

A small frown furrows his brow. "I see. And why are you going to such ferocious friends so early in the morning? ...Do your parents know about this little adventure of yours?" I turn away from him, hiding my face. "Ah, I see. You didn't want to tell them because you didn't want them to stop you," he surmises.

I spin back to him, a pleading look on my face. "Please don't tell them! Please don't make me stay! I have to help!"

"Help with what?" he asks curiously.

"I have to help in this war," I state. "It's my fault things have gotten this bad. I'm the one that figured out how to fix the Gift Stealer... and now Patrick is laying siege to all of Zilferia. I have to stop him, Chet," I plead, grabbing his hand and peering up into those deep green eyes of his. "I have to stop him, because every life lost is a life on my hands..." I can feel tears welling up in my eyes, and I blink them away. Now is not a time for crying. I've done enough of that already. There's no need for more tears. They don't solve anything.

Chet's face softens. "Surely you don't blame yourself for this war?"

"No, not the war... just the advantage I gave Patrick," I explain.

He frowns. "So, just how do you mean to turn the tides?"

"I'm going to see if I can get us all united. Patrick can conquer every one of us because we are all divided and see little hope. I need to gather my friends, get it so we can all work together, and save hope once more."

"Hope cannot win a war, Crystal."

"Hope grants power beyond what would be possible otherwise," I argue. "Hope is what keeps us going beyond what the enemy believes we can go. Hope gives us an advantage. Hope and friendship. There is strength in numbers, but there is greater strength in the bonds between individuals. Then we do not fight simply for ourselves, but for more. We would be fighting for this entire realm."

He nods slightly. "I am touched by your speech," he says, smiling. He rubs his hands together. "So... where do we start?"

I smile up at him. "Probably the Sohos. I haven't seen them in quite a while."

He grins back. "Sounds great."

<<<Hunter>>>

As Hunter follows his sister out the door, his mind is whirling. *She plans to* unite everyone and empower them with hope? Hope can easily be crushed with enough pressure from fear... but still. This isn't good... just how far should I go with this pretense? ...Should I just grab her now and haul her back to the hideout? Patrick told me not to... but he has no idea of her determination to stop us. He told me that the fake journal would convince her to come to us willingly... He stops walking suddenly.

Crystal turns around. "What's wrong?" she asks.

He smiles calmingly at her. "Oh, nothing. ...I was just wondering what happened to the journal we found at the Dragon Hunter's hideout," he asks innocently.

She grins at him and pulls the little book out of her backpack. "I kept a hold on it the entire way back to the Village. I packed it so it would be safe with me."

"Have you read any of it yet?" he asks urgently.

"Well... no," she slowly replies. "Why?"

"If it contains clues to Patrick's plans, then we can tell the Sohos of them, as well as begin preparing to fight back," Hunter replies, making it up as he goes along.

She takes the bait. "Oh! That's true! ...Should I read some of it now?" she asks. He almost laughs out loud. *It sure is a good thing I thought of having her read it. Even if it doesn't convince her yet, it should slow her down long enough for me to toss more doubt into her mind or find another way to sabotage her plans.*

"Sure, why not?" he replies nonchalantly, once again doing a fabulous job of keeping his real thoughts and feelings buried.

"Do you want to hear what it says?" she asks, sitting down on the grass. He sits next to her and can feel her nervousness increase as the distance between them diminishes. *It's so obvious that she likes this 'Chet' character, and using the Gift to amplify it was honestly such a stroke of genius. She's so easy to manipulate now.*

"Why, yes, I am very interested in what Patrick has written in there." It's not a lie. He really is intrigued by what he thinks will cause Crystal to be buried in doubt and eventually come to them willingly. "If you want to read it out loud, you can, although I can see it just fine," he continues, scooting even closer to her. Their clothes brush and the blush on her cheeks turns to crimson, although she pushes through it, pretending it wasn't there.

"I... um... well, do you want me to read it?" she asks nervously.

He smiles reassuringly at her. Their faces are mere inches apart. It's quite odd pretending to have a crush on his sister, but he's done stranger things. "I would love to hear your sweet voice even more," he murmurs. As predicted, this causes her blush to spread all the way down into her shirt. The tips of her ears are dark red.

"I... I..."

"Or I could read it, if you wish."

"I... I think it would sound better if you did," she finally squeaks out. Smiling a little, he nods and accepts the book from her, making sure their hands brush while doing so. He catches a little shuddering gasp from her as he does so. *She's so easy to manipulate...*

He opens the little leather book to the first entry. "Might as well start from the beginning," he explains. She nods, seemingly having lost her voice. Her hands are clenched in her lap, betraying her inner war while the rest of her seems at ease. He grins. *Maybe Patrick was right... she will not be hard to convince.*

"Dear new Diary... or Journal... whatever thing others call these infernal booklets that contain my inner thoughts." Hunter almost laughs. He can hear Patrick's voice in the journal as though it was his actual one. He sure did a good job forging it. **"I have decided that I should record the things I have done recently- and will do in the future- for others to read of my accomplishments later. Hunter could benefit from what I have to say. I shall give him this booklet at a later point, I suppose."** He glances over at Crystal. She's frowning, but doesn't say anything. He's frowning too- but for an entirely different reason than she. *This... this is almost uncanny how much it sounds like Patrick. Could I have grabbed the wrong journal?* Scoffing at himself, he brushes off these worries and continues reading. Patrick was a mastermind, he's sure he meant for it to sound like this.

"For now, I shall speak to you as though I could be reporting these things to anyone. For who knows when Hunter will be disposed of anyway..." He stops reading entirely then. *What did he mean by that?* He panics.

"When Hunter will be disposed of?!" Crystal repeats. *Please, repeating it doesn't lessen the confusion.* "He's planning to get rid of Hunter? I should have rescued him while I was in there... who knows if he's even still alive?!" she starts panicking. He quickly reaches out and grabs one of her hands, attempting to comfort her.

"Crystal, I'm sure he's fine..."

"No! Chet, he's going to kill Hunter once he's no longer of use to him!" She continues, but he doesn't hear her. A chill runs down his spine. *What if she's right? What if he really does mean to kill me- or have me killed- once I can't help him anymore? ...No. No, surely not... This is just Patrick playing to Crystal's assumption that he's a bad guy,* he decides. He's not thoroughly convinced, though.

"Crystal!" he says, cutting her off. With a shock, he realizes that tears are pouring down her face and she's clutching his hand tightly. He softens his voice and tries to sound comforting and reassuring. "I'm sure he didn't mean that... he probably just thought that he might be killed in their war against the dragons and such. I mean, there are a lot of casualties in a war. I'm sure Patrick hopes that he doesn't get killed- but hoping isn't everything," he adds. He's almost convinced himself of this, so the surety in his voice helps calm Crystal down.

She nods. "Yes... yes, I'm sure that's it..." She sniffles and subtly wipes her nose. "I'm sorry... please, continue," she says with a deep breath.

He nods slowly. "...Yes. Okay. Well, here goes...

"Today, I marked the dragons as our first targets to dispose of. We shall utterly destroy their entire race, and then the Sohos will be vulnerable once more, and we shall march upon their hidden village. It shouldn't be too difficult to find. Once the dragons are gone, their source of power will be depleted, and they'll be vulnerable as babes. Once they are terminated, the entire Village will quake and tremble and fear me and my might... but I shall not put them out of their misery yet. I shall first destroy the annoying fish that still think they can best me. If my men were in their territory, if they were to venture into the water, then the foul creatures would stand a chance. However, with my technology coming straight from both First Earth and Quagon, those large chunks of seafood don't stand a chance. It won't take long to finish them off. And then, when the Kingdom is cowering at my feet, I will descend upon them, leaving only Alexander and Pearl. Then, when I kill Alexander, I shall give the lovely Pearl a choice. Join me, or die. Painfully."

Hunter looks over at Crystal and can see that her face is pale. "Well, it did have his plans in it," she finally chokes out.

He nods. "That's the end of the first entry. Are you okay?"

She tightens her lips and nods determinedly, although he can see it looks like she's about to throw up. "Yes..." She takes a deep breath and calms her shaking body. "I guess we should go to the dragons first to see if they're still okay," she determines, "since Patrick was going to kill them first. I need to make sure Eric, Gale, Tatiana, and Victor are still okay..."

"Yes, yes of course," he reassures.

Crystal glances at him. "Are you sure you want to come? Dragons can be kind of hard to handle..." He can't help but grin at this, remembering how he conquered the strong heart of Vincent the Proud. "...Why are you smiling at that?" she asks in confusion.

"I... um..." He didn't expect her to catch that smile- or for it to even slip out. "I'm sure I'll be fine with you there to protect me," he finally says.

She blushes. "W-well... I-I guess I'll do my b-best..." she stammers. He laughs and stands, holding out a hand to help her up.

"Well then, let's go. We can continue reading the journal later. We have enough to think about for the moment anyway," he finishes. She nods, her face still pale from the things unfolded in Patrick's journal.

"Right," she whispers, leading Hunter towards the dragons' hideout.

9

Nathan's waiting, lying on his bed until Zarafa comes back for him, his eyes closed. He isn't sleeping, but daydreaming as he waits. Zarafa had retrieved him for breakfast, then locked him back in his room for a few hours. He was starting to get quite bored, so he had lain down and quietly rested until the time that she returned to let him out of the room, everything prepared for his search for the lost Dragon child.

His thoughts wander to Crystal, as they always seemed to do. He remembers her determination and the way she hid her fears from everyone… he even had to pry her feelings out of her at first. But later on, she opened up to him and seemed to trust him. He smiles. It warmed his heart that she would do so since she hid her inner thoughts and feelings from everyone she could, it seemed. She had always made him feel special… and now he owed it to her to let her have a rest while he took over finding her brother for a while. She deserved to have a break, so he would do what he could to help her have one. *As long as she's on Second Earth, she'll be safe.*

The sound of the vampire's footsteps coming down the stairs pulls him out of his thoughts. He sits up and turns toward the door, suddenly feeling anxious. It was time. Zarafa had left him in the room while she had gone to find the first place they should look for Rex Dragon.

The door opens, and the perfect, almost glowing face of the vampire lady appears, smiling. "I believe we have a working plan," she announces, her light accent pleasant in his ears. "Come with me, I'll show you," she continues, turning and leading the way up the stairs. Nathan follows her, excitement mingling with anxiety. How were they supposed to search all of First Earth before the end of the weekend? He only had today and tomorrow before he had to go home.

When he voices his concern, she just laughs. "Who says we have to find him this weekend? Just come back next weekend and we can continue."

He laughs a little at himself. "Of course... sorry, I guess I'm just not thinking," he explains sheepishly.

She smiles kindly at him. "It's not a problem. It happens to the best of us."

"...Yeah."

He then follows her silently down the hallway until she stops at the last door to the left. She opens the door, then steps back so Nathan can enter. He steps through the doorway and finds the room filled with technology, most of them showing maps on screens or holograms. There's a main one in the center of the room, taking up most of the space. Above it is suspended a huge globe hologram with different colored dots in certain places around it. Nathan immediately recognizes it as First Earth.

"What are all the different colored dots for?" he asks.

Zarafa steps up beside him, also peering at the globe floating before them. The top of it reaches a few feet above her head. "Each one represents a different search team. The 'dot' expands to include where they have each searched automatically. Once all of First Earth is covered, we will move on to a different realm." She swipes at the hologram with her hand and it spins away, replaced with a much different one. This one is almost all water.

"Quagon," Nathan states.

She nods. "This is where we are likely going to search next if Rex is not here." She changes the hologram back to First Earth by swiping at it in the opposite direction she had before.

"I see. Which search team am I a part of?" he asks curiously.

"We are the crimson one. Notice how tiny it is? Once I give you something with a tracking device in it, the dot will expand while you explore."

"So I'm a one-man team?" Nathan asks in surprise.

"Well, I'll do what I can to help you, but for now, yes. You are alone in your group. However, now that you've accepted the job, it will be the highest priority to find you..."

"If I were to work with another person, I would want it to be Crystal," he interrupts, determination clear on his face.

"I know," Zarafa murmurs, her voice soft with sympathy. "But it could also be dangerous, with the Dragon Hunters searching as well. We think it would be best if you were to work with someone. It's up to you, of course. However you want to find the lost Dragon boy."

"Okay," he says. "So where's this tracking device?"

She smiles at his eagerness to begin. "Come with me." She turns and exits the room, Nathan following close behind. She goes a few doors down and uses a silver key to unlock the matching silver door, leading the way inside. The room is plain with a simple table in the center of the room. There are shelves with a few books on the walls.

Reaching behind one of the empty shelves, Zarafa pulls a bag out of a hidden compartment that Nathan hadn't been able to see from the doorway. Setting the bag on the table, she pulls out a variety of items. A couple of rings, a few different bracelets, a watch, a hat, a necklace, a pair of gloves, a cloak that resembled that of a Dragon Hunter's, a few coins that were unfamiliar to him, a quarter, and a pen.

"Go ahead," she invites. "Pick one. You must carry this with you at all times while keeping a sharp eye out for anyone who looks like they could be part of the Dragon family and are around sixteen or seventeen years old. Should you lapse, we'll have to backtrack and redo parts that weren't recorded. The item you choose will stop recording the instant it is no longer touching the intended part of your body- for instance, if the hat is not on your head or the ring on your finger. So make sure to pick one you won't take off and lose... although you will want one that is inconspicuous—like that cloak there," she adds, pointing to the Dragon Hunter's cloak. "While it may be handy blending in with the Dragon Hunters, that is not your purpose."

"Right," he says, examining the items. He finally picks up a ring, figuring that it will be easy to keep track of since it will be on his hand where he can see it, unlike a lot of the other things on the table. The gold band of the ring seemed to have minuscule words etched into it with bronze. It gleamed in the light streaming from the windows. "I'll take this one," he says, fingering the cool metal.

She nods appreciatively. "Lovely choice." Packing the rest of the items back into the pack, she stuffs it into the secret compartment, then ushers him out of the room, shutting and locking the door behind him. "Feel free to get a snack from the kitchen while you wait. I'll try to locate the best place for you to begin your search, then find a way to get you there as well."

"Sounds good," Nathan agrees, walking to the kitchen as she heads into yet another room.

In the kitchen, a servant greets him with a bow. "Master Nathan! My name is Todd, and I will be aiding you with anything you need during your stay here in my Mistress's house."

Nathan nods politely to him, feeling uncomfortable being waited on by this man around his age, possibly a little older than him. "Um… well, before I go, I was just thinking that I should get a backpack and fill it with supplies," he suggests.

Todd nods hastily, immediately backing out of the kitchen. "Yes! Oh, yes, of course! I shall go fetch one now for you, sir!" Before Nathan could ask him to just call him by his name, the servant is gone. He then sits at the counter on a barstool, tapping his fingers with nervous energy.

This was really happening.

<<<Zarafa>>>

"He doesn't want a partner."

Patrick sighs. "I thought as much." His face shows that he's not worried about this.

Zarafa frowns at him, concerned at his *lack* of concern. Her hands still on her hips, she says, "Well, what are we going to do about it? We need him to get close to Bryce, don't we?"

"Yes," Patrick replies, his voice soft and sarcastically patient, as if he was dealing with an incompetent child. Zarafa's lips harden into a thin line and her eyebrows furry slightly with anger. He doesn't notice, however, and continues. "I know that. Don't worry. I have it all under control." With a curt nod, Zarafa turns off the hologram square and storms out of the room, trying to let her anger simmer. However, the embers of rage had already been lit in her heart.

And she had to admit, it felt good.

<<<Nathan>>>

"Master Nathan!"

Nathan turns to see Todd, who has already returned with a loaded backpack. "That was fast!" he comments, a little surprised.

Todd beams at the praise. "Yes, well, most of the supplies were already set out. I simply organized them into this pack! There isn't much anyway since all you really need is a teleporter to take you back here, where you can grab anything you need."

Nathan nods. That explained the small, light backpack. "So what's in here, then? Besides the teleporter."

"Mostly just food and a stack of pictures of what Rex might look like based on his family traits," he explains, placing the backpack onto the counter beside Nathan.

"Good," Nathan nods. "I was wondering how I was supposed to know what to look for. He could look just like Crystal—or he could be completely different, and I wouldn't recognize him for who he really is."

Todd nods. "Mistress Zarafa seems to think of everything."

Nathan frowns a little, contemplating this. "Yes... yes she does."

<<<Bryce>>>

Bryce walks purposefully down the sidewalk, his piercing blue eyes looking neither to the left or to the right, just straight ahead. He knows his destination. His dark cloak billows behind him in the breeze. He is powerful, and the people he passes by shrink away from him in fear, subconsciously able to feel this. Finally, he reaches the end of his walk. He raises his gloved hand to knock, but the door opens before he can.

Zarafa sighs with relief. "Good, you're here."

"Where's the boy?" Bryce asks, glancing around.

She frowns. "He is cautious and wary. I was unable to convince him that he should have a partner in the search. He already left."

"Then I will come up with a plan," he declares.

"Do you need my help?" Zarafa asks.

"No," he growls, pulling his gloves on tighter. "I've got it covered." And with that, he strolls back out the door. Zarafa stands there watching him go, confused, but also assured that he will be able to do what he says he will.

Nathan will accept him as his partner willingly, and the plan will begin to fall into place. She smiles and closes the door behind him.

<<<Nathan>>>

Nathan wanders through the streets, passing by a few dark alleys that he feels a little uneasy about entering, but then he remembers that he needs to be looking *everywhere* for Rex—even and especially in the most unlikely of places. Fingering the straps on his backpack, he steps cautiously into one of these dark alleys. He stops and lets his eyes adjust before stepping forward. Through the gloom, he sees that there's nothing but a dumpster at the end. He turns to leave the alley and finds a dirty gloved fist in his face.

He falls to the ground, blood dripping from his nose. He snarls and shifts into a tiger. He's shocked when the man calmly pulls something out of his sleeve and holds it to his mouth. He shoots a dart into Nathan's shoulder. He reverts back to human form and is unable to move. He watches, wide-eyed, as the man kneels by his head, sneering. His thin lips pull back to reveal yellow teeth. "Greetings, Zilferian. I don't know who you are, but you obviously have some Gifts. And that makes you valuable to Patrick." Nathan is unable to respond to this with anything but his breathing, which becomes more rapid. The man grins and scoops Nathan up, helpless, in his scrawny yet strong arms and turns to go.

He is also met with a fist to the face. He drops Nathan, who lands on the ground with a groan. He's in a position that he can't see his rescuer, but he can see the black boots that step over him to the thin man, who is hastily scrambling away, fear on his face. The boots calmly follow the man until he's backed up against the wall beside the dumpster. Nathan can see that the rescuer has a black cloak, not unlike those that the Dragon Hunters were always wearing. Fear rushes through his veins once more. He isn't his rescuer- he just wants to take Nathan to Patrick himself!

Nathan struggles to sit up but only manages to prop himself up on his elbow. At least the paralyzing effects from the dart were already wearing off. He watches the cloaked man carefully as he beats the other man, who eventually scrambles past the cloaked newcomer and races out of the alley as fast as his long legs can carry him, completely ignoring Nathan, who now pulls himself to his feet. The cloaked man turns and surveys Nathan, who stands there panting and watching him wearily. "What do you want?" Nathan finally asks.

"Nothing," the man replies. "I just saw that you needed help, so I helped you."

"Do you know who I am?"

"…Yes. You are Nathan Anderson, friend to the Dragon family, and a searcher for Rex Dragon."

"So, you know Zarafa?" Nathan asks, slightly less wary.

"Yes. We are… close friends. She wanted me to be your partner in the search, but she informs me that you do not wish to have a partner."

"Why do you have a Dragon Hunter's cloak?"

"I just came from one of their meetings. I pretended to be a Dragon Hunter to blend in. My job is to learn their secrets. It's how I knew that one was lying here in wait for you."

"Oh." Nathan relaxes, assured that this man doesn't mean him any harm. He just saved him, and he knows Zarafa, and he spies on the Dragon Hunters. This man is a friend. "What's your name?"

"Bryce."

"No last name?"

"No. It makes it harder for the Dragon Hunters to find me if I've been discovered, you see. One can never be too careful."

"True," Nathan admits. "Well, thank you for helping me. I think I'll just be going now."

Bryce raises an eyebrow skeptically. "And do you know where the next Dragon Hunter lies in wait? No, of course you don't. You also don't know what other tricks they have up their sleeve that they'd use to capture you."

Nathan sighs. "What are you saying?"

"I'm saying that you need me. I know the Dragon Hunters' next moves, and I know how to protect you."

"I don't want a partner," Nathan replies, Crystal's image flashing behind his eyes once more. He had only one partner. No one would be replacing her.

Bryce sighs. "Listen. I know I'm no Crystal Dragon, but I can help you. In fact, if you really don't like me that much, then I could just follow you at a distance and keep the Dragon Hunters off your tail. Or I could travel with you and protect you that way, as well as advise you and otherwise help you where I can."

Nathan looks the man up and down. About two or three inches taller than him, he seems to be in his late twenties or early thirties. His piercing blue eyes have a look in them that tells you he knows more than he's letting on. His black hair goes down to his ears. He looks built to fight, but is obviously also intelligent, judging from the glint in his ice-blue eyes. Nathan sighs, unable to deny the fact that he would probably make a great search partner. Still…

"I'm sorry. It's just… I don't think I can bear working with anyone other than Crystal. I'm sure I'll be able to manage on my own."

Bryce nods gravely, accepting this. "It's your choice, Nathan. But just remember that I'll be here for you whenever you change your mind."

"Okay. Thanks," Nathan replies, turning and walking away. He sighs with relief as he steps back into the sunshine. *Could this weekend get any weirder?*

<<<Bryce>>>

Bryce stays in the shadowy alleyway, watching Nathan's back as he walks away. His finger taps thoughtfully on his whiskery chin. *This boy will obviously take some convincing. However, I don't think that anything I do now will speed this along. I'm sure eventually the boy will come to me, but I cannot wait forever. …It appears I may need Zarafa's help after all.*

He strides out and turns to face the way he came, walking once more towards Zarafa's house. As he travels, he forces himself to avoid looking at any woman around him. They all looked like his lost wife, and he was tired of seeing her everywhere. He's almost to his destination when he feels a sudden weight on his back, pushing him face-first to the ground. Someone pins his arms and legs down. Bryce recognizes the feeling of the Dragon Hunters' leather gloves. "What are you doing?" he growls. "Who put you up to this?"

"Oh, this was all my idea," a raspy voice replies in his ear. "I know where your loyalties truly lie."

Growling, Bryce attempts to throw off the person on his back, but the man just laughs and hollers as if riding a bull. Bryce then cocks his head to the side, trying to catch sight of who was on his back, accusing him of being a traitor. Before he can, a huge shadow rolls over them. A giant talon appears before Bryce's gaze, scooping up the man on his back before flinging him into the air, screaming. The man recovers and flies away, his thin hair tossed every which way in the wind. The last man jumps up and races away, becoming a blur.

Bryce sits up and surveys the giant eagle that saved him, which lands in front of him before shifting into the shape of a boy. He offers him a hand to help him up. "I've changed my mind," Nathan says, smiling. "It appears you need me as much as I need you."

Bryce chuckles and accepts the extended hand. "It appears so. I'm delighted you changed your mind."

"So," Nathan says, sticking his hands in his pockets. "Where do we start?"

<<<Nathan>>>

By the end of the day, they hadn't found anything. As they walk back to Zarafa's place, Nathan's head hangs a little lower. Bryce seems to notice. "I would be astonished if we found him today. The Dragon Hunters have been searching for Rex for over a year now. They've actually searched enough of First Earth that they don't think he's in this realm- of course, he may have slipped through the cracks, but that's why Zarafa came up with such an ingenious plan to make sure that doesn't happen to us. Although the possibility that he's on First Earth..."

"Yeah, I get it," Nathan says glumly. "It's alright, I understand... it's just still a little disappointing, you know?"

"Yes," Bryce acknowledges. "Just try not to dwell on it too much."

Nathan just nods. It isn't just this that has him bogged down today. He can't find Greg, he misses Crystal, everything that happened recently has him a little unbalanced... but mostly he misses Crystal. Somehow searching for Rex, though monotonous with Bryce, would be fun and adventurous with her. If there's one thing Crystal's good at, it's keeping his life interesting... and while it also makes his life become more dangerous at times, her presence still was a comfort to him. He feels... almost more at home with her than with his own family, as crazy as that sounded.

Zarafa greets them when they reach the house. "Bryce! What a pleasant surprise. What are you doing here?" She asks, her eyes moving between him and Nathan, a clear question on her face.

Bryce smiles. "Nathan changed his mind about wanting a partner in his search."

"Why, that's wonderful!" she gushes, letting them inside and closing the door behind them. "Any luck today?"

"No," Nathan sighs. "Not yet."

"Ah. I'm sorry about that... but at least you still have tomorrow before you have to go back to school."

"Should I even be going to school?" Nathan asks. "If finding Rex as quickly as possible is our number one priority, then I can skip school for a while, I'm sure."

Zarafa shakes her head, though. "No, Nathan, that would not be the best idea. It may take years to find Rex- the Dragon Hunters have already been searching unsuccessfully for the boy for about a year. We need you to still get an education and have a life outside of the search."

"What can I do to help during the week, then?" Nathan sighs in resignation.

"Well, you could study those pictures I gave you for what we believe Rex may look like," she suggests.

"Yes, that would be best," Bryce agrees. "Every member of the search time is asked to memorize at least the general idea of just who we're looking for. You might as well get started on it when you're not out searching."

"...Alright," Nathan agrees.

"Great!" Zarafa beams. "Now then. Who's hungry?"

<<<Greg>>>

Greg wanders the streets, sniffing the ground. *Where did Nathan go? Surely he couldn't have gotten far... those two creatures are too small to carry him long distances... but then again, I can't smell any tracks from him or the creatures. They all seem to have just disappeared...* The dedicated Familiar trundles on, nose to the ground. Suddenly he catches the sour scent of the red creature that grabbed Nathan. Spinning around, he's seized tightly around his chest and dumped into a rough sack, which is then tied off.

"Rosulkip! Come here!" Greg hears the red one call out. "I caughted the rat!"

"*I'm a Familiar!*" Greg protests. Both creatures ignore him.

"Oh, goody!" the pink creature squeals, clapping. "Now what we do with it? Eat it?"

Greg shivers in disgust and fear. "No, Rosulkip. This is boy Nathan's rat. Zarafa wants to be taken far far away where Nathan won't find it, and it won't find him."

"Oooh, I love playing the hide-and-seek-it! Can I hide it? Please?"

Greg's stomach lurches as he suddenly flies through the air in the bag, landing with a hard thump, then lifted into the air once more. "Fine. I tell Zarafa we'd found it."

"Okay!" The childish voice of the pink creature pipes, racing away.

If there was food in Greg's stomach, he would have thrown up.

<<<Angela>>>

Angela stands impatiently in front of the door after she rang the doorbell. She can hear the slow steps of Nathan's grandma as she shuffles to the door and finally unlocks it. She peers curiously up at her, but Angela doesn't have time to go about this gently. "Where's Nathan?"

"Why, he went to a friend's house for the weekend," the grandma says. "He'll be back to school on Monday."

Angela's stomach clenches in worry. Had she already failed in her assignment? "Okay. Thank you… um, if he gets back early, will you please tell him to call me back?"

A twinkle of understanding lights in the old lady's eyes. "Of course, dear. And I presume you are the famous Angela Dove that my grandson's been speaking so highly of?"

This throws her off track. Nathan had been thinking about her? And telling his family about her?? "I… um, yes."

The grandma's smile widens. "I'll be sure to let him know you stopped by."

"Thanks," Angela says. The grandma nods and shuts the door. Angela stands there frozen for a minute. Did Nathan Anderson… actually *like* her? She shakes it off. She didn't have time for those thoughts. She had to report.

She heads back home and locks herself in her room before opening her laptop. Soon enough she logs into her account and the face of the 'bus driver' appears on her screen. "Ah, Angela. I was beginning to worry. Is everything alright?"

"I'm not sure," she admits. "I don't know where Nathan is. His grandma says that he's at a friend's house."

"Then he's probably at a friend's house. Why are you so concerned?"

She sighs. "You know why, T! I was handpicked *by the Queen* to keep an eye on him! If I've failed her now... if the Dragon Hunters got to him already..."

T raises a hand to try and calm her. "Angela. I'm sure he's fine. Just relax until Monday. If he doesn't show up by then, we'll search for him. There's nothing we can do right now as it is."

Angela slowly lets out her breath. "Yes, of course, you're right... I'm sorry, T. Don't tell the Queen about this until we can be completely sure, alright?"

"Of course," the bus driver assures, a twinkle in his blue-grey eyes. "I won't breathe a word about it. Besides, I'm sure the Queen has other things on her plate at the moment."

"Why? What's happening in Zilferia?"

T just shakes his head. "It doesn't concern you, and there's nothing you can do about it anyway."

"Please, just tell me!" Angela begs. "I hate being out of the loop!"

"I'm sorry, I'm afraid I can't tell you. By order of the King and Queen. ...It concerns Crystal, you see. And if you knew anything about Crystal, Nathan would find out. You would be acting differently, and he is intuitive enough to pick up on it. He would get it out of you, too."

"No, I'm a much better actress than that!" Angela protests. "He still thinks I'm just an average girl from this realm."

"Good. Keep it that way. I'll see you on Monday."

Angela sighs. "Right. See you, T." He then signs off and Angela is left alone with her swirling thoughts.

10

"So," Chet says as we walk. "Your friends are Dragons, wild people who live with dragons, and man-eating merfolk. Do your parents know about this?"

"Yes," I reply, leading the way up the hill to where I first encountered Tatiana and Victor. "Although they don't know that I'm risking my life to go and see them."

"Risking your life?"

"Yeah. The Dragon Hunters are still out there, aren't they? And they're out for blood. I can only imagine what they would do to me if they captured me again..." I shiver, trying to force the memories of what happened last time from my mind. No way is that happening again. Nothing could convince me to go back, and if they try to take me back with force, I will fight with all my might against it. No holding back. I would rather die than end up back in Patrick's clutches.

Chet comes up beside me and puts an arm around my shoulders, drawing me into a hug. I hide my face in his neck, trying not to cry. "Hey. It's okay. I'm here, remember? I won't let them take you back. I promise. Okay?"

I stay in his arms for a few more seconds before pulling away, sniffling. "...Yeah. Thanks. ...I'm really glad you're here."

"Me too," he replies. We reach the top of the hill. I climb onto one of the big rocks that little Eric used to climb up when he was little in order to scan the skies for dragons. I feel a pang in my heart. Oh, how I miss that little guy-although he's probably not so little anymore. When I gave him up for the dragons to take care of, I didn't ever imagine all of these things happening-the dragons nearly being wiped out, me losing my Gifts...

I take a deep breath and shove those thoughts out of my head. I must become better at managing my emotions. Losing my Gifts and my dragon part can't destroy me. I won't let it.

"What are you doing up there?" Chet asks, peering up at me, one gloved hand shading his eyes.

"Hoping that a dragon will see me."

He laughs and climbs up to stand beside me. "You know, for most people, that would be considered a death wish."

"I'm not most people," I say, turning back to survey the sky.

"Yes... you sure aren't," he says. Somehow, I get goosebumps when he says this. I try to ignore him and just keep a sharp eye out for dragons, but I'm aware of his every minuscule movement. My skin feels gradually warmer. "What if there aren't any dragons around here today?" He asks.

"Then we wait."

"What if they don't come by here tomorrow either?"

"Then we walk to Dragon Mountain... unless you would rather head back to the Village, of course," I add.

"No, I want to stay out here and help you," he says. "Although there is something we could do while we're waiting."

"What?" I ask, dreading his answer. I don't really want to read more of Patrick's journal.

Unfortunately, that's just what he suggests. "Read the next entry of the journal. ...We could learn something valuable," he adds as if he can tell what I'm thinking. I sigh. He's right, of course. It contains valuable information that would be wasted if I don't ever read it. Plus, the sooner I read it, the better off I'll probably be in the long run.

I sigh and sit down on the boulder, pulling the journal out of my backpack as Chet sits down beside me. With trembling hands, I open it and flip to the second entry.

"Today was yet another success. Crystal Dragon and Nathan Anderson have left Zilferia. Now my plans may be able to speed forward. I had the ingenious idea of having Crystal Dragon finish building my Gift Stealer in order to destroy her from the inside. She is dying of guilt, I am sure of it.

Not only that, but Hunter now controls her Gifts. Making the enemy less powerful and strengthening my ranks all in one swoop... perhaps I will begin kidnapping certain Villagers and taking their Gifts and giving them to my men and myself.

"Hunter was my experiment. So far, the Gifts have taken to him well. Better than just well, in fact. He has been able to twist his sister's Gifts to take new form... rather than just befriending animals, he is able to control them. I very much look forward to what other developments happen in Hunter's case. If he is able to twist her other Gifts just as splendidly, then perhaps I will give him the rest of the possible Gifts to obtain. I'm sure he could force them to obey him just as he did the rest. He is strong-willed. He is like me. I have chosen the next leader of the Dragon Hunters well."

<<<Hunter>>>

Hunter only half-listens as Crystal reads the entry out loud. His mind is occupied doing other things. *"Vincent the Proud, heed my call."*

The reply is prompt in his mind. The broken voice of the once proud dragon echoes through his brain. *"What do you want?"*

"Come to me. Pretend you do not know me. Pretend to be who you once were. Do not let Crystal Dragon see into your mind and do not let her see anything that happened since she left. Tell her whatever you wish that keeps her on the dragon's side and on mine as well. Remember, I am not Hunter, I am Chet. You do not know me."

"Yes... master," Vincent hesitantly replies. Hunter then feels him leap into the air and begin flying towards them. With a satisfied smile, Hunter returns his attention to his body.

Crystal is staring at the journal. Hunter peers over her shoulder to see what has her so wound up this time. He catches the last few lines that are praising him. No, that's not it... ah. The part about Hunter's abilities with Crystal's Gifts. That's probably the part she finds distressing. It makes sense, though. She nearly bursts into tears at any mention of any Gifts whatsoever. Reading about how he was 'twisting' her Gifts to better serve him... she's probably in pain.

Why would Patrick include that in his fake journal? The point wasn't to make her hurt, it was to change her mind about us. ...Right?

107

He puts an arm around her shoulders. "Are you okay?"

She's shaking from the effort to not cry. "I'm not sure. Hunter's... controlling animals? Why would he do that? Taking away their free will? There's probably nothing worse. Not being able to control their own body... just imagine how much pain they would be in because of it..." Despite himself, Hunter feels a pang of remorse. He'd never thought about what the animals thought or felt. They were just... animals. They existed to further his purposes. No, they don't have any real thoughts or feelings. They just existed to be broken. Hunter feels comforted in this thought.

<<<Crystal>>>

Chet gently takes the journal from me before my shaking hands drop it to the earth. He unzips my backpack and sets it inside before zipping it back up. I slide down off the boulder and stand on the earth, pulling my arms in close to my sides in an effort to comfort myself. But I cannot be comforted. The more I learn about my poor, brainwashed brother, the more saddened I get. Can he ever be saved? Or will he forever be a slave to Patrick's words and lies? How much longer will this go on? Torturing animals and people, killing dragons, stealing Gifts? Has Hunter gone too far off the deep end to be pulled back?

Chet walks toward me and opens his mouth to say something, but I'm distracted by a black speck on the horizon. "Chet! Look!" I say, pointing to the dot as it grows steadily larger. "It's a dragon! And it's coming this way!" I could feel like dancing. At least one dragon was still alive. Surely this means that others are alive as well?

I recognize the dragon as it arrives. "Vincent?" I gasp. The once proud black dragon lands before me. He holds his head high, as always, but his scales have lost their luster. They are more grey than black. His wings droop and his tail remains still. He doesn't seem to feel any emotion seeing me again. This surprises me. I would think that he would be frustrated or something, but instead, he seems defeated. *"Vincent, what happened?"*

"Dragongirl... where have you been to not know what has been happening? The Dragon Hunters are killing us by the hundreds. Gale still believes you can help us," he snorts. *"The foolish old dragon."*

"He's still alive?" I gasp happily. *"Oh, Vincent, this is wonderful!!"*

"Nothing is wonderful anymore, Dragongirl. There are some among us who believe that if you were here… that perhaps we might have been delivered from such destruction." He shakes his head sadly. *"However, now that I see what pitiful state you are in- no Gifts, no dragon part- that their hopes were very clearly in vain."* He turns to go.

"No! Vincent, wait!" He stops and swings his head around to peer at me. His eyes no longer shine like they used to and I feel an immense sadness weigh on my heart. How could the Dragon Hunters do this to such beautiful, wonderful creatures? *"Vincent, I need you to take my friend and I with you to see Gale."*

"Why?" he asks. *"There's nothing you can do to help."* A tear slips out of my eye as I drop my head from shame. He's right. How am I supposed to help these mighty creatures when I can't even help myself? *"That's what I thought,"* he continues, turning to face the way he came once more.

I suddenly freeze as a thought enters my mind. *"Wait!"*

"What is it?" He growls impatiently.

"I might be able to help you."

"How?"

"If you take me to Gale, I can consult with him. Maybe he can figure out how to get my dragon part back. He said himself that no one can take it away from me- maybe he knows a way for me to reaccess it… he might even have an idea for what to do about my Gifts as well!" Vincent pauses, probably debating if this is too much of a stretch. *"Please, Vincent!"* I beg. *"This is probably my last and only chance to get my Gifts and dragon part back! I really want to help you and the rest of the dragons! It is not my wish to see you be driven to extinction! Please, let me try this! Don't give up on me yet."*

Chet glances from me to the dragon and back to me. I wonder what he's thinking. He probably has no idea what's passing between Vincent and I. I'll have to explain it to him later. Vincent still seems to be undecided. Then he turns back around and bows his head to me. *"Very well, Dragongirl. Just as we are your last hope, you are ours. It just may be worth it to investigate and see if the old dragon knows anything. Climb aboard."*

I'm elated. I quickly clamber onto his back, waving Chet up as well before Vincent can change his mind. He scrambles up behind me, bringing my backpack, which I forgot about. As Vincent crouches to take off, Chet wraps his arms around my waist from behind. I can feel his muscles tense as we take to the air. Within a few of Vincent's strong wingbeats, I can tell he's not about to relax. I lay a comforting hand on his and turn my head a bit so he can hear me. "It's alright. Vincent won't let us fall."

He nods and releases his tight hold on me a bit. "Sorry," he says. "I've just never seen a dragon up close like this before... let alone flown on one."

"It's alright, I understand," I assure him, unable to keep from grinning. "After all, not many people have."

Whereas Chet is uncomfortable on the dragon's back, I am completely at ease. I'm a little surprised how much I missed watching the clouds fly by beneath me and everything else zooming by in a blur. I take a deep, cleansing breath of the cold air rushing past and can't help but laugh out loud at the feeling of freedom that comes from flying. Chet relaxes further the longer we fly.

I'm actually a little disappointed when we arrive at our destination—a ways past Dragon Mountain.

"Isn't Gale in Dragon Mountain?" I ask Vincent.

He laughs. *"No. That's just where we meet for meetings, so the Dragon Hunters won't find us. Gale lives here."*

'Here' is a mountain almost as large as the volcano they call Dragon Mountain. I slide down Vincent's side and land softly on the ground beside him, Chet landing easily beside me. I take a step towards the mountain.

"Wait," Vincent warns. *"You don't need to go inside. I'll just go and get Gale and he'll come out here to meet you."*

"...Okay," I say, a little confused, watching as he walks into the cave entrance.

"I wonder why he doesn't want us to go in there?" I wonder out loud.

Chet shrugs. "Maybe that's where he's hoarding meat or gold or something."

I glance at him, surprised. That sounded like something a Dragon Hunter would say... well, he was one for a while, and I surmise that this must be the cause. Chet isn't a person who doesn't care about others. I know that much after the time that I've known him. I suddenly think of Nathan with a pang. I miss him so much I catch my breath in surprise. How could I have hardly thought of him since I got here? What's wrong with me? I shouldn't be here with Chet, I should be here with Nathan!

Chet glances at me, a worried look on his face. Before he can say anything, though, the colossal mass of golden dragon walks out of the cave. Chet's eyes widen and his mouth falls open. Fear is evident in his eyes. I feel a flash of protectiveness. I reach forward and take his hand, showing him that I'm still here. He just stares at Gale as he walks closer. He looks like a deer in the headlights, and I can tell he's about to bolt.

"Chet... Chet, it's fine. Gale's nice. Super nice. He's very wise and kind and he's going to help us. He's not going to hurt you..." It takes some effort, but Chet forces himself to relax some, although from the tightness of his grip on my hand, I can tell he's still anxious.

"*Dragongirl!*" Gale's surprised voice sounds in my head. I've missed that voice. "*Crystal Dragon... oh, how much you have missed over the past few months.*"

"*Fill me in,*" I ask. "*I want to help you.*"

He lowers his head nearly to the ground so he could look me in the eye. Chet releases my hand and scrambles backward several feet. "*Crystal Dragon, it seems that you need me more than we need you at the moment.*"

"*Yes, but after you help me I can better help you! ...I found a drawing of the designs for the Dragon Slayer machines! I can figure out its weakness, and once I have my Gifts back, I may be able to take them down from the inside.*"

"*Hmm,*" he says, raising his head a bit. "*Interesting. Well whether you could help my people or not, Dragongirl, I would help you. We are basically kin, and we help our kin, even if the humans do not. Dragons will remain honorable, even to the bitter end.*"

"*Thank you, Gale,*" I say, a tear falling from my eye. Could this be it? Could I finally be getting my Gifts and Dragon part back?

He nods, a twinkle in his eye. "*Come with me. Let us sit and debate about how to proceed.*"

"*Wait... what about Chet?*"

Gale doesn't turn around. "*He can wait out here. This is between you and me.*"

I start to follow Gale. Chet runs up and grabs my hand, a pleading look on his face. "Don't leave me," he begs.

"I'll be back soon," I assure him. "I need to talk to him to see if I can get my Gifts and dragon powers back. I have to go, Chet. You'll be okay out here, I promise," I say before pulling my hand away.

He nods bravely, then whispers, "Please hurry, though." I smile and nod before racing after Gale.

He crouches and lets me climb up onto his back before he soars up to the top of the mountain, reaching it in just a few mighty wingbeats. He then lands and I slide off. He lies down with a weary sigh before turning his head to face me once more. *"So, child. You lost your Gifts, and you believe that you lost your dragon part as well, is that it?"*

"Yes," I reply, confused. He already knew that. Why was he asking me again?

"Well, I'm fairly certain you haven't lost either part."

"What?" I am so confused now. Of course I lost my Gifts! They had been torn right out of me!

"No one can take away something that is a part of you. Your Gifts are who you are. Should they take away something that makes you you, you would cease to exist. Even if this wouldn't happen with your Gifts, it certainly would with your dragon half. Between that and your Gifts, you would truly cease to exist if they could actually take that away from you. You are who you are, and no one and nothing can ever take that away from you. No one can change you unless you let them."

"But, Gale," I protest, *"they did take my Gifts away! And they may not have taken away my dragon part, but they repressed it so I can no longer become a dragon. ...Tell me how to fix it! Please!"*

He sighs, and a warm gust of air washes over me. *"Crystal Dragon, that is something only you can do. It is a part of you—I can't find that for you. You have to find yourself."* I'm nearly in tears now. This isn't helping me at all. *"However, I believe I can think of something that might help you to find yourself."*

"What?" I ask, desperate to know. *"I'll do anything!!"*

"The Mermaid King might be able to do something for you, if he had his Trident."

I frown. *"I'm not actually sure what happened to the Trident. The last I saw it... I gave it to Vlad. The person who was pretending to be Vlad, that is... oh no! Does Patrick have it?"*

"I do not know," Gale says sadly. *"I'm afraid you're going to have to find out. Your other option could be to see the Sohos to help you recover your dragon part. They know more about dragons than any other human."*

I nod. It sounds reasonable, and it's a much better lead than I had before. Now I at least have something to aim for, rather than just sitting back and doing nothing while all of Zilferia falls apart. Which reminds me... *"Gale?"*

"Yes, child?"

"I didn't just come for me. Patrick is waging war on Zilferia—which you already know, of course—but he's focusing on one group at a time. He is dividing and conquering. I need to get everyone on Zilferia on one side or another. It will give us

hope and strength through the bonds of friendship and a united purpose—to save all that we love and hold dear. Our friends, our family, our homes… everything will be obliterated if we allow Patrick to continue. You are the first group that I've visited thus far, but I am planning on traveling to the Sohos and the Merfolk as well as those in the Village to band together. …Will you join us?"

Gale looks at me gravely with those huge golden eyes of his. "Yes. It is for the best… although the clan of black dragons may be difficult to convince. They are still prideful and would rather be destroyed than accept the help of humans. What remains of the other clans though… well, from what I've seen, they will be willing to accept help no matter the source. I will gather as many dragons as I can. Whenever you need us, call my name with your mind and your voice as you did before, and we will come to you. I may call on you in the same way if we need aid as well."

I feel like crying I'm so elated. "Thank you, Gale."

He shakes his head, his entire body rumbling with laughter. "Oh, Dragon-girl. I should be the one thanking you. You came back to Zilferia for the sole purpose of helping us and everyone else residing on Zilferia, despite the risk to yourself. It is the least I can do to accept your plan to proceed in this desperate war." He bows his head to me. "So thank you, Crystal Dragon."

"…You're welcome."

<<<Hunter>>>

Hunter paces, one hand on his sword and the other hand running through his hair. *Gosh darn it! What is taking that girl so long? Eventually one of these dragons is going to see who I really am and alert all the rest of them!* He thinks worriedly, eyeing the mouth of the cave as yet another dragon wanders out of it. *How many dragons are in there, anyway? Is that where they're keeping their injured dragons?*

He's just about ready to go charging up the mountain when he spots the huge golden beast gliding towards him. *Finally. Now we can get out of here…* He's surprised to see how happy Crystal is when she comes racing towards him after sliding off of Gale's back. *What did the dragon tell her? Obviously there's no way for her to get her Gifts back, nor her special little 'dragon powers,' so why would she be so happy?*

"Chet! I got the dragons to agree to fight with the Sohos, the merfolk, and the Villagers! Isn't this wonderful?"

"Oh, yes, magnificent! I knew you could do it!" he cheers. *Hmm. She's hiding something from me... that isn't the only reason she's so happy and hopeful. There's something else...*

"Vincent will take you two home," Gale says, his eyes piercing Hunter's. *Oh crap!* He thinks, filled with horror. *I forgot to avoid his eyes! He can see exactly who I am!* "...Hunter Dragon. Now, why are you walking around pretending to be someone you're not?"

"It's none of your business," Hunter replies tartly.

"Hmm..."

"You aren't going to kill me, are you?"

"...No," He says after a moment of hesitation. *"Not just yet. However, if I ever see you around here again..."*

"I won't come back here," Hunter promises, actually meaning it for once. There's no way he could stand up to this ancient dragon- or the rest of the dragons packed into that cave.

Gale nods. *"Then be on your way."*

"You're not going to tell Crystal about me?" He asks, confused.

"No. And before you ask why, I have my reasons—which I will not share with you at this time. Perhaps at a later point, when we can meet at a much happier occasion."

Hunter stares at the dragon, more confused than he had ever been in his life before. Crystal turns to him. "You coming, Chet?"

"Uh, yes, of course," he stammers before clambering up to sit behind her once more.

"Goodbye, Gale!" she calls, waving to the golden dragon as they fly away.

Hunter sure had quite a bit to ponder from the developments of the day.

<<<Crystal>>>

"So. What next?" Chet asks as we watch Vincent fly away once more.

"Next we go to the Sohos."

"Are we going to stop by the Village first?"

"No," I reply. "We can't go back just yet... someone is guaranteed to stop me there. I don't have time to stop. I need to get over to the Soho's as fast as I can, then head back to the Village."

"Okay," he says, shouldering the backpack. "Lead the way."

"You really don't have to come with me, you know," I say. It's not that I don't want him to come with me... some things are just easier done alone. Especially since I have this nagging feeling that I shouldn't tell him about my new chance to get back my Gifts and dragon powers. I don't know why I have this feeling, but I've been in Zilferia long enough now to know not to just brush such feelings aside.

"I know. I want to come with you."

I think fast. Something tells me he just really shouldn't go with me. "Okay, but I need to get word to my parents that I'm okay, though. They're all probably freaking out. Last time I disappeared..." I swallow the guilt down. I don't have time to feel bad about my decision- it's necessary to save all of Zilferia!

Chet's face softens in understanding. He hands me the backpack. "Alright. Tell me how to find you, and I'll come find you as quickly as I can after telling everyone that you're okay." I tell him the way to the spot that the Soho's dragon dropped me off the last time I saw them—excluding that detail, of course. It would take too long to explain everything. "I'll be back before you know it," he says, winking at me before speeding away. I blink. *He has the Gift of speed? Since when?* I shrug and turn towards the Sohos. I'll think about it later. Right now, I have a job to do.

When I arrive at the spot, I find that Zeke and Kate are already standing there waiting for me. Kate rushes forward to hug me tight when she sees me. "I'm so relieved you're okay!" she says.

"Same here," I say. "It seems the Dragon Hunters have been stirring up quite a bit of trouble while I've been away."

"I'm afraid that's an understatement," Zeke says grimly. "Come. We have lots to talk about."

I nod and follow him into the clearing, where the huge dragon awaits me. I climb on and hold tightly onto one of the spikes on its neck. It pushes off powerfully from the ground and rises quickly. I then feel a sudden change in the air, as if we are in a different place... yet it still feels like Zilferia. Did we just pass through a magical barrier, like the ones around Patrick's castle? This solution seems to make the most sense to me, so I decide to go with it.

Realizing I've never reached out to this silver dragon before, I make an attempt to speak with him. *"Hello!"* I begin.

I'm met with a slow, grudging response. *"Greetings, Dragongirl."*

"What's your name?"

"I much prefer to spend my time in silence, if it's all the same to you," he sighs, the huge gust of air released rushing back to my face, warming it against the cold wind. *"I am old, and tired of everything. I stay with the Sohos because it does not require me to do much. They all leave me well enough alone most of the time."*

"Ah... I see. Sorry."

When we land at the Sohos' village, I'm shocked to see that there are not many people there. "Where is everyone?" I ask.

Kate looks at me sadly. "This is just our medical center now, for those who get injured because of Patrick's Dragon Hunters. Everyone else is in an army base about a twenty minute march from here."

"...Oh," I say.

Zeke turns to me, intensity in his eyes. "Crystal, I think it's safe to say we both need to get the other up to speed with what has been happening, don't you agree?"

So I tell them all that happened since I last saw them. It all seems so long ago. The last time I saw the Sohos, I was still in the Games! As I talk, we walk up to Zeke's house high in the trees and sit on his balcony. I start summarizing more as I see the sun slipping down from its apex in the sky. I'm running out of time.

Kate's eyes are filled with tears by the time I finish my tale with me traveling here, hoping to get the Sohos to unite with the Dragons, Merfolk, and Villagers. "Oh my goodness! One so young, having to go through so much..."

"Everyone else on Zilferia is suffering just as much as I," I insist, hating it as always when all the attention is directed onto me.

Zeke shakes his head in concern. "No one else had their dragon part ripped away from them. That's... that's probably even worse than losing their Gifts. And somehow you endured both trials..."

I take a deep, shuddering breath. "...Gale said you might be able to help me in that regard."

Kate frowns. "How? What does he think we can do?"

"He thinks that my dragon part is just blocked because it would kill me if he actually took that much of me away. He thinks that you can do something to help me 'find myself,' as he worded it."

Kate shares a glance with Zeke. "Well, I do have one idea. But we're going to need some help," she says.

"Anything," I reply. She nods and leads Zeke and me back over to the silver dragon. Kate whispers into its ear, and it soars into the sky once more.

"Where's he going?" I ask.

"Just be patient," Kate laughs. "You will see soon enough."

So I sit down on the grass and wait. As I wait, Zeke tells me what happened to the Sohos, although I already knew most of it. The Dragon Hunters had been attacking them- although not focusing on them nearly as strongly as they had the dragons. Still, Sohos had been both killed and kidnapped by the Dragon Hunters, and now their numbers are dwindling. One of the kidnapped people, a captain, a leader of a section of the army that got taken, found his way back. He told Zeke and Kate how Patrick and sucked the Gifts right out of him and his men. Half of them died because of the process.

Zeke doesn't know what they do with the Gifts. I take a breath and prepare to tell him when I'm cut off by the return of the enormous dragon- and following along right behind him is another dragon. This one is dark green, lithe, and beautiful. It is obviously young, but not as young as Eric was when I found him or let him go. My head goes up to its shoulder. The young dragon lowers its head to peer at me. I'm instantly lost in his eyes. Immediately tears well up in mine and I throw my arms around his neck.

"*Eric*," I cry.

"*Crystal*," he responds, not sounding like his carefree younger self any longer- but also not like the other dragons. His voice isn't as high as it used to be, but neither is it so low that it shakes the earth, like Gale's does.

"*Oh, Eric, I missed you!!*"

"*I missed you, Crystal*," he replies. "*Living with Tatiana and Victor was fun at first, but I wanted to go back to you. I didn't understand at first why they wouldn't let me see you… but then my friends' parents and other family started dying around me… death was all around us. I still thought of you every day.*"

"*I thought of you every day too*," I say. "*At least, almost every day.*"

Kate steps up, and I reluctantly release Eric's warm scales. "Eric is here to help you." He bobs his head in agreement.

"How?" I ask. "Gale couldn't help me… how can Eric?"

"Because," Kate says, grimly holding up a cup. "I think that drinking dragon blood may help you."

"...Dragon blood?" I glance worriedly from Kate to Eric.

"It won't hurt," Eric promises. *"Kate says you only need a little. Just a scratch. I'll be fine."*

I'm shaking. Drink dragon blood? "Now while normally this would be suicide for a human to do..."

"Wait... what?" I interrupt her. "Suicide?"

Zeke explains. "Humans who wanted the power of a dragon would sometimes kill a dragon and drink its blood in the hopes that its magic would be infused into them deeply enough that it would turn them part dragon. ...They all died if they tried."

"But you are already part dragon," Kate continues. "Plus you would only drink a sip, not an entire quart like they tried to do. I seriously doubt it would kill you, but it might help to bring out your dragon side."

I glance from Eric to Kate and back again. "If Eric's willing, then I guess I'll try."

Kate nods and turns to Eric. "My needles are not sharp enough nor long enough to penetrate your skin between your scales. Otherwise, I would simply draw blood that way. As it is..."

Before she can even finish, Eric raises a claw and slashes at his 'wrist' on his other foreleg and holds it over the cup as Kate holds it out. About five great drops of blood splash into the cup before the cut stops bleeding so heavily. Eric lowers his forearm, and all three of them turn to me expectantly.

I accept the cup from Kate with shaking hands and lift it to my lips. Closing my eyes, I take a sip. The instant the blood touches my tongue, I drop the cup, gasping. A little of the blood makes it down my throat, but for the most part, I spit out about half of what I got in my mouth in the first place. I collapse to the ground, gagging. The blood burns! It tastes like liquid fire, and is the consistency of... well, blood. The blood seems to thicken around my tongue and on my throat, and I gasp for water. Zeke whistles a runner over and tells him to grab some water for me. He's back in a few seconds with a cup of water, which I guzzle down thankfully. The rest of the blood washes down my throat and I'm able to breathe again. I sit up, gasping as the other dizzying effects of the dragon blood take hold.

My eyesight is suddenly as clear as if I was using my dragon eyes, the base of my fingernails hurt, my brain suddenly feels like it's been asleep all my life and only now just woke up, and every nerve in my body tingles. The tingling fades first, thankfully, as does the pain in my fingers. My brain slows down a bit, but it's still more active than usual.

"I can see... why people... die from drinking very much of it," I gasp, my eyes watering.

"Yes... well, we chose Eric because he's young. His blood is more magical and potent than most," Kate says, sounding as if she's choking from shock. I glance up at her, but she doesn't meet my eyes. She's unusually pale while Zeke regards me with curiosity in his eyes. "What?" I ask. "What happened?"

Zeke just waves over another runner, who then grabs a mirror. Zeke hands it to me without a word. I glance in it and am surprised to see that my eyes are a mix of my normal eyes and my dragon eyes. I'm a little unnerved by the sight and quickly avert my eyes. I then notice my fingers. My fingernails have turned into claws. "Um... is that supposed to happen?" I ask, casting my eyes around the rest of my body, which seems to be just fine.

"Honestly, we weren't really sure what would happen," Kate says, glancing at me then looking away again. "There hasn't exactly been another Dragongirl who got her dragon part... buried... before."

"So, we also don't know if this change is permanent or not," I murmur, glancing at my hands once again.

"No, not for certain. But since you are able to control if you want to be a dragon or not at will- normally- we think that this should behave the same," Zeke says.

"What if it doesn't go away?"

"Then I suppose the King's Village will just have to get used to having a dragon-princess among them in the flesh," Zeke says. "How about you get some sleep. We can take you back to the Village in the morning."

"Yes, we'll know by morning if that change is permanent or not," Kate says, trying not to make it evident that she's avoiding looking at me.

"...Alright," I say sadly, allowing Zeke to lead me toward one of the empty houses in the trees.

"Crystal! There you are!" I bolt upright in bed, frantically searching the darkness with my eyes, which I immediately notice are back to normal. Someone turns on the lights and I'm able to see who it is.

"Chet," I sigh, laying back in bed. "You scared the living daylights out of me!"

"Sorry," he says apologetically. "I couldn't find the meeting place for a while. I only just got here. I was worried I wouldn't be able to find you."

I instantly forgive him. He really sounds pretty worried. "So how did my parents take the news?" I ask.

"As well as you'd expect," he says, sitting by my feet on the bed. "They were outraged that you just left without telling them, then they sent me back out to find you and bring you back as soon as possible—whether you want to or not."

I laugh. "Don't worry, I'm coming back in the morning."

His eyes grow serious. "No, Crystal, you need to go back now. If you wait for morning it may be too late."

"Wait... what?" I say, sitting up and fully paying attention now. "What do you mean?"

"I saw the Dragon Hunters on my way here. They're coming to attack the Sohos again. Which means, you can't be here when that happens."

"But I need to help them..."

"Yes, but you can't now, remember? No Gifts."

I wince, but then that reminds me of the next thing I need to do—find the Mermaid King's Trident and return it to him. Hopefully, he can heal me enough that I'll get my Gifts back, like Gale said. "Alright, let's go," I say, swinging my legs out of bed as he stands up. He helps me get my jacket on, and I put on my boots and we head out the door.

Dawn hasn't yet come, but it's no longer dark. The sky is grey and there's a magical feel in the air. I breathe in the calm, clean air and relax. Everything is right with the world here. Here, I can feel at peace.

At least, that's what I think until I hear the first scream.

<<<Hunter>>>

Hunter freezes at the sound. His men weren't supposed to attack yet. This could ruin everything! ...But at the same time, it might help him. Saving Crystal could get him some bonus points in her eyes, and that's never a bad thing, especially when he's trying to get her to like him and trust him.

Zeke, the leader of the Sohos, comes running up. "Crystal, you have to go... who's this?"

"This is Chet," she says. "He's a friend."

Zeke's eyes narrow at him. "You're a Dragon Hunter." He draws his knife. Hunter forces himself to hold still.

"I was, because Patrick forced me to join. Crystal rescued me."

"Well, Nathan really rescued both of us," she explains.

Zeke sighs. "Fine, I'll give you the benefit of the doubt." He turns to Crystal once more. "Crystal, you have to get out of here, right now. And good luck with the Merfolk," he calls before racing away to join his people.

Crystal turns to Hunter. "How are we going to get out of here quickly without being noticed?"

He shrugs. "We'll just have to be careful." He takes her hand and begins running toward the dragon. "This is how you got here, right?"

"Yes... how did the Dragon Hunters get here? I thought there was a magical shield around the place," she says.

"I don't know," Hunter says, helping her onto the dragon before climbing up himself.

"Take us back," Crystal says to the dragon, who then takes wing, flying quickly. They land within minutes. Crystal slides down the side of the dragon, breathing hard from the speediness of the flight. "Let's... go. Before-" she ducks and an arrow whistles over her where her head just was.

"Too late," Hunter says, standing between them and their invisible assailant. "Run! I'll be right behind you!"

"No! I'm not going to leave you!"

"GO!" he roars. He doesn't have time for this. She needed to get away so he could take care of the guy who just shot at her. She scrambles away. Once she's out of sight, Hunter turns back to the man who still lurks in the shadows.

"What the heck do you think you're doing?" he demands, shifting back into his own form and speeding up to the man, grasping him by the collar of his cloak. "Did you not hear my orders? Do not harm the girl!"

"She... she wasn't harmed," the panicked man stutters. He's bigger and older than Hunter, but is clearly terrified of him nonetheless.

"Yes, because you got lucky! You need to think before you shoot, dang it!"

The man drops to his knees before him, bowing his head. "I'm sorry! It won't happen again!"

"No... it won't," Hunter says, pulling a knife out of his sleeve. "I don't have room in my ranks of men for those who do not obey me." He then drives the knife down into the man's neck. He falls to the ground, gasping and choking on his own blood. Hunter swivels to the other boy who still lingers in the shadows, fear in his young eyes. "Spread the word. I will have no mercy on those who disobey me." The boy nods hastily and races away.

Hunter sighs and wipes off his knife on the now dead man's cloak before sheathing it once more. He then turns and stalks after Crystal, shifting back into Chet as he goes.

When he catches up to her, he finds two more of his men dead at her feet with what looks like claw marks in their throats. "Crystal? What happened here?"

She glances up at him, tears in her eyes and confusion on her face. "I... I don't really know. They... they attacked me... and then... then they were dead. I... I don't..." she breaks off, sobbing.

Wow, she sure is an emotional mess, Hunter sighs to himself before taking her into his arms. "Hey, it's okay... you're fine... you are fine, right?" he says, holding her at arm's length and looking her over.

"Yes, yes I'm fine... sorry, it's just... I'm just so confused and lost anymore... I don't know what I'm doing."

"You're going to the King's Village," he says, looking at her worriedly. *What happened to her? How could she not remember where we're going?*

She shakes her head. "No, I remember that... I just don't know what I'm doing here, on Zilferia. I can't help anybody, and I can't do anything..."

He glances at the bodies of the two men. "Um, I wouldn't say that you couldn't do anything..."

She just sighs and shakes her head, done crying. *Girls,* Hunter exclaims to himself. "No... but we need to go before more of them come. And we need to hurry." She looks at Hunter meaningfully.

"Right... then are you okay with me carrying you? I don't want to hurt you by dragging you along behind me," he explains. Truthfully, this way she wouldn't slow him down quite so much.

She nods. "That's probably the best thing to do." He then picks her up. She clings to his neck and buries her face into his shirt as he speeds away toward the Village.

His arms and legs are burning by the time he arrives. Not because Crystal was heavy, but he's not used to running as fast as he can while carrying someone else. He sets her down outside of the castle doors gratefully. She goes up and knocks on the door, then opens it and walks in. She is immediately grabbed by Alexander Dragon and pulled into a hug.

"Don't you ever do that again," Pearl scolds, smiling with relief at seeing that her daughter is fine. "There's a war going on, you can't just go wandering around—especially without your Familiar," he adds as Nora flaps into the room.

"I know," she says, finally able to pull away from Alexander. "I wasn't just wandering around. I was trying to help with the war."

"How?" Thaddeus asks, walking up.

"Well, I got the dragons and the Sohos to agree to work with each other," she says. "I know how to contact the dragons, as well as the Sohos," she pulls the feather of a river-bird out of her boot. It glimmers in the light. "And they know how to contact me as well."

"Well that's great," Alexander says, "but don't do it again, okay? We can always send someone else to do whatever it is that you're wanting to do."

She shakes her head. "No, you can't. The dragons would kill anyone else on sight, as would the Sohos and merfolk."

"Merfolk?" Pearl questions.

"Um..."

"It doesn't matter," Alexander presses. "You aren't leaving again without our permission and more than one guard. Not that you didn't do a good job," he continues, turning to Hunter, who's just standing there awkwardly. "It's just that more than one would be better."

"Oh, yes, I understand, sir," he says. "I just figured that it would be better than letting her go out alone, as I'm sure she would do if I didn't follow her."

"Yes, and thank you for that," Pearl says. "But next time, don't let her leave at all. Am I understood?"

"Yes, my Queen," Hunter replies, bowing to her slightly.

She sighs. "Please stop saying that. I thought we had gotten past that! Just call me Pearl."

"Sorry... Pearl."

Thaddeus steps up. "It's early. The sun hasn't yet come up, I think that these two youngsters should get some sleep."

Crystal sighs. "I don't think I can even fall asleep at this point."

The family cook, Matilda, then comes in holding a tray with two cups of hot chocolate on it. "Well then good thing I thought to make you two some hot chocolate! I added something to help you sleep," she continues with a wink to Crystal.

She takes one gratefully. "Thank you, Matilda."

Hunter takes one as well. "Yes, how thoughtful."

<<<Crystal>>>

I take the drink up to my room. I sit carefully on the huge, plush bed and just cradle the hot chocolate in my hands for a while, trying to figure out the images whirring through my brain. When I was running after Chet told me to go, I had stumbled. When I got back up, there were two Dragon Hunters in front of me. Rather than just killing me or taking me hostage, they decided to pummel me with words instead. They told me how worthless I was and how doomed I was, trying to fight against an entire army with my small, nearly powerless band of friends.

As they spoke, I was filled with such anger that my vision turned red. The next thing I knew, my dragon eyes came out, and claws erupted from my fingertips. The men were so surprised they didn't stand a chance. I cut them down in seconds. My anger cooled, but once it did, I was so terrified of myself that I was left shaking and crying. I didn't know what to do. What had that dragon blood done to me?

I sigh and peer into my cup of hot chocolate and realize that it's not as hot anymore. I raise the cup to my lips and swallow some of it. I then set the rest of it down on the table and curl up under the covers on my bed and fall asleep.

Thankfully, I don't dream.

11

Nathan jumps as his cell phone vibrates once again. It was the fifth time that morning that it had gone off, and it was only nine thirty. He was still eating breakfast. He sighs and sets down his fork. "I'll be right back," he says to Zarafa, who nods. He walks into another room and pulls the phone out of his pocket. It was Angela, again. Why would she be calling so often on a Sunday? There must be something terribly wrong, Nathan figures, so he finally answers it.

"Angela? What do you want?" He didn't mean to be so harsh, but his nerves were tight nowadays.

Her voice is filled with relief when she replies. "Nathan! Oh, I can't tell you how glad I am to hear your voice again!"

"What's wrong?" he asks.

"Nothing. I was just hoping that nothing was wrong with you... I was worried that ugly red monster that attacked while we were on the bus came back and got you."

Nathan pauses. "Why would you think that?"

"Because I saw it outside your house yesterday. I was really worried!"

It was outside his house yesterday? But yesterday he had been here, with Zarafa, who controlled the little beasts. "I'm fine," he says. "...Was there a pink one with the red one?"

"Um, yes, I think there was," she confirms. "The red one had a bag. It looked like they were looking for something."

"But they left?"

"Yes."

"Well, that's good..."

"Nathan? What's wrong?"

"Nothing. I'm just... thinking. You don't have any idea why they were there?"

"No. The only thing I could think of was that they were looking for you. I'm glad they weren't, although I thought that they might have already got you since you weren't around. I've been calling you a lot because I was so worried!"

"Well, there's no need to be worried anymore," he replies. "I'm just hanging at a friend's house. I'll see you on the bus on Monday, okay?"

"Yeah, okay," she says, sounding much happier. "I'm glad you're alright, by the way."

"Yeah, me too," he says before hanging up.

Before he goes back in to finish his breakfast, he stops and thinks. Why were Rosulkip—and the other red monster whose name he keeps forgetting-snooping around his house with a sack? What were they looking for? He has an idea, but he sure doesn't like it.

They probably found and took Greg.

<<<Angela>>>

Angela slowly lowers her hand, the cell phone still clenched tightly in her fist. Nathan was worried about something, and it was obvious. Was T right? Did he already suspect her to be spying on him? ...That she knew about Crystal? She shakes her head, chiding herself. Of course not—she's just being paranoid. What was he worried about, then? Obviously he was fine... was it because the creatures knew where he lived? Possibly. But she had a feeling it was something more than that... Greg! His Familiar!

Suddenly she has a flashback to when she was back on Zilferia, an average citizen... back when she didn't know as much as she does now that she's a spy/guardian for the Queen. Back when Nathan and Crystal were still in the Games. She remembered the stunning red-tailed hawk, Nora, that

Crystal got. They had developed a bond instantly. Greg and Nathan had as well…

Picturing the rat, Angela swallows. She doesn't really like rodents, but she isn't as squeamish about them as many girls are.

She sighs. It appears that she'll have to look into why the Dorff were really there. Although Angela doesn't need to discover anything to tell her that the Dorff are bad news.

After all, they were enlisted into Patrick's service. They served the Dragon Hunters.

<<<Nathan>>>

Bryce strides into the room just as Nathan finishes his last gulp of orange juice. He doesn't stop to say hello.

"Nathan, come with me. Now."

Nathan stands, confused, but follows Bryce as he leads him to the door, which he left open when he came in. "Um…"

"No time for questions. I will fill you in as we walk."

"Okay…" Nathan grabs his backpack as he nearly jogs to keep up with Bryce's long legs and shuts the door behind them.

"I just came from a Dragon Hunters' meeting," he begins as they start down the hill that Zarafa's huge house is set on. "They are planning something big. It all goes down in about an hour."

"…What does?" Nathan asks, not looking forward to the answer.

Bryce doesn't answer him. "I figure we should be there to watch it all go down and try and prevent some of it if we can."

"Wait, we're going *towards* the Dragon Hunters??" Was his search partner stupid, or suicidal?

"Yes. You can blend in as an average citizen, and I can blend in as a Dragon Hunter." He looks down at Nathan with his intense gaze. "Are you up for this? There are far more opportunities for you to help take down the bad guys if you stop running and hiding from them."

Nathan frowns. "I don't run and hide." Bryce nods, accepting this as him going along with his plan, but Nathan still isn't sure. He follows reluctantly. Something tells him that this is a very, very bad idea.

<<<Angela>>>

Angela fidgets, waiting for word to come if the rat is still in Nathan's room or not. She had sent Auna to find out, but it was taking a little longer than she expected. Finally, there's a light tapping on her window. She rushes to it and lifts it up.

The small, fragile-looking fairiye flutters in. She's about as tall as Angela's pointer finger, and her wings, thin and delicate, extend to either side of her. Long white-blonde hair drifts around the tiny face, going down far enough to nearly reach the end of her light blue-green dress. The fairiye kicks her tiny feet excitedly as she hovers in the air, the sparkles on the light green shoes catching Angela's eye. She's shaking with nervous energy and her bright blue eyes lock onto Angela's as she relays the information, which is just what she was dreading when she asked her to go look for Greg.

"The Familiar is not present in the house, nor in his favorite places around the neighborhood. I cannot sense his magic anywhere."

Angela sighs. *"Thank you, Auna."*

The small fairiye lands on her right shoulder and puts a tiny hand on her face. *"Are we going to go look for him?"*

"Yes. Nathan needs his Familiar to keep him safe whenever we can't be there with him."

"You mean when you *can't,"* Auna laughs. *"His eyes can catch me and see through my cloaking spell. I can't be with him anyway."*

"Even more reason for him to have his Familiar. He needs as much protection as we can provide. I will NOT fail in my mission from the Queen."

Auna drifts up in front of Angela's face and tilts her head to the side thoughtfully. *"How do you know he didn't take Greg with him?"*

"I don't for sure," Angela sighs. *"I just know that I can't leave this alone. I can't sit still and do nothing if there's some way that I can help. The Queen is trusting me to take good care of Nathan, and that's what I intend to do. ...But I hope you are right and Greg is with him."*

"When are we going to look for him? Today's Sunday. You know Walter and Ramona don't approve of you going anywhere on Sundays. And after that, you have to go to school, play your sports, do your homework, and keep an eye on Nathan. We can't look out for both Greg and Nathan at the same time."

"I'll think of something. We need to go find him now. Who knows what those Dorff may have done to him? We could be too late if we wait too long."

She then walks over to her backpack and dumps the school stuff out on the bed before filling the pack with magical tools, food, and anything else that might help her in the hunt. She pulls it on before opening her door and walking downstairs, finding her parents quietly reading. "Mom?"

Ramona carefully puts a bookmark in the book before setting it down next to her before looking back up at her daughter, tucking some of her short blonde hair behind her ear. "Yes, dear?"

"One of my friends texted me, and she's having a really hard time today. She lives near here... can I go over and see if I can make her feel better?"

Her mom grins and her dad looks proud. "Of course. Take however long you need, just try and be back for dinner."

"Okay, I will. Thanks."

"Bye," Walter calls as he and Ramona pick up their books once more.

"Bye," she responds before closing the door behind her. She turns to Auna. "Lead the way."

<<<Nathan>>>

When they get to the spot, Bryce says to split up, but he'll be close by and keeping an eye on Nathan as he investigates. Before he can protest, Bryce had already disappeared. He sighs and walks around, not having any clue what he's supposed to be looking for. He peeks into the windows of the stores he passes by, other people quickly walking past him. He still finds it a little strange to see people on First Earth walking rather than using hoverboards. He was used to Tanguay, where everyone had enough money for all the technology that kept coming out.

He goes into a few of the more interesting stores, but everything seems to be as it always is. Nothing seems to be wrong. Nathan relaxes. Bryce must have just heard wrong. Or maybe the Dragon Hunters changed their minds about coming here to do... whatever it was that they were going to do.

He changes his mind once he sees something flicker by the window in front of him. That fairy again... the one he saw on the bus! ...Or he thought he saw. He wasn't sure if he did or not, but his stay on Zilferia told him to follow his instincts- and his instincts were telling him to follow the fairy. So he darts into the store bathroom and turns into a small moth before darting out the window in pursuit of the fairy as it zips along.

After following it for a short time, he realizes that it seems to be searching for something. He decides that he needs to talk to it, so he shifts back into himself and dashes into a cooking shop, buying a simple glass jar before speeding back outside. After peering around, he spots the tiny person standing on a bush, eating a blackberry. He sneaks forward until he's close enough to use his Gift to control the wind and push the fairy into the jar. She almost gets away regardless of the considerable gust, but Nathan manages to snatch her out of the air and dump her into the jar, clamping his hand over the top.

Lifting it up to eye level, he regards the fairy with interest. The beautiful, delicate fairy's wings flutter nervously as she stares back at him, hands on her hips. Suddenly he hears a light, clear voice in his head and knows instantly that it's the fairy's voice. *"Well, Nathan Anderson, you caught me. Now what are you going to do with me?"*

"Just ask a few questions," He replies, deeply intrigued by the magical creature. *"Which realm are you from?"*

"Lii, originally," she replies, folding her arms to show her discontentment at being stuck in a jar.

"How did you get here?"

"Through a portal, obviously."

"Why?"

"...I'm on a mission."

"And what mission would that be?"

"You don't need to know that," she replies, sticking her tiny tongue out at him. He grins and tries to keep from laughing.

"What are you looking for?"

"...Your Familiar, Greg."

Nathan freezes. *"Greg? How do you know about him? As a matter of fact, how do you know about me?"*

The small creature sighs. *"I reside with Angela while I am here in this realm. She told me about you."*

Nathan pauses, then decides to decipher this later. *"But Angela doesn't know that I have a Familiar —"*

"No, but those with magic can sense other magic users. I am attempting to find Greg because I believe that he was taken by the Dorff. ...Unless he's with you?" Her icy blue eyes quickly scan him.

"No, I don't have him with me. We were separated. Why would you believe that he was taken by the two Dorff?"

"Because the Dorff are known to only work for Patrick's Dragon Hunters," she tartly replies. *"By the way, this jar is completely unnecessary. Let me out and I will still talk to you."* Nathan frowns. *"I'm kind of suffocating in here,"* she continues. Nathan notices that she's leaning against the glass like she can barely support herself.

"Oh, sorry!" Nathan says, lifting his hand from the top of the jar. After taking a few deep breaths, she jumps into the air and stands on the lip of the jar and tilts her head at him inquisitively.

"Why are you so surprised?"

Nathan swallows. *"I... um... just didn't realize that there were Dragon Hunters on First Earth."*

The fairy laughs. *"You're kidding me, right? There are Dragon Hunters on every realm!"*

"Wait... all of them?" He repeats, instantly thinking about Crystal. If there were Dragon Hunters on Second Earth...

"Yes, all of them," she sighs.

After a few seconds, Nathan again decides to move on before the fairy gets bored and leaves before he can ask anything else. *"What is your name?"*

"Auna," she smiles. *"By the way, I am not a fairy, I am a fairiye. Fairies are the cousins to the Fairiye, and they are less intelligent and less adept at using magic than us, although we do look similar."*

"Oh... sorry," he says.

Auna suddenly freezes. *"Angela's in danger!"*

"Wait... what?"

"I have a bond with her much like you and your Familiar's bond," she explains impatiently, lifting into the air, her wings becoming a blur. *"She needs us, now! Follow me!"* she gasps as she darts forward. Nathan quickly shifts into a magpie and follows the fairiye as she zips away so fast he can barely keep up with her. They find Angela within a couple of minutes.

She's surrounded by five Dragon Hunters, their hoods hiding their faces. Angela is spinning in circles slowly, trying to keep all of them in sight at the same time. The Dragon Hunters press in closer to her, but she lashes out at them, pushing them back. Nathan can see the fear in her eyes as she continues to glance around at the men, a challenging glare attempting to hide the fear.

Nathan quickly lands and shifts back into himself before shifting into a large wolf and charging into the midst of them, leaping onto the nearest man and biting into his neck before breaking it with a sharp twist of his head. He lands on top of the body and stands there, hackles raised, as he bares his now bloody teeth at the rest of the men, who turn to face him instead.

<<<Angela>>>

Auna flutters up in front of Angela as the large silver wolf distracts the Dragon Hunters. *"Angela! Let's get out of here! Now!"*

"Um, right!" she replies, backing away from the fight, even as she is unable to tear her eyes from the scene as the wolf is tackled by all of the Dragon Hunters at once. She gasps, afraid for the wolf- or whoever it is that shifted into the wolf, since there are no wolf packs around these parts, plus wolves don't act like this- but her rescuer darts out from under them with nothing but a scratch on its shoulder. It glances at the cut, bares its teeth in anger, then savagely rips a chunk of meat from one of the man's legs. He goes down, screaming.

Angela can't take it anymore. She turns to Auna. *"I have to help!"* she says before turning and racing towards the fight. Auna sighs, but follows. She needs to protect Angela as best she can, even if the foolish girl won't listen to her.

Luckily, the wolf had already taken down three of the five Dragon Hunters and the last two were fleeing, so Auna didn't have to worry about her too much. Angela then rushes to the side of the large grey wolf, the people still remaining around them gawking. "Thank you for saving me!" she gasps gratefully, her arms around the wolf's neck for a moment in a small hug. "Who are you? How did you know where I was? ...Were you sent here for me?"

<<<Nathan>>>

Boy, I sure wish she would stop talking to me so much, Nathan sighs to himself. *I need to get out of here.* He snarls at the girl so she would back away. He dips his head to her in farewell before turning and loping off into the trees in the park nearby. Once far enough away from people, he shifts back into his own form, gasping at the sting of pain in his shoulder. Grimacing, he tears the sleeve off of the shirt, wrapping it around the wound as well as he can. Then he remembers Bryce and decides that he needs to find him and update him on what happened with the Dragon Hunters as well as with the fairiye, Auna.

He starts walking back out of the park, but stops. Should he tell Bryce about Auna? After all, he trusted the fairiye, although he wasn't quite sure why. And she had told him… that the Dorff were known to work only for Patrick.

But that can't be right, he tries to reassure himself as he begins walking again, slower. *The Dorff obeyed Zarafa, and she had already been proven to be working for the King and Queen- not that jerk, Patrick. But what if I'm wrong? What if that wasn't Alexander Dragon that I saw in that hologram? What if Zarafa tampered with it before she let me see it? What if she and Bryce have been lying to me this entire time?*

Though Bryce could be misled as well. Even Zarafa could have no idea who she's actually working for. Then again, what if the fairiye's facts were wrong? What if the Dorff were working for good now? He groans and stops walking for a second. *Too many 'what ifs!' I need to find out who's telling me the truth, and I need to find it out now!*

He suddenly hears men talking in low whispers behind a group of trees. Nathan quickly and quietly edges over to them, listening intently.

"Curse Bryce! He should have been controlling the boy- not gallivanting who knows where, doing who knows what! He failed in his job, and therefore caused us to fail in ours." There are murmurings of agreement at this. "So what should we do about that?" He continues, sneering.

"Kill him!" An exited, nasally voice suggests.

"Torture him?" A sly sounding voice chimes in.

"No, no, he's a favorite of Patrick's. We can't do that, or we would jeopardize our own standing with him."

A quiet voice finally peeps up. "We… could tell Patrick things. Things that would make Bryce seem…like a true traitor. Things that would raise us in Patrick's eyes, and get Bryce either killed or evicted from the group. Although he already has his insignia, so obviously he cannot be allowed to leave."

There's a pause. Nathan can feel his breath coming fast and hard. He tries to quiet it. His head is spinning. *So, is Bryce fooling these Dragon Hunters? Or is he fooling the King and Queen? Whose side was he really on?*

This insignia... was it like a brand on the Dragon Hunters? Did it enlist them to Patrick's service forever? Where was this sign, and how would he find it? Would that help him confirm who's on who's side? Or would it even prove anything? After all, Bryce could have gotten it simply to get closer to Patrick and it didn't actually mean anything.

Nathan backs away from the group, tripping on a root and falling on his back with a loud gasp. There's rustling from the direction of the voices and before he can even scramble to his feet, he is yanked into the air by multiple pairs of rough hands. He stands, panting, and sweeps the area with his eyes. He's surrounded by six Dragon Hunters- two of whom had been in the group attacking Angela just a few minutes previous.

"Nathan Anderson," the strongest looking one comments. He was one of the ones attacking Angela and seems to be the group's leader. "What a... surprise."

Nathan cocks an eyebrow. "Is it? Or am I just an unpleasant inconvenience? I heard you talking. You knew I was here."

The man looks surprised, then laughs. "Oh, dear, no. I had no idea you were there. I did, however, know that you were the wolf that tore down three of my men and escaped with barely a scratch..." he reaches out and tears Nathan's hastily made bandage from his wound. Nathan doesn't flinch, just watches the man carefully and steadily. "Hmm," he says, wiping some blood off of his arm with his finger and casually inspecting it. "It seems to me that a steeper price must be paid for the loss of my men, don't you agree?" The group surrounding Nathan tightens and the men chuckle eagerly.

Nathan slowly eases into a crouch and prepares his mind to shapeshift or manipulate the weather. A dark storm front rolls in and rain starts pouring down. Nathan doesn't move an inch, waiting for the Dragon Hunters to make the first move. They watch him just as warily. Finally, one of them flinches as Nathan's piercing gaze suddenly shifts to his. Nathan quickly leaps, transforming into a cougar, tearing out the man's throat before the man can hardly lift his hands to defend himself.

He then feels the icy bite of a metal blade in his hind leg. Swiveling around, he swipes at the man who cut him, slicing open his chest with his long, strong claws. Nathan quickly transforms back into himself, ducks under another attack, and changes into an eagle, taking to the air and winging away from the group of Dragon Hunters.

He doesn't get far before he's suddenly stopped in midair, unable to advance any further. Glancing down, he notices one of the men with his eyes locked on him, his hand extended in a claw as if he was grasping Nathan, ready to pluck him out of the air. He's chanting as he does so. As Nathan strains against the magical bonds holding him back, the man begins pulling him closer. Panicking, Nathan shifts into himself, nearly landing on the warlock, who dives out of the way just in time.

Panting, Nathan stands again, grimacing and trying not to put any weight on his injured leg. The first man, the leader, grabs him from behind and pins him. As Nathan struggles, the warlock stands, brushing some mud off of his cloak. Glaring at Nathan, he advances, once again stretching forth his hand and slowly walking towards him while chanting.

An aching pain begins to overtake Nathan, starting in his feet and spreading upwards. Desperate, Nathan changes into a snake. The instant he does, however, the pain instantaneously overtakes his entire body, filling him with agony as it intensifies. He's shocked when he reverts to his normal form without evoking his Gift. The leader makes a move to grab him again, but it's not necessary. Nathan collapses to the ground, convulsing in pain as the Dragon Hunter continues to chant.

After a few more minutes, he stops, just as Nathan was on the verge of unconsciousness. Two men pick him up by his arms. He hangs limply from their grasp, struggling simply to breathe. The magic-wielding Dragon Hunter turns to the leader. "It is done."

The leader grins widely. "You did it, then? You took away his Gifts?"

"To the best of my knowledge, yes. But we should keep him under observation to see if my spell holds true. We don't want him to be getting his Gifts back any time soon."

"That we do not. ...Very well, we'll take him with us." He motions to the two men holding Nathan up, who can barely stand on his own two feet. "Let's go."

<<<Angela>>>

"Come on now, Angela, let's get you home," Auna urges, hovering by her shoulder. Angela stays where she is, standing still and staring after the place where the silver wolf who saved her had disappeared.

"Who was that?" she murmurs.

"Does it matter? We need to get you home!" Auna insists.

Dark clouds then quickly roll in. Within a minute, Angela is drenched from the fat raindrops. Shivering, she turns from the park at last. "Okay," she finally concedes. "Let's go."

<<<Bryce>>>

Bryce curses to himself under his breath. He had lost track of the boy. Who knows what trouble he may cause without his supervision? Knowing his luck, the boy could have stumbled across the Dragon Hunters as they tried to accomplish their actual goal rather than the diversion that Bryce and his helpers had set up.

Rain starts coming down in driving sheets, and he curses again as those around him scramble for shelter. This rain wasn't predicted in the news, which meant that the weather was induced by a Gift. He just hopes it had nothing to do with Nathan. Not only would he never hear the end of it from the other Dragon Hunters, but things could go drastically wrong should Nathan discover things meant to stay a secret.

A girl walking fast from the direction of the park suddenly bumps into him. "Oh, sorry!" she exclaims, lifting her head. Angela. Now he knows that Nathan had indeed discovered their real goal. He growls in anger. The boy just complicated- if not ruined- everything!

The girl's eyes widen as she takes in his cloak and gloves. Bryce sighs. He was hoping to save this for later. It was a rather rare thing, after all. There was a limited amount of times that he could use it.

Angela turns to run, but another, smaller Dragon Hunter stops her. "Bryce," he says calmly, keeping his eyes on the girl. "We can do the job ourselves..."

"No," he responds, shaking his head as he pulls out a vial of black powder that's about the size of his pinky finger. "She is not part of my job."

"Your job," the other man replies, sneering, "is to keep Nathan Anderson occupied and ignorant. Use him to find Rex if you must. This girl?" he continues, grabbing Angela by the arm as she tries to flee, "This girl was assigned to protect Nathan, and to keep him from knowing that anything is amiss."

"And isn't that exactly what we're trying to do as well?" Bryce calmly replies.

"Not exactly, and you know it!" the other Dragon Hunter replies, exasperated. "Our job is to keep him occupied, to keep him from knowing anything about our designs in Zilferia, and especially Second Earth. He absolutely cannot know about Crystal. You know how he would react. He cannot know about any of this, and as helpful as it may be to use him to find Rex, that is not our main priority, and you know it!"

"Oh, shut up already," Bryce sighs, pulling Angela from his grasp. She spins to face him, her eyes wide with fear.

"Please," she whispers. "Please... don't hurt me..."

Bryce looks into her eyes, shining with unshed tears, and feels a pang in his heart. His wife had looked so similar to this girl. Of course, everyone claimed that he saw her everywhere, in many girls. With a swift, decisive move, he opens the vial and tilts her head back a little with his other hand. "Don't worry," he murmurs softly, wiping some of the powder on her eyelids as she remains frozen in place with fear. "I'm not going to hurt you." He spreads more around her ears. Her eyes flutter back open, but now they are devoid of the fear they once held.

She looks at Bryce in wonder and confusion. "What... what did you..."

"Shh..." He gently replies, lying her softly on the ground. "Sleep well," he adds as her eyes close and her breathing slows and deepens.

"Well wasn't that just touching," the other Dragon Hunter mocks. "Saving her life by erasing her memories. You know it's only temporary, don't you? It may not be our job to remove her, but it is someone else's. She won't last long."

Bryce sighs and stands, closing the vial and tucking the rest away. There's only two-thirds of it left. "John, I will do what I have to do to protect the innocents."

John scoffs. "The innocents? Dude, wake up, we are Dragon Hunters! Not only that, but we are at war! In order to complete our mission—and Patrick's vision—there will be casualties. Besides, this girl is not innocent. She's from Zilferia, and she's on a quest for Queen Pearl. That practically makes her enemy number one."

Bryce stalks toward him menacingly. "She. Is. Just. A. Girl. I want her to stay out of this. Little girls do not belong in war."

John sighs and shakes his head. "Fine, fine. We'll leave her be." He turns and flips his hood back up over his brown hair. "I don't know how you ever made it to your status with that soft of a heart in the first place," he sighs quietly, knowing Bryce heard regardless. With that, he vanishes.

Bryce kneels by Angela's head and looks at her peaceful, sleeping face. With a trembling hand, he shifts a lock of hair off of her face. How was it possible that she looked so much like his dead wife? He strokes her cheek gently with the back of one rough finger before quickly standing and striding off into the rain.

Time to find Nathan.

12

A warm hand on my face wakes me. My hand jumps up to cover the hand as it cradles my face. My eyes flutter open sleepily. "Chet?" I ask quizzically. "What's wrong?" His face is only a couple feet from mine, and his green eyes sparkle mischievously—more like the Chet that I first met than the one I have been seeing for the past few days.

"Nothing's wrong," he murmurs, smiling at me.

"Then why are you in here?" I ask, sitting up as he removes his hand and leans back a little. "What time is it?"

"No one else is up yet," he says. "Now might be a good time to…"

"Visit the merfolk?" I finish for him.

He raises an eyebrow. "Um, I was going to say read the journal before you have to do other things, actually…"

"Oh," I say. I don't want to read that dumb journal. I want to finish uniting Zilferia against the Dragon Hunters. I need to go visit the merfolk. "Oh!" I suddenly exclaim, remembering what Zeke told me the day before.

"What?" Chet asks quizzically.

"Nothing…" I start to reply before I remember that he had been recaptured by Patrick since I was gone. "Actually, there is something. While you were at Patrick's castle, did you happen to notice… a huge Trident?"

"No," Chet replies, looking increasingly curious. "I think I heard Patrick ranting about how Vlad's impostor never gave the Trident to him, though.

Said he must have hidden it somewhere. He tortured him to get the information out of him, but just before he told him the location, he killed himself by jabbing a knife in his throat."

"So, Patrick doesn't have it? And he has no idea where it could be?"

Chet looks at me a little strangely. "No. Why?"

"Well, I promised the merfolk that I would give it back to them if I could. I think it would be the best way to not be killed on sight if I'm returning it to them."

"Ah. Sounds reasonable," he concedes, laughing a little and standing. "Well if we're going to search for it, then you should get dressed. I'll see if I can grab us some breakfast real fast before anyone else gets up."

"Okay. Thanks," I reply, swinging my legs out of bed as he closes the door behind him. As I get dressed, Nora wakes up.

"And just where do you think you're going? Thinking about leaving me behind again?" she asks. I can hear the hurt in her voice. *"My job is to protect you and advise you. I can't do that if you keep leaving me behind and making foolish decisions."*

I pull on some black, waterproof pants. They adhere to my skin once I put them on so there's less resistance as I swim, I suppose. The dark green shirt does the same. "Nora, I'm just going out to find where Vlad's impostor hid the Trident so I can return it to the merfolk. I probably won't even leave the Village today, plus Chet will be with me. And you are welcome to come as well."

"Good, because I'm coming whether you want me to or not," she responds, flying to perch on my shoulder once I put on a black jacket and a matching pair of slim, water-proof shoes.

Chet doesn't bat an eye at Nora when she joins us for breakfast. "I found some leftover pancakes in the fridge," he says, placing a plate of steamy blueberry pancakes in front of me. He pulls out a chair for me. Smiling, I sit down as Nora flaps up to the post on the chair to wait. "So, what's the plan?" He asks me as he sits down and grabs the syrup.

"Well, I was thinking about talking to Thaddeus to see if he has any ideas of where the impostor could have hidden the Trident and after that, I guess we just look for it."

Chet raises an eyebrow as he takes a large bite of pancake. "You know how long it could take us to find it?" He swallows. "This is not really a one-day venture." He eyes my outfit. "So you didn't really have to get all ready to go out and meet the merfolk yet."

I shrug. "Better safe than sorry. I would rather return the Trident to them as quickly as possible."

"So your parents can't stop you?"

"Well... yes, but also because it will help them fend off the Dragon Hunters." *And because there's a chance the King could heal me so I could get my Gifts back.* Again, I don't add this part. My gut instinct tells me that I shouldn't let Chet know about my Gifts or my Dragon part. I'm not really sure why, but I'm not one to go against my instincts.

"Ah. I guess that makes sense." His brow furrows in thought as he glares at the pancakes on his plate. I can't even begin to guess what he's thinking about, so I just shrug and start on my own pancakes.

<<<Hunter>>>

Dang! Getting Crystal on our side seemed so easy when Patrick asked me to do it! Why are all these snags coming up? Why is she trying so dang hard to unite Zilferia against us? Why isn't the journal destroying her like Patrick promised it would? Sure, it's distasteful to her so she doesn't want to read it anymore, but that's not enough!

If we actually do find the Trident, how am I supposed to prevent her from delivering it back to the merfolk without blowing my cover? I can't just sit back and let the merfolk regain their primary weapon against us! Hunter lets out a heavy sigh and pushes one hand through his hair and stands abruptly. *That's it. I need to contact Patrick and let him know what's going on. I need him to advise me on what to do.*

"I'll be right back," he says to Crystal, who nods.

He then shoves his way outside, breathing heavily. He absolutely did not want to do this, but it seemed it was now necessary. He quickly makes his way into the surrounding woods, glad that it was early enough that few peeping eyes were out and about.

After going a ways into the woods, the sounds of the Village fade. The forest is quiet. Hunter feels a pang. He missed the song of the trees, the noises of the animals roaming freely through the trees. He missed the sounds of life. Hopefully the Dragon Hunters will quickly win this war, and everything can go back to how it was before.

With trembling hands, he pulls off his gloves and lets them drop to the earth. He then holds his right hand up to the light. A silvery blue tattoo shimmers on the back of his hand. It's in the semblance of an eye.

Hunter takes a deep breath and lightly brushes the image with the index finger of his other hand. The eye turns a fiery orange and moves, blinking and looking around. Hunter tries to contain a shudder as his skin crawls with the peculiar feeling the magic induces. "D... Dravyn..." he says, trying not to stutter. "I need to talk to Patrick."

The eye stares at him for a few seconds before the fiery ink swirls and forms the image of Patrick's face. "Hunter?" It inquires, its voice faint. "Why would you contact me this way? What's the emergency?"

Hunter is beginning to sweat. The magic required to use his Eye was taxing. He didn't have long to relay his message. "I wouldn't have done it unless there wasn't enough time to contact you another way and receive your answer in time as well."

"Well spill it, boy! And hurry, I have urgent matters to attend to."

"Yes, sir. ...It seems Crystal is more difficult to persuade than you lead me to believe. She's trying to unite the dragons, Sohos, and merfolk and give them *hope*. Not only that, but today she means to set out and find the Trident and return it to those fish."

"Hmm," Patrick murmurs thoughtfully. "It would indeed be a setback should they have their Trident back, but it would be even worse should your cover be blown. You are the only inside man I have left."

"Wait, what? What happened to the others?" Hunter asks, beginning to shake from the toll of the magic from the Eye.

"Old Thaddeus and Vladimir were hunting them down. I ordered the last few to flee. You are the only one left completely undetected. Keep it that way. Earning Crystal's complete and utter trust should cement your standing with the others as well. As for the Trident issue... try and distract her as often as you can. Should you find the Trident before she does, do not let her know of the location and lead her elsewhere. At the end of the day, deliver it to me as she sleeps."

"What if she finds it before I do?" He inquires.

"Then just go along with it. If you must, steal it from her as she sleeps and take it to me. If for some reason you cannot do this, then allow her to deliver it to the oversized fish. It will be a small setback, but once we get the girl to come to me willingly, the war will be over. This spark of hope she's been attempting to spread will be smothered forever, and we will rule Zilferia!"

Hunter doubles over and empties his stomach of his last couple of meals. "Urngh," he groans, wiping his mouth with the back of his hand. He turns back to the Patrick on his other hand. "I won't fail you."

"I trust that you will not. Oh, and next time you need to contact me and it's too taxing—like this conversation—then stand before a mirror and recite these words: *Llacym deehkc irtap.* I shall replace your reflection in the mirror, and there are only minor effects to that spell. Farewell, and don't forget to get Crystal to read more of the fake journal! We must crush her hope before it grows out of control."

The orange-red outline of the man then swirls and is replaced with the eye, which stares at him once again. "Thank you, Dravyn," he says to the eye, which blinks at him before becoming inanimate once more, the ink cooling back to its original silvery-blue appearance on the back of his right hand.

Hunter collapses to his knees and takes a shaky breath as he feels the strain of magic finally ease. He wipes his mouth again and grimaces. *Llacym deehkc irtap.* He would need to remember that. There was no way he was using the Eye again unless he had absolutely no other choice and it was a life or death situation.

After putting his gloves back on, he ambles back to the Dragon mansion. The Hunt was about to commence. Hopefully he could find the Trident before Crystal did.

<<<Crystal>>>

I finish braiding my hair and begin pacing. What was taking Chet so long? What was he doing? The door then opens and I spin around. "Chet," I gasp in relief, taking a few steps toward him. I stop when I see the look on his face. "Chet, are you okay? You look... sick."

"Just a bit of an upset stomach," he replies. "I'm fine."

I hesitate. His face is grey, and he's leaning against the doorway like he doesn't trust his body to hold itself up for very long. *"He said he's fine,"* Nora says. *"Let's just go before your parents get back."*

"Alright," I concede, knowing we need to hurry. "Let's go." I brush past Chet with Nora flying above me. He falls in behind us, his breathing a little ragged. I wonder what happened to him. He seemed fine before he left, and then when he came back, he appeared exhausted and sick.

"Crystal, I'm fine," Chet says, as if he knew what I was thinking about. "We just need to find this Trident of yours, okay?"

"Yes, of course," I concede, sighing. I look around. "I have no clue where to start though."

"May I make a suggestion?" Nora asks.

"Of course!" I reply gladly. *"What is it?"*

"Thaddeus was an advisor and worked alongside the fake Vlad as well as the real one. And if we can find Vladimir himself, he should know a few hiding spots that he is privy to. We might be able to find it that way."

"Nora, that's brilliant! Why didn't I think of that?" I chuckle. "Nora says we could just talk to Vlad or Thaddeus," I inform Chet.

"Great, that sounds like a good lead," he says. "Show me the way."

I'm not sure where Vlad lives, so I head over to Thaddeus's house. After knocking, I can hear him scrambling around inside for a few seconds before the door swings open to reveal his tall, lean shape. His beard hasn't been trimmed for a while and has now advanced down his neck and become a little untidy, giving it a scraggly look. His face droops like he has little energy left. "Ah, Crystal. I wasn't expecting a visit today. Come in, come in," he says, gesturing Chet and me into his house. "Welcome, Nora," he greets Nora, who favors him with a slight bow, wings outstretched.

Chet hesitates at the doorway. "Hey, Crystal, I think I'll see if I can go and find Vlad. Together one of us should be able to find the Trident, right? Maybe two parties searching would be faster and more thorough than just one."

"Okay, sure," I say. "That sounds like a good idea. Just meet me back here in two hours for lunch?"

"Alright, sounds like a plan," he says, waving to me as he turns and heads away. Thaddeus shuts the door behind him and turns to me.

"What are you two searching for?" He inquires curiously as he sits down across from me at his little wooden table, brushing aside a pile of old, musty books.

"The Mermaid King's Trident," I reply.

Thaddeus raises a grey eyebrow at me. I suddenly realize that there are a lot more white hairs then there used to be. Not too long ago, it was all grey. Now there's a dusting of white. It makes me sad, like somehow age didn't apply to Thaddeus, it wouldn't affect him. It wasn't allowed to. Now I see the evidence that even Thaddeus can be weighed down by age and stress.

"Why would you be looking for that?" he inquires.

I take a deep breath and let it out slowly. "It's kind of a long story."

"I have all day," he says.

"Well, I need to hurry," I murmur, almost talking to myself. "So I'll just shorten the tale."

"Sounds good to me," Thaddeus says, settling into his seat. "Go ahead."

"Okay… well, I think I know how to get my Gifts and maybe my dragon part back," I begin.

"Really? How did you discover this?"

"Um… I went to see the dragons yesterday," I say. "As well as the Sohos."

"Ah, right. I heard about that. What did you learn?" He's now leaning forward, anxious to hear what I have to say.

"Well, Gale suggested that neither my Gifts nor my dragon part should really be able to be removed from me. He speculated that perhaps if the Mermaid King had his Trident back, he could use its magic to help remove whatever is blocking me access to my Gifts. As for my dragon part, he suggested that I go to see the Sohos since they know more about dragons than any other human. So, I went to them, and they had their dragon find Eric, who then gave me some of his blood to drink…"

"Wait, you did *what?!*" Thaddeus exclaims, standing and looking me over. "And you're okay?"

"I didn't have very much," I clarify. "And I'm fine now… but these weird things happened when I swallowed it." He sits back down and watches me intently. "My eyes were a mix of both dragon eyes and normal, and claws replaced my fingernails."

"However, neither of these symptoms seem to be present at the moment," he notes, still just watching me.

"Yes, they receded after I went to sleep in one of their huts. But when I got angry, the claws came back, as did the eyes. I lost control of myself and killed two Dragon Hunters."

"Did Chet see this transformation?"

"No, he was dealing with other Dragon Hunters," I reply. "And by the time he got back, my anger had faded and the claws and eyes went back to normal."

"Hmm," he murmurs thoughtfully, leaning back in his hair and stroking his beard with one hand. "That is interesting indeed. I have never heard anything of the sort. Of course, there's never been another Dragongirl since Alex's time. This is all new experimentation."

"So, we don't know if it will end up working or not," I sigh. "Or if I'll end up being stuck like this forever."

"Well, we can always try our best," He comforts, standing. "And I think I may know where the impostor Vlad hid the Trident- granted it hasn't been disturbed since he left it there."

"Well then let's go!" I exclaim, rising with him and heading to the door with Nora perched on my shoulder. He chuckles a little and opens the door, following me out. *"I sure hope the Trident actually works."*

"I do as well," Nora replies.

<<<Hunter>>>

Hunter casts about the nearby houses with his mental probe, searching for thoughts that would reveal where Vlad is. He needed to find him, and quickly. Luckily, he was nearby, so he locates him without much trouble.

He walks up to a hut that looks the same as Thaddeus's and knocks. He hears a surprised exclamation from within before the man scrambles for the door and unlocks it. "Chet?" Vlad peers around him, as if looking for someone else to be with him. "To what do I owe the pleasure?"

"Crystal and I are looking for the Mermaid King's Trident," he explains, stepping past the man into his house. It's not nearly as tidy as Thaddeus's place.

"The Trident?" Vlad repeats, closing the door and turning to him. "Why are you suddenly interested in that?"

"Crystal wants to return it to the Merfolk," Hunter replies. "She wants to unite them, the Sohos, and the dragons, but doesn't want to go back without their Trident. It's kind of a peace offering so they don't kill us," He explains with a small smile. Those fish couldn't harm him. He's practically the Prince of the Dragon Hunters. Invincible. Powerful. Cunning. "Would you happen to have an idea of where the Trident could be?" He presses.

"There are a few spots I could think of," Vlad replies. "But if Crystal's the one that wants it, why are you here and she isn't?"

"She's with Thaddeus. We figured if we split up it was more likely that one of us would find it, plus it would be faster to scour the Village in two groups rather than one."

"Ah, I see. In that case, come with me," Vlad replies, leading the way back out of the cluttered house.

Hopefully we can find it before Crystal does... I need to present it to Patrick. I would rather it didn't end up back in the hands of those fish. That could cause a kink in our plans, despite Patrick's assurances that it won't make much of a difference. If only Crystal would read that journal. I'm not getting very far in causing her to doubt herself. If anything, she's more driven than before to fight—which is the opposite effect that Patrick predicted.

She seems to make my life a lot more difficult than it needs to be, he sighs.

<<<Crystal>>>

"Every once in a while, I noticed the impostor Vladimir sneaking away into the woods. That's probably when he contacted Patrick and the two transferred information. However, I do believe that there was one other place he might have gone. The Trident may be hidden there," Thaddeus says as Nora and I follow him through the Village toward the edge, near the forest. Thaddeus stops just before an old, dilapidated building. "Here we are."

"You think he hid it in here?" I question dubiously, wiping dirt off a window and peering through. The small building seems to have a bunch of boxes stacked all around. Dusty cobwebs cling to just about everything.

"No," Thaddeus explains as he unlocks the door. "I think he hid it in the area that the tunnel beneath the store leads to."

"A tunnel beneath the store?" I repeat as I cautiously step inside. The air is stale and musty here, and there is a layer of dust on everything, including the floor.

"Watch," Thaddeus says, waving his hand at the dust on the floor. Patches of it, each about the size of a footprint, begin to fade away, then glow a light, faint green.

"The impostor?"

"Yes," he confirms, carefully following the tracks through the maze of boxes. "These are his footprints."

I suddenly notice something. "They only go in one direction. He never came back out..."

"Oh, he came out alright, just not the way he went in," Thaddeus explains.

"Wait, why do the footprints disappear there?" Nora wonders, flapping over to where the tracks do indeed vanish.

Thaddeus approaches the spot and crouches. "This is the entrance to those under-ground tunnels," he says, touching the spot of the floor where the tracks end and closing his eyes for a few seconds. There's an audible click, and a section of the floor slides back, revealing an opening just wide enough for a person to squeeze through. Thaddeus turns back to me. "Ready?"

I take a deep breath. Ready to get my Gifts back? Definitely. Ready to help unite Zilferia? Yes. Ready to plunge into uncertainty to retrieve something that the Dragon Hunters are also searching for? Ready to face an unknown, potentially dangerous future? "Yes," I say with confidence. I'm prepared to no longer be so afraid. I'm ready to take the next step.

"Then after you, Princess," he says, stepping back and leaving the way open for me. I take a deep breath and approach the hole in the ground. I only see darkness below.

"Um... there's no ladder or anything..." I point out.

"Just jump. It shouldn't be far," he assures me. Shuddering, I turn back to the hole... and jump.

I fall quickly before landing on the hard ground. I land a little awkwardly and roll my ankle. I gasp and fall to the side to get out of the way of Thaddeus. I pull my ankle closer to me and examine it with my fingers since it's too dark to see much but the faint light from the square of light above. Sure enough, I sprained it. I carefully stand and gently put some weight on it. It may hurt a little, but I can walk.

"Come on down," I call out to Thaddeus. Nora flies down to me before Thaddeus jumps. He lands perfectly.

"Are you alright?" he asks.

I nod. "I just twisted my ankle a little. It's okay though. I can still walk."

"Good," he says before closing the hatch above with a flick of his wrist. A faint light can now be seen to Thaddeus's left.

"I'm assuming that's where we have to go now?" I ask.

"No," Thaddeus says, turning to face the opposite direction. "That's to fool others who come into a trap. The true direction lies this way." He once again waves his hand and reveals the continuing green footprints.

We follow the prints for a while until we come to a thick wooden door. *"Isn't it odd that we haven't encountered any traps yet?"* Nora notices.

"Yes, it is," I confirm. "Thaddeus is there a trap behind this door?"

"Not exactly," he sighs. "It's more of a test."

"A test?" I repeat, confused. "What kind of test?"

"A test that I cannot pass, nor Nora..."

"Let me guess. Only I can do whatever is necessary on the other side of this door." I sigh. "Why is it always me?"

"Well because I must use my magic to hold the door open for you so you do not remain trapped in there forever should anything go... awry, and because Nora is a bird and a human must enter."

"What will I have to do?"

Thaddeus hesitates. "I'm not entirely certain."

"Wait... so you knew about the rest of this place but not this part? Why is that?" I question him.

He sighs. "Because I created this place. However, the room inside changes to defend whatever is inside. It doesn't defend every item the same way, you see," he explains. "Just... remember what I taught you last year," he offers as a last bit of advice before grabbing the door handle and heaving it open with an obvious amount of effort. "And please hurry," he grunts as he holds the door open.

I nod and step cautiously inside.

I instantly come face-to-face with a large... man... dressed in black armor. He has bulging muscles and a hood covering his face, but the thing about him that most attracts my gaze was his large, white, feathered wings. His head slowly lifts and his eyes open, revealing glowing white orbs that seemed to pierce into my very soul. My mouth falls open as I attempt to say something, but words seem impossible.

His voice is deep and shakes the ground beneath me. "I am Tzadkiel. I am the archangel that represents Justice, benevolence, and grace. You have come to me seeking a weapon of great power."

"Y...yes," I manage to squeak out.

"I am the guardian of this object that you seek. How do you intend to win it from me?"

"I... I don't know," I murmur, feeling helpless tears rise to my eyes. "I cannot and will not fight you for it, for I know I would lose. I will not attempt to find it without your aid, for I know you will not allow me to. ...I suppose the only thing I can do is to beg for you to grant it to me. Please trust me when I tell you that I mean to use it to bring about Justice."

The archangel pauses. "I can sense that you are telling me the truth. However, can you bring about Justice while also being benevolent?" I don't reply. I'm shaking in the frigid air that permeates the area. I cannot think of an acceptable answer to him. If I tell him yes, I definitely can, then that will seem prideful and make me seem less likely to be telling the truth. But if I tell him no, he will definitely not grant the weapon unto me. "Well? Do you believe that you would be benevolent to those whose lives you will hold in the balance while you control the Trident?"

I force myself to say something. "Oh, Tzadkiel... I know not how to answer you. I only wish I could show you... is there some way for me to prove myself to you? To show that I can be benevolent?"

Tzadkiel's eyes gleam from under the hood. "You impress me, Crystal Dragon, with your words, but mostly with your purity of heart. However... there is one test I must administer unto you to test your worthiness of this great weapon."

"Anything," I pledge.

"Very well," he says, flapping his wings and rising into the air. He then spreads his wings so each tip reaches the far walls of the cave-like room. "This is your test. I will be watching how you conduct yourself. Close your eyes."

I obediently close them, waiting with baited breath for my 'test.' After a few seconds, I feel the rumble of Tzadkiel's voice once more. "Open your eyes. React to the situation as you normally would. I will be watching."

When I open my eyes, I am no longer in the cave, and Tzadkiel is nowhere to be seen. I am in Patrick's castle. My lungs immediately seem to seize up and refuse to take in air. "Please..." I gasp. "Please... not here... Tzadkiel... please... take me somewhere else..." But there is no response from the absent archangel.

My vision starts to fade as I begin to slide into a full-out panic attack. I sink to my knees on the cold stone floor. Suddenly, I hear footsteps and a familiar voice. My head shoots up at the sound. Patrick. My vision snaps back into clarity and my lungs take in air once more. Patrick... the cause of all this sorrow and pain. What better way to put an end to it all than to put an end to *him?* I jump up and seem to fly over to him, pinning him easily against the wall. I am strong, powerful. I can do whatever I want to do.

Patrick's face is one of complete fear. Sweat shines on his brow. "Crystal Dragon... how nice to see you again."

"Shut up," I sneer, holding a sword that had appeared out of nowhere to his throat. "It's time for you to die. After everything you've done... you deserve that much and worse."

"Ah, but you are too good to kill me. Remember the last time you had that opportunity?"

"I'm a changed girl," I growl, pressing the blade against his skin. A drop of blood rolls down his neck into his shirt. "*You* did that when you stole my Gifts. I am not the same person anymore."

"So, you think killing me is justice?" he pants nervously.

I hesitate. Is it justice? Yes. ...But is there a better way to bring about the Justice the people deserve? A more... benevolent way?

I back away from Patrick, releasing him from the wall. I'm breathing heavily. "Killing you is Justice. But there is also a better way. I'm taking you to my parents. You will be put on trial before the Village. If you are there condemned for your wrongdoings, so be it. But I will not be the one to end your life in cold blood, even if that's what you would do if our places were reversed."

I close my eyes, and when I open them again, I am back in the cave with Tzadkiel standing in front of me. I can see a slight smile on his face where the hood doesn't completely cover. I'm confused and breathing heavily. "What... was that?" I pant.

His smile widens. "You passed. You passed the test of Justice versus Benevolence. You found a balance between the two, even when confronted with your worst enemy. You have earned the Trident," he finishes, waving his hand. The Trident materializes by my feet. I glance down at it, then back up at the archangel.

"Thank you," I say.

He dips his head to me slightly. "Now go, Crystal Dragon, and return Benevolent Justice to the world. Restore the balance." I blink, and he's gone.

I carefully reach down and pick up the heavy Trident. The metal is cool in my hand as I heft it and turn back to the door. I found it at last.

<<<Hunter>>>

Vlad leads Hunter to an old, abandoned store filled with old boxes covered in dust. He is filled with disbelief and disgust. This stupid 'advisor' led him astray, wasting time and giving Crystal a head start to the actual location. He growls in frustration.

"Follow me," Vlad invites as he opens the door. Hunter stalks past him angrily.

"How can this be where he hid the Trident??" he demands.

"The most likely place for the Dragon Hunter to hide the weapon would be in the vault beneath the store," he patiently explains as he leads the way to the back of the store. "Watch," he advises as he sweeps his arm over a section of the floor, which then lifts and slides away, leaving a hole in the floor.

"Are you certain this is where the Trident is?" he asks, peering into the darkness of the hole.

"It is my best guess," he sighs.

"Very well," Hunter says, and jumps down into the hole, landing in a crouch. Vlad comes down behind him, closing the door above them.

"This way," he says, walking in the opposite direction of the only light visible.

Ignoring the crazy old man, Hunter walks towards the light. Vlad calls out behind him, but he takes no notice of him and continues forward. He's suddenly tackled by something from behind. "Arg!" He cries as he falls. "Vlad, what is wrong with you? Get off me!" A hysterical laugh that sounds nothing like Vlad's comes from by his ear. "Who are you? Get off me! Leave me alone!"

The voice laughs again. "Oh, but why would I do that?" It's a higher, more mischievous sounding voice than Hunter expected to hear. "We were just beginning to have a little fun! Oh, what wonderful misfortune you came this way!" The hysterical laughing comes again.

"What are you?" Hunter grunts in frustration as he tries to stand. "And why do you sound like a monkey when you laugh?"

The laughter stops abruptly. "Monkey, did you call me?" The creature leaps off his back and lands in front of him, lifting his face with its hands until his face is mere inches from the creature's. "Do I look like a monkey to you?"

Truthfully, it did look very similar to a monkey. Only instead of hair, it had rough, leathery grey skin and bronze eyes with no pupils. As the monkey-like creature skittered back a little, Hunter sat up and peered closely at it. It had a long tail like a monkey, and four limbs that were like both arms and legs. It wore bronze cuffs on its 'wrists,' and its hands had only three fingers. There were strange, dark markings on its body, which seemed to swirl like smoke.

"What... what are you?" Hunter gasps, standing.

The creature laughs again. "I am Abonsam. I am the spirit of trouble and misfortune. And you, Hunter Dragon, are full of misfortune and seem to cause unfathomable amounts of trouble, for both yourself and others."

"Excuse me?" Hunter rages.

The Abonsam scrambles around him. "Yes... poor boy, kidnapped by the one you now most admire, yet seem to know not much about, somehow... you embrace evil without even knowing that it is indeed evil which you perform..."

"Shut up, you stupid little beast!" Hunter cries, pulling his sword from its sheath. "You don't know what you're talking about!"

"Tsk tsk," the Abonsam continues, perching on his head. "And even now, the misfortune of failing in your task to keep Crystal from the Trident."

Hunter freezes. "What? What do you know about that?"

The spirit chitters and flies into the air, hovering in front of Hunter's face, his legs folded like he's meditating. "Crystal is just down the hall—where Vladimir was leading you—retrieving the Trident as we speak. She is amazing, that one." Hunter scowls. "Whereas you... ah, the trouble you go through trying to prove yourself. How unfortunate," it cries in hysteria as it cartwheels through the air. "Such delicious agony," it crows as it settles to the ground before him once more.

"I don't have time for this," Hunter growls, turning to go back the way he came. He only takes a few steps before he runs into an invisible barrier. "What the heck?"

The Abonsam laughs once more, hands on its stomach. "Oh, silly Dragon

Hunter Prince," it chortles. "You cannot leave without giving me something in return."

"Why, you stupid little imp! I'll cut you to ribbons if you *don't* let me go!" He cries, swinging his sword threateningly.

"Ooh! Ooh hoo! Stupid boy! This is not my rule! It's the rule of this room- of my prison! It is not my choice!" Hunter growls and swings his sword. It passes harmlessly through the Abonsam's arm. It just sits there and smiles. "Done trying to harm a spirit now, boy?"

Hunter rages. "What do you want? I have gold, I have magic spells, I have Gifts that I can use to give you whatever you want! So tell me, creature, what do I have to do to get out of here?"

"Hmm," The Abonsam murmurs, scampering over his body before sitting back. "I don't want anything that you have."

"Then how am I supposed to get out of here?" he cries in agony.

"There is still a way!" The spirit laughs. "There is always a way. Even for me, there is a way for me to escape my prison... although it takes another..."

"So, you want me to help you get out? Done. What do I have to do?"

"Do? You do nothing. Do nothing!" It laughs as it suddenly rushes him and hits his chest with an icy cold blast of spirit air. Hunter gasps and collapses to the ground as he feels like his heart freezes. He hears the spirit inside his head. *"Now hurry, dumb boy! Run! Get out of this room before we both die! Run!"*

Hunter staggers to his feet and forces his way through the invisible barrier, which feels more like Jell-O than the wall it had felt like before. Just as he decided he was probably going to suffocate, he finally pushes through and collapses back to the ground. A grey mist oozes out of his pores and condenses into the Abonsam, which leaps around in joy. "Free! Free! Free at last! Now to go join Abonsam brothers! 'Tis not good to be alone! Bye, dumb boy!" It crows with joy before jumping up and disappearing through the ceiling.

"Chet?" Vlad's voice reaches the nearly unconscious Hunter's ears.

"Vlad..." he groans before passing out.

<<<Crystal>>>

"You got the Trident!" Nora and Thaddeus exclaim at the same time.

I grin. "I got it," I confirm, holding it tightly. "Now let's get out of here."

As Thaddeus leads the way, I share my memories with Nora since it's faster than telling the story. *"Wow! That's impressive! I knew you had that in you! After all, how could the Dragongirl not be benevolent and also bring about Justice? That's practically your calling! It's part of what makes you the Dragongirl!"*

"Wait, what?"

"Oh, um… we Familiars had kind of a prophesy, although nowhere near as clear as the Dragon's prophesy of you. Ours is old, but it says that when Benevolent Justice is the most needed, the Dragongirl will come, and she will bring back the peace."

"And you waited until now to tell me this?"

"Well, honestly, I thought it was more of a tall-tale," she sheepishly confides. *"I didn't recall it until now."*

Thaddeus turns to me as we emerge from a tunnel leading out of the underground room I was just in. "I assume you are going to go return that to the Merfolk now?"

"Um…"

"Don't even try to lie to me," he says, his stormy grey eyes twinkling. "You're wearing waterproof clothing, plus I know you. You want to hurry off and go save the world while your parents are gone and can't put in a word edgewise."

"I'll be safe," I promise. "They won't hurt me. In fact, they might even help me."

He raises an eyebrow. "Help you? How?"

"Gale the Gold has a theory that the Trident might be able to help me… regain my Gifts." Thaddeus's jaw drops in surprise. I press on. "And if it works on me, then it might also work on everyone who's lost their Gifts," I add, hoping to convince him to let me go- although I'm going no matter what he says.

"Why that's… amazing…" He looks at me seriously. "Go. I cannot guarantee that I won't tell your parents what you're up to, but I will do what I can to stall and get you some time before they try and follow. I'll see if I can get Chet to help me stall them as well," he adds with a wink.

"Thank you so much," I say gratefully as I turn to Nora. "Um… are you sure you can come with me underwater?"

"Unfortunately, my magical abilities have not progressed that far yet. I will

remain with Thaddeus until you return and also aid in stalling your parents. ...
Good luck, Princess."

"Thank you, Nora," I say in appreciation. "The fastest way to get to them and back is probably by using the Trident," I murmur.

"Do you know how to use it?" Thaddeus asks incredulously.

"Yes. I just need a minute to remember the password," I say. "You start on stalling my parents. I'll be fine."

"Very well. Good luck, Crystal," he says, giving me a quick hug before hurrying off with Nora following.

I turn to the Trident. What was the password again? I think the Mermaid King said that it was the name of the one who made it... I think it started with a D? "Demeter," I suddenly remember. At the mention of the name, the Trident warms in my hand and develops a green glow about it once more. A warm buzz of energy flows from it into my fingers, which then travels throughout my body until I feel like I'm vibrating with excess power.

"Take me to the Mermaid King," I command it, tapping the ground. Everything around me swirls and changes. I'm underwater once more.

"Crystal Dragon. Long time no see," says a familiar voice.

I turn and see the Mermaid King. "Oh, good!" I gasp. "You're alive."

"Yes... it appears that I am," he smiles, swimming closer to me, his rainbow-like scales shimmering in the underwater light. "As are you... yet you appear concerned. What is it, child? Come, tell me everything over lunch. You are always welcome at my table, you know."

I smile and follow him to the large table where I met him the first time, hope filling my heart for the first time in a while. My plan might actually work. Maybe I'll actually be able to do this.

<<<Hunter>>>

Hunter wakes up in the Dragons' palace. He groans and rolls off the bed he's lying on, but falls to the floor. He's astounded by his weakness. *A spirit residing in my body shouldn't have this kind of toll on me. Of course... I had also used the Eye just before that, so apparently, the two combined are extremely taxing.*

"Oh, Chet, darling!" The Queen cries, coming up to him as he struggles to sit up on the floor. "Alexander! Come in here and help me with Chet! He fell off the bed!"

At that, the King rushes in. "Oh, poor boy," he says as he picks him up and puts him back on the bed.

"Um, I'm okay..." he assures them, confused at the love they seem to have for him- well, Chet.

Pearl won't have any of it. "Matilda! He needs some of your special hot chocolate!"

"Coming right up, my Queen!" the cook calls as she hurries up, holding a tray with a pot and a cup on it. She quickly pours the hot chocolate into the cup and hands it to Hunter. He glances down at the gently steaming liquid.

"Um, what is this for?"

"It will help to warm that icy skin of yours," she explains, "and help you to regain your strength." This sounds good to him, so he carefully lifts the cup to his lips and takes a sip, and then a gulp.

His eyelids then begin to feel heavy. "Hey, I don't want... to sleep..." He protests, yawning.

Alexander gently takes the cup from his hands. "It's alright, you'll be better in no time," he assures Hunter as he drifts back to sleep.

13

"*Angela?!*" The mental probe pierces the empty air as the raindrops slow and eventually cease to fall altogether. "*Angela, where are you?!*" The source of the cries is a small fairiye, which flits around anxiously, peering into stores and even under bushes.

"Auna?" A weak sounding voice whispers.

"*Angela!*" A flood of relief hits the small fairiye as she zooms over to the source of the voice. "*Angela, what happened?*" Auna asks in concern, placing one small hand on the girl's cheek. "*You were right behind me! At least, I thought you were.*"

Angela slowly sits up, leaning against the wall of the store behind her. "I… I don't know," she murmurs sleepily. "I was following you when I bumped into someone… the next thing I know, I wake up from lying on the ground."

"*Anything else?*" Auna presses, searching her from top to bottom. *She looks fine…*

"Um, my brain is kinda fuzzy… it's a little hard to think," Angela offers.

"*Hmm.*"

"Do you know what happened to me?" she asks the fairiye balancing on her knee.

"*You had your memories erased,*" Auna replies. "*That much I'm certain of. It was probably a Dragon Hunter who did it. If I knew how he did it, I could find a way to reverse it..."*

"Do you think T would know?"

"Possibly," Auna says, lifting back into the air. *"But we can worry about that later. First, we need to get you home."* Angela stands and takes a deep breath. *"Are you alright?"* Auna asks.

Angela smiles grimly. "I guess when I signed up for this war, I didn't really think I'd be in any danger. I'm not in Zilferia on the main front. I thought I would be safe here." She gives a terse laugh. "I guess it's time to start acting like a soldier in this war. It's time to step up and play a bigger role in this."

"And I'll be right here to help you!" Auna offers.

Angela smiles. "Good. I can't do this alone." She straightens her jacket. "Time to get started."

<<<Bryce>>>

Bryce and John crouch on the roof near Angela as she begins walking home, watching her. "I doubt she knows where the boy is," John warns.

"Yes, but she has his phone number," Bryce murmurs as he begins creeping down the roof to keep up with Angela. "So once she calls him, you just need to work some magic and follow the signal from her phone to his, leading us right to the boy."

John lets out his breath in a huff. "That's easier said than done," he complains.

Below them, Angela stops. "Before I go home, I should check and make sure Nathan's okay," she says to the fairiye accompanying her, pulling out her small blue phone.

"Get ready," Bryce whispers.

John nods tersely and outstretches his arms toward the girl. He quietly begins chanting. *"Langi sehtwo llof... yobeh temwoh shoitan itseds tio tlangiseh twollof... langi sehtwo llof..."*

Angela holds the phone up to her ear after dialing the number. It rings, but Nathan doesn't answer it. "Hey Nathan, it's Angela again. I was just checking to make sure you were alright... I heard there was a large fight

today. I... was just worried, that's all. Um, call me back when you get this."
She ends the call and sighs.

Bryce turns to John, who stops chanting and lowers his arms. "Did you find it?" He whispers urgently.

John is shaking and sweaty. "Yes," he confirms, panting.

"Alright then, let's go," Bryce requests, nodding to John to lead the way.

John takes a deep, calming breath and shakes off the magic-induced fatigue before turning towards the park. Bryce risks one more glance at Angela before he follows his fellow Dragon Hunter. They race across the rooftops before sliding to the ground from a smaller house, landing at a run. Bryce isn't sure why, but he feels that time is of the essence. After entering the park, John slows and looks around.

"The signal wasn't very strong," he explains. "So I wasn't able to pinpoint the phone's exact location."

"Nathan!" Bryce calls, his voice echoing through the moisture-filled air. "Nathan, it's Bryce! Where are you?" He waits for a reply, but although the air is still and calm, no response is heard. Bryce feels sick as he sinks to his knees in the mud. "I've failed in my mission," he mourns quietly. "I've lost the boy..."

Above him, the clouds are thinning and beginning to blow away, revealing the solemn blue sky. A beam of sunlight falls on the two Dragon Hunters and reflects off of something half-buried in the grass near the roots of a tree. Bryce quickly stands and rushes over to grab it.

It's Nathan's phone.

<<<Nathan>>>

Nathan's vision fades in and out as he is taken with the Dragon Hunters as his body struggles to not completely shut down. He's numb and unfeeling and doesn't even react when they strap him into the saddle of a beast the size and bulkiness of a small rhino. He hardly cares that its legs are bulging with muscle and narrow towards the foot, from which long, strong claws erupt. He can hardly feel its long, dinosaur-like tail swishing anxiously, nor feel the pounding of its massive heart. The heat radiating from its thick, leather-like skin doesn't bother him, nor do the large, green eyes with a second set of transparent eyelids covering them.

He doesn't feel a rush of excitement or fear as the beast, alongside a few others that the Dragon Hunters ride, suddenly lunges forward and tears deep gashes into the ground as it rapidly accelerates. He doesn't care when he feels a blindfold slip over his eyes and tie behind his head. He isn't wary about where he's going.

He doesn't feel anything until his brain finally processes what happened. They took his Gifts away with magic. That wasn't how they took Crystal's away from her... *Crystal.* The name sparks some feeling back into him, and his fingers twitch and tingle. A warm feeling then floods his body and heat pulses through him, filling him with energy.

Jabbing his elbow back, he hits the man behind him in the gut. He tumbles off the side of the beast with a surprised yelp. Nathan scrambles to remove the blindfold, then inspects the creature to find a way to control it. He can't find anything resembling reigns to direct it. Ahead of him, the other Dragon Hunters begin to slow.

"Come on, come on!" he gasps, pulling at the beast's head. It doesn't turn. Ahead of him, the Dragon Hunters are climbing off of their rides, even as Nathan's begins slowing even further. Finally, Nathan bails out and rolls off the side of the beast. He hits the ground hard, breaking a couple of ribs and spraining his wrist.

The Dragon Hunters shout in surprise as Nathan's beast arrives riderless. Nathan hauls himself to his feet once finished rolling and coughs up blood. *I need to find a medi-bot...* he thinks as he takes a shaky step away from his captors.

Taking a deep, raspy breath, Nathan plunges into the treeline.

<<<Bryce>>>

Bryce kneels by some deep gouges in the ground. "Beasts from Ponorama," he murmurs, standing and turning to John. "The fast ones."

John frowns. "Then how are we supposed to keep up?"

Bryce turns to face the direction the tracks lead. "We'll just have to travel fast and hope they only went a short distance," he sighs, gesturing for John to join him as he begins running. After a while, they slow to a stop, panting lightly. "Do you hear that?" Bryce asks, turning to John, who nods slowly.

"Someone's coming back this way."

"Into the trees," Bryce orders, dashing into the tree line and crouching beside a large tree in the undergrowth with John to his right. Their breathing slows and steadies, and soon the only sound was that of someone stumbling toward them. The person's breathing is harsh and ragged, and their footsteps sound weak, and they stumble often. Bryce makes a signal to John, who nods. Bryce then tenses in preparation as the person comes closer.

His intended target stops near him, their breathing so shallow and raspy that they pass out, their body falling hard onto the ground. Bryce turns to John and raises a quizzical eyebrow before standing and walking over to the person. He freezes when he identifies them.

"Who is it?" John asks, sliding up next to him. "Is it anyone we know?"

Bryce moves some bushes aside so his companion can have a better view of the body. "I do believe so."

John's eyes widen in disbelief. "By the Great Eye! What happened to him?!"

The boy then moves, groaning and blinking his eyes open as Bryce kneels beside him. "Bryce..." he sighs wearily.

"It's alright, Nathan. I'm here. You'll be fine. Just don't move. Now tell me what happened," Bryce urges, keeping his voice calm although he can hear the other Dragon Hunters coming closer.

Nathan's eyes are beginning to roll back in his head. "Ribs," he gasps. "Wrist... fell off... ran... tired..." and then he's out again.

Bryce carefully picks him up and turns to John. "We need to get him to Zarafa. Immediately."

<<<Auna>>>

"Auna, it will just have to wait until Monday," Angela sighs as she tugs a shirt over her damp hair. "Mom told me to take a shower and stay inside. You know as well as I that if I push too hard, it only gets worse."

Auna follows as Angela sits on her bed, easing a brush through her hair. *"I know,"* she sighs. *"I'm just worried that it might be too late to reverse the Forgetfulness by then."*

"Well, it's probably a better option to risk that than to push mom to never let me leave the house for anything but school. How am I supposed to help Nathan- and fulfill my duty to the Queen- then?" Angela retorts, setting down the brush and picking up her phone, checking it to see if Nathan responded to her call. He hadn't.

The fairiye balances on the doorknob. *"What if whatever the Dragon Hunter made you forget was extremely important to helping keep Nathan safe? What if you accidentally heard their plans or something?"*

Angela sighs and turns back to Auna, hands on her hips. "We'll just have to trust that we can get by without the information until tomorrow."

"What about finding his Familiar?"

"I can't go anywhere. If you feel up to it, you're welcome to search for him. I would recommend looking for those two Dorff first. They're bound to know where he is."

"Fine," Auna concedes. *"It's getting dark anyway. You go eat dinner. I'll be back in the morning to report."*

"Thank you," Angela sighs. "Good luck." With a polite nod of her head, the fairiye flits out the window.

That girl may not listen to me, but perhaps T will. Surely he will understand the dire situation we are in, Auna decides, winging her way over to his hideout. When she arrives, she knocks on the door of the bus. There's no movement from within, so she pushes it open and slides through. Leaping to the top of the stairs, she looks around. No one seems to be home. She lifts back into the air and turns to go.

"Leaving so soon?" A gruff voice behind her asks.

She spins around. *"T? What... where did you come from?"*

The old man grins. "Surprise ya, did I? I thought you knew about my secret?"

Auna sighs. *"I know a few of your secrets, but I doubt I will ever reach the end of them. You seem to have more than most."*

He chuckles. "True enough," he concedes. "So what can I do for you, my dear fairiye?"

"It's Angela."

He instantly looks concerned. "What? What is it? What happened? Is she okay?"

"I think so... well, yes, but she's had her memories erased, and I have no idea how... I was hoping you could help her."

"And this couldn't wait until tomorrow?" He questions.

Auna groans. *"Not you too! You know as well as I that the effects may become permanent if a solution is not found quickly."*

The old bus driver turns and begins heading toward the back of the bus. "What is it that you believe she forgot?"

"*Well, I don't know for sure,*" the fairiye pouts, folding her arms. "*I just know that it had to be important for a Dragon Hunter to wipe her memories. Perhaps plans involving Nathan? The whereabouts of his Familiar?*"

"What makes you so sure it was a Dragon Hunter that did it?"

"*There were lots of them in the town today, plus who else would ever need to—or know how to—erase her memories? ...What are you doing?*" she questions, hovering over his shoulder as he stands facing the back wall of the bus.

"What am I doing?" He chuckles. "Well, I'm going to see if I have a cure for Angela's little problem. This will take a while. You may want to go and do something else in the meantime. Come Monday morning, I may have the answer to your dilemma."

"*Alright,*" she sighs. "*Just be careful. Your cover can't be blown no matter what, remember?*"

He laughs at this. "How long do you think I could be a double spy without knowing that? Don't worry, the Dragon Hunters have no idea who I am. All they know is that I supply them with their potions, and that's all they really care about. Now go, be on your way."

"*Farewell, T,*" Auna calls as she squeezes out the door once more. *Now then. To find the Lost Familiar.*

<<<Greg>>>

Greg wakes in the dark. For a moment he's disoriented- at least, until he catches the sour scent of the Dorff. He wriggles around and gets to his feet. He's still in that cursed bag that he was first captured in, with no idea where he is now. All he knows is that the pink monster, Rosulkip, comes in to feed him now and then. She only slips small bits of rotten Zilferian food through the opening, then closes it again before he could even think about jumping out of the bag.

Today he had a plan, however. He was going to get out of his stinking prison and get back to Nathan if it was the last thing he did. He had to warn the boy... he was in more trouble than he realized. And if he was too late to get to him...

He stops and shudders, his tail wrapping into a nervous knot. Now was not the time to think about such things. He just needed to get out of there as soon as possible.

"Mousy! I bring foods to eat!" the annoying voice of the pink Dorff announces as she stomps over toward him. "Be good mousy and get more foods!" The top of the bag opens and she dumps the food in. Greg doesn't move, figuring that playing dead might help his plight. "Mousy? Mousy no hungry?" A yellow eye appears in the opening of the bag. Greg lies still, eyes mostly closed, waiting. "Is mousy... dead?" The bag opens wider. *Wait for it,* Greg urges himself. *Wait for it...*

A rough pink hand closes around him and pulls him out of the bag. The instant his body clears the dirty cloth, he swivels and bites the Dorff's hand. She squeals and releases him. He falls to the ground. Rolling back onto his feet, he takes off running, dodging the large, boil covered feet of the now stomping Rosulkip. He's in an old farmhouse. Surely there was a rat hole in the wall somewhere. He begins skirting the walls of the room. *There!*

He shoots into the hole just as a foot crashes down behind him, missing his tail by the width of a whisker. "Whew," he breathes in relief. "That was close."

"Who are you?" A high voice inquires. Turning, Greg sees a young mouse.

"Why, hello there," he greets. "I'm Greg. ...Do you know of a way I can escape this house?"

"Sure, mister!" The little black mouse happily chimes. "Follow me!" At that, the brown mouse turns tail and skitters away. Greg cautiously follows him. After a while, the walk turns into a climb.

"Where are we going?"

"To the top. You can slide down the rain gutter once we emerge onto the roof," he says. Sure enough, after a few more minutes the two emerge onto the roof, which is slick from recent rainfall.

"Thank you," he says, turning to the mouse.

"No problem. I don't get many visitors. Come again soon?"

"...Maybe," Greg says. With a nod, the mouse disappears back into the house. *I can't believe it. I'm free at last!*

After a few minutes, he hears something in his head, faint at first. *"Greg? Greg the Familiar to Nathan Anderson... oh, this is useless. I'm never going to find him."*

"...Hello?" he calls back curiously. "*Who are you? How do you know Nathan?*"

"*Greg?*" the voice chimes back excitedly. "*Is that really you?*" The voice grows clearer, and he realizes that whoever it was is getting closer to him.

"*Yes, I'm Greg. How do you know who I am?*"

"*Just a moment... I have almost reached you.*" At that, a beautiful fairiye comes flying toward him from the sky. "*I am companion to Angela Dove... she and Nathan know each other.*"

"*Ah, that explains it. Except... how is that possible? I thought Angela was a normal girl...*"

"*A 'normal girl' originally from Zilferia,*" the fairiye explains.

"*From Zilferia? But...*"

"*No time,*" the fairiye sighs. "*I need to get you back to her, so she can get you back to Nathan. He needs you.*"

"*You have no idea,*" he sighs. "*Alright, lead the way.*"

<<<Zarafa>>>

Zarafa opens the door, exasperated. "Bryce, I was..." her voice trails away when she catches sight of the boy lying limp in Bryce's arms. "What happened..." He brushes past her into the house, a sense of urgency about him. John steps in behind him. "Who is—"

"Nathan was attacked," Bryce interrupts, lying him on one of Zarafa's couches. "By the group of Dragon Hunters whose mission was to capture or kill Angela Dove- as she goes by in this realm. Apparently, Nathan got in the way of that mission, so they decided to..." he pauses and looks him over. "Do... whatever they did to him... in revenge."

"What *did* they do?" she asks, coming over to him. The strong smell of blood caused her teeth to ache and begin to sharpen. With a surge of strength, she forces them back. The boy is not a meal.

"We're not sure," John says, stepping up beside her, hands in his pockets. "We kinda just... found him like this."

"All we really know is he was captured, and he escaped," Bryce explains. "He is hurt and needs healing so he can tell us what happened."

"So, you came to me," Zarafa smugly determines.

Bryce sighs exasperatedly. "Yes. So please, help him... *without* biting him," he says, eyeing her teeth as they begin to sharpen again.

"Yes, yes, I know," she replies tiredly. "Stay here. I'll be right back." She then goes to a dark blue door and unlocks it. She heads straight to a certain drawer and opens it with a wave of her hand, withdrawing a vial of rich, dark orange liquid. After retrieving a needle, she speeds back down the stairs and uses the needle to deposit a single drop of the liquid into the boy's veins. A light glow spreads from the area and eventually envelops his entire body, shimmering and dancing over his pale skin. It fades within a matter of seconds.

"His breathing has returned to normal," Bryce reports, relieved.

"Of course, it has," Zarafa scoffs. "Did you ever doubt me?"

"No, of course not," he replies after a second. "So how soon until he..."

Nathan groans and opens his eyes. It takes a few seconds for them to focus on Bryce's face. "Bryce..."

"Yes, I'm here," he assures him, kneeling by his side. "Do you think you can tell me what happened?" he cautiously ventures.

"Yes... but I won't," he tartly says, sitting up on the couch.

"Why not?" he inquires, concerned.

"Because I don't trust you," he simply says, standing.

"Why don't you trust me anymore?"

"Because... well, because of everything. The Dragon Hunter's cloak that you *always* wear, what those Dragon Hunters said about you..."

Bryce curses under his breath. Of course he heard the other Dragon Hunters ranting about him. Just his luck. "Nathan..."

"No. Don't talk to me. I don't want to see you or hear from you until I can decide who you *really* are."

"Nathan, I told you, I'm a spy..."

"Yes, but for which side?" He shakes his head and walks toward the door, taking his phone from Bryce's hand as he goes. "I'm going home. Don't bother me. I may or may not come back next weekend... it depends on what I find out about you."

"Um... okay..."

"Goodbye," he says, removing the tracker ring from his finger and tossing it to Zarafa before shutting the door behind him.

Zarafa turns to Bryce. "That went well."

"Shut up," he groans, holding his face in his hands.

<<<Nathan>>>

Nathan remains where he is for a few seconds, breathing hard. Bryce may or may not be a Dragon Hunter. He may or may not have made another enemy today, and he may or may not have ruined everything for him finding Rex before Patrick did. Either way, what's done is done. Now the only thing left to do is return home and rest, then head out and find Greg. He clenches his fist. *If they took him... those two Dorff will regret it for sure...*

He walks home in a haze, not really knowing what to do, but wanting to go home. When he emerges onto his street, he gets another call from Angela. He doesn't answer it, too tired to deal with anyone right now. When he gets into his house, he just climbs up to his room and quietly slips inside. He then slips into bed and falls asleep, exhausted and drained from the day's events. *Tomorrow... tomorrow I will find Greg, and I will find out the truth. I will wring it out of that fairiye, Angela, the bus driver, the Dorff, and everyone else who's been lying to me. Tomorrow, there will be no more secrets.*

Nathan wakes up in the morning before his alarm goes off. He sits on his bed for a few minutes, staring at the wall, thinking of very little. Then he tries to create a simple gust of air in his room. Nothing moves. He sighs and leans back against his wall. So it was true, then. He really did lose his Gifts. One tear races down his cheek before he shakes himself and gets into his shower. *It doesn't matter. I don't need them... I can figure out the truth myself. Gifts aren't everything. I can't let this destroy me... between Crystal and I, one of us needs to be strong... or at least pretend to be. We were alright before we even knew about the Gifts. There's nothing to state that anything even has to be different now. I'll be fine.*

When he climbs onto the bus, T doesn't wink at him. Today, he just says, "We need to talk. Find me during lunch. Bring Angela." Nathan nods. *Well, that's good. Now I can get those two to tell me what's going on, at least. And if I can get Angela to summon her little fairiye, she can also tell me what she knows.*

When Angela climbs onto the bus, he notices dark circles under her eyes. She sits in the seat behind him. "You look..."

"Angry?" he suggests.

"No. Tired. Tired of everything."

"Well, thanks. You look tired too."

"That's not what I meant..." she sighs. "You and I need to have a heart to heart."

"Yes, we do. T says to meet with him at lunch so we can all three of us have a 'heart to heart.'"

She nods determinedly. "Alright. Sounds good."

"Good." After that, they don't talk the rest of the ride to school. In fact, they don't speak in their first class, or even their gym class together. During lunch, he opts to skip eating.

"Come on, Angela," Nathan announces when he finds her sitting with her friends, eating lunch. "It's time to talk."

Ignoring the stares of the other girls, Angela nods solemnly and stands, dumping the rest of her food in the trash before leading the way out of the school. They find T's bus parked by the tennis courts.

"Ah, you made it," the old man greets, opening the door after he knocks on it.

"Yes," he tartly replies. "Now who are you, really?"

He laughs. "Well you sure jump right to the point, now don't you? But first thing's first. Angela, dear, I do believe I have something for you." He hands her an eye dropper filled with a murky liquid.

"What is it?" she murmurs in confusion, holding it up to the light.

"That is what I asked him to procure for you," a proud voice says. They look up to see Auna entering through a window. *"It will help you remember whatever it is the Dragon Hunters caused you to forget."*

"What? You did this last night?" Angela repeats, confused. "But... I thought you were out finding Greg last night."

"I was. I just made a stop here first."

"Wait," Nathan interrupts. "You were looking for Greg? ...Did you find him?"

"Why don't you ask me yourself?"

"Greg!" Nathan gasps, relieved. He turns, and sure enough, the Familiar is perched happily on the top of the stairs.

"Did you miss me?"

"Oh, Greg! What happened to you?!"

"All in good time," Auna intercedes. *"There is much to tell you, Nathan. Too much to fit into this lunch break. Besides, we first need to recover Angela's memories —they might hold the key to everything."*

"Right," Angela confirms nervously. "So I just... put a drop in each eye?"

"And another in each ear," T adds.

The girl carefully lifts the dropper into the air, then tilts her head back. A drop falls into each of her eyes. She blinks them away, her eyes red like they are irritated. After putting a drop in each ear, the group gathers around with bated breath to see if it worked.

After a few seconds, Angela shrugs. "I guess we waited too long..." she suddenly passes out, falling back onto one of the seats on the bus.

"What happened?" Nathan inquires anxiously, peering over her. "Is she okay?"

"Yes," T explains patiently. "The Knaowkuf powder put her to sleep to hide the memories. The way to get them back requires much of the same."

"Knaowkuf powder?" Nathan repeats, confused.

"It is a rare, memory-erasing powder from Ponorama," T explains. "And the cure for it comes from the same plant."

"So how long until..." Nathan's question is interrupted by Angela gasping and sitting back up.

"It worked," she whispers, her eyes on Nathan. "But you're not going to like what I found out..."

"I don't care," he replies. "I need to know the truth. From *all* of you," he continues, turning to look at each person, fairiye, and Familiar in the bus.

T glances at his watch. "Well, you certainly can't know everything right now, lunch is just about over." Following his remarks, the school bell rings. Nathan glares at the bus driver as though it was his fault.

"Fine. But after school, there will be no more secrets. No more lies."

"No more," Angela whispers affirmatively.

"I'll meet you at home, Nathan," Greg says, scooting out the door.

Nathan follows him off the bus, not looking back to see if Angela is coming as well. He's angry that they would keep him in the dark for so long and doesn't feel like forgiving any of them just yet. He may not even forgive them after they tell him everything.

That remained to be seen.

<<<Angela>>>

Angela fidgets in her seat, anxiously watching the clock on the wall. In just a matter of minutes, Nathan would find her and demand to know everything… and she wasn't sure how much she could keep from him. When he pleaded for them to stop keeping things from him, she could hear the hurt in his voice, as though he was being betrayed. There was no way she could lie to him now. She would have to trust that it was for the best for him to know everything, although the Queen had told her to keep him in the dark for as long as possible. After all, that's obviously no longer possible, since he was so determined to wring the truth out of them all.

The bell finally rings, and Angela leaps out of her seat, already packed up and ready to go. She hurries through the door and nearly bumps into someone very familiar. "Jake," she sighs. "Now is *not* the time…"

"Oh, but it is," he sneers. "We need to talk."

"Too bad. I have to catch my bus."

"Oh, it won't take long… I just wanted to warn you that if you tell that idiot boy anything about us you will regret it."

"I'm afraid I don't have any idea to what you are referring," she replies, playing dumb.

"You know what I mean. You may remember what Bryce said to you, but Nathan is not allowed to know. If you tell him our plans, I will make sure to personally make your life a living hell."

"How? You can't touch me," she smugly retorts.

"You may have a small amount of protection, Zilferian, but your *brother* does not."

"Chet? But… but he…"

"We recaptured him," Jake sneers. "Now ponder that before you go blabbing things that aren't meant to be shared." He backs away. "Might want to hurry and catch your bus," he finishes before walking away.

Angela and Nathan step off at her stop, and she opens a note that T had slipped her as she passed him. *'I'm afraid that I cannot meet you at your house today,'* it reads. *'You know how you can contact me. I'll add what little information I can to help Nathan find the truth that way.'* She sighs and tucks the note into her back pocket.

"T can't join us," she tells Nathan, who scowls. "Not physically, at least. But don't worry, he can jump in for a little later if needed."

"Fine," he concedes. "But Auna will be joining us, right?"

"Yes, and Greg."

"Greg knows no more than I do," he puffs.

"That was true before he was captured," she confirms as they begin walking to her house. "But he has discovered things since then."

Nathan's face grows stormy with anger. "Why is it that I know less than everyone else does about things that concern *me*?!"

"Um... Nathan?"

"What?!" he bites back.

"Are you... alright?"

"I'm fine," he growls.

She just nods and continues walking, keeping as much space between them as possible. *He's so moody all of a sudden. He wasn't like this before the weekend... I wonder what happened to cause this change? It has to be more than frustration at being kept out of the loop...*

"Mom, dad, I'm home," she calls as they open the door.

"Ah, good," Ramona says as she walks in from the kitchen. "Oh, Nathan! We weren't expecting you today, dear."

"He just needed some help with some homework," Angela jumps in before he can reply. "Is it okay if he stays for a while?"

"Of course," Walter confirms from his spot at the table, lowering his tablet. "There's always enough room at the table for another person," he chuckles heartily, winking at Nathan.

"Oh, it probably won't take that long," he cautiously replies.

"Yes, well, if it does then you are welcome to have dinner with us," he smiles at him, returning to his tablet.

"Oh... well, thank you."

"Come on, my room's this way," Angela intercedes, leading the way up the stairs. She carefully closes the door behind them and drops her backpack on the ground by her bedside table before sitting down with a huff on her bed. Nathan remains standing.

She sighs. "Don't worry, Greg and Auna will be here in a minute," she consoles him. He doesn't reply, standing with his arms folded and his eyes focused unwaveringly on the window. It's only a couple of minutes before the two arrive, but to Angela, it feels like an hour. The tension in the air between her and Nathan makes her feel sick with guilt.

"Okay, no more stalling," Nathan declares, turning to Angela. "Tell me everything."

"I... I don't even know where to start..."

"How about you start with who you really are," he says without emotion. "Since I'm sure you even lied to me about that."

"Are you sure you don't want to sit down?" She offers. When he doesn't move, she sighs and begins her story. "Alright. My name is Angela Adkins. I... I grew up in Zilferia." She hesitates and watches Nathan's response. He nods for her to go on, his face a mask of indifference. "M...My family and I... grew up in the King's Village, near the edge. When Patrick started adding to his ranks... he... he took my family," she says, choking back a sob. "I wasn't home at the time of the incident... I was gathering herbs in the woods while my brother went hunting. ...When we got back, our parents were missing... My brother was enraged. He charged after them, following their tracks until he caught up with them. When he realized that it was Patrick who had taken them, he didn't stop. He tried to attack Patrick... he didn't even get close to succeeding, of course, but Patrick decided to enroll him in his army. They never saw me, for I was hiding amongst the trees... after they took Chet from me, I hurried to find the King and Queen, hoping that they would help me. The Queen informed me that although she couldn't waste resources on one boy, she would try her best to rescue my family and make sure they stayed safe.

"She also needed help. So I agreed to help her and also gain her assistance in rescuing my family, which is how I ended up here. She wanted help in watching the comings and goings of the Dragon Hunters in certain realms and warn her of whatever technology they took, things like that. So for a while, I simply spied on them for her. Which wasn't hard, they almost never take off those stupid cloaks. Every once in a while, when I returned to report, I was allowed to stay for a short time." She looks up at him shyly. "I saw you. You and Crystal... in the Games. I saw snippets of the Games themselves, and I was there when you first met Greg..." She stops for a second.

"Sorry, that's off-topic... anyway, so when you were going to be sent home, the Queen gave me a new assignment. I was to stay here and keep an eye out for you... make sure that you were safe from the Dragon Hunters. I'm sorry to say that part of that was keeping you ignorant of the danger in the first place. Believe me, that was not my call," she continues, begging with her eyes for him to believe her. "Anyway, when you got here, I also got word that Chet was okay, and that you rescued him... and that the rest of my family was dead." A tear slips out of her right eye. "I was about to demand that I be allowed to go back and be with my brother until I saw you... up close." A slight blush begins to rise in her cheeks. "I decided that Chet would be fine... I had the Queen promise me that he would be looked after, and she said that he could even live with them in their castle."

"So, you were assigned to babysit me?" He restates dubiously.

"Um... more to keep the Dragon Hunters from getting close to you. Although I don't know why she trusted me with this mission so much..."

"Why not?" he asks, finally softening and kneeling in front of her. "Why wouldn't she trust you?"

Angela lowers her head ashamedly. "I... I'm one of the rare people from Zilferia that... doesn't have any Gifts," she finally chokes out, another tear falling from her right eye, followed by one from her left. She quickly wipes them away with the heels of her hands ashamedly.

Nathan sighs and leans back. "Then that's something we have in common."

She looks up at him, confused. "But, I saw you, in the Games..."

He shakes his head before she can continue. "I did then. I had them up until yesterday, actually. ...A group of Dragon Hunters attacked me. They had a magic-user with them and he... took away my Gifts, somehow." No tears fall from his eyes, but she can see the heartbreak on his face. She stands and pulls him into a hug. After a few seconds, he puts his arms around her and holds her close, his face nestled in the soft indent at the bottom of her neck. She can now feel him trembling. Her heart breaks for the poor boy. Not only did she fail in her job, but he lost his Gifts because of it. The only thing worse than never having Gifts is to know the taste of freedom they offer... and then lose it all.

"I'm sorry," she whispers in his ear, her voice cracking.

He pulls back. "Why?" he asks, confused.

"Because it's my fault," she sadly informs him. "It was my one and only job to keep you safe from them. You lost your Gifts because of me."

He takes her face in his hands and pulls up her chin so she'll look at him. He looks into her eyes. "This is not your fault," he softly assures her. "... Thank you for telling me the truth," he murmurs, softly kissing her forehead.

He turns to Auna. "Alright, what's your story?"

The small fairiye hovers at eye level and looks at him seriously. "I am Angela's companion. The Queen sent a request to Lii for a fairiye to be sent to help her in her task to watch and help you, and mostly to keep you safe. I now also report to the Queen, so Angela no longer has to leave your side. It is much faster that way as well, since I can travel through realms at will."

"Truly?" Nathan says, awed. "That's amazing."

"It is the biggest thing that sets us apart from our cousins, the fairies. They also cannot bond with their companions as deeply as we can."

Nathan takes a deep breath and turns to Greg. "Now then. What do you have to tell me? What did you find out over the weekend?"

The Familiar scoffs. *"You make it sound like it was a voluntary field trip. I was captured by those two creatures —"*

"Dorff," Auna supplies.

"Those two Dorff... *and stuffed in a bag and kept in an old, dilapidated farmhouse. I eventually escaped... but while I was in that bag, I heard them talking about the Dragon Hunters' plans. I heard that they were going to attack Angela, and I also heard that Zarafa talks to Patrick regularly using a Hologram Square or something like that..."* Nathan frowns heavily at this. *"....and that Bryce's job was to keep you from disrupting any of the Dragon Hunters' plans... he just decided to use you to find Rex as a bonus. He's practically Patrick's right-hand-man. If Hunter was killed, Bryce would be next in line to lead the Dragon Hunters."*

Nathan stumbles back, sitting down hard on Angela's bed. "I should have known..." he groans.

After a few minutes, he turns back to Angela. "You have more to tell me," he ventures. "What is it?"

She sighs. "Well... Jake is a Dragon Hunter, not... not my ex," she confides.

He nods tersely. "And what about your... parents... downstairs? Who are they really? Do they know about any of this?"

She shakes her head. "No. Vladimir came with me the first time and changed their memories... they think that they are my parents. And no, they know absolutely nothing about Zilferia or Dragon Hunters."

"Alright," he accepts, nodding. He takes a deep, cleansing breath. "Is that all? Does anyone have anything else to tell me?"

Angela fidgets a little. *I should tell him... but I can't. Jake told me... he threatened Chet if I told... although he already knows most of it now anyway thanks to Greg...* "I do," she suddenly gasps before she covers her mouth with her hands, looking mortified.

"You do?" he inquires, turning to her. "What is it?"

She sighs. There's no going back now. "When T helped me restore my memories… I remembered that I was with Bryce and another Dragon Hunter after you saved me from the group of Dragon Hunters that had me trapped yesterday."

"What?" he says, looking confused.

"I know you were that silver wolf," she says tartly. He looks surprised, then nods.

"So, what did you remember?" he asks. After she tells him, he looks more shocked than ever. "Crystal? Are you sure they specifically mentioned her?"

"Yes," she sighs. "But they only mentioned that you 'can't find out about her.' I have no idea what that means."

"I do," he replies, fire burning behind his eyes. "It means she's not safe. And I'm going to do something about that."

14

---

unter wakes alone. He sighs with relief. *Good. Now no one will get in my way...* He cautiously slides his legs out of the bed, feeling the cold limestone floor underneath his feet as he makes his way around the bed. He casts his eyes around the room and catches sight of just what he's looking for- a mirror. The full sized mirror, rimmed in gold patterns, reclines against the wall by the dressing room. Hunter stumbles over to it, casting in his mind for the spell that Patrick told him just the day before.

"*Llacym deehkc irtap,*" he murmurs, leaning against the wall. After a few seconds, his reflection swirls and changes.

"Hunter! I wasn't expecting to hear from you so soon," Patrick says, smoothing his cloak. "What's wrong?"

"Crystal got the Trident," he coughs. "I bet she's with the fish right now. I'm sorry, I tried to beat her to it, but I just…"

"It's alright," Patrick assures him. "But what happened to you? You seem worse than when you used the Eye, and this spell isn't nearly that taxing." Hunter quickly tells him of the Abonsam, keeping the explanation as quick as possible as he feels his meager reserves of energy drain away. "Ah… this is good," he broods.

"Um… how is that good?" Hunter questions.

"Because Abonsam gather together in 'family' groups. They are never alone—unless they are trapped, like the one that you met. When they are together, they normally raid houses, cause 'misfortune,' the like."

"And this helps us how…"

"Since one of them was inside of you, you have the power to summon and control it. And since they travel in packs, the others should follow, particularly since I sense that this particular Abonsam is the leader of his pack."

"And what would I do with a group of Abonsam?"

"They can turn invisible, intangible… completely undetected. They are the perfect spies or thieves, or whatever it is we decide to use them for."

"Oh." He could see the use for that.

"So, how is our little Princess doing? How broken is she?"

Hunter sighs. "Not much at all. The diary doesn't seem to be fazing her much beyond distaste. Are you sure I grabbed the right one?"

"Of course," he scoffs. "What do you take me for, a fool? I made sure to put the fake on the shelf, just like I told you."

Hunter freezes. "The shelf?"

"Yes," he sighs exasperatedly.

"But I got that from the left table…"

Patrick's face goes from cocky to dismayed to furious in the blink of an eye. "YOU DID WHAT?!"

He gulps. "Um… so I suppose that wasn't—"

"THAT WAS MY ACTUAL JOURNAL, YOU FOOL!"

Hunter hastily backpedals. "Um, but this can easily be fixed, right? I mean, if you can find the fake and then send it to me, I could switch them…"

Patrick's rage cools somewhat at the prospect. "True… for your sake, I sure hope this works. I will contact you with instructions after I hide it near you. And for Dravyn's sake, boy, don't mess it up again!" With that, Hunter's 'reflection' swirls and looks like him again. He sags against the wall, his meager store of energy spent. *Great. Could our plans get any more screwed up?*

<<<Crystal>>>

"Hmm," the Mermaid King contemplates, staring at me over his plate of uneaten squid. "You tell quite a tale, Crystal Dragon. I have never heard anything of the like in all my years under the sea."

"But you can help me, right?" I plead, desperation clear in my voice. "Um... now that you have your Trident back," I continue, trying to relax a little.

He gingerly strokes the glowing gold weapon as it lies on his lap. "Yes... I suppose it wouldn't hurt to try. Although I cannot guarantee that you will get your Gifts back," he warns as he pushes back his chair.

I stand and face him, turning away from my own uneaten food. "I am aware, but it is a risk well worth taking," I assure him, taking a deep breath to calm my jittery nerves.

"Yes... I agree," he says, sighing as he levels the Trident at me. "Are you ready?"

"Ready to get my Gifts back? Definitely. Ready to lose my last hope? ... This just better work," I reply with a slight smile.

He chuckles in return. "I hope it does as well... not only for you, but for the sake of all of Zilferia," he reminds me seriously.

"Yes... for all of Zilferia," I gulp.

The King pauses before taking a deep breath and beginning his chant. "Heal. Fix all that is hurt, return all that is lost. Return control to whom it belongs... Heal, fix all that is hurt, return all that is lost, return control to whom it belongs..." he repeats as the Trident glows brighter.

At first I don't feel anything, but after a few seconds, I black out. I can no longer see anything, although I feel like I am still fully aware and conscious. I cast my eyes about, searching for something- anything- and finally catch sight of what looks like a chain of pools in the soft light. Where they should be connected, a stone wall stands strong, keeping the waters separated. The stagnant water seems dull and lifeless in each indistinct pool. Stooping, I begin pulling rocks from the first wall. I only remove about half of it before I feel a tugging, like someone is trying to pull me back. I fight and remove another stone before suddenly the scene swirls away, replaced by the King standing before me, looking tired and lowering his Trident.

"Well?" he inquires. "Did it work?"

I pause, searching within myself. I don't feel any different. "I don't think so," I sigh.

The King returns to his seat wearily. "I am sorry, Dragongirl. I do wish there was something more I could do to help you. Perhaps your own people will know what to do now," he suggests.

I stand and wipe away a tear that had leaked out of my eye- as futile as that is while being underwater- and face the King. "It is doubtful that they can help either... this was my best chance," I sob.

"Then perhaps you will find a way to find your Gifts once more yourself."

I sigh. "Maybe. Although-" I'm interrupted by a loud conch shell blowing. "What was that?" I ask, quickly turning back to the King.

He groans and drops his head wearily into his hand. "That is our signal to warn my people that the next Dragon Hunter attack has begun." He swims up to me and peers down into my teary eyes. "You must go."

"Wait!" I stall. "You will help us, right? Zilferia can protect itself from the Dragon Hunters, but only if it unites! Only if we *try* and *believe* can we accomplish what seems to be impossible! I know we can do it! Please, you must join us! I will not stand by and watch you be eradicated!"

The King chuckles. "My, you are insistent. Very well." He plucks a scale from his tail and hands it to me. I admire the palm-sized object in the underwater light. Although mostly green, it shimmers in the light with all the colors of the rainbow. "Hold this tightly and request for it to take you to me, and it will do so. Or you can request to see me, and my image will appear in the scale and we can speak that way, if you wish. However, it only works once, and can only transport one. I may also speak to you through it the same way that you would use it to speak to me." He bows to me. I watch, unsure of what to do. "Good luck saving Zilferia, Princess. I await your command."

"Oh, I'm not a war general or anything!" I hurriedly assure him, laughing a little.

"Aren't you, though?" he smiles. "You gathered these three, very diverse groups together. Who else do you think we would *all* follow into battle? Like it or not, you are now our leader." He pauses at the look on my face. "Hey, you can do it. You have it in you, whether you believe you do or not. You will prove it to everyone—especially yourself— when the time comes. Trust me, you will," he assures me, cupping my face in his smooth hands and putting his forehead gently on mine. "You will. I trust that you can lead us all to victory." He then steps back as the alarm sounds once more. "However, for now you must go back to your own people. Farewell, Crystal Dragon...

our Savior. Until next time," he winks before lowering the Trident to point at me. "Transport," he instructs it. My eyes cling desperately onto his as they become the last thing I see. Finally, they too disappear.

<<<Patrick>>>

Patrick rages and storms through his castle, leaving a wake of trembling followers and broken objects in his wake. He rants to himself as his long strides hurdle him down the hallways. "That miserable boy... what an imbecile! Can't even tell the two journals apart... even as the girl started to read it! Hunter *must* prevent her from reading too much, or else his cover could be blown! Worse, she would never voluntarily return to me... and Zilferia would regain the hope she's been attempting to re-instill! I would lose this war! And that is *not* an option!" He suddenly stops in front of a door. "I *will* fix this," he mutters as he bends down, removing a key from a tiny hole in the wall beside the door. "Dravyn need never know about this. I can certainly fix everything before Dexter comes to check up on me..." He unlocks the door with a quick flick of his wrist. Withdrawing the key, he turns and tosses it to the Dragon Hunter Guard behind him before turning and entering the room.

He quickly heads to the bookshelves where Hunter was *supposed* to 'find' his fake journal. He withdraws the thin book, his hand shaking. He was right. Crystal had his actual journal. He breathes out angrily. The boy could have ruined everything. Perhaps it was time to replace him as his right-hand man. Bryce would do nicely, working hand-in-hand with Zarafa. He had already proven that he could get along with her, and that was more than could be said of most of his men. Plus, he already had his insignia. All that remains is to tell him of his decision to reinstate him.

He whirls back to the door, fake journal in hand. Time to fix this mess.

<<<Crystal>>>

I blink as my parents' castle swims into view before me and stumble a little as I'm released from the spell. Clutching the mermaid scale to my chest, I walk up to the door and knock. Three, then eight, and finally, one knock to tell those inside that I am not a Dragon Hunter. The door is hurriedly unlocked, and the next thing I know, I'm enveloped in a bear hug from Alexander. He lifts me into the air and Pearl closes the door behind me.

"Um, hi, dad," I wheeze into his chest. He sets me down, then kneels in front of me.

"Oh, what are we going to do with you?" he sighs, smiling.

"What he means is, we're glad you're back and that you're safe," Pearl laughs, coming up to hug me as well.

"I went to see the merfolk…" I start.

"We know," Alexander sighs as Thaddeus and Nora come up behind him.

I rush on before he can stop me or lecture me. "I returned their Trident, and they agreed to help us in the war," I inform them, holding out the scale for them to see. "He said that we can contact each other with this."

Alexander takes it carefully in his large hands. "This is Kaifeng's scale," he murmurs. "How did you get it?"

"He gave it to me," I say, taking the scale back.

Nora lands on Pearl's shoulder and cocks her head at me. *"So what exactly happened down there? Did your plan work?"*

"No… I'll tell you about it in a minute," I respond as the cook, Matilda, hurries up.

"Oh, you poor thing!" she gushes. "You must be exhausted! To bed with you!" she orders, shooing me out of the room. "I shall bring you dinner. You just stay in bed and recover from your escapades! …Oh," she gasps, turning to Pearl. "I'm sorry, your majesty… she can do anything you desire, of course… I- I didn't mean…"

Pearl smiles kindly at the cook. "It's fine, Matilda, I was about to have her do the same thing." She turns to me. "Do as she says, dear. We'll talk later. Oh, and don't think about running off again," she adds as she walks away. "I'm going to have a guard—who *isn't* Chet—stay by your door. Possibly even two of them."

"What?!" I gasp in outrage. "So you're just going to lock me in my room? Keep me prisoner?"

"No, it's for your own safety," Alexander reassures, looking sad. "We can't have you continuing to risk your life so recklessly." He then turns and follows my mother as she walks away from me without a backward glance. Seething, I turn to head back to my room with Nora following me. I may be kept here for a while, but during that time I can at least do something productive.

I can read Patrick's journal.

<<<Hunter>>>

Hunter wakes on the floor by the mirror. Groaning, he hauls himself to his feet. Just as he's about to get back into bed, there's a sound from the mirror behind him. Turning, he sees Patrick standing there once more. "Hunter," he quickly says. "I have the fake journal, and I'm sending it to you as we speak." There's a sound outside of Hunter's door. He quickly turns back to Patrick.

"Don't send it right here. Someone's about to come in. Send it... just send it later. I'll contact you. Now go! Hurry!"

"Very well. I shall be waiting," he says as his image fades away, just as the door to Hunter's room opens.

"Chet, darling, what are you doing out of bed?!" A worried Queen inquires as she hustles into the room and leads him back to the bed. "You aren't strong enough to be out and about yet."

Hunter contains an irritated sigh as she tucks him back under the covers. "But what about Crystal?"

"Oh, she's fine, dear," she assures with a smile. "She came back about an hour ago."

"But what if she tries to leave again?"

"She won't... I'm having her room guarded." She sighs. "It's for the best, I'm afraid."

"Oh, yes, I do agree with you," he says as she places another pillow behind his head. "She is acting kind of outrageously lately. It's best to keep her contained. Who knows when the Dragon Hunters will strike, after all," he says. *Thank Dravyn, she's finally being contained... now hopefully she won't be doing so much damage to our operations. Regardless, I should encourage Patrick to speed up the rate of destruction among the Dragons... even if that means marching straight into their stronghold. I do know where it is now, anyway. Besides, I control a large chunk of what's left of the dragons. With that kind of force, we should be able to finish off the rest that are not being controlled... and from there, we shall easily destroy the Sohos.*

The Queen frowns, looking quite saddened. "Yes, I'm afraid so... I absolutely cannot have my daughter wandering around, let alone without any protection! She'll see that I'm right soon enough..." she stands slowly. "Just ring this bell here if you need anything," she offers, gesturing to the small copper bell on the bedside table.

"Alright. Thank you... Pearl," he says. She smiles sadly at him as she leaves. As soon as she does, he jumps out of the bed and returns to the mirror. "*Llacym deehkc irtap,*" he mutters.

"Ah, good. I was beginning to worry," A flustered Patrick says as soon as he swirls into focus in the mirror. "Now then, I'm sending the journal over."

"Just put it on the bed or something," Hunter groans.

"What's your problem?" Patrick asks. "I've never seen you this down before."

"It's nothing. ...Well, it's everything. And on top of it all, Crystal is locked in her room."

"Oh dear... she's not..."

"She probably is," he sighs.

"Curse that child!" Patrick rants, clenching the book in his hands until his knuckles turn white. "Hunter, you *must* switch this, as soon as you can! There's no time to waste!"

"What do I do with the other journal?" Hunter asks as Patrick narrows his eyes at the book in his hands.

"Just place it where you retrieve this one," he says as it disappears from his hands. "Then contact me and tell me that it's ready and I will take it back."

"Yes sir," He says, backing away from the mirror and quickly walking over to the bed. He picks up the journal. It's thinner than the real one, but is similar enough that Crystal will hopefully not notice he switched them out. He stuffs the small book into his back pocket and walks cautiously to the door. He quietly opens it and peers out. No one is in sight. He quickly ascends the stairs to Crystal's section of the palace and comes face-to-face with Susan Parker and Reed Agee. He barely contains a groan. Of course, it had to be these two guarding Crystal.

"Can I... talk to Crystal, please?" he asks politely.

"No," Susan tartly replies, looking bored.

Reed sighs. "Sorry Chet, but the Princess isn't being allowed many visitors at the moment."

Well, this is frustrating. "Yes, the Queen told me about her... quarantine... and I think I can help."

"Oh? Can you? What makes you think you can prevent her headstrong ways? It's not that easy, you know," Susan murmurs, leaning in close to him.

"Susan..."

"Back off," she shoots back before Reed can continue. "Let me interrogate the boy." He sighs and relents. "Now then... where were we?" she murmurs.

"I was about to tell you how I can help Crystal's urge to continually place herself in danger," Hunter calmly replies while simultaneously blocking her mental ray from entering into places he didn't want it to go. He lets her see Crystal's seeming infatuation with him, but not much else.

After a few seconds, she leans back. "Very well. Just know that I will have to report this to the Queen," she warns.

"Of course," he says, turning the handle of the door and entering Crystal's large bedroom. She's lying on her stomach on her plush bed, surrounded by pillows as she reads the book in front of her. Her head darts up when he enters, and something strange seems to pass over her. But as fast as it came, it's gone.

"Chet!" she cries, racing over to embrace him. "I heard what happened to you."

"Did you?" he remarks, wondering what it is she heard.

"Yes... Thaddeus told me about the Abonsam that was in that other room... and how you had to give it something in order to escape. I don't know what it did to you, but I was told you came out and Vlad found you unconscious and cold as ice! He quickly took you here, of course... and you look better," she notes, looking him up and down.

"Yes, I've been sleeping and recovering while you've been... locked in here. What have you been doing this whole time?" Hunter asks curiously, although he fears he already knew the answer.

"Oh, just reading a little bit of Patrick's journal," she casually says. It's clear from her voice that she had discovered something, and that she was certainly not going to tell him what it was.

"And did you find anything interesting?" he probes.

"Not particularly... just that he and Susan have quite a past, really," she remarks.

"Oh?"

"Yes... but I don't want to talk about all that," she says, pulling up close to him and looking deep into his eyes. "We might as well have some *fun* while I'm here, don't you think?"

"Uh..."

"Come on!" she invites, grabbing his hand and tugging him along behind her. "I have a pool, a ping pong table, my own chef, and a gorgeous balcony that looks out over everything... take your pick!"

"Um... whatever you want to do, I suppose..." he stalls. "Although I don't have much of my energy back, so I don't know that I'll be that much... fun... today," he warns.

"So the Chef and the balcony, then?" she quips cheerfully, tugging him through various rooms until they stop in one that is bathed in heavenly smells. Hunter's stomach gurgles loudly, surprising him. He hadn't realized he was hungry.

"Steve!" she calls, smiling.

"I am already here, milady," A well-dressed man says, stepping up from behind a counter. "Your friend's stomach called me out," he chuckles, winking.

Crystal grins, delighted. "Wonderful! Would you happen to have anything for us?"

"When do I not, Princess?" he smiles as he leads them to a table. "I shall be right back with something for you both," he says, bowing slightly to each of them before turning and returning to his cooking station.

As soon as he leaves, a red-tailed hawk appears out of nowhere as she lands on the table between them. The Familiar cocks its head to the side as it relays some information to Crystal, whose mood instantly dampens. She nods, and the bird climbs onto the girl's shoulder and begins preening itself.

Curious, Hunter sends a mental ray outward to pierce Crystal's mind and discover what it was that she was keeping from him and is immensely surprised to detect a wall around her thoughts, smooth and impenetrable. He gapes in surprise.

"Chet? Is something wrong?" Crystal casually asks, intelligence gleaming in her stormy blue-gold eyes. *She knows what I tried to do!* Hunter realizes, panicking. *Just what did she read in that journal?!*

"No, nothing's wrong... I just... need to go to the bathroom," he says, rapidly creating an excuse to leave.

"Alright. It's just down there," she says, pointing back the way they came. Hunter hurries off without another word, anxiety causing his thoughts to roll and boil. How could this happen? He had to switch those journals before she discovered anything else... although he's sure that whatever she found thus far would already harm their designs for the war. He just had to keep it from getting any worse, if possible.

He races back into Crystal's room and hurries over to the bed. Sure enough, Patrick's journal lies open with a sketch of the Dragon Slayer device sitting beside it. He quickly switches the books, stuffing the actual one in his back pocket before taking a deep breath and hurrying back to the snack room with Crystal.

"Hey," he greets as he slides back into his seat across from her.

"Hey," she replies, her mood obviously stormy.

"What's wrong?"

"Nothing. ...I'll tell you later," she sighs, picking up a French fry and sadly munching on it.

"Alright... if that's what you want," he says, snatching up a cinnamon roll.

<<<Crystal>>>

I feel like crying. Those things I read in Patrick's journal are true; Nora just confirmed them. She felt him trying to read my mind, and she saw him switching the journals. Still... I'm going to give him one more chance to prove to me whose side he's really on. One more chance to save my heart, one more chance... before I alert Thaddeus to his deception.

After a few minutes, I know that I can't really eat anything. I'm too distraught to stomach anything. So I wait until Chet/Hunter is done eating his cinnamon roll, then have him follow me to the balcony. I'm not sure what I'm going to say to him there, but I know I need to say *something*.

I open the door and breathe in deeply, enjoying the fresh, early-fall air. I collapse into a chair by the edge of the balcony. Chet/Hunter sits cautiously in the chair next to me. He watches me for a few seconds, then turns to look at the view. After a few minutes, I sigh. "It used to be so much more... just so much more beautiful. Pristine... full of life," I point out as I stare at the burned sections of the forest and the blackened sections of the sea where the Merfolk reside.

"Yeah," Chet/Hunter agrees, looking out with a little bit of sorrow on his face. I carefully observe him. "Hopefully it will be better again once this war is over."

"Yes… but if the Dragon Hunters are victorious, it will never be the same as it was."

"Oh?" he says, cocking an eyebrow at me. "And how do you know that?"

I stare at him in disbelief. "Seriously? Okay. Who started this war?"

"Well, that depends on who you ask…"

"I'm asking you."

"…Your parents."

"And why do you think that?" I ask, trying to keep my rage down and try and help my poor, lost brother to understand.

"Because…"

"Because that's what Patrick told you?" I intercede, my face hard as I stare at him. His eyes widen in surprise and disbelief. I press on before he can say or do anything. "When I was in his clutches, he told me a great many things too. However, they were so obviously wrong that I felt sick that you were being led astray so easily… Hunter, listen to me." His face hardens when I speak his name, and my stomach sinks. So it *is* true, then. "Hunter…"

"Shut up," he says, standing. "You don't know what you're talking about. Patrick has told me nothing but the truth." His body ripples and becomes that of Hunter's. "You know, I gave you the wrong journal. You were supposed to read a fake one that would convince you to come back to us willingly so you would be on the right side…"

"The right side?!" I retort, also standing. "You don't even know what you're talking about! Patrick started this war! He loves destruction- he wants me back to see if he can break me emotionally! He thinks it would be oh-so-satisfactory if he saw me breaking inside!"

Hunter's breathing heavily now, clenching his gloved hands. "Liar."

"I am not the liar," I assure him, reaching back and pulling the journal out of his back pocket. I start flipping through the pages, trying to find the right spot. He snatches it out of my hands before I can find it. He's seething in anger. I back up a step, suddenly fearful. What have I done?

"You are going to come with me, whether you like it or not," he says, putting a hand on my head and concentrating. I can feel the barrier around my mind that Nora helped me with begin to wobble. I stumble back, putting my hands up and trying to push him away, but he just follows me, seeming to grow stronger by the second. "You cannot fight me," he growls as the barrier around my mind finally crumbles. Nora flies up and beats at his face with her wings, but he backhands her so she flies hard into the wall, breaking a wing.

I sink to my knees as I feel his thoughts forcibly enter mine and seize control. *So this is how all those poor animals he controlled felt...* It's almost an out-of-body experience. My mind is in a haze. I hear his thoughts pierce through the haze. *Stand,* he orders. I struggle to my feet without really realizing what I'm doing. *Alright, Vincent, we're ready now,* I hear him say. In my blurry vision, I see the black dragon descend and hover beside the balcony.

Hunter turns to me. *Climb on to him. Hold on tight, do not fight him or me. Do not call for help.* My feet stumble over to the dragon and before I can stop myself, I leap onto his back. Hunter climbs on behind me. Within a few wingbeats, I am being borne away from the castle... towards Patrick. I start panicking, but there's nothing I can do. My body won't do anything to disobey Hunter's orders. I am helpless as my poor, misled brother takes me back to the one place I most dread to return.

<<<Thaddeus>>>

Thaddeus sighs. "Alexander, what do you think the girl could possibly be doing? She's still locked in her room."

The King continues pacing. "I have no idea... I just have this feeling..."

"Fine," Thaddeus concedes. "I'll look in on her with magic." He leans forward in his chair and holds his hands palm up on the table. Closing his eyes, he begins muttering. After a minute, he gasps and his eyes fly open. "Oh, Dragonfire..."

"What? What is it?" Alexander pleads, knowing that Thaddeus would never be so vulgar unless it was something big. "Where is she? What is she doing? Is she..."

"Alexander," Thaddeus interrupts. "Crystal is... she's been kidnapped... again." The King gasps in horror. "I saw her... on the back of a dragon... that was being controlled by Hunter."

"My own son..." the King collapses into a chair and drops his face into his hands. "What are we going to do?"

"We have to stop them before they can get back to Patrick. They seem to be traveling alone for now." The King jumps up and strides to the door. "Um… Alexander, what are you doing?" Thaddeus inquires.

"Getting my daughter back," he growls as he yanks the door open. "Don't let Pearl follow me. Send as many soldiers as you can find after me. I'll get her back myself if I must," he declares as he storms out the door, slamming it behind him.

<<<Hunter>>>

Oh, what have I done? Hunter groans to himself as they fly. *I just kidnapped my sister! What will Patrick say about this? He told me to let her come of her own free will… but he also said that I need to make sure my cover isn't blown…* he sighs. *I guess that I'll just have to risk Patrick's wrath… surely he'll understand…*

Still, he's tense and nervous by the time they touch down just outside the boundary line for the Dragon Hunters. After helping Crystal down off the dragon, he turns to address their ride. *Thank you, dragon, that will be all.* The black beast takes off without a word. Hunter feels proud of himself for how thoroughly he had taken over the proud creature.

"Please… please don't do this, Hunter," Crystal whimpers, dread etched clearly on her face. The fear in her eyes was so evident that he actually paused. Why was she so afraid? Patrick wasn't going to do anything to her but talk. It's not like he was going to take her Gifts away again or anything. There wasn't any reason for her to fear like this.

"It will be fine," he sighs as he leads her across the boundary line. However, the further they walk into Dragon Hunter territory, the more unruly she becomes. She even fights hard enough at one point to turn and start running back the way they came, despite his order to not try and escape. *She really is terrified,* he realizes. *I just need to show her that there's nothing to be afraid of.* After renewing his hold on her mind, they continue toward Patrick's castle. The instant it comes into sight, she collapses. Sighing, he picks her up and carries her into the building and past the small red dragon now standing guard in place of the porcupine-tiger that he had killed to gain Crystal's trust.

Once inside, he signals a guard over and hands him the unconscious girl. "Follow me. Don't drop her," he warns before heading to where he knew Patrick would be.

He knocks on the door. "Patrick, sir, I have returned with… an update," he gulps. "May I come in?" The door is opened by a Dragon Hunter from the inside. Taking a deep breath, he steps inside with the guard holding Crystal right behind him.

Patrick doesn't turn from his chair, keeping his head down as he works at some papers on his desk. "What is it, Hunter? And why are you contacting me this way rather than with the mirror? You need to stay with Crystal."

"Um… sir?"

"Yes, yes! Out with it!"

"Things… didn't exactly go according to plan."

"What do you mean?" he sighs, finally spinning around in his chair. He freezes as he catches sight of Crystal, then groans. "What happened?"

Hunter breathes a sigh of relief. He understands. He's not going to punish him. After Hunter explains the situation to him, he sighs. "Very well. I suppose it might be better this way regardless. She was dangerous while she was out and about- especially with my journal. I can break her just as well from within these walls."

"What should I do with her?" Hunter asks, glancing at the unconscious girl.

"Put her in the room next to Chet's. I have an idea for how to begin breaking her," he says with a grin.

"…Sir? I thought we were showing her that she's on the wrong side in the war?"

"Yes, yes, that's what I meant, of course," he sighs, turning back to his work. "Now go, get her out of my sight. I'll deal with her tomorrow."

15

"Nathan, you don't even know for sure if they did anything to her or not!" Angela protests, following him as he storms down the street. "They were probably just saying that for... for insurance or something! Or maybe they just meant plans for way... WAY down the road!" She continues to argue, although he doesn't seem to be listening. She grabs his arm and spins him around to face her. "Stop, dang it!" she finally says.

"Why?" he retorts, fire burning in his eyes. "Why should I stop? Why should I just leave her alone- all alone, to face the Dragon Hunters with no Gifts?"

"Because you don't have any Gifts either!" she bursts out, regretting it the instant it leaves her mouth.

He stares at her in disbelief. "That was a low blow," he rumbles angrily.

"But true," she whispers cautiously.

Greg finally catches up to them. *"Nathan... I know you are angry and hurt... and I know you just want to protect her, but..."*

"But what?!"

"...You are not prepared to take on the Dragon Hunters at this time... Provoking them now could have catastrophic consequences... such as them hurting Crystal. You should take some time to make a plan. Use your new knowledge to help take them down from the inside. Don't do something stupid. Calm down... and think."

Nathan takes a few deep breaths and his temper cools. "Fine," he breathes. "But I *am* saving her."

"I believe it," Angela murmurs, looking half in awe and half disappointed.

"I'm not going to school tomorrow... or ever again until this is fixed," Nathan resolves.

"And how long do you think that would take?" Angela inquires.

"I don't know," he says as he walks up to his house. "But I also don't care. School is nowhere near the most important thing right now."

"Okay, then I'll skip school too," Angela declares.

Nathan spins around in surprise. "You don't have to do that, you know."

"Yes, I do... and not just for the Queen." Nathan looks surprised, then nods gratefully.

"Thank you."

"So, how are we going to do this?" Auna asks.

"We're going to do what they're least expecting," Nathan replies. "We're going to change the rules."

<<<Zarafa>>>

"It's your own fault for treating this like a game," Zarafa smugly scolds. Bryce stops his pacing to whirl around and glare at her.

"I was *not* treating it like a game!" he bites back. "I was doing what Patrick instructed me to do!"

"Yes, and then you decided to play with the boy. I'm not overly surprised it blew up in your face," she mocks. "You know all this happened because you took him back into town when you knew perfectly well that he tends to get into the middle of our operations. Just wait until Patrick finds out..."

"He *won't* find out!" he desperately cries. "And if you tell him, I'll tell him about you and Dalwork!"

She frowns. "Fine, fine. But what are you going to do to fix all of this?"

Bryce collapses into a chair with a sigh. "I have no idea. I need to show him that I'm on his side somehow."

"I might have an idea," Zarafa reluctantly says.

"Really? What is it?" he pleads. Before she can reply, there's a loud beep echoing through the house.

She sighs. "That would be Patrick. I'll be right back." She then heads to the Hologram room. After a minute, she comes back out. "He wants to talk to both of us," she announces, looking at him seriously.

He gulps and follows her into the room. Sure enough, Patrick's hologram hovers above the blue square on the floor. "Bryce."

"Greetings, Patrick," he greets, bowing. "To what do I owe the pleasure?"

"This is just an update," he assures, then pauses, frowning. "Crystal Dragon has become a bigger pain than I had anticipated. Hunter had to grab her and take her back to my castle by force... He has made far too many mistakes, I'm afraid... so you are reinstated as my right-hand man." Bryce's face freezes in shock.

"...Sir?"

"I know, you never expected to get back to that rank since your betrayal, but it was long ago, and I have decided to forgive you. However, Hunter is still next in line to lead the Dragon Hunters. So really, you are his right-hand man as well."

"Th... thank you, sir," he says, offering another deep bow. "I shall do my best to aid you both."

"I trust that you shall... which is why I need you here. Crystal needs more maintenance than Nathan does. I'm sure Zarafa can keep his nose out of our business just fine on her own." The two glance nervously at each other.

"...Yes, sir. When do I leave?"

"Two days. I will provide a portal. For ease of you finding it, I will place it just outside this building."

"Yes... thank you, sir."

Patrick nods. "Good. I will see you in two days." The hologram then shimmers and disappears.

Bryce turns to Zarafa. "So, what was that plan of yours?"

<<<Nathan>>>

"Two days?" Nathan confirms.

Auna nods as she lands on the table between him and his grandma. "*Yes. Patrick is providing a portal just outside Zarafa's house for Bryce to be able to return to Zilferia.*"

"And you are *completely* sure that he said that Crystal was back in his castle?"

"Yes. Her brother Hunter took her there because she was becoming 'too much of a pain...' his words, not mine," she adds when she notices the fury passing over his face.

"Well then, Nathan," his Grandma Beryl says, leaning back in her chair. "It seems that you just need to be ready to also hitch a ride in that portal in two days."

"You also need to be prepared," Greg adds. *"The portal will likely put you directly inside the castle. You need to plan ahead of time how you're going to get both of you out of there."*

"Yes, I know," he sighs. "I'll work on it."

"And I'll help," Angela declares. Nathan shakes his head at her. "What? I can help, even without Gifts! I can talk to T. I'm sure he knows of something that can help you."

"Fine. ...I just don't want you to get hurt," he admits.

"I won't," she promises, smiling at him. He smiles back.

"Um, anyway, I have a plan for how to be inside Zarafa's place when the portal is made- that's the easy part. The hard part will be planning what to do after I get through the portal..."

"T can probably help with that," Angela offers.

"Great, let's go," he decides, standing.

"Hold up there, tiger," his Grandma Beryl chuckles. "You should have dinner first. Besides, your parents and sister will be home soon. You should leave after they head out again."

"May I stay for dinner?" Angela asks.

Beryl grins delightedly. "Of course, dear! You are always welcome in this house," she warmly informs her.

"Why, thank you," Angela replies, surprised.

The whine of a machine desperately in need of repair then reaches their ears. "Sounds like they're home. Auna, you might want to wait outside," Beryl says, opening the door for the fairiye. "Greg, you too. You know the Andersons can barely tolerate you as it is," she says with a wink as the Familiar follows Auna out.

The door opens, and the intimidating form of John Parker Anderson fills the doorway. "Hey dad," Nathan greets. "You look tired."

"Oh, I'm fine," he chuckles warily. "Just a little over-worked. I'll get used to the hours, don't you worry yourself about it. Now then... who's this pretty girl? Nathan, you didn't tell us you had a girlfriend already! What's your name?" he asks, walking over to her.

"Oh... I'm Angela... but we- we aren't..."

"She's not my girlfriend, dad," Nathan explains, his cheeks flushed as brightly as Angela's.

"Ah. Pity," he says with a wink.

"Oh, Parker, you leave those two alone," Nathan's mom scolds as she comes in, holding little Anna's hand. "Hello, Angela," she smiles at her. "I apologize- we weren't expecting company for dinner."

"Oh, of course... I can go if you..."

"Nonsense. It's fine," Parker assures her kindly. "Now then," he continues, clapping his hands together. "What should we eat?"

<<<Zarafa>>>

"Oh, calm down and just eat," Zarafa sighs, twirling a silver fork in her hand.

Bryce sighs and takes a bite, forcing himself to swallow the Zilferian food. "Just tell me your plan already! How are you going to get Nathan to trust me again? He's so suspicious..."

"I know," she sighs, setting down her fork. "But there are a few options open to us. ...Unfortunately, most of them involve me receiving the blame, from both Patrick and the boy."

Bryce leans forward, a gleam of hope in his eyes. "Tell me."

"Don't be so excited," she sighs. "There are a couple of things we could do, but I would prefer it if we tried the one that would have less extreme consequences for me first."

"Alright, fine," He quickly agrees. "So come on- what is it?"

"Well, one thing that would work would be to... well, to use a form of mind control..."

"Wait. You don't mean... biting the boy?" he nervously asks, eying her mouth.

"Yes, actually, I do."

"Patrick told you specifically not to do that..."

"I'm not going to turn him into a vampire!" she says exasperatedly.

"Are you sure? I heard it's difficult to control the urge once your... you know... are in his... and you're..."

"I have done it before, and I can do it again!" she grunts, standing and pushing her chair back from the table. It goes flying and breaks against the wall behind her. "Besides, he isn't involved in any prophecy or has any magic... he is no longer special, so his blood won't have nearly as strong of a hold on me as you may think. *Don't* underestimate me."

Nodding, he nervously watches as her eyes return back to normal and her teeth dull once more. "Alright," he says, his voice quiet and tight. "Alright. ...What if that doesn't work?"

"Simple. I just tell him that I'm controlling you and that you have no idea who you're working for. To sell it, I'll arrange him walking in on us as I pretend to bite you. You know, as if you had just discovered what was going on and I had decided to kill you."

Bryce's face goes white as a sheet. "No. No no nonononononono. Oh, Dravyn, I'd rather die!"

Zarafa sighs, her hands on her hips. "Oh, please. Stop being so dramatic. There's no need to curse like that... why are you trembling so hard? I said *pretend* to bite you."

Bryce, no longer in the regal position he usually favors, is backed against a wall with his arms wrapped tight against his sides as he quivers. "You know... what happened to my... wife, don't you?"

"Yeah, something about her leaving you for another guy or something?"

"No, that's not the true story," he admits, pain written on his face. "The truth is... that I had a friend... who was a vampire. His brother... fancied my wife. I didn't find out about it until it was too late... until I returned home from a long hunting trip to find him holding her limp body as he drained her of blood... replacing it with his vampire venom. I drew my sword and ran him through immediately. He turned to ash- my sword had recently been coated in Viglax, you see, because of the hunt I was on. My wife was unconscious the rest of the night... and woke the next morning. I thought she was fine... she said she felt sick, but I thought that it was just the usual morning sickness that comes when women are pregnant. I took her to the hospital since she felt the baby coming... the doctors said the baby was healthy... but my wife... died soon after delivering her. The next night, Patrick came and recruited me into his army. I had to leave my beautiful daughter behind... I have no idea what became of her."

"So, you blame this vampire for your wife's death?"

"You know as well as I that she died because she didn't complete the transition. I learned after her passing that the process had to be completed or the person transitioning would die, just as she had."

"I see… just to make sure, though… her skin was pale?"

"Yes. With a dark purple bruise ringed with gold larger than my hand on her neck, at the place that creature's fangs... well, you know."

"Ah. I would say that she died thanks to the vampire bite, then," Zarafa acknowledges.

"Yes. She did."

"And that's why you have a secret loathing for me. Don't bother," she adds as he opens his mouth to say something. "I can tell these things. Very well, I don't have to pretend to bite you. I could be about to destroy you some other way."

"Anything would be better than a vampire bite, even a fake one."

Zarafa nods, accepting this. "Very well. So, will you do the honors of calling the boy, or shall I?"

<<<Nathan>>>

"Mmm," Angela moans as she sets down her fork and leans back from the table. "That was delicious, Mrs. Anderson. Thank you for allowing me to stay over for dinner."

"Any time," she assures, a broad grin on her face, enamored with the girl like everyone else was.

"Well, I really must be going," Angela announces, standing.

"Oh, must you? We have some pie if you're still hungry…"

Angela chuckles. "Oh, no, I'm afraid I couldn't take another bite! Thank you very much, though."

"Any time," Nathan's mom assures her. "Oh, Nathan, will you walk her home, please?"

"Of course, mom," he says, standing and taking their dishes to the sink before pulling on his jacket and opening the front door for Angela.

"I love your family," Angela smiles as they walk toward her house.

"Really? I was worried you would think they were a little overbearing," he chuckles.

"Oh, they certainly are, but it's just adorable," she assures him. Nathan watches her perfect lips as she talks. He doesn't know what it is about her, but he feels drawn in by everything she does. He loved spending time with her. She had a way of helping him to forget everything in his life that's going wrong.

"So, what are we going to do about Zarafa and Bryce?" she asks as they near her house. He sighs. So much for that idea.

"I'm not sure yet. Can I call you tomorrow when I figure it out?"

"Of course," she grins. "I'd love for you to call me," she adds with a flirtatious wink as they stop on her doorstep.

He grins, and suddenly everything in his body tells him to kiss her. So he does, taking two steps up to her and cupping her face with one hand. The next thing he knows, he was kissing her. Her body softens in his arms as she relaxes and begins kissing him back. She tasted like honey and... like magic. After a few more seconds, he pulls away, releasing her. His face is slightly flushed and his heart pounding as he says, "Goodnight," and turns away.

Behind him, he hears a soft, "Goodnight."

<<<Angela>>>

Angela stands stone-still on her porch, shock seeming to glue her in place as she watches Nathan walk away. Her lips tingled from the unexpected kiss. It wasn't her first, but it was different than any other kiss she had ever felt. There was definitely something special about him, although she couldn't quite put her finger on it.

After a few more seconds, she turns to head into the house and is stopped by a stunned fairiye. *"What was that?!"* She gasps.

"It was a kiss..."

"Yes, I know that!" she sighs. *"What I mean is, what do you think you are doing?! You are supposed to be protecting him, not falling in love with him!"*

"Hey, he kissed *me*, not the other way around!" she protests.

"Yes, but I can tell from the grin on your face that you enjoyed it." Angela attempts to frown, but the smile quickly reappears on her lips.

She shrugs. "What does it matter? I can still protect him. If anything, this should make it easier to help him."

Auna shakes her head exasperatedly. *"Fine. Don't listen to me. But I can guarantee that this blossoming 'romance' will not end well."*

<<<Nathan>>>

Nathan pauses and looks back as he hears her door close. He then looks down at his chest and puts a hand over his heart, which is fluttering strangely. *What* was *that? He wonders. That may have been my first kiss, but even so, I can tell that most aren't like that... then again, most girls aren't from Zilferia, and I bet they don't taste like magic. ...Hmm,* he contemplates, running his tongue over his teeth. *At least I think that's what magic would taste like.* His lips still tingled from the faint electric surge that had passed over him when he kissed her, and every other part of his body thrummed with energy.

He pauses in front of his house, trying to swallow his grin before he goes in. After a minute, he walks into his front room to find his grandma watching him. *She knows!* He panics irrationally before scolding himself for being so paranoid. Of course she doesn't know.

"So, do you and Angela have a plan yet?"

"Um, no, I'm working on it," he says, although his brain is definitely not focusing on that at the moment. "I'll call her in the morning once I finish... um, planning."

She cocks an eyebrow at him. "Hmm. Alright then. You're just lucky you're the last one of the family to leave in the morning, as well as the first to get back. Otherwise, your parents would know that you're skipping school."

"Nathan?" Parker calls up from the basement.

"Coming, dad," he replies before finishing his conversation with his grandma. "I know, but I could fake going to school anyway since T is also in on this." He then turns and joins his dad downstairs. "Yeah, dad? What is it?"

"Angela get home alright?"

"Um yeah, she lives barely a street away. She's fine."

"Did you kiss her goodnight?" he asks, winking.

A blush instantly leaps to Nathan's cheeks before he can stop it. "Um..." His brain isn't fast enough to come up with a reply.

His dad's booming laugh echoes loud enough that Nathan's mom comes in from the other room. "Shh," she scolds. "I just put Anna to bed! What is wrong with you?"

Parker continues his hearty chortling. "Nathan kissed her!"

"What?" she spins to face her son, peering at his face. "Is that true?"

"I… uh…"

"Oh my goodness, it is!" she gasps, sitting down in her rocking chair. "I can't believe this day has already come… your first kiss! …That *was* your first, right?" she confirms.

"Yes," he sighs, giving in.

"I told you she was his girlfriend," his dad chuckles, winking at his mom, who is still sitting a little stunned in her chair.

"No, she's…" Nathan starts protesting before he stops. Wasn't she practically his girlfriend now? After all, he had kissed her. Whether he had planned it beforehand or not, that meant he liked her. And since she had also kissed him back…

"Nathan!" Beryl calls from the top of the stairs. "You forgot to feed Greg again!"

He sighs with relief since this gave him an excuse to leave. "Yes, grandma, I'm coming," he calls back before racing up the stairs, the laughter of his dad following him as he makes his escape. When he reaches his grandma, he notices a glint in her eyes. He sighs. "You knew, didn't you?"

"Ah, young love," she chuckles. "It's so hard to hide, isn't it?" she smiles as she rubs his head affectionately as though he were a dog. "Go on, then. You know how Greg gets when he doesn't get his dinner," she laughs.

"Yeah," he murmurs, opening the sliding door with a touch of his hand and stepping back out into the brisk night air.

"*You* kissed *her?!*"

Nathan sighs. "I really don't need to hear this from you, too."

"*Yes, you do,*" Greg insists as he scurries up to him. Nathan kneels and begins putting his Familiar's food in his dish as he listens to his scolding. "*What were you thinking?*"

"*Hmm, I don't know, I guess I was thinking about how beautiful, funny, and fearless she was and how much I wanted to kiss her. Why do you have such an issue with it?*"

"*Because I happen to know another beautiful Zilferian girl who is also fearless and whom you admire and always have! I happen to know…*"

"That's enough," Nathan growls as he stands back up. "*Crystal and Angela may have some things in common, but I can tell you that Crystal doesn't think about me that way- and probably never will. Angela, however, likes me just as much as I like her. Crystal and I are just friends, and that is all it will ever be. So why should that stop me from having a girlfriend? I bet she has a boyfriend anyway,"* he sighs.

Greg's tail droops, as does his head. *"Fine. You do what you please."*

"Thank you."

"However," he adds, looking back up at him. *"Just promise me one thing."*

Nathan groans. *"What?"*

"Promise me that you won't forget about Crystal, and that you won't give up on saving her because of Angela. Promise me that you will work just as hard to save Crystal as you would have if tonight had never happened."

He's surprised. He and Crystal may not be involved the way he and Angela were, but that didn't mean he didn't still care for her. *"Of course."*

"Good," the Familiar nods before shoving his nose into the bowl of food. As Nathan heads back inside, he hears Greg murmur one more thing to him. *"You had better get started on that plan, then."*

Nathan tosses and turns in bed, unable to fall asleep. Sighing, he sits up and looks at his clock. It's nearly four in the morning. He groans and wipes his face with his hand before pulling back the sheets and stumbling into the bathroom. The light flashes as soon as the door opens. He turns the faucet on and holds his hands underneath to catch the cold cascade of water. He splashes his face a couple times, then turns off the water. He looks into the mirror and watches the water dripping off his face, trying to empty his mind. His swirling, confused thoughts have kept him up all night, and he hadn't come to any solid solution to his dilemma.

He grabs a towel and dries his face, then lies back down on his bed, his hands under his head as he stares up at the ceiling. After a few minutes, he sits up and grabs his phone, turning it on before pausing. Who could he call at four in the morning for help? No one could really help him. ...No one in this realm, at least.

He sets down the phone and stares at his watch instead. The last time he had tried to use it, it hadn't worked, but he had a feeling Zarafa had had something to do with that. Maybe this time... He lifts the circumference of the watch. Holding his breath, he twists it to the right to contact Crystal.

After waiting for a few seconds, he turns it to the left to reach Thaddeus. It doesn't work. He groans and unfastens the watch from his wrist. Clasping it in both hands, he closes his eyes and focuses his mind. *Maybe I can somehow push through whatever spell Zarafa put on it...* That's his hope, at least. So when a measure of energy rushes through his body and out of his hands into the watch, he's stunned. *Did I just use... magic?*

"Nathan?" Thaddeus's voice rises faintly from the watch. Nathan uncovers it and finds his old mentor's face hovering above the watch in hologram form.

"Thaddeus!" he cries in relief.

"Nathan, what's wrong? What's happened? We lost touch with you! Are you alright?"

"Um, yeah, I'm alright, I guess," he replies, thinking about his lost Gifts. "But Crystal... what happened to her?"

Thaddeus's face falls. "Ah. You heard. ...Wait, how did you find out about what happened to Crystal?"

"There... there are a bunch of Dragon Hunters on First Earth," he explains, a little reluctantly. "And I... well, they told me they were working for Alexander Dragon..."

"Wait... so you are on good terms with these Dragon Hunters?"

"Um, I suppose you could say that. They're trying to get me to trust them."

"Good... this is good."

"How is this good?" Nathan inquires skeptically.

"It's good because this means that you can get inside information," he says thoughtfully. "Although they are pretending to not be Dragon Hunters, since you know where they are, you could do some snooping and tell us what you discover."

"Well, I did find out that Patrick is going to put a portal to Zilferia by Zarafa's house for Bryce so he can help... with Crystal," he chokes out. "So, I'm assuming it will take him directly into Patrick's castle."

"You plan to follow him in," Thaddeus realizes.

"Yes. I need to go save Crystal. Who knows what that evil creep is doing to her now? Who knows how much time she has left? Thaddeus, I have to go." He pauses. "But I contacted you so I could ask for your advice. Getting in there won't be a problem, but getting us *both* out... I'll need your help."

"Indeed... however, I cannot be of much assistance to you until you arrive on Zilferia. Luckily, we have a spy who is currently on First Earth. His name is…"

"I know," Nathan interrupts. "I already met T."

Thaddeus looks surprised. "Oh! Well, splendid! That will save you time. Contact him as soon as you can, he should have some potions and such to help you. There is also someone else who you can contact if you are in need of aid…"

"Angela doesn't have any Gifts. Unless you mean Auna," he speculates. "She could definitely be quite helpful since she can travel between realms."

Thaddeus's face is now displaying open shock. He finds his voice after a few seconds. "You already met the fairiye and know about Angela… well then…"

"Yeah how about next time *don't* try and keep me out of the loop, alright? Who knows what could happen next time if I don't know everything?" he adds bitterly.

Thaddeus narrows his eyes suspiciously at him. "Nathan? What happened that you aren't telling me?"

He sighs. "The Dragon Hunters… there was a group—not Bryce or Zarafa—that was angry with me… we fought for a while… then they had this magic wielder and he… I don't know, really. He might have taken my Gifts or just locked them away or something, but the point is that I don't have my Gifts anymore," he states bluntly.

Surprise and compassion swim in Thaddeus's eyes. "Oh, my dear boy…"

"Don't," Nathan interrupts. "Just don't. Forget about it and move on, alright? And don't tell anyone about it either. I don't want anyone to know. I'll be fine."

"Nathan, you know what this means, don't you?"

"I know quite a few things that not having Gifts changes. I know what happens now. I watched Crystal go through it. Don't worry, I'll be fine."

"I know you will. However, I was referring to the fact that you are the first person this has happened to due to magic. Patrick will be on the hunt for you so he can keep you under observation."

He sighs. "You don't need to beat around the bush. I'm his new experiment. Got it. However, if that gives me an edge for getting Crystal out of his clutches, then I'm all for it."

"Nathan—" He slams the circumference of the watch back down, cutting him off. No one can talk him out of rescuing Crystal. He will do whatever it takes to keep her safe, even if that means sacrificing himself.

<<<Bryce>>>

"Here it is," Zarafa announces, handing the tablet over to Bryce. "I told you it would be easy to find his number."

Bryce glances down at the number. "How are we supposed to explain how we got a hold of his number, though?"

"If he asks, tell him it doesn't matter. Just pretend to be desperate and panicking- as though you had just discovered who I am and who I work for and you need to hurry and relay the information before I catch you. Plead with him to come over as soon as he can."

"It's barely five in the morning. Should we wait?"

"No, this is perfect. It's more likely for you to be snooping around early in the morning than at any other time. Besides, we want to catch him before he gets to school. Now go on, show me your acting skills," she urges.

He sighs. "Fine. But if he doesn't buy this..."

"Then we'll go on to the next plan. And don't worry, I'll save the mind control as a last resort," she assures.

"Good," he says, turning on his phone and dialing Nathan's number. He picks up after only two rings.

"Hello?" He sounds confused, but not drowsy as though he had just woken up.

"Nathan! Oh, good, you answered!"

"Bryce? What are you..."

"No time!" he gasps, glancing at Zarafa, who nods encouragingly. "I need to tell you something vital, are you paying attention?"

"Yeah..."

"I know it's early, but what you said before struck me. I know you don't trust me and I understand why. See, this morning I broke into Zarafa's house and snooped around. I learned that she's been in contact with Patrick! You were right about her! The thing is, after I discovered this, she heard me in her house and even at this very moment she's trying to catch me! Nathan, I swear I had no idea! I thought Zarafa was working for Alexander, just like you did! We've both been duped! Hurry, I need your help! Please come help me get away from her! She's going to kill me or turn me into a vampire or something! Please, I need your help! I'm in Zarafa's house. I'm hiding in her kitchen, in the cupboard! Nathan, I need—" He then hangs up abruptly.

"Well done," Zarafa appraises him.

"Do you think he's really going to come?"

"Knowing that boy? Definitely. He has a soft spot for those who are in trouble. Now come on, into the cupboard with you," she laughs, directing him to the kitchen.

<<<Angela>>>

The sound of her phone ringing pulls Angela out of her sleep. She yawns and sits up, rubbing her eyes sleepily and reaching over to stop the insistent sounds. She's about to deny the call until she sees who it is. "Nathan!" she gasps, sitting up and attempting to straighten her unruly hair. She finally answers the phone. "Hello?" she says, trying to mask the drowsy tone in her voice.

"Angela, I need your help- fast," he immediately announces.

"Um, okay? What is it?"

"Bryce just called me. He's still trying to get me to trust him. He's saying that he found out that Zarafa is working for Patrick and insisting that he had no idea and he was just following orders and such... anyway, he wants me to rush over there as soon as I can and help him out. I don't know what to do, though. Would it be better to pretend and buy his story or just not go or... what?"

"Okay... why are you calling me?"

"Because you are smart and one of the few people I can trust with this and also because you're on speed dial and I need to make a decision fast."

Her heart skipped a beat. She was one of his main contacts in his phone? He really did like her! "Um. Okay... well, I think that it would be easier to get inside information if you pretended to buy his story. Plus if he thinks you're on his side, it could protect you from the other Dragon Hunters. At least until you go through the portal, that is. In fact, you might be able to trick him into giving you some weapon that could help you free Crystal."

He laughs. "I knew you were brilliant. Thanks!"

"Wait," she calls before he hangs up. She hesitates. "Do you need a ride? Your parents will notice if your car is missing."

"What about your parents?"

"We have a tennis game today, remember? I always drive to school on game days before the bus comes so I can drive myself home afterward."

She can hear the smile in his voice as he replies. "Like I said— brilliant. I'll be over in a few minutes." He then hangs up. Angela sits on the edge of her bed holding her phone in both hands with a huge grin on her face.

She hears a sad voice in her head. *"Well if you're going to go, you should hurry and make yourself presentable,"* Auna sighs as she flutters over.

"Right. Thanks," she smiles at the fairiye as she quickly changes and brushes her teeth. She is just putting her hair into a ponytail when she hears his voice beneath her window.

"Angela?"

She rushes to the window and leans her head out. "Just a second. I'll meet you in the front by the car."

"Alright," he replies, grinning as he heads around the building. Angela quickly grabs a hat and some sunglasses, then eases her door open and tiptoes past her parents' bedroom. She races down the stairs, her socks muffling the sounds of her footsteps. Picking up her tennis shoes, she cracks open the front door and steps out onto the porch.

"Hey," Nathan greets her, smiling. His hair is a mess, but he's breathtakingly handsome all the same.

"Good morning," Angela replies as she sits on the top step, slipping her shoes on. "Ready?" she asks, standing.

"Sure. It helps that you're here," he adds.

"Well, I can't come inside with you," she warns as she unlocks the car. "Bryce would recognize me- and Zarafa might as well."

Nathan sighs as he slips into the passenger side and closes the door behind him. "I know. But you're here with me now."

She smiles at him as she starts the car. "I sure am."

16

My sleep was dreamless. This is the first thing I notice as I begin waking up. I *always* dream when I sleep, so the fact that I had none helps to startle me awake. Rather than emerging from an imaginary scenario, I swim forth out of darkness that seemed to occupy every niche of my brain. I feel drugged when I open my eyes and everything looks grey and nothing holds still. I'm disoriented as well, and it's hard for me to remember what happened.

I sit up and put a hand on the stone wall next to me. Maybe *this* is my dream. Surely this is a nightmare. It's the only explanation. Why else would I be back in Patrick's castle?

The door opens, and I wince away from the harsh light, covering my eyes. "Crystal?"

Hunter. The sound of his voice causes an inexplicable rage to surge through my veins, and I lurch to my feet and stumble over to him. "You... you..." I can't seem to say more than that one word, and I can't figure out why my body isn't really responding to me.

"Stop." This one word uttered from his traitorous mouth is enough to cause my uneven steps toward him to cease. I peer up at him, mere inches away, yet unable to reach him.

"Why... why would you..." tears well up in my eyes and stream down my cheeks, soaking the simple cloth shirt I am wearing. That's when I notice that I am wearing a black shirt and black pants. "Why… why am I… dressed like…"

"You are dressed like a Dragon Hunter because you are one," Hunter murmurs in a voice that seems to calm me, even though I do not want to be reassured.

"What? I'm not… a Dragon Hunter… you are," I sob as my tears begin to abate.

"You joined me," he informs me, his face so close to mine that I'm lost in his multi-colored eyes. *Wait… I thought he had brown eyes…* "I told you the truth, and you believed me. You realized that you were fighting on the wrong side of the war, and you decided to join Patrick and me."

My brain doesn't want to process this. "…I did?"

"Yes. And you love your friends the dragons, the Sohos, and the merfolk, and you don't want to leave them, but you realized that the best way to help them is to show them the truth like I showed you the truth," he assures.

"Yes… I love my friends," I whisper, clinging to that phrase. I know that that part is true. Surely the rest of his story is true too? I look around the small room. "Why am I in here?"

"You, um, hit your head earlier, and we were afraid that you would forget the truth and that you would continue fighting for the wrong side of the war," he explains.

"So now that I remember, can I go wherever I want?" I ask innocently. I don't remember anything, so I decide to trust Hunter. He is my brother after all, right? Besides, he sounds trustworthy.

"Uh… yeah, of course… not yet though," he hurriedly adds as I take a step toward the open door behind him. "We have to try and help you some more, and make sure that you remember the truth first. Okay?"

"Okay," I mildly agree, sitting on the edge of my bed.

"Good," Hunter sighs, turning to go.

"Will you come back soon?" I ask.

He turns around, surprise and a little compassion on his face. "Yeah. Real soon," he assures me.

I smile. "Good." He nods awkwardly and slowly steps out, shutting the door behind him and locking it.

I lay back on the bed and stare at the ceiling. *I wonder what it is I forgot when I hit my head. I don't really remember much of anything… I hope Hunter can clear that up for me soon.* I pause. *How did I even know his name in the first place, though?* After a while, I shrug. I suppose selective memory loss is probably not the strangest thing that's ever happened to me.

"*Crystal!*"

I open my eyes and find a tiny person hovering over me, her wings fluttering like a hummingbird's. Her long white hair whirls in mesmerizing patterns as the movement from her wings causes the strands to dance.

"Hello," I say, sitting up and smiling at her. "What's your name?"

"*My name is Auna. I'm a fairiye. I've come to check in on you.*"

"Hi, Auna. That's very kind of you. I'm fine, though."

"*Hmm,*" she murmurs, flying to a spot near my face. "*Nathan is worried about you.*"

"Okay, well tell Nathan that I'm fine. Hunter's taking good care of me." I'm not sure who this Nathan is, but he must be one of my friends if he's worried about me.

The fairiye then frowns. "*May I look into your memories?*"

"Sure," I shrug.

"*Thank you.*" She then places a soft, tiny hand on my right temple and closes her eyes. Unsure of what to do, I shut mine too. After a few seconds, I see glimpses of… something. A boy with light shining on a thin layer of snow on his hair. A big man with an even bigger grin and a thin woman who seems to radiate love and kindness. Dragons, merfolk, treehouses. A boy who changes into Hunter. Then these memories are suddenly swallowed up in the dark fog that seems to permeate every part of my brain.

I sigh and open my eyes. The fairiye looks at me sadly as she removes her hand. "*I'm so sorry Crystal,*" she says.

"Why?" I ask, confused.

"*…I'm sorry for the loss of your memories,*" she explains.

"Oh. Well don't worry, Hunter will find a way to help me remember," I smile at the tiny person.

"*I'm sure… I have to go now, Crystal,*" Auna says as she flies back to the center of the room. "*Don't tell anyone I was here, okay?*"

"Okay. Bye," I say, waving as the fairiye begins to glow, then fades away and disappears.

<<<Hunter>>>

"You say you completely repressed her memories?" Patrick repeats, pausing in his pacing.

"Yes," Hunter sighs, reclining in his chair. "She doesn't remember who she is. She's like a child now—simple-minded and submissive. She believes anything I tell her without question."

"Interesting… your powers have grown strong," Patrick appraises him, putting a gloved hand on his shoulder. "I'm impressed."

"Thank you, sir," he replies, knowing this is the proper response.

"Now then, what to do with the girl? Dravyn is quite impartial to mind control, but of course, it is a far better alternative than letting her wander around causing damage to our designs. He wants her on our side and so do I although we would both rather she do it of her own free will."

"Perhaps that will come later," Hunter suggests. "After we give her fake memories and she believes in them- and in us- I could lift my control from her mind, and she can see for herself that this is the life she should have chosen from the beginning."

"Hmm," Patrick murmurs as he sinks into his plush chair. He leans forward and rests his elbows on the table between them and peers into Hunter's eyes. "That just might work," he contemplates, then grins and stands once more. "Wonderful. That will be your main job now."

"For how long? …Sir."

"For however long it takes," he states, walking toward the door and opening it. "You start now," he adds before shutting the door behind him.

Hunter sighs and turns to the Dragon Hunter standing beside him. "Come on, then. Let's go."

<<<Patrick>>>

Patrick's long strides propel him down the hall, and there's a slight bounce in his step. Finally, his plans are proceeding at a decent pace. He pauses by the girl's room and turns to the guard who's standing beside the door. "Open it," he orders.

The guard bows. "Yes sir," he quips as he slides the key into the lock, then swings the door open. Patrick steps inside, his cloak billowing magnificently behind him. The door closes behind him. "Crystal?" he addresses the girl sitting on the edge of the bed, her hands folded peacefully in her lap and her head bowed.

She looks up. "Patrick," she states, although there's no hint of recognition on her face.

"Yes. Do you remember me?" he cautiously probes.

She shrugs. "I feel like I should, but I don't. I don't even know how I knew your name." She sighs and resumes staring at her hands. After a few seconds, she looks up at him. He's surprised to see her eyes swimming with unshed tears. "Can you help me get my memories back?" she pleads, her voice breaking with sorrow. "I don't even know who I am. I feel so lost... disconnected. Like I'm floating in space... all alone. Hunter told me some things, but I'm still just so confused," she sobs, a tear finally falling from each eye, splashing on her arm.

Patrick is surprised to feel a flash of pity course through his body at the sight of the broken girl. He hadn't even tried to break her, and here she was, begging him for help. He thought that was what he had wanted, but looking at her now... Hunter was right. She was like a child.

"Um..." He's not sure what to do. Should he comfort her? Hunter had suggested showing her the life she could have had if she had joined them in the beginning... although it might take even more than that. It might take making her feel welcomed here, as though she had another home with them. "Yes, of course I'll help you get your memories back..." the words had hardly come out of his mouth before an overjoyed child-like Crystal bounded up to him and ensnared him in a bear hug.

"Thank you!" she cries, her voice muffled by his cloak. Patrick remains frozen, uncertain of what he should do. After a few seconds, he gingerly puts his hands on her back. She pulls back and smiles at him. "Can I see Hunter now?" she asks. "I miss him."

"Certainly," he says, backing away and clearing his throat tentatively. "I'll go get him for you right now." He stares at her happy smile before he turns and exits the room. *Well, that was odd. I don't know if I'm ever going to get used to the strong-willed Crystal Dragon being so submissive and open to me.* He shrugs. *It doesn't matter,* he decides. *All that matters is that she's helping us, not hurting us.*

He had hardly resumed walking down the hallway before the back of his right hand begins to burn. Gasping, he yanks off the glove covering his Eye

Insignia. The silvery-blue shape rises from his hand and shifts into a burning orange. It then rearranges to represent the head of the man Patrick most dreaded to see.

"Dexter," he breathes.

The head nods to him politely. "Greetings, Patrick. I have contacted you to inform you that I will be at your castle in approximately two days to observe the progress you have made in the war on Zilferia. I trust you will be ready." With that, the image reformed into the eye, which then settled back onto Patrick's skin and cooled into the silvery blue it had started out as.

He stoops and retrieves the discarded glove, slowly slipping it back onto his hand. *Great. Just what I needed. An investigation from Dexter. ...Hunter better have Crystal prepped by then.*

<<<Alexander>>>

The King takes to the air, barely bothering to shut the door behind him. He pushes all the energy he dares into flying, hoping that he can quickly catch up to Hunter. ...*His* Hunter. A tear is ripped from his eye, and it has nothing to do with the wind speeding past. His heart aches as he contemplates just how far off the path his son had wandered. No. Not his son. Not anymore. Although he had held to the hope that he would return to them someday for those seventeen years, that hope had vanished when Thaddeus informed him that he had kidnapped his daughter and delivered her into the hands of his enemy.

His son was gone. All that remained was a dangerous boy who was a bane to him and everything he cared about. He was a problem.

One that needed to be removed.

<<<Hunter>>>

Hunter stops outside of his sister's door, hesitating. The Dragon Hunter with the key chuckles as he slips it into the lock. "I'm sure she'll be thrilled that you're back. She sure is getting a lot of visits. What do you mean to do with the two from the Village Council?"

"Nothing, I suppose," he wearily replies.

"...Nothing, sir?" the guard repeats, confused.

"That's right. Nothing. The Princess is our number one priority."

"But... sir..."

"And Patrick's decisions are *not* to be questioned," he growls, glaring at the man.

He gulps. "Yes, sir. My apologies, sir. I never meant..."

Hunter sighs and pushes the man aside, opening the door himself and slipping inside. Crystal looks up at him and beams. "Hunter!" She greets him with a hug.

"Um, hello there," he says, patting her on the back. "I wasn't even gone that long... it's only been a few minutes."

"I know," she smiles as she pulls away. "But I like it when you come and talk to me. Whenever you're gone, I feel... like I'm floating. In an ocean... completely lost, completely alone, just... drifting." Hunter frowns. The image didn't inspire feelings of delight. "But then you come," she continues, beaming. "And suddenly I have an island, where I'm safe, and I may not know where I am, but I know that I'm not in the water anymore and that's enough."

"Right," Hunter says, pulling out of the hug that follows her statement. "Well let's see what we can do about that pesky ocean."

Crystal's answering grin seems to light up the room. "You're the best, Hunter!"

"Right... well, where to begin..."

"Who am I?" she asks as she sits on the bed.

Hunter breathes a heavy sigh as he sits beside her. "Well, you are a princess."

Her eyes light up. "Really?"

"Really," he laughs. "And I'm your brother. Our mother and father... don't live here. But that's okay because all we need is Patrick."

"All we need is Patrick," she repeats, her eyes wide as she greedily drinks in every word he says.

"Our parents are leading the other side of this war we are in."

"War?"

"Yes... they want to protect dragons—they are beasts that terrorize and kill people," he solemnly informs her.

"No," she gasps, not blinking as she stares at him, anxiously waiting for more.

"Yes. Patrick wants to save everyone from the dragons, but the King and Queen want to stop him. So, they started this war."

Crystal hesitates. "But people die in wars, don't they?"

"Yes," he nods. "That's why it's so important we quickly show them that war is bad, and that they are wrong. We need to show them that dragons are evil and hurt people, just like war does."

"How?"

"Uh..." Hunter hesitates. How *are* they doing that? "We... well..."

He's saved from having to reply thanks to Patrick opening the door. "Ah, Hunter. I'm sorry Crystal, but I need your brother's help for a bit. May I?"

"Of course," she says. "Anything for you, Patrick."

Hunter's eyebrows nearly shoot into his hairline. That is one thing he *never* thought he would hear her say—perhaps sarcastically, but never with such sincerity.

"I'll be back later," he promises as he leaves.

"I'll be here," she happily replies, waving as he steps out the door.

Patrick turns to Hunter. "Are you sure you didn't do anything other than repress her memories?"

"Well, I can't be sure," he admits. "It's the first time I've done anything like that... but she sure is acting oddly."

"That she is... it's like the fire in her completely went out. It's more than her just losing hope to fight against us," Patrick contemplates as they walk away. He pauses, then shakes his head. "But that's not what I wanted to talk to you about."

"What is it?" Hunter asks curiously.

Patrick sighs. "The King is coming toward us. He's alone, for now, but I want you to go subdue him."

"Me? But there are plenty of men who could take him. Scourge, for example..."

"I don't want your friend to go out there," he sighs. "I want to show Alexander, once and for all, that you are *not* his puppet. You know where you belong, and you are willing to fight to stay there."

Hunter nods. "I'll call Vincent."

<<<Hunter>>>

215

As the King flies closer to his enemy's hideout, he invokes his other Gift and turns invisible. Soon after he does, dragons begin appearing out of the forest as they fly through the barrier surrounding the Dragon Hunter's hideout. They fly towards a section of the King's Village that had not yet been raided by the group.

By the time they reach the Village, the dragons are flying high in the sky, so many that they block out the sun. One of them, a black one, is leading them. A person is riding it. The dragon flies unevenly, suddenly swinging to the right or the left once in a while before continuing on as it had before. The group swoops down above a village, fire flying from their mouths, setting buildings on fire.

One of the dragons suddenly gets hit by lightning. Everything is confusing after that, people flying around amid fire, water, and lightning. Dragons begin falling from the sky. People running, screaming… dragons roaring, diving, and tearing with their claws. Blood; blood everywhere. Huge groups of people trying to flee; others arriving to help. A voice booms amid the chaos, but it barely cuts through the noise. The dragons turn to escape and only one remains behind- the one that led them- the one with a person on its back. It spins in a circle, eyes searching the skies.

The King flies at it, still invisible, and uses his Gift of Strength to punch the dragon towards the ground. It falls a ways down, but pulls up at the last second, growling. The person on its back shouts and the King is revealed. He looks up, panic written on his face as the dragon's head comes closer.

"My King!" The shout comes from one of his soldiers just before he dives in front of him, shielding him with his body. He screams as one of the dragon's teeth pierce his body. "Go, my King… we are here to save you," he whispers before he dies.

The dragon, dismayed that he didn't get his intended target, drops the body of the other man. It falls silently to the ground. The Dragon and its rider turn to the King. "Father," the boy spits in disdain.

The King's eyes glow with anger. "You are no son of mine," he growls.

"Oh?" Hunter sneers. "Are you disappointed in me? Not to worry. I'm just as disappointed in you."

Alexander pauses. "What? What do you mean?"

Hunter's grin grows. "You mean you don't know? I'm disappointed that my 'father' has no backbone. No determination to fight for what he believes in. No honor, no valor, no wisdom. Who are you, really? Take away your crown, your Kingdom, your Queen, and what are you?" He pauses. "You. Are. Nothing." With that, he raises his arm, summoning a bolt of lightning. He smiles at Alexander. "And soon, you will be no more."

Alexander dodges the lightning strike, then redirects it into the dragon's wing. As the beast roars in pain, the King again disappears- although not before the dragon whacks his left arm with its thick tail. Alexander then turns and flies away from the fight, tears in his eyes as he hears Hunter's victorious laughter. Once he's away from the burning section of his Village, he spots a group of refugees below him. He lands and is instantly surrounded by the guards Thaddeus had sent after him.

"My King?" One of them addresses him as he bows a little.

"Soldier. Lead this group of Villagers to my castle. Afterward, send your men around to the others in the outskirts of the main Village. Tell them... tell them to evacuate."

"But... sir, where will they go?"

"We will find room in the main Village—in my own castle if necessary. It's time to fortify ourselves for this war... and begin to fight back," he declares, his eyes burning with rage.

"...Yes, my King," the soldier acknowledges, bowing once more before heading to the front of the group of people rescued from the outer Village.

"War has come to the people," the King whispers sadly.

<<<Hunter>>>

Hunter grins as he watches the King take off after landing for a little while. He was victorious- but of course he was. How could he fail? He was the Prince of the Dragon Hunters. He was a god to the dragons. Soon the other races on Zilferia would willingly follow them, especially once Crystal was secured into their ranks. No one would stand against them then.

He guides Vincent to join the other dragons back at their hideout so he can return and continue talking to Crystal. It really shouldn't take long to get her on their side for good, at the rate she's absorbing his words.

17

Angela stops the car at the base of the hill where Zarafa's place is and turns to Nathan. "Are you sure I can't come with? I could hide. I could go around back where they can't see me or anything..." she stops and sighs at his look. "I know, I know, it's not worth getting caught. I just don't want you to go in there alone."

He smiles at her in a way that makes her heart flutter. "I know. Don't worry, I'll be quick and careful."

"You better," she sighs, putting the car in park and turning her body towards him. "I'll be ready for a quick get-away," she promises earnestly. "I'll help in any way I can."

"I know," Nathan laughs, reaching forward and cupping her soft face in his hand. He leans forward until their noses touch.

"I love you," Angela whispers, her heart aching.

Nathan's grin stretches so wide it hurts. "I love you too," he says before sliding his nose down the side of hers and gently kissing her. Heat seems to seep from his lips into her heart, lighting a fire she knows will never die. He was so achingly perfect, and Angela still was in shock that she was here, kissing the boy of her dreams.

Far too soon, she feels him slowly pull back. Her eyes flutter back open and he takes a deep breath. "Here goes nothing," he mutters before opening the car door and stepping out into the wind.

Angela watches him as he hikes up the hill away from her as her smile slowly fades. Her boyfriend, her new, gorgeous, perfect boyfriend, was heading into danger.

And she could do nothing to help him.

<<<Bryce>>>

Bryce opens the cupboard door and peers out. "Is he here yet?" he whispers.

"No," Zarafa sighs. "Not yet. Now get in there and hold still! I'm going to go around the house. Be prepared for when the boy comes in." Bryce strains his ears and hears her shut the door behind her. The house is eerily silent and Bryce sighs in resignation, settling back into the cupboard. Hopefully that boy won't take too...

"Ahh!" he cries as the door is suddenly ripped open.

"Shh," Nathan hisses. "Zarafa is outside. We can hurry and make our escape now."

"Nathan?" he gasps, his hand still on his heart. "Dragonfire, you're quiet!"

He raises an eyebrow. "I'm sorry, I thought you said you were in trouble. My bad for being quiet!" He sighs. "Now come on. At this point, Zarafa should be in the back. We should head out the front- and quickly!"

He then leads the way out of the kitchen. Bryce watches him, wide-eyed. Never. Never before had he been caught unaware- by *anyone*. Who was this boy, exactly?

He follows Nathan out the front door, silently shutting it behind them. Nathan waves for him to follow, and he does, although his mind is still spinning, trying to figure him out. Finally, he shrugs. He must have just been off his game for a moment. And really, who could blame him? He was trapped in a vampire's kitchen! Really, it was impressive he could deal with the vampire at all, let alone make himself vulnerable to it.

Once they were away from the house, he spots a car parked below them. "Is that your getaway car?" he asks Nathan.

He nods and turns. "But you aren't coming."

"What?" Bryce is completely astounded. He 'saved' him, but won't allow him to use his getaway car?

Nathan puts his hands on his hips. "I still don't trust you. I helped you get out, and I'm sure you can do the rest yourself. I'll call you later if I decide to give you a chance," he adds as he turns and walks away, pulling the hood of his jacket over his head.

Bryce just stands there in the wind and watches him, more mystified than he had ever been before. *What am I going to do with this boy?*

<<<Nathan>>>

Nathan opens the door when he reaches the car, sliding in with a sigh. Angela quickly inspects him. "What's wrong? Are you okay? What happened?"

"Nothing," he murmurs. "That was so weird. I just walked in, opened the door Bryce was hiding behind, lead him out, then left him. He barely said anything, and I hardly even saw Zarafa."

Angela breathes out a sigh of relief. "Well, that's good! I was worried you got hurt or something!"

"No, I'm fine," he assures her with a small smile. "Just... thinking is all." He takes a deep breath. "But we can always do that somewhere else. Let's get out of here."

"Amen to that," Angela chuckles, pulling away from the hill.

<<Bryce>>>

Bryce watches the car drive away, still standing stock-still partway down the hill. Once the car moves out of sight, he turns and trudges back into the house. He collapses heavily on one of Zarafa's couches and stares at the wall on the other side of the room.

The door opens moments later and Zarafa walks in. "What are you doing? Nathan should be here any minute! Get in that cupboard!"

Bryce doesn't move. "He already came and left, Zarafa," he sighs.

"Wait... what?" she repeats, startled. "Seriously? I didn't even notice him?"

"Neither did I," he murmurs, standing and turning towards her. "How is that even possible?"

"I have no idea," she admits, shock still evident on her face. Her perfect red lips dip into a frown. "There's no way he could put up a cloaking spell around himself and kept it up so completely while he was walking around and talking with you... I am assuming you did talk to him?"

"Yeah... not much," he admits. "He seemed pretty intent to get out of here before you caught us or anything."

"Does he trust you again, then?" she inquires.

He sighs and shakes his head. "I don't think so. He 'saved' me, then quickly left. He may trust me again, given time."

Zarafa groans. "Time is the one thing you don't have! You're leaving tomorrow to join Patrick in Zilferia!"

<<<Angela>>>

"Don't worry, Nathan," Angela consoles. "Auna can easily get into Zilferia- and Patrick's castle- undetected. She can talk to Crystal."

"That's not what I'm worried about," Nathan sighs, watching as his house comes into view. His parents should have left for work by now, so only Grandma Beryl should be in the house. He and Angela decided that that's where they would hide out until the Dragon Hunter dilemma had been taken care of. "I'm worried that Crystal will be... well..."

"They shouldn't be doing much to her," Angela says as she tries to comfort him, parking the car on the street beside Nathan's house. "They already took her dragon part and her Gifts, right? What else would they be doing to her?"

Nathan shakes his head. "I don't dare imagine. Knowing what Patrick has already done... who's to say he won't do worse?"

"I'm sure she's fine," she smiles comfortingly at him. "Either way, we'll know for sure how she is when Auna gets back. Just try and relax for now, alright?"

"Right," he sighs, smiling back at her. "Thanks."

"It's what I'm here for," she laughs before opening the car door and stepping out. Nathan follows suit, then leads the way up to his front door. The door opens before he can even reach out a hand to it.

"Nathan!" Beryl gasps in relief. "You're back!"

"Yeah, I'm back," he smiles.

"How did it go?" she inquires, waving them both into the house.

"Fine. Extremely well, actually. I was in and out pretty fast."

"They didn't notice you?"

"Nope. I got Bryce out really quickly, then just left him." he sighs as he sits down on the couch. "I told him I don't trust him yet."

"Why is that a bad thing? You *don't* trust him!" Beryl exclaims.

Angela sits beside Nathan on the couch. "Because he needs to have an excuse to be over there tomorrow when the portal to Zilferia appears."

"I see… that could complicate things, then," Beryl contemplates.

"It doesn't matter," Nathan growls, standing. "I *will* save her. I'll find a way. I will *always* find a way."

Beryl smiles at him. "I'm sure you will, sweetheart. Just promise me you'll be careful."

"I'll take care of him," Angela promises, steely determination in her eyes.

Beryl smiles at her. "Thank you, dear," she says before sighing and standing. "Keep me updated, please."

"I will, grandma," Nathan says.

"We're about to send Auna to check in on Crystal," Angela offers.

"Oh, good. Tell me how that goes."

"We will," she smiles.

After Beryl walks off, Nathan turns to Angela. "Where *is* Auna?"

"She's coming," she promises, closing her eyes. *"Auna, it's time."*

"I'm on my way."

"When will she—" Auna's appearance cuts off his question. "Never mind."

"Traveling down the street takes almost no effort, nor much time," Auna laughs. *"Now then, you wish for me to check on Crystal?"*

"Yes. She's in Patrick's castle," he says. She nods and vanishes. He turns to Angela. "That's it?"

"Yes, but it will take her a while to get back. Come on, let's go do something fun before your parents come home," she smiles.

<<<Zarafa>>>

"Oh, stop sulking," Zarafa sighs. "That chicken is just going to get cold," she adds, taking another bite of her own.

Bryce leans back, setting down his knife. He wipes his face wearily with his hand. "Zarafa..." She frowns and sets her fork down. "What are we going to do now? We don't have long."

"Less than twenty-four hours, to be exact," she sighs. Bryce glances at the clock. It's true, Patrick said the portal would be placed by the back door at exactly four o'clock and would only remain open for five minutes. "So what's your plan?"

"That's what I was going to ask *you*," he groans.

"You won't like my idea," Zarafa warns. "There are many things we *could* do, but very few that actually stand a chance at persuading Nathan that you are on his side. I can only think of one thing that's likely to have a very great effect on the boy..."

Bryce sighs in resignation. "Fine, we'll do it."

Zarafa arches an eyebrow in surprise. "Really? But I thought..."

"It's our last resort," he says, looking up at her. She's shocked by the deep fear in his eyes. "I have to do it. I've got no other options, and we both know what would happen should Patrick discover that I failed him. Again."

<<<Nathan>>>

Nathan fidgets. "Why isn't Auna back yet? She left hours ago!"

Angela smiles patiently at him and reaches out for his hand, pulling him down beside her on the bed. "When fairiye jump through realms, time passes differently for them. For Auna, it's probably only been ten minutes or so since she arrived in Zilferia. She should be back soon. I bet she's on her way right now," she explains.

Nathan relaxes a little and smiles warmly at her. "Oh, what would I do without you?" he asks.

She grins back. "Probably find some other way to rescue Crystal yourself."

"I don't know if I could do it alone," he sighs.

"I'm sure you could," she assures him. "You're amazing. Besides, the only thing I'm doing is keeping you from going crazy with worry," she laughs.

"No, that's not true," Nathan insists, turning towards her and taking both of her hands in his. "You are amazing and very helpful. You found out about Crystal being in trouble in the first place, you helped confirm who's on whose side here, you and Auna helped me find Greg. I really don't know what I would do without you. ...I love you."

"I love you too," she whispers, leaning in and softly kissing him. After a few moments, their kiss grows more demanding. She kisses him harder, pushing her right hand up into his hair and teasing the soft strands between her fingers. She feels him slip his hand onto her waist before sliding it onto the small of her back, pulling her closer to him.

"Okay, seriously, Angela? What do you think you're doing? And Nathan- you should be focusing on saving Crystal!"

Angela pulls away from Nathan with a gasp, blushing. "Auna... you're back." The fairiye hovers in the air before the two of them, her tiny hands on her hips.

"Auna! I... um..." Nathan clears his throat, his face red for the first time that Angela had seen. "Uh... so, um, what news on Crystal? Is she okay?"

"Not really," Auna sighs, letting her arms hang at her sides.

Nathan jumps up, worry and panic flashing onto his face. "What? What do you mean? What are they doing to her?!"

Auna turns to Angela. *"You can tell him,"* she declares before feeding her the details of the encounter through their link.

Angela pales.

Nathan's frantic eyes dart between the two, anxious for an explanation. Angela draws a trembling breath and turns to face him. "I'm so sorry," she starts. He stares hard at her face, waiting with bated breath to hear the news. "Crystal's brother Hunter... he's using some form of mind control on her. He took away her memories and told her... well, he told her that she joined them willingly. She has no other memories, so she believes them. They have her, not only physically, but also... also mentally," she breathes, watching him carefully for his reaction.

His face is hard as stone. "Nathan..." she gently probes, unsure of what's going through his mind.

He doesn't reply. Walking over to where Greg had been sleeping for the past couple of hours and scooping him up, he grabs his backpack and heads to the door. "Whoa, wait!" Angela calls, scrambling to her feet. "Where are you going?"

"To talk to T," he shortly says, opening his bedroom door.

"What... why?" she asks, feeling lost and confused.

"He restored your memories," he explains as he leads the way down the stairs. "Maybe he can do the same for hers."

His grandma looks up from her book as they walk past the couch she's sitting on. "Nathan? What's going on?" She glances up at Auna.

"I'm going to go see if T can get me something to help rescue Crystal," he says as he opens the front door. "I'll be back soon. Tell mom and dad that Angela and I are practicing tennis or something."

"Don't worry, Beryl, I'll take care of him," Angela promises, pausing at the door.

She smiles kindly at her. "Thank you, dear. He needs someone like you."

"Thank you," she responds, touched.

"Now go," she laughs, waving her out the door. She quickly catches up to Nathan, who's waiting for her on the sidewalk.

"Lead the way," he says.

"*Hmm... wh- what? What's going on?*" Greg mutters sleepily as he yawns and stretches, poking his head out of the pocket of Nathan's sweatshirt. Nathan quickly fills him in as they walk. "*Are you sure this will work?*" the Familiar questions. "*It's not even close to what happened to Angela. It's not because of some herb, this is because of a Gift, possibly even two. It may not even be reversible,*" he warns.

"I know," Nathan acknowledges, walking faster. "But it's worth a shot. I will..."

"Save her. Yeah, we got it," Angela interrupts with a sigh.

Nathan stops and spins to face her. "Alright, what is it?" he asks. "What's wrong? Are you mad at me?" he questions, looking her seriously in the eye.

"No," she frowns. "I'm not... mad at you."

"Then what? What is it?" Angela shakes her head and continues walking. Nathan grabs her hand, stopping her. "Angela. Tell me what's wrong."

She lowers her gaze and lets out her breath in an annoyed huff. "It's just... you're obsessed! You go on and on about how you will save her, whatever the risks... and I... I just..."

"Just what?"

She shrugs and looks at him again. "I guess I... well, I get a little jealous."

He frowns, looking genuinely confused. "But... why? I love you!"

"Yeah, you keep saying that," she mutters, glaring at the ground sorrowfully.

"Hey. Angela." His hands cup her face, lifting her chin until their eyes meet. "I *do* love you. Crystal is my friend, and she's saved my life dozens of times. I can't just stand by and do nothing when she's in Patrick's clutches. Hey, look at me!" he pleads as she starts to turn away. "Don't you think for a *second* that I wouldn't do the same for you."

"Really?" she whispers, lifting her gaze reluctantly.

He smiles gently at her. "Of course."

She softly kisses him. "…Thank you." Then, throwing back her hair, she smiles at him. "Well then. Let's go see if T can help."

Nathan knocks on the door of the bus, then turns to Angela. "T seriously *lives* in the bus?"

"Well… it's not exactly a normal bus," she smiles. "It holds many secrets. I don't think even T knows them all. What I do know is that it can, like Auna, travel through the realms. There is also a magical door in the back that leads to a room that… changes."

"Changes?" Nathan questions.

"Yes… I'm not really sure how it works," she admits. "Just another one of his secrets, I suppose."

"Indeed, it is," T says, opening the door for them. "I have more secrets than you youngsters can ever imagine," he chuckles, waving them inside.

To Nathan, the inside of the bus looked completely ordinary- right down to the heart with *A+J 4ever* in it carved into the back of one of the seats. "Wait a second!" he exclaims, turning to T. "You drive a *magical* bus to school? With a bunch of *teenagers* on it?! Aren't you worried that someone would eventually find your 'magic door' and open it?"

The bus driver laughs. "Tell me, Nathan, even with your experience with magic on Zilferia, can you find the door?"

Nathan frowns. "What?"

"Go ahead," he says, waving towards the back of the bus. "Try and find it."

Nathan turns with an exasperated sigh. There's no door in sight. Walking along the aisle between the rows of seats, he peers at the walls, the floor, the ceiling, even under and between the seats. Finally, he turns and walks back to T and Angela. "There's no door," he declares.

T grins and winks at him. "Look again."

When Nathan turns around, he's shocked to find not only one door, but many different doors around the circumference of the bus. The seats have all vanished. One door, larger and more splendid than the rest, stands in the center, touching nothing but the floor. Although it was made of what appeared to be plain, black wood, the door seemed to call to Nathan. Angela comes up behind him, also seemingly drawn to the magical door.

"How..." Nathan lets his question hang unfinished as he reaches his hand out to the door. Rather than grasp the shining golden doorknob, he trails his fingers along the smooth wood as he slowly walks around it. Angela follows him, her eyes dazed as well. T watches them carefully as they return from behind the door. "How..." Nathan can't seem to complete his sentence, but his eyes convey his confusion as he stares at the mysterious bus driver.

"How else?" he smiles in response. "Magic."

"The door's magic, or yours?"

"Or the bus's?" Angela adds.

T's grin widens. "I always knew you two were smart for your age. Very perceptive. The door's magic is actually the main source of the bus's power, and I happen to have... a connection with the door."

"So... it's the magic of all three?" Angela questions.

"Something like that," he smiles, clapping his hands together. The doors promptly disappear. "Now then. To what do I owe the pleasure?"

Nathan snaps out of his stupor. "It... It's Crystal," he swallows.

T's face loses its former lightheartedness. "What has befallen the Princess?"

"Hunter kidnapped her," Angela gravely informs him, her gaze flicking over to Nathan. "He used his new mindreading and 'befriending animals' Gifts to control Crystal... he wiped her memories—"

"*Suppressed them,*" Auna corrects.

"*Suppressed* her memories," Angela corrects with a quick glare at the fairiye. "And replaced them. She thinks she willingly joined the Dragon Hunters." T's frown deepens and worry lines crease his forehead.

"We were hoping you had something that could help her," Nathan adds.

T doesn't respond at first, frowning and lost in thought. After a few minutes, he nods thoughtfully. "Gifts are tough to deal with... but I just might have the thing to help lift the fog in Crystal's mind."

The relief that floods Nathan's face causes a pang of envy to enter Angela's heart once more. "Really?! Oh, T, you're a life saver!!"

He chuckles. "Don't thank me just yet. Thank me once we know it will work- and that you will be able to get it to her."

"I can get it to her," Nathan pledges. "...So, what is it?"

He smiles. "I need to make it, first, as well as make sure I have all the ingredients."

"You make it sound like you're cooking," Nathan laughs.

"I am," he winks. "Now then, I'll just keep Auna here with me and send her with it when it's done. Alright?"

"Alright, that's fine," Angela says, waving for Nathan to follow her off the bus.

"Thanks again," he says to T as he passes him. "You don't know how much this means to me."

"Oh, I think I do," he murmurs, a far-away look in his eyes.

228

18

"Thaddeus!" The call thunders through the Village as the King storms up to his castle. *"Thaddeus!"* He calls again, ripping his door open with his right hand. His left he holds tightly to his chest as it throbs in pain. He resists the temptation to look down at it. The white-hot pain emanating from it tells him it's broken. He doesn't need his eyes to support the fact.

Thaddeus races down the stairs. "Alexander! You're alright!" He breathes a sigh of relief.

"Not exactly," he grunts, gesturing to his injured arm. "Hunter's blasted dragon broke my arm. I need you to fix it with magic."

"Of course," Thaddeus mutters, holding his hands over the arm, his eyes closed. Alexander takes deep breaths to keep from crying out as the pain intensifies, then fades away at last.

Panting, he nods to Thaddeus. "Thank you."

"Of course," he replies wearily. "While you were gone—" he begins before he's cut off by the king.

"Tell me in a moment," he sighs. "First, I must warn you- I have ordered that all those in the outskirts of the Village must be relocated in the center. We will make fortifications and prepare ourselves for the war that has been thrust upon us."

Thaddeus watches wide-eyed as the King lowers himself onto one of his plush couches. "What... where are we going to put them all?"

"In the houses reserved for contestants in the Games, in portable housing set up in the Square, in my own castle if needs be," he replies, his vacant eyes focused towards the flames dancing in the old stone fireplace. "The only room that will be off-limits is Crystal's room. I'm not giving up on getting her back," he grunts determinedly, turning his haunted gaze towards Thaddeus once more.

"Speaking of Crystal," Thaddeus begins, sitting across from the King, "I was finally able to contact Nathan."

"Oh? That's good. Is he coming to help us?"

"Yes... well, more to help Crystal."

"How does he mean to get into Patrick's blasted castle?"

"He knows some Dragon Hunters on First Earth who are pretending to be working for you. He learned of a portal Patrick means to place there to bring Bryce back to his castle."

"Bryce?" the King stirs uncomfortably. "That monster is coming back?"

"Not exactly," Thaddeus continues. "Nathan is going to prevent him from traveling through the portal—he's going to be the one transported directly into Patrick's castle instead. He's going to break Crystal out and return her to us."

Alexander shakes his head. "That foolish boy," he mutters, admiration in his voice. "How does he mean to succeed?"

"With the help of our spy."

"T?"

"Yes."

"Then perhaps he may yet prevail..." he murmurs, standing once more. "Let's go and discover what we can do to aid that poor boy," he declares.

<<<Crystal>>>

I look up hopefully as the door to my room is opened. "Hunter!" I cry, leaping to my feet. "You're back!" I feel relieved. I hate sitting here alone.

"Hey," he smiles back. His brown hair is knotted like he'd been through a massive windstorm.

"Are you okay?" I ask, concerned.

He runs a hand through his hair, straightening it. "Yeah, I'm fine. It's just... a little windy out there."

I nod. That makes sense. "What were you doing?"

He doesn't reply immediately. Walking to the chair beside my bed, he sinks into it. "Just walking along our borders. I had to make sure that we weren't being attacked by the dragons or Sohos."

"Sohos?"

"They are dragon sympathizers. They fight against us."

"So, you and Patrick are fighting against the dragons, Sohos, *and* our parents?" I gasp. "Isn't that hard?"

He smiles at me. "It's not that bad. We have a lot of people helping us, too. Plus it's not like they are all attacking us at once. They take turns."

"Oh, okay. Are we winning the war?"

He laughs. "Well we're pretty early into the war, so no one is really winning yet, but... yes. If things stay like they are now, then we will win for sure."

I grin. "Good. I don't like people getting hurt, and that's why we're trying to stop the dragons, right?"

"Right." He opens his mouth to say something else but is interrupted by a dull thump on the other side of the wall, followed by someone screaming.

"Hunter? What's going on over there?" I panic, racing over to the wall and putting my hands against it.

"Um... that's just another dragon sympathizer," he explains. "Patrick is asking him what his people's plans are."

"Is he a Soho?"

"Well... no. He's from the King's Village. His name is Chet. You can't talk to him—he'll tell you lies. Okay? You can only trust Patrick and me until we finish restoring your memories."

"Okay," I say, sitting back down on my bed. Something at the back of my mind tells me that if Patrick was simply asking him questions, he wouldn't be screaming like that.

The door to my room opens again and Patrick sticks his head in. "Hunter, I need to speak with you."

"Will he be back soon?" I ask anxiously, loath to let him go again.

"Of course. He'll be back with dinner in an hour. I just need him to help me plan what to do next in this war."

"Okay," I sigh. "Good luck."

<<<Hunter>>>

"What's wrong?" Hunter inquires as soon as the guard locks the door again.

"I know I said I wouldn't disturb you while you're talking to Crystal, but something has come up," Patrick explains, stalking down the hall towards his council room.

Hunter almost has to jog to keep up with his long strides. "And? What happened?"

"Dexter contacted me. He's coming tomorrow. You must have Crystal prepared by then."

"Oh," Hunter says, realizing what this means. He had only met Patrick's superior once, but it was enough to convince him that he never wanted to meet the man again. "How am I supposed to have Crystal totally ready by then?"

"Do whatever it takes. Have one of your dragons kill a prisoner while she watches. That should convince her that we're fighting for the correct thing. After that, treat her as an equal in our cause. She can have her own room, a new set of clothing, unlimited access to the castle. That shouldn't be a problem since most of our prisoners are in the other building now. She won't run into anyone who convinces her to let them go."

Hunter nods. "Sounds like a good plan. I'll get started immediately."

"No, not immediately," Patrick corrects as he stops at the door to the council room. "You are still a part of our council, and we need to decide our next course of action." With that, he pushes open the heavy wooden door. The stiff iron hinges complain at the movement. Those in the room turn at the sound. The eight of them had been leaning over a sturdy wood table conversing across a map of Zilferia that was spread across the surface of the table.

"Patrick." They all bow in unison. "Hunter." They bow again, and Hunter feels a flash of pride. These men were loyal to him. As well they should be—he was the Prince of the Dragon Hunters! Everyone answered to him or Patrick. Sure, he had to obey Patrick and his superior, Dexter, but he had more power than most, and more power than anyone his age in any of the realms. He had a gift to lead, and luckily he was in a position to utilize it. Alyssa, of course, was about his age, but despite her place in the council, he was still much more important than her to their group.

"Galwart, report," Patrick demands the nearest and oldest man of the group.

Galwart bows before responding. "Patrick. We were just discussing which of the groups we should attack next."

Hunter sighs impatiently. "The Dragons, obviously. They are the most powerful, and the Sohos draw their strength from them. By wiping out the dragons, the Sohos will be vulnerable. We'd be killing two birds with one stone, essentially."

Patrick nods. "Indeed. However, time is of the essence. We need to impress Dexter when he visits tomorrow evening. It is of the utmost importance."

"Well, it would probably be fastest to attack them at their stronghold," one of the men states. "However, since we don't know where that location is…"

"I do," Hunter interrupts. At the back of his mind, the huge Gold dragon whispers his warning to not return. He ignores it and turns to Patrick. "Crystal took me there. She was hoping to get the dragons to agree to fight with the Villagers."

"And she was successful, I presume," Patrick sighs. "Well, regardless, it won't matter after we blow them all sky high, now will it?"

<<<Thaddeus>>>

Thaddeus spins the circumference of his watch and waits expectantly. "Thaddeus?" Nathan's face appears, hovering over his wrist. "I haven't talked to T yet."

"No, that's quite alright. I actually contacted you to make some suggestions for how to proceed once you arrive."

"Oh. Well great, what is it?" he inquires impatiently.

"Patrick has, over the years, taken many things that would aid you if you could find them. Among them are Crystal's rewards from the Games- such as the Matter ring and lightning shoes. And, most recently, clothing made from Glaoud skin."

"What's Glaoud skin clothing?" he asks, confused. Thaddeus swiftly explains the purpose and origin of the skin. "So, it will make me invisible?"

"Practically, yes. But that's assuming that you can find and access his treasury where these items and more are sure to reside."

"Don't worry, it shouldn't be a problem," Nathan assures him. "I'll send Auna over to scope it out. And while I'm in there, I'll rescue Zelda and Y'vette as well. I'm not sure what state they'll be in after being there so long, but I'll see what I can do."

"Just don't get caught," Thaddeus cautions. "Don't try and achieve more than is safe to attempt. We still need you here. We don't need you in Patrick's clutches."

Nathan laughs harshly. "Of course not. Especially since I'm his new experiment." He sighs. "Although I'm sure you guys will want to study me as well."

"Only enough to discover how to reverse the damage," Thaddeus assures.

Nathan just shakes his head. "Whatever. I've got to go. Good luck with everything."

"You too," Thaddeus manages to get out before Nathan closes his watch, ending the conversation. Lowering his arm, he turns to face the King.

"Are you finished?" he asks, his fingers nervously wrapped around a sword tied to his belt. Thaddeus is surprised at the sight of it.

"I thought you said you were never going to touch that sword again."

Alexander frowns and looks down at the black hilt. "I have no choice. It is a worthy weapon, despite its history. I need it now more than ever, and cannot afford to continue shirking it. I shall forge a new legend to accompany the blasted thing. Evil cannot follow it around forever."

"...Right." Thaddeus shakes his head wearily and turns away. "Ready?"

"Yes. Pearl has called the council together. The only ones left are us."

"Shall we, then?" Thaddeus invites, waving his hand for Alexander to lead the way.

<<<Hunter>>>

Finally, Hunter thinks as the meeting ends, pushing open the door as he storms out of the room. "Hunter, don't forget to grab Crystal's dinner," Patrick calls after him.

"Yes sir," he replies, irritated. He heads to their lunch room and grabs Crystal's tray. One of his men carries his and follows him up to Crystal's room. The guard quickly opens the door.

"Hunter! You were gone for so long!" Crystal cries when she catches sight of him. "Is everything okay?"

"Yes, it's fine," he sighs, handing her the tray and lowering himself into the chair by her bed. He accepts his tray from the other man, then sends him away. The door closes softly behind him. "Now eat quickly. I want to show you something," he tells her.

"Really? What is it?"

"I just want to introduce you to one of my friends," he says, munching on a carrot. "He's really nice, you'll like him."

"Do I get to go outside?" she asks eagerly.

"Yes," he responds, unable to keep from smiling at her excitement at this. She bounces eagerly and quickly finishes off the food on her tray.

"I'm done! Can we go now?"

Hunter laughs and sets the remainder of his food aside. "Sure. Let's go." As he leads her out the door, he feels a pang of regret. She was so happy and excited to go outside. Maybe he should just wait to have a dragon kill one of his men until later. She was so innocent... he didn't want to destroy that fragility.

When he opens the door leading out of the castle, he turns and observes Crystal as she steps slowly onto the dirt with her bare feet. Her wide eyes gaze around at the pitiful surroundings. She points to the place that she had thrown a grenade not too long ago. "Were you guys attacked recently?"

"Yeah, something like that," he chuckles.

A soft breeze picks up. Crystal gasps as she feels the movement. She opens her arms as if embracing the weather and tilts her head up to the sky, keeping her eyes open despite the glaring sun. She then laughs. Hunter is stunned. He had never heard her laugh before... not even in his guise as Chet. The sound lifted his own heart and made him want to rejoice with her.

He shakes his head. No, he couldn't be allowed to get distracted. Patrick had given him direct orders to have her observe a dragon killing someone. Although he now regretted getting her attached to said person before so the experience would be more impactful. He didn't want to witness her loss of childlike joy.

But it had to be done.

"Princess Crystal!" One of his subjects, the bravest of them all, jogs up to them. He was not too much older than he and Crystal, but he had the heart of a lion. He had volunteered for this venture. Hunter admired his dedication.

Crystal lowers her arms and turns to Hunter. "Is this your friend?"

He forces a smile. "Yes, he is. He mentioned he wanted to meet you. Crystal, this is Kristich."

Kristich bows to her, his smile reaching his ears. "It's a pleasure to meet you, Princess," he says, taking her hand and slowly raising it to his mouth. Crystal giggles when he kisses her knuckles, his whiskers tickling her skin. "I was extremely gladdened to hear the news that you have switched sides in this war."

"I need to show my friends the truth," she simply replies, repeating what Hunter told her during their first session.

Kristich's smile widens. "You are admirable, my lady. Whatever you need, I am at your service."

"Why, thank you," she replies, beaming.

Hunter sighs and reaches out with his mind for the nearest dragon. It was a small purple one. *"Come to me and obey your directions."*

"Yes, master," it replies before lifting into the air. It doesn't take long for the beast to arrive.

"Dragon!" Kristich cries. He doesn't waver as he sees his oncoming fate. "Princess, you need to get out of here! Go with Hunter! I shall slay this beast and save you!"

Crystal gasps and weakly follows as Hunter tugs her away from the doomed man. The dragon descends, breathing a torrent of fire, which Kristich dodges. He dives under the dragon and slashes at its belly. The dragon roars, then spins and sinks its teeth into the poor man's chest.

"No!" Crystal cries, tugging at Hunter. "We have to save him! Hunter!"

Hunter just grimly shakes his head. "It's too late," he sighs. The dragon then turns to face them after dropping the body. It growls at them, its teeth red with Kristich's blood.

"Stay behind me," Hunter orders, shoving Crystal behind him as he draws his sword. She cowers as he takes a few steps forward, mocking the dragon. He dances around it, making it confused. Then he hollers and dashes forward, driving his sword into its brain. It convulses, cutting his leg as it does so. He hisses in pain and watches with satisfaction as it dies.

He turns to find Crystal in tears. Lowering his sword, he holds it by his side as he walks over to her. "Crystal? Crystal, what's wrong..." She turns from him before he reaches her and races into the castle, her face hidden in her hands. He groans tiredly and hands his sword to a Dragon Hunter waiting by the door. "Make sure I get this back in perfect condition," he orders before following his sister, his cloak billowing behind him as he strides through the hallways. He turns a corner and is surprised to find Crystal with her face buried in Patrick's chest. As her tears slowly soak his clothing, Patrick looks to Hunter for an explanation. "What happened?" he mouths.

Hunter just shrugs, then walks forward and places his hand on one of her quivering shoulders. "Crystal?" he gently asks as she flinches at his touch. "What's wrong?"

She suddenly swivels and faces him. Her face red from crying, she shouts, "What's wrong? *What's wrong?* I'll tell you what's wrong! Your friend is *dead*, that beautiful creature is *dead*, and you're a *murderer!* What's more, I don't feel safe here! I don't think I'm really safe *anywhere!*" She then races towards the Dragon Hunter who guards her room, tears the keys to her room from his belt, and takes off running down the corridor towards her room.

As the guard chases after her, Patrick turns to Hunter. "What *happened?*" he demands.

"I... I just did what you told me to do," he whispers. "She just... didn't take it very well."

He shakes his head tiredly and walks away, gesturing with his hand for Hunter to follow him. "Well, that was a disaster. We may have to move to more drastic measures to impress Dexter when he comes to visit."

"What do you mean?" Hunter inquires as he walks just behind him, holding back a wince as the scratch the dragon dealt him stretches, tearing further. *I must get this leg looked at as soon as possible*, he surmises.

"The dragons. You know where their stronghold is, and we *must* impress Dexter." Hunter nods. He had met the man only once before, but he knew that he didn't ever want to see him again. He was definitely one you didn't want to disappoint.

"I understand," Hunter begins slowly. "But do we even have time to do so? Dexter is coming tomorrow evening, correct?"

"Yes. That's why you will be taking as many men as we can spare, as well as all the Dragon Slayers. Have your dragon squad carry the machines so you can move faster. However, I do want to make sure you get back before Bryce arrives. We will need to inform and prepare him for Dexter's impending visit."

"Yes, sir. I won't fail you," Hunter pledges.

"I trust that you won't," Patrick responds, his eyes gleaming.

19

Angela groans with exhaustion as she hears her phone go off- *yet again.* She reaches over and answers the call without bothering to look and see who it is. There's only one person who would be calling her that early in the morning. "Nathan. You do realize you just called me five minutes ago, right?"

"Yes," he answers. "I just wanted to check and see if Auna was back yet."

"That's great," Angela yawns, sitting up in bed. She looks over at her clock and is disappointed to see that it was nearly two. "But like I said, you called me just *five minutes* ago. Nothing is going to happen in five minutes- especially not at a time that every other sane person is asleep. Just... get some rest. Okay?"

"You'll call me when Auna gets there with the cure for Crystal?"

"Of course."

"And..."

"Good*night,* Nathan," she interrupts, quickly hanging up. She holds the phone in her hand and waits for a moment, half expecting it to ring again. When the phone remains blissfully silent, she breathes a sigh of relief and sets it on her bedside table once more. Snuggling back up under her covers, she takes a deep, calming breath and closes her eyes.

It feels like mere moments after this that yet another noise rouses her. *"Angela! T was successful in the cure!"*

"That's great, Auna," Angela mutters into her pillow, not bothering to open her eyes. "Just put it by my phone. I'll get to it in the morning."

As the fairiye does so, she sighs with exasperation. *"Alright, then. You get your beauty sleep for your new boyfriend. Don't even worry about the welfare of the Princess! Don't thank T for working through the night by immediately getting it to an anxious Nathan or anything. You just take care of yourself."*

Angela opens her eyes and prepares a retort, but discovers that the fairiye is gone. She sighs and rolls onto her back, staring at her ceiling. After a few minutes, she closes her eyes and tries to sleep. Rest seems to escape her, however, so after an hour she groans and swings her legs out of bed. Standing, she shuffles over to her bathroom.

After switching on the light, she peers at her reflection in the mirror. Her bloodshot eyes had bags hanging beneath them and her face was pale. Sighing, she brushes her teeth and applies her makeup. It doesn't completely hide the bags, but it helps a little. After brushing her hair, she walks back into her bedroom and calls Nathan. He picks up on the second ring.

"You got it?"

"Yeah, I got it."

She can almost hear his grin on the other end. "Awesome! I'll meet you outside your window." He hangs up before she could say another word. Tucking the phone into her pocket, she finishes lacing on her tennis shoes.

It's only now that she inspects the 'cure' for Crystal. The amber liquid bubbles slightly in the clear glass syringe which contained it. The syringe was pretty large, about the width of two of her fingers, and it was mostly full. *I wonder if she has to ingest all of this,* Angela thinks to herself as she carefully slips the cure into her purse, which she then slings over her shoulder.

She's careful to make as little noise as possible as she slinks past her 'parent's' room and out the back door. She sits at one of the tables by the pool to wait for Nathan. Unsurprisingly, he arrives soon after she does. "Angela," he murmurs when he reaches her. "Where is it?" She looks at him despairingly and points to her purse.

"Before we talk, we need to get away from the house," she whispers to him. "Mom's a light sleeper."

He looks a little impatient at this, but nods and takes her hand. They walk into one of the last remaining groves of trees in Pargunma, stopping once their neighborhood is far enough away for them to be able to speak freely.

"Angela…" Nathan starts. She hands him the syringe before he even finishes asking for it.

"That's it," she says, watching as the faint glow from the liquid lights up his face in a golden glow.

"Wow," he murmurs, gently caressing it with his fingertips. "Does she need all of it?"

She shrugs. "I don't know. It would probably be best to give her as much as you can, though."

He nods. "Of course." He looks up. "Where's Auna?" he inquires.

"I don't know," Angela sighs. "Do you need to talk to her?"

"Well I wanted her to ask T some questions for me, if that's possible," he frowns, looking at her a little strangely.

"Alright. I'll call her," she says before reaching out with her mind. *"Auna?"*

"Oh, you're up," the fairiye quips irritatingly. *"Wonderful."*

"Shut up," Angela groans. *"Just come here. Nathan has some questions he wants you to ask T."*

"T's asleep, but he gave me some instructions for the cure," Auna responds as she appears between her and Nathan.

"Great," Nathan says, turning his attention to the fairiye. "What did he say?"

"He said that only half of the solution is required to restore Crystal's memories, but he doubled it in case something goes wrong and you need more for whatever reason. He also said that it could be given to her directly through a vein, or you could put it in her food or drink. Does that answer your questions, Nathan?"

"Yes. Thank you," he smiles, again returning his attention to the object in his hands. He takes a deep breath and looks up. "I guess it's time to put the final touches on our game plan, then. However," he adds, turning to Angela. "When this all goes down, I need you to stay here, out of harm's way."

<<<Bryce>>>

Bryce paces the floor in front of Zarafa, who remains deathly still on the couch. He shakes his head vigorously, his hands anxiously raking through his dark hair. "I can't do this. I really don't think I can do this." Zarafa doesn't respond. Her comments earlier in the day, as well as the day before, had done nothing to comfort him. It was up to him to console himself.

"I mean, there's only so far I can go," he mutters, gripping his hair so hard his knuckles turn white. "There's only so much I'll do for Patrick- and I'm pretty sure this plan crosses the line there is simply no way I'm letting your fangs near my neck," he shudders.

"Then what do you plan to do?" Zarafa sighs, weary of his endless pacing. "That is the last resort for us being able to convince Nathan you're on his side."

"But what if even that isn't enough?" he moans, spinning to face her. His face twitches like a mad man's. "What if *nothing* we do will convince the boy?"

"Then I could always bite him. Influence his mind with magic."

Bryce groans and shakes his head vigorously. "If Patrick found out…"

"Patrick *won't* find out," Zarafa assures, standing and putting her hands on his shoulders to hold him in place. "Look at me." He forces his eyes to meet hers. "I will *not* let Patrick find out. Even if he does, I promise that all the blame will fall on me. Okay?" As he starts to turn his head away, she jerks it back to face her own. "Okay?" she growls.

His face sags as though defeated. "Okay," he agrees. "I suppose it's the only way… as long as you can control your bloodlust."

She scoffs as she releases him. "What do you take me as? An amateur?" She laughs. "Please. I've had decades of practice. Trust me, I can handle the blood of one hardly significant boy."

<<<Nathan>>>

"Sounds like a pretty good plan to me," Beryl says after a few seconds of silence. Nathan nods and looks around the table at the others gathered there. Greg says nothing and neither does Auna, but when his gaze falls on Angela, she decides she has to speak up.

"Yes, it's great…"

"Except?" Nathan sighs.

"Except I have no part in it," she explains.

Nathan frowns. "That's because I'm not letting you into the line of fire for me."

"Maybe it's not all about you," Angela retorts, tears stinging her eyes.

"Maybe it's because I need to do this for myself, for the Queen, for the Princess, for the overall war, *and* for you. Either way, I want a part in this plan of yours. If you don't let me help, I'll just take things into my own hands," she threatens.

Nathan stares at her for a minute, trying to weigh the possibility that she would actually do such a thing. Finally, he shakes his head. "I can't let you put yourself in danger," he proclaims, standing. "And you won't follow up on your threat." He pauses at the smoldering look in Angela's eyes. "I'm doing this for your own good," he assures her, walking around the table and kneeling in front of her, holding her right hand in his own. He looks deep into her eyes. "Please believe me when I say that I'm doing this because I love you and can't bear to have you get that close to danger. I don't know what I would do without you, and I don't want to have to find out." Angela wipes away tears and nods, not trusting her voice. She didn't want to give away the plan that was already cooking in her brain. Nathan didn't have to know that she was going in, regardless of his pleading.

Nathan stands and steps away, a veiled pain in his eyes as his grandma leans across the table towards her. "Angela, I understand your concern better than you know… you are more than welcome to stay here with me when it all goes down." Angela frowns. That's guaranteed to put a kink in her plans, but Beryl's look was so insistent that Angela finally gave in and agreed.

"Now then," Beryl continues, turning to Nathan. "When do you expect to be back? It's not fair to leave your girlfriend here alone, you know."

"Oh, it shouldn't take long," he says, looking relieved that Angela wasn't still pushing to go. "Once I get Crystal back to her castle, I'll have Thaddeus put a portal back here. Angela should be safe enough in the Dragon's castle, right?"

"I'm sure," Angela quickly inputs before he could start to doubt the safety of Zilferia.

"*Now the only question is how we should get this started,*" Greg comments. "*Should we sneak up on the building and simply slip through the portal, or should we try and trick them again?*"

"*I say sneak up, unless they call and try to get Nathan to come over again,*" Auna decides. "*Which isn't very likely, but in the event that they do decide to try and deceive Nathan again, we should stall until at least three thirty so he could still be there when the portal opens. If we must fight to get through, then so be it.*"

<<<Bryce>>>

"How do you plan to get him here this time?" Bryce asks, his eyes darting over to the clock once more. "The portal opens in an hour. We need him here *now* if we're going to do anything."

"I know," Zarafa sighs. "That's why I'm going to have to resort to more drastic measures to get him here and get him here *now*."

"What are you going to do?" he questions.

Ignoring him, Zarafa picks up her phone and dials Nathan's cell number. It rings twice before he answers it. "Zarafa? What…"

"No time for pleasantries," she quickly interrupts. "If you don't come to my house *now* and give yourself up to me, I will kill Bryce."

"I don't care about him," comes the response. "Kill him if you wish; that's just one less Dragon Hunter that I'll have to deal with myself."

Zarafa's nostrils flare open and her eyes dilate like a cat's. "Fine. Then I'll kill Angela. One less girlfriend for you to *deal with*, as well as one less spy for me to dispose of later."

There's silence on the other end. Finally, his tight voice replies. "Zarafa, if you value your own pitiful existence, you will not touch a hair on her head. …I'm coming over now, not because you told me to, but because I decided the world would be much better off rid of you and Bryce. You might want to flee before it's too late," he threatens before hanging up.

Zarafa lowers the phone and looks to Bryce. "Change of plans. I don't have to bite you. Nathan's coming to kill us both. Obviously getting him to trust you is a waste of time. I'll just bite him and let the consequences fall as they may."

Bryce nods, his face still pale. "It sounds as though we have indeed arrived at our last option."

<<<Angela>>>

Nathan lowers the phone, shaking. Angela glances at Beryl, who nods her onward. Reaching out an unsteady hand, she gently touches him on the shoulder. She can feel him shaking in anger beneath her hand, his skin burning through his shirt.

"Nathan?" she gently probes. When at first there's no reaction from him, she opens her mouth to say something else.

Suddenly spinning around, he takes her face in his hands and kisses her. After a few seconds, he breaks away, breathing hard. "I'll never let them get you," he promises before whirling back around and striding out the door.

Angela just stares after him as Greg hurries out the door to join with Auna close behind. Beryl chuckles. "He's so like his grandpa was, it just warms my heart."

~

"Well," Beryl says, turning to Angela. "Are you going to chase after him or not?"

Angela stares at her in surprise. "What?"

"I told you I knew how you felt, didn't I? I know you won't let him go on this mission alone. Just be safe, alright?" she smiles sadly at the girl, patting her on the shoulder.

Angela grins back, tears of gratitude swimming in her eyes. She pulls the grandma into her arms. "Thank you," she whispers.

Beryl's eyes sparkle like they haven't in years as she smiles at Angela. "Go," she urges.

Angela doesn't need to be told twice. By the time Nathan's car reached the end of the street, she was on her way through the neighborhood, running like she had never run before.

<<<Nathan>>>

Nathan brings the car to a stop at the bottom of the hill and pulls out Crystal's cure, cradling it in his hands before tucking it away again. Taking a deep breath, he turns to face his companions. "Ready?" he asks.

"Um, not exactly... what's the plan?" Greg anxiously inquires.

Nathan shrugs. "We don't have time to make another plan. We'll just have to improvise." Greg squeaks unhappily, but doesn't say anything else. "Alrighty, then. Let's go," he declares, opening the door.

He stands and shivers against the brisk October air before starting up the hill. Soon, he was warm enough from the exercise that he had to remove his jacket. He drops it in the grass, figuring that it would only slow him down at this point. He slows as the huge house comes into view. Everything is still, both inside and outside of the house, but Nathan isn't fooled. He knows that Zarafa wouldn't actually run from him.

He turns to Auna. "You said you can see portals, right?"

"*Yes,*" she confirms.

"Good. Please alert me when you see it." He glances at his watch. They had about ten minutes until the portal was supposed to appear. "Until then, I guess I lure Zarafa into a trap and kill her. Bryce too, if I have time."

"*What trap?*" Greg asks, whiskers twitching nervously.

"The one I'm about to make," he replies, grinning and examining his surroundings. "Let's get started," he crows, rubbing his hands together.

<<<Angela>>>

Angela crouches behind a tree, panting. The vampire's house was in view. She had to be more cautious from this point. She couldn't risk getting caught. Too much was on the line. *We need weapons,* she decides. *They should have some in her house somewhere…*

Keeping low to the ground, Angela smoothly races towards the building, taking cover behind anything she can along the way. She reaches the back corner just as Nathan stalks past, his eyes intent on the woods. Greg and Auna follow him. Angela stiffens as the fairiye pauses and instantly throws up mental shields around her mind to mask her presence from Auna. Angela breathes a sigh of relief when she continues on with Nathan. Once the trio is out of sight, she continues around the house. She soon discovers what she had been searching for- an unsecured window.

Cautiously sliding open the blacked-out window, she peers inside. She only sees a couple of tables and some official-looking papers. After slipping through the window, she closes it and waits for her eyes to adjust to the dark, dusky atmosphere. That's when she notices the black lockbox in the corner.

After glancing around once more, she scuttles over to it. Crouching, she explores the midnight-black box with her fingertips. The cold sting of the gleaming silver lock contrasts the soft, velvety darkness of the rest of the container. Lifting it, she's surprised to find that although it was about the length of her arm, it was quite light.

At this point, her curiosity was overwhelming. Banging on the small lock, she's frustrated when it doesn't break. Her bobby pins won't work on it, either. *It must be enforced with magic,* she realizes.

She's ready to leave the strange box behind, but something stays her hand. Finally, she resigns with a sigh. *Whatever's in here sure better be worth it,* she groans. Condemned to keep the mysterious object, she searches for a way to transport it with her.

A black strap lying where the box had previously been catches her eye. It's made of the same dark material the box was fashioned from, she realizes when she picks it up. She grins with relief and attaches it on either end of the case before lying it on her back. The strap cuts diagonally across her front, going from her right shoulder to her left hip, holding the box in place on her back while still granting Angela free range with her arms.

Satisfied, she rises to her feet once more before heading to the door. After unlocking it from the inside, she cautiously slips her head into the hallway, darting it back and forth, eyes alert for any sign of movement. When there is none, she creeps out into the hallway, the plush carpet absorbing all sound.

Stepping carefully, she makes her way down the hallway until she reaches the next door. She holds her breath nervously as she eases the door open. Hopefully she could find a weapon before she chanced upon Zarafa or Bryce, and also before Nathan discovers her and sends her home.

<<<Nathan>>>

Nathan fidgets as the time gradually ticks by. "Where the heck are they?" he murmurs, disquieted. "There's no way they actually left... unless they got the portal open earlier!" he gasps as the possibility of just such a thing suddenly presses itself upon him. He leaps to his feet and turns to Auna, who pulls herself out of her hiding spot to face him.

"I'll go and see if that is indeed the case," she offers before vanishing. Nathan fidgets in her absence, already feeling loss. What if their chance had already slipped through his fingers? What if *Crystal's* chance had been lost- all because he lost his temper for a while? Sorrow threatens to swallow him up in its gaping maw, and he struggles to not get sucked in.

It feels like an eternity yet also like no time at all had passed by the time Auna returns. *"The portal has not yet come. I cannot sense the residue of one having been used recently,"* she promptly informs him.

Nathan nearly crashes to the ground in relief. "Good, then we can still make it." He inspects his watch once more. "Two minutes left... I guess killing Zarafa will have to wait for another time," he remarks with a light chuckle, tucking a very relieved Greg into his shirt pocket.

"Let's go-" A scream ripples through the air, immediately chilling him to the bone and freezing the words in his mouth. *"Angela!"* he cries, tripping over his feet as he races towards the cry.

Soon, another sound follows the first. "Oh Na-than!" the sing-songing voice of the vampire taunts. "I have your pretty little thief of a girlfriend... come here and kill me if you dare!"

Nathan slows just before he emerges from the trees, berating himself. He had to be smart about this. Odds were, this was a trap, and Bryce was hiding nearby, ready to grab him when he rushed Zarafa. Peering into the clearing, he checks to make sure Angela isn't in immediate danger. Zarafa's just standing next to her as she kneels in the grass, her hands resting on the ground beside her knees. An odd box lay on her back and she seemed to be unable to rise. Knowing that Zarafa had access to magic, Nathan figures that her inability to move was due to a spell. *Wait... that box looks... familiar...* scolding himself, he shakes the thought from his head. Now was the *worst* time to be thinking about that.

Turning, Nathan follows the tree line. *"Bryce is to your immediate right,"* Auna informs him, buzzing anxiously by his right shoulder. He nods and circles around the unsuspecting Bryce. Leaping forward, he grabs him from behind, pinning his arms behind his back. He yelps in surprise, but is unable to wrestle free.

Muscles burning from the effort of holding the larger man in place, Nathan leans forward to murmur into Bryce's ear. "Walk forward, slowly. Don't try to get away or I'll just kill you."

Bryce stumbles forward with clumsy footsteps, forcing his body through the undergrowth he had been cowering behind. Nathan presses him onward until they emerge from the cover of the trees.

"Why, Nathan, aren't you just *full* of surprises." Zarafa hisses, her eyes dilating and her teeth sharpening in her anger. Yanking Angela to her feet, she holds the girl in front of her as a shield, mimicking Nathan. "Looks like we've arrived at a stalemate," she snarls.

"Not quite," Nathan shoots back, his mind racing to think of the best way out of their situation.

"No, I do suppose you're right," Zarafa admits, calming herself down. "After all, this girl means much more to you than Bryce does to me," she points out with a feral grin.

"True, but you would never risk angering Patrick... to you, his wrath is much worse than mine. If I were to kill Bryce, Patrick would punish you in horrendous ways, am I right?" Her pale face is the only reply he needs. "That's what I thought. Now, hand over Angela." Zarafa's face contorts with pain and conflict. Finally, her hands spring open, releasing her captive. Angela immediately scrambles over to Nathan's side, quivering.

"Now let Bryce go," she snarls, her eyes flicking over to the side. "And give back what you stole."

"The portal is here," Auna announces to him and Angela.

Nathan starts edging towards the portal, keeping his hold on Bryce. Zarafa's eyes begin to smolder. "Give him back *now*," she demands.

"Auna, how close am I to the portal?"

"Take two more steps to your left and you will pass through it," she replies.

"Very well, I will release him," Nathan declares out loud. He turns his head to Angela. "Are you planning on coming through the portal with me?" he whispers.

"Yes," she murmurs, hesitance in her voice. Nathan frowns. She shouldn't be so afraid to tell him so. He was just trying to keep her safe! He gives a terse nod, accepting Angela's plan. Neither realm was safe for her anymore, and he would rather have her by his side anyway.

In a sudden movement, he shoves Bryce into Zarafa, sending them both tumbling to the ground. "Go, go, go!" he shouts, pushing Angela towards the portal. She vanishes into it, as does Auna when she follows just behind her. Nathan has only taken a step towards it when a burning hot blade slips through his calf. He turns to see Bryce's vengeful eyes looking up at him. They're the last thing he sees as he plummets backward into the portal.

<<<Angela>>>

Angela gasps when she emerges from the portal, her head swimming. She still wasn't used to the thrill ride of traveling between the realms. Shaking herself to try and banish the leftover feeling from the ride, she turns back to the portal. She's just about to panic that Nathan missed the portal when he tumbles through. It closes behind him. He collapses to the ground, his head heavily whacking the stone floor.

"Nathan!" she cries, kneeling beside his head. "Auna, what happened?"

The fairiye shrugs her tiny shoulders helplessly. *"I went through the portal before I noticed anything was amiss. I'm sorry, I don't know what transpired to cause Nathan to collapse like that."*

Greg slips out of Nathan's shirt and scuttles around to his right leg. *"Bryce stabbed him just before he got to the portal... he's bleeding pretty badly,"* he remarks, his tail knotted in worry.

"Okay... okay, so we just need to bandage it up... stop the bleeding," Angela begins, scrambling to find something to tie over the wound. There's a burned, abandoned Dragon Hunter cloak lying nearby, which she folds and ties as tightly as she can on Nathan's cut. Then, unsure of what to do, she sits and pulls his head into her lap.

"Please... please wake up," she murmurs, stroking his face. "We don't have long before we're likely to be discovered... and I don't know what to do," she finishes, a tear slipping out of her right eye.

Nathan then stirs. "Angela..." She feels his body stiffen in pain as his nerves scream at him once more, reminding him of his cut. He pants from the effort, but is able to force himself to his feet. He sways unsteadily, then leans a little on Angela when she lends him her support. He turns to Auna, gasping. "Auna, you said you found where Patrick kept his weapons and spoils of war... please lead us to it."

Auna hesitates. *"Wouldn't it be wiser for you to administer the cure to Crystal while Angela grabs the weapons? We don't have much time... each second is precious,"* she presses.

Cursing his foggy brain, Nathan agrees. "Alright, fine. But please hurry, Angela," he says, looking her in the eyes. She peers back into his pleading eyes, glistening with tears, and nods.

"You can count on me," she assures him before slipping away.

<<<Nathan>>>

Following the path Auna had outlined in his mind, Nathan pushes against the wall for support. Each of his uncertain steps threaten to cast him down, but he presses on. *For Crystal... for Crystal*, he repeatedly chants in his mind. The words give him the strength to keep moving, although his leg howls in horror at the pain it had endured and yet still was forced to suffer through.

At the last turn before he reached Crystal, he turns to Greg. *"Alright, your turn. Show me what you can do."* The rat quivers when he's set down on the floor, then takes off like a bullet, streaming around the corner. The guard in front of Crystal's room screams, and the sound reverberates off the stones around them. *The clock truly is ticking now,* Nathan grimly realizes as he steps toward the flailing woman.

Her back was turned to him, thanks to her single-minded focus on Greg, so it's easy for Nathan to reach out and tug her sword from its sheath. She spins at the sound, but Nathan instinctively runs the cold steel through her gut as she lunges at him. He winces and drops the sword immediately. Who had he become?

Shaking off such reflections until a later time, he stoops and removes the key to the room from her belt. Standing and leaning against the wall, he slips the key into the lock, twisting it until he hears a clear *click.* Pushing the door open, he steps into the room, eager for his first look at Crystal in months.

Naturally, he's caught off-guard when he's tackled to the floor.

"Who are you?" Crystal demands from the perch on his back. "What did you do to my guard?"

Nathan grunts as she shifts her weight, crushing his lungs. "I'm... Nathan... your... friend," he gasps out.

She hesitates, then rolls off him. "I don't remember you," she simply states, watching him with wide, curious eyes as he sits up.

"That's okay," he pants. "I can help you remember everything," he adds as he pulls out the syringe, which had miraculously survived.

Crystal eyes it suspiciously. "How do I know you're not lying? What if you're trying to kill me?"

Nathan's eyes fill with tears as he observes her. Her childlike behavior wasn't the only thing changed about her, she was almost a completely different person. His heart aches inside of him, as though it's trying to reach out and find Crystal itself. "Because," he finally says, "I sent Auna, the fairiye, to find you. Do you remember that?"

"Yes, Nathan sent her..." she murmurs, her eyes narrowed thoughtfully at him.

"And do you trust Auna?" he presses.

"Yes," she replies. "She gives off a good feeling, like I can believe her," she states.

"And I don't?"

She runs her eyes over him, then shrugs. At this, Nathan feels like wailing and gnashing his teeth in horror, loss, and sorrow. He struggles to swallow these feelings. "Well... if you trust Auna, you can trust me. You need to take this medicine," he assures her, holding the syringe out to her. "I can help you with it," he offers when she hesitates.

Biting her lower lip, she nods and holds her left arm out for him. He takes the soft, pale arm of his lost friend and lays it in his lap as he prepares the needle. Concentrating, he slips it into the main vein, then squeezes half of the golden liquid in before retracting the syringe. He returns the container to his pocket, then watches Crystal's face intently, waiting for the change.

After a few seconds, she shrugs. "I guess your cure thingy didn't work."

Her nonchalant words strike his heart, and he hurt like he never had before. He was now devoid of hope, and *she* was devoid of hope- only she didn't even know it. He had lost his best friend, yet she was sitting right in front of him. *What am I supposed to do now?!* He screams inside his mind, feeling the energy drain from his bones. ...*What am I supposed to do?*

20

The boy, Nathan, kneels in front of me, just staring at my face. His eyes swirl with unexplained sorrow. On impulse, I reach out and take his hand. He gazes hopefully into my eyes. "Listen," I begin. "I'm sorry your elixir stuff didn't work..." The boy shakes his head and stands, turning away from me.

"No," he says, breathing heavily and raking his hands through his hair in frustration. I stand and watch him curiously. "No, this isn't right... *why didn't it work?!*" he cries, spinning around and rushing up to me. Taking my face in his hands, he presses his forehead to mine. Anxiety causes him to be stiff and intent. "Please... please remember," he begs.

Something about the look in his eyes causes something to click in my brain. A burning sensation instantly spreads from the area he had slipped the needle into. Gasping, I stumble back, pulling away from him as my veins throb. The golden liquid flows around my body, then seems to gather in my brain.

I collapse to the ground, unable to control my body. Behind my closed eyes, memories once blocked parade by at a blinding pace. My eyes fly open once I reach the end, and I sit upright with a gasp. Nathan is kneeling beside me, looking panicked.

"Nathan!" I cry, pulling him into an embrace. I feel as though I've just woken from a dream. A long, terrifying dream.

"Crystal," he sighs, relief seeping out of him. "I thought I'd lost you," he mumbles into my neck. I shiver at the feeling.

"You won't be getting rid of me that easily," I tease, pulling away and smiling at him.

"So, your memories are back, then?" he confirms, running his eyes over me as if checking for damage.

"Yes, I remember everything," I smile. "And once we're out of here, I'll tell you all about it."

He smiles back. "I'm sure we both have noteworthy tales." He pauses as a girl with something strapped to her back appears at the doorway. "In fact, I need to introduce you to someone. Crystal, this is Angela. Angela, Crystal."

"It's a pleasure to finally meet you in person," Angela says, her eyes flicking over to me for only a second. "But I'm afraid we don't have time to exchange pleasantries at the moment." She drops a duffle bag at Nathan's feet. "I grabbed the things you mentioned specifically, as well as a few others. Matter Ring, Glaoud skin clothes, Lightning shoes, etc. However, as I was leaving, someone saw me. He ran before I could stop him…"

"Patrick's on his way," I finish for her, dread seeping into my bones once more.

Nathan gives a sharp nod. By the look on his face, I can tell his mind is buzzing as it races to piece together a plan. "Alright," he declares, stooping to open the bag. "Let's suit up." He hands me the Glaoud skin outfit. "This lets you disappear, right?"

"Pretty much," I confirm, slipping it on over my other clothes.

"Angela, I want you to take the Matter Ring," Nathan says, slipping it onto one of her fingers. I watch them carefully, noting that there seemed to be more than just friendship between them. I feel a pang in my heart, then banish it, scoffing at myself. Why should I be jealous? Nathan's free to have a girlfriend.

Then I realize I have *every* right to be jealous. Angela was gorgeous, obviously fit and sporty, and close to Nathan. She's probably close to a lot of people, whereas I'm not even close with my own family- *either* one. I had few friends as well. Angela seemed like the perfect girl. I already resent her.

The sound of pounding feet interrupts Nathan as he slips on a pair of Lightning Shoes. Dropping the laces of the remaining shoe, he quickly spins towards me. "Stand by the wall and put your hood up. Don't move- don't let them see you." To Angela, he says, "They can't grab you while you're wearing that ring- unless they have one of their own." Pulling a sword out of the bag, he turns back to us. The long, slim sword gleams in his tight fist as it tilts, catching the light. It seemed to be made of white gold. The hilt was studded with a big blue jewel and seemed to fit perfectly in his hand.

"I'll fight them off," he finishes. I gape at him in surprise, but Angela speaks up before I can.

"You're going to fight off an unknown number of *trained soldiers* by your-self? And on your injured leg, no less!" she cries, gesturing to his right leg. It's only then that I notice the injury. His leg was bleeding heavily, although part of a Dragon Hunter's cloak helped to staunch the flow.

"What happened?!" I gasp.

"I'll tell you later," he grunts as the Dragon Hunters nearly reach us. "But I'm fine," he finishes as the first of the Hunters reaches the door. He looks in and pales when he doesn't see me there, thanks to the Glaoud skin.

"Patrick's gonna kill me," he groans.

Another man appears beside him. "Not if you capture Nathan! The girl, though, we can kill," he sneers, stepping into the room and facing Nathan. It takes everything I have to hold still.

"Angela, get behind me," Nathan growls. She reluctantly gets out of the way. Behind the man, three other Dragon Hunters arrive. They stop and watch.

"Put down the sword, boy," the man directs. "Unless you want to lose some fingers, that is," he snickers.

In a single, fluid motion, Nathan flings the sword forward, his arm straightening until the sword plunges into the man's gut. He falls to the floor, a ghastly gargling sound erupting from his throat as blood begins spilling from his mouth. Nathan pulls the sword free and glares at the other men.

"Attempt to kill or harm my friend here or myself, and I *will* kill you. However, if you wish to join us and take refuge from Patrick's wrath, you are welcome to flee with us- provided you give up your weapons."

One of the soldiers turns to whisper to his companion. Carefully leaning forward, I manage to catch his words. "We only have to preoccupy him until Patrick and Hunter return. If we can keep him here, we might be rewarded... or at least escape punishment for losing the Princess." The other man nods, then takes a deep breath and steps into the room towards Nathan.

"Boy, you could kill us all, but it would never solve your problems. You will still be Giftless, still be hunted by Patrick, and Crystal will still be ours.

Regardless, the more strife you cause us, the more he will cause *you*. Your loved ones..." He doesn't get to continue his sentence. With one angry surge, Nathan removes his head from his shoulders. Angela screams and moves away from the blood that follows, although it passes through her regardless, thanks to the Matter Ring.

As Nathan stands, panting with fury, his sword slowly dripping blood onto the floor, I remain still. Shock freezes my bones. What had I just heard? Nathan... Giftless? I watch him as he stares down the rest of the Dragon Hunters, snarling like a wild animal. How had I not noticed before? Something had drastically changed him... and now I knew what it was.

"I don't have time for this," Nathan growls at the three remaining soldiers before leaping forward and cutting them down. Two are killed before they could react, but the third is quicker on his feet. Pulling a knife out of his sleeve, he severs the muscle in Nathan's sword arm.

With an outraged shout, he shoves the man into the wall so hard he cracks his skull. Blood shows in his teeth as he smiles, panting his final breaths. "No matter," he chuckles wetly. "It's too late for you now. Patrick will return in a minute... plus that knife was laced with poison only we can cure!" With another gasping chuckle, the man finally dies.

Nathan falls to his knees.

"Nathan!" I cry, tearing off the hood and leaping forward. Angela follows a second behind.

Nathan remains on his knees, his face pale as he covers his wound with his other hand. "I'm fine," he whispers, his face constricted in pain.

"We *have* to find that cure before Patrick gets here!" Angela gasps, throwing me a pleading look. Irritation flashes through me at the implication that I would ever leave him.

"I'll—"

"No." The faint word startles Angela and I, and we both turn to Nathan.

"What?"

"I said no," he repeats, staring deep into my eyes. "I came here to rescue you, and nothing—not Hunter, not Patrick, and certainly no poison—is going to stop me from finishing that mission."

"Nathan..."

"*No,*" he growls, taking my shoulders in a surprisingly firm grip. "Just this once, listen to me. Just please... take care of yourself for me."

I take in his face through vision blurred by tears. "But who's going to take care of *you*?" I whisper.

"I am," Angela declares protectively.

"No," Nathan stubbornly repeats. "You have to... go with... her," he gasps, clenching his arm tightly.

"No! I'm not leaving you!"

Nathan struggles to his feet and takes her face gently in his hands. "If you love me... you will do this for me."

Angela's face hardens as she stares at him, her jaw clenched tightly. After a few seconds, a tear slips from her left eye and slides down her cheek. She gives a sharp, decisive nod, then turns to me. "Let's go."

"What?!" I cry in surprise. "How could you leave him? He'll die..."

"He'll die if he doesn't get the cure. We just have to chance that Patrick wants him to stay alive. I'm not abandoning him, I'm giving him his best chance," she explains, her voice cracking from strain. "We'll come back for him."

I hesitate, then nod reluctantly. "Fine." I turn back to Nathan and am dismayed to find him shaking and pale. Sweat drips from his face and his eyes are unfocused. I cradle his head in my hands, then lay my forehead on his. "We'll be back for you," I promise in a hushed voice.

He blinks but doesn't otherwise respond. Taking a shaky breath, I stand and turn back to Angela. "Fine. Let's go."

<<<Hunter>>>

Hunter fidgets as he sits on Vincent's hard, scaly back as he flies after Patrick on the return trip from the mountains. From what Patrick had told him about Dexter, he would probably arrive at the castle soon. They were speeding back in a race against time. Hunter curses the fact that Patrick even made him come out in the first place. Their armies had been able to transfer the Dragon Slayer machines without him before, and he's angry that Patrick had not only made *him* go out, but he himself had gone as well! Really, both of them should have stayed.

His desperation to please Dexter must be blinding him, Hunter realizes, shaking his head in exasperation at his foolishness. *He's going to get us both punished sooner or later,* he sighs, closing his eyes and trying to relax. The dragon's hard scales chafe against the insides of his legs as they hit another gust of turbulence and Hunter grimaces, opening his eyes again. He would probably have someone make a saddle for the beast soon. It was getting a little past the point of discomfort to fly bareback. He was worried the flesh on his legs would be scraped clean off should he need to grip on even tighter with his legs. While riding a dragon into battle would be an asset to them, neither he nor his men had yet to attempt it. Riding was painful if you had to stay on for too long, and the extra padding in their pants wasn't enough most times.

He would also need to find a way to keep them warm. At the rate the wind tore past them when they flew—especially when they were pressed for speed—it quickly stole the warmth from their faces and hands.

Hunter's musings are put aside as he notices the half-dead trees that mark the edge of their territory. *Finally! We still need time to prep Bryce for Dexter's arrival. Hopefully we'll have time to get everything ready before he arrives... although Bryce has probably been waiting for a while for us.* He shrugs to himself as he directs Vincent into a dive toward the ground. *Oh well. Bryce could use some chilling out anyway. He always likes to take charge, even when it's not appropriate for him to do so. I think he needs to learn his place. Patrick doesn't care that he speaks out of turn because of his ideas... which isn't fair. No matter what my idea is, I get scolded if I don't present it in just the right way at the proper time!*

These thoughts put Hunter into even more of a sour mood by the time they touch down outside of the castle. Sliding down Vincent's lowered neck, his feet finally touch the long-awaited firm ground. He pauses, then turns to Patrick, who is stiffly clambering from his dragon.

"Patrick..." he begins.

"Later," he immediately replies, turning to enter the castle. "I am weary from the flight, and we have work to do. Now is not the time to burden me with your complaints."

"Patrick, something is wrong," Hunter insists. "Where is everyone?"

Patrick frowns as he also notices the lack of Dragon Hunters. "The few men that I left behind should be welcoming us back," he comments, tugging his sword from its sheath before turning to Hunter. "Lead the way. I've got your back."

Hunter nods, unsheathing his own sword and stalking quietly up to the door. He eases it open and peaks inside before opening it wider and slipping through with Patrick right behind him. They then jog quietly to Crystal's room, for Hunter's instincts tell him that this has everything to do with her. He freezes when he rounds the corner and finds her guard run through just outside the door. A pool of blood stretches out around her- far too large to be composed of hers alone.

Hunter breaks into a sprint and tears into the room. He nearly trips over the five corpses slumped by the doorway. Gagging at the strong metallic smell from the blood, he quickly scans the room. Sure enough, there was no trace of Crystal. With a groan, he steps back out into the hallway to report to Patrick.

"She's gone."

Patrick's face is like a stone, but Hunter knows that underneath, he is devastated beyond words. "We have to find her. *Now,*" he orders. Hunter nods and begins jogging down the hall, although he knows it's pointless to look. If Crystal was gone, it was because she was taken, and there was no way whoever had torn her away from them had stuck around with her.

He pauses outside of a room with the door cracked open. He knew for a fact that this door was always closed. Taking a deep breath and steadying his sword hand, Hunter eases the door open softly. He finds Nathan Anderson lying there, a pool of sickly blood slowly growing around his arm. He seemed to have just recently passed out from the wound after crawling there, Hunter figures. He groans and wipes at his face with his free hand. This boy was growing seriously tiresome. He would just leave him there to die, but he knew that Patrick wouldn't be pleased if he did.

Sighing, he kneels beside the boy. *Well, let's just see what we can do about that arm. Then hopefully Patrick will let me execute this daft, irksome Dragon Lover.*

<<<Crystal>>>

Angela crouches beside me in the undergrowth near Patrick's hideout as he and Hunter land. We watch breathlessly as they hurry into the building. I turn to Angela once they disappear inside. "Okay, let's go."

"What if they don't find Nathan in time?" she worries, her hands clenched anxiously on the handles of the duffle bag.

"They will," I assure her, although I'm not so sure myself.

"What if they don't want to heal him, though?" She adds, turning and meeting my eyes. "What do we do then?"

I hesitate. "We can't do anything but trust Nathan," I finally sigh, standing. She reluctantly follows as I turn towards the Village. We reach it without incident, although Angela tripped once and spilled the contents of the bag onto the forest floor. After we quickly picked everything up, I carried the bag.

I turn to Angela just before we enter the Village. "Angela, what's with the box?" I ask, referring to the long container strapped to her back. I had been wondering this since I first saw her, and I wanted to ask before we got swept up in whatever craziness happens next.

She pauses. "Honestly? I have no clue. I found it and I just have a feeling that whatever's in it can help us." I slowly nod, accepting this for now, then step into the Village. After a minute, I turn back to Angela. "Where is everyone?"

She frowns heavily. "I have no idea." The outer part of the Village was completely deserted. Doors to houses hung open, and the insides seemed to be ransacked. "Let's keep moving," Angela whispers before cautiously continuing deeper into the Village.

As we pass through the area where contestants had slept during the Games, there's movement behind us. I freeze and look to Angela. She nods, confirming that she had also heard the sound. I carefully set the duffle bag down and turn around with Angela. We wait for a few tense moments before our eyes catch movement as someone steps around the corner.

"Evomt nod!" Angela cries, throwing out her hand in the direction of the stranger. The man freezes, and I laugh when I recognize who it is.

"Angela, let him go. It's Thaddeus!"

She blushes. "Oops. Cigameh tesa eler," she says as she lowers her hand. "Sorry about that, Thaddeus," she apologizes as he retrieves his staff. It's with sadness that I realize he uses it more than he used to. He really was getting older.

He chuckles and waves it off. "Don't worry about it, my dear. It's my fault for sneaking up on you." His eyes fall on me, and they fill with tears. "Crystal," is all he says before opening his arms. Without hesitation, I rush into them, hot tears already coming from my eyes.

"Thaddeus," I cry. He puts a hand on the back of my head comfortingly.

"It's alright. You're alright now." He looks over my head at Angela. "... Where's Nathan?" At the mention of his name, I truly break down.

"Oh, Thaddeus! He was poisoned by a Dragon Hunter and he said that only Patrick has the cure so we had to leave him although we really didn't want to and we're both just so worried that he's not going to make it because Patrick might not even want to cure him of the poison and…" I can't manage to explain any more as my heart breaks for my hero.

Thaddeus just holds me as I cry and doesn't say anything for a moment. When he does speak, it has nothing to do with Nathan. "Let's get you two to the castle." I retrieve the duffle bag, my tears having ceased their race down my face. As Thaddeus hustles us towards the looming building, Angela questions him.

"Thaddeus… what's going on? When we were walking through the outskirts of the Village, it was abandoned."

He sighs wearily. "Alexander has gathered everyone into the center of the Village- some are even living in the castle itself. He is going to begin training an army in the morning." The setting sun illuminates the weariness written in every line on his face as he speaks. "We don't have enough soldiers to fight off the Dragon Hunter's constant attacks. Alexander is recruiting younger and older men to help fight, and should a woman volunteer, he's even ready to accept their service as well. He's preparing to launch an attack on Patrick, and I fear that even Crystal's return won't dissuade him from continuing his plans. He's been pushed past the brink with the last attack on you, Princess," he adds, looking down at me with his sad, grey eyes.

"Should I invite the Sohos to join us in the Village? It would strengthen our numbers and maybe make dad feel less… anxious," I suggest. "Plus I think they are running low on numbers too. If we combine forces, it would help us both." Thaddeus looks thoughtful.

"I don't know who these Sohos are," Angela joins in, "but if they are willing to fight with us, I say that we do as Crystal suggests. It could only help, right?"

Thaddeus laughs and nods. "Indeed. You may summon them whenever you wish," he adds to me, "but first thing's first; your parents are very anxious to see you." We had finally reached the Dragons' castle. Thaddeus knocks—three, eight, one. At the sound of the last knock, the door is hurriedly pulled open.

"Thaddeus, you…" the man, one from the Village Council, I realize, pauses when he sees me. "Ah, Princess. Your parents will want to know of your safety. Shall I fetch them?"

"Yes, please do," Thaddeus accepts. As the man hurries away, Thaddeus collapses onto one of the couches in the room. Angela and I sit down across from him. I notice that she keeps the box strapped to her back, although it can't be comfortable. "So, Angela," Thaddeus begins, leaning forward with his elbows resting on his knees. "I'm most curious of everything that transpired on First Earth. Nathan didn't tell me everything, and he wasn't willing to share how he lost his Gifts regardless."

She winces at this. "Well, it was kind of my fault," she confesses. My breath catches at this and my eyes pin her down. *What did she do?!*

He looks at her in concern, his grey eyebrows low over his brooding eyes. "How is this any fault of yours?"

Angela lowers her eyes. Before she has the chance to respond, Pearl and Alexander hurry into the room. "Crystal!" Pearl cries, rushing forward, arms wide open. I stand and am pulled into a tight embrace. "Oh, my baby girl!" she cries as she holds me close. Before she can release me, Alexander's crushing arms wrap around us both. He doesn't say anything, but I feel a great tear land on my shoulder near my neck.

"Whoa, hey, guys, I'm fine," I gasp out, my lungs getting crushed. "I promise," I continue when the crushing arms don't release me. Then they finally spring open, releasing me. Pearl cups my face with one soft hand and gazes into my eyes as if trying to memorize every last detail.

Alexander's face just looks drawn and tired, but deep sadness sparkles in his stormy eyes. "I'm sorry, Crystal. I'm so, so sorry…"

"It's not your fault," I sigh. "You had no idea about Hunter…"

"No, but I should have," he growls, sinking into the seat beside Thaddeus.

"That's ridiculous," I argue. "How on earth could you know?"

"Crystal's right," Pearl sighs, laying a comforting hand on his shoulder. "Hunter fooled us all."

I hesitate. "Well… that's not completely true," I admit. I swallow as every pair of eyes in the room land son me. Their questioning, accusatory gazes cause my breath to rattle as I explain about Patrick's journal and how I pushed Hunter about the things therein, which lead to my kidnapping. "So really it's all my fault," I sigh, finally raising my eyes from the carpet, which I had been staring at exclusively during my confession.

The looks on their faces make me wish I hadn't. While everyone carries surprise in their eyes, it's Alexander's look that scares me the most. Utter disbelief clouds his face, but a fierce, draconic anger burns in his eyes. He stands and shakes his head at me. "It seems we have to go even further to secure your safety," he growls before laying a heavy hand on my shoulder and spinning me around. Before I can wrap my head around what's happening, he's marching me to my room. My instincts tell me that I won't be allowed to leave it any time soon.

"No!" I scream, pulling back from him.

"This is for your own good," he growls. I stare at him in astonishment. Thaddeus was right. He really had snapped. He grabs my hand in a carelessly crushing grip and begins tugging me away once more.

"Alexander Jacob Dragon!" Pearl finally snaps out of her stupor and stomps over to us. "What do you think you're doing?! This is our *daughter...*"

"I know," he replies, his eyes burning. "I'm doing what I have to, to protect her." As he drags me away, no one moves to stop him, frozen in shock. I continue kicking and screaming, but my pleading falls on deaf ears. When we reach my room, he shoves me in and slams and locks the door behind me. I pound on it, still screaming at him, even after he walks away. Finally, exhausted, I lean against the door and slide to the ground, sobbing.

Nathan may have rescued me from Patrick, but who was going to rescue me from my father?

<<<Angela>>>

Angela sits petrified on the couch as she watches the King drag his daughter away, her hands clutched into tight fists on her knees. She doesn't stop pressing her fingers into her palm, even when little red crescents from her nails appear in her skin and her knuckles turn white. She whips around to face Thaddeus. "What the heck was that?! Thaddeus, he..."

He shakes his head, cutting off her words. "I know. The King has... changed."

Angela snorts derisively. "Yeah, I'd sure say so!"

Pearl lowers herself gently into the seat beside Thaddeus, tears gathering in her eyes. "Alexander has had too much pressure on him since we awoke. He is a good man, just... lost," she whispers.

Angela feels a pang of remorse for her rash words. "I... I'm sorry, my Queen... I didn't mean..."

"No, I know… It's perfectly alright," she sniffles, waving a dismissive hand at the girl.

Thaddeus hesitates at her side. "Would you like me to show Angela to her room?" He offers.

She glances at him, surprised at herself for not thinking about doing so earlier. "Why yes… of course. My apologies, Angela. I'm afraid I am quite out of sorts today."

"It's no issue, my Queen," Angela hurriedly assures her, standing and dipping into a curtsy. Picking up the bag that Crystal left behind, she turns and follows Thaddeus from the room.

The instant they are out of Pearl's sight, he turns to Angela, lowering his voice. "Your room is supposed to be just beneath Crystal's… but I hate to leave her alone- for many reasons. Would you be… willing to stay with her?"

"Sure, Thaddeus. No problem," she replies. "I'm always happy to help." *The Princess may get on my nerves, but there's one benefit to spending so much time with her,* she muses. *She can be my backup when I leave to rescue Nathan. It's foolish for me to go alone, and I doubt mad King Alexander would spare me any other warriors- if he'd even let me leave at all! Crystal and I could get away for a while, I'm sure of it.*

Thaddeus looks relieved as he leads her up the stairs to Crystal's 'room.' "Thank you. It just wouldn't be good for the Princess to be alone- both because of her track record for frequent kidnappings and because… well, it's never really good for anyone to spend too much time alone."

"Yes, that's very true on both accounts," Angela acknowledges. "Don't worry, I'll keep an eye on her."

Thaddeus nods his thanks, relief clear on his tired face. "Well, here we are," he says, gesturing to the door before them.

Leaning forward, Angela takes note of the Phoenix on the door. "That's cool," she comments.

"Yes… remind me to tell you the story behind it another time," he smiles. Then, opening the door, he ushers her inside before locking it once more behind her. Taking a deep breath, Angela turns to find the bedroom empty.

"Crystal?" She peers into the massive closet, but she isn't there either. "Crystal? It's Angela!" When there's no response, panic flutters in her chest. Dropping the bag, she races through the Princess's many rooms, finally bursting into a room that smelled of food. A man stands there, watching her with wide eyes. "Where is she?" Angela demands. His quivering finger directs her to the final room, the balcony.

<<<Crystal>>>

I can hear someone shouting at me. The words are muffled thanks to the distance between us, but I know they'll soon find me. Lifting my face from the towel, I stand and walk towards the balcony, dropping the towel beside the pool. I've just reigned in my tears, but they soon start up again as I quicken my pace. Whoever's here will undoubtedly set ever more restrictions on me, and I just can't face that right now. I fly past my cook, Steve, without really seeing him. My gaze is focused on the one obstacle between me and relative freedom.

My hands close around the handle of the door, and with a desperate yank, it flies open. Staggering onto the balcony, I collapse to my knees, and once again the floodgates burst open wide. My face is coated in tears within seconds. Blinking them away, I stand and walk to the railing on the edge. Just a few inches away is the open air. Air, untainted by the stifling stench of control. Air... freedom... just out of reach. So close...

"Crystal!" The sharp voice is like a physical blow. I stagger back from the railing, only now noticing how close I had been to toppling over it. Pulling the hand that I hadn't realized I had stretched out back to my chest, I turn to face the intruder.

"Angela." I'm a little surprised. I figured dad would send Thaddeus or someone from the council to talk to me.

"Crystal, I know you're distraught, but jumping won't help anyone- it certainly won't help Nathan." Her bright hazel eyes shine with restrained anger as she glares at me, her hands on her hips. She thought I was going to jump?

"Angela, why..."

"I know you feel trapped, hopeless, and powerless," Angela interrupts, "but I can help you with that."

I pause, thrown by her words. "Wait... what? How?"

She gives me a small smile and relaxes her stiff stance. I guess she thought she'd talked me out of jumping. "I'll teach you how to use magic."

My eyes widen in surprise. I don't know what I was expecting, but it certainly wasn't that. "What... magic? Are... are you serious?"

She sighs impatiently. "Of course. I'll need backup for when I go rescue Nathan, and the more useful you are, the better."

I frown at the word 'useful,' but shrug it off. She's right, after all. "Okay, makes sense," I say. "But how are you going to teach me to use magic? What... what if I *can't* use magic?"

She laughs a little, then gestures for me to sit. She joins me on the cold stone, sitting cross-legged directly across from me. "Crystal, you can use magic. Everyone has access to magic. It just takes a little skill and a lot of practice to get very good at it. The more you practice, the easier it becomes, and you can advance to more difficult aspects of magic as your tolerance for it increases."

"My tolerance for it?"

"Magic, unlike Gifts, is taxing," she explains. "See, Gifts are a part of you. They use energy from your body. Using them is as easy as breathing. Magic is..." she hesitates for a moment. "Magic is how we use energy around us and focus it to obey our will. Our bodies become... a filter, of sorts. A magnifying glass. If you take in too much energy—magic—it can be overwhelming to your body, although everyone does have a little magic inside of themselves to use as well. Commonly you get headaches, nosebleeds, or dizziness, although sometimes you can get seriously sick and weak. If you continue using the magic past that point, you could end up fainting, going into a coma, or dying." She pauses, taking in the look on my face. "But that's rare, and for most spells, you can release the magic and end the spell at any time. You'll never get to that point, don't worry. We're going to be starting you off easy."

I take a deep breath, hold it for a few seconds, and release it gradually. Once the last bit of air escapes past my lips, I draw in another breath and look back at Angela. "Alright. How do we begin?"

She smiles at me and takes my hands in hers. "Close your eyes," she murmurs, "and focus on what you can feel around you." I do as I'm told. At first, I just feel the usual things—the breeze that plays with my hair, my nose as it begins to itch, the hard stones beneath me. Then as I turn my focus onto Angela's hands as they grasp mine, I notice a warmth that isn't normal body warmth. This is... almost electric. I instinctively tear my hands out of hers and rip my eyes back open. I stare at my fingers, which look the same as always. Breathing heavily, I look back up at Angela.

"What the heck was that?!" I demand.

"I was letting you feel my magic," she patiently explains, reaching a calming hand towards me. I flinch away from it. "It's nothing to be afraid of. Crystal, you have a similar magic inside of you. Everyone's magic has a distinctive feeling to it, although it's hard to perceive at a beginner's level. Now that you know what to look for, you can focus on finding it inside of yourself. ...It's something you have to do before we can continue." Just as she finishes speaking, I hear Thaddeus yelling up, magic carrying his voice.

"Angela! Your dinner is ready!"

She looks at me with worry in her eyes. "Don't worry," I laugh dryly. "I have my own chef. I won't starve. Go ahead. I'll be here when you get back," I chuckle sarcastically. *As if I had a choice. I can't leave my room anyway.*

She nods slowly and stands. "Alright. Try and get in touch with your magic while I'm gone, okay? The sooner you can use magic, the sooner we can go and rescue Nathan."

Yes, of course, everything's about you and Nathan, I internally sigh. "Of course," I respond, standing as well. "I don't want to leave him in there any more than you do," I point out. I expect a witty retort, but she just turns and walks away. I watch her go, her perfect hair swinging in time with her flawless model catwalk. Bitter jealousy suddenly wells up in me, and I struggle to swallow it back down. *Nathan deserves a perfect girl like her anyway,* I tell myself.

The thought doesn't ease my pain.

<<<Angela>>>

Angela hesitates before leaving Crystal's bedroom, fingering the soft strap that still held the mysterious box to her back. Looking down at the duffel bag filled with curious, yet-to-be-explored items, she sighs. *I really don't want to draw undo attention to the box. It's best kept secret... at least until I can figure out how to open it and find out what's inside.* Despite this, she finds it difficult to release the box, even after she pulled it over her head. Holding it in trembling hands, she finally crouches and slips it into a hidden area of Crystal's closet. She can't shake the feeling of its importance.

Standing, she takes a deep breath before unlocking the door with magic and relocking it behind her. Walking down the stairs, she pauses and places a hand over her stomach. It's tight with anxiety. Taking a shuddering breath, she struggles to relax. *Crystal will get the hang of using magic... surely the* Dragongirl *will be able to learn quickly enough to help me save Nathan. I just have to believe that he'll be there to save. I have to believe that Patrick would rather keep him alive than let him die. If I can't believe that he's still alive... I... I don't know what I...* She crumples to her knees, fighting back tears... choking on them.

Finally, gasping, she stands, quickly wiping the tears off of her face. With a surge of sheer will, she forces the tears to stop flowing. Coaxing a smile to her face, she throws back her shoulders in a stance of confidence. *Everything will be fine. There can be no room for doubt.* Thus renewed in her belief, she continues down the stairs and into the kitchen.

<<<Crystal>>>

Returning to my bedroom, I head into my walk-in closet. Flipping a switch on the left, I watch as the hidden drawer of jewels emerges from its spot in the wall. Unlocking it using another finger scanner, I reach in and pull out the large feather I had hidden there. I hold it up to the light, once again briefly admiring the shimmering blue-green colors before drawing it to my lips. "This message is for Zeke," I murmur, just as he had instructed me. "Zeke, it's Crystal. The Village needs more strength—as do the Sohos, I hear. Please come and join us in the Village. Bring everyone! We can help protect each other from Patrick's attacks. ...Um, end message," I finish. Quickly lowering the feather to the ground, I hastily back up a step.

The feather then seems to light on fire, just as Zeke had warned me. The feather is swallowed up in light, then suddenly vanishes. Blinking away the afterimage of the feather, I turn and close the drawer that had held it before stepping out of the closet. Assured that I had done my part, I head towards my snack room to get something to eat, although I'm not sure how much I'll actually be able to stomach.

In order to save Nathan, I'll have to learn how to use magic- something that I doubt I'll be able to do, despite Angela's assurances to the contrary. Taking a deep breath, I shake off my doubts. I can and will do this. I have to.

It's for Nathan, after all.

21

*Z*eke walks up the steps leading to his house, his head lowered dejectedly. He stops and slowly lifts his head to face the open sky as it glitters with stars and sighs heavily. *Oh, what I would give to join those stars in the sky! So free and without a care. What I would give to be unshackled from the worries of the world and the stresses of war and leadership…*

"Zeke?" The sweet, familiar voice lifts his spirits only slightly.

"Kate," he responds affectionately, finally lowering his face from the sky. "What are you doing up so late? The sun set a while ago."

"I could ask you the same question," she softly reprimands. "Why are you still up?"

He blows out a puff of air tiredly. "How am I supposed to be able to sleep when we are on the losing end of a bloody war? We're losing people left and right…" Kate comes up and places a soft, pale hand against his sun-kissed cheek, causing the words to die in his mouth.

"Hey. Don't lose hope, okay? There's always a chance. Crystal's still fighting- we need to do the same."

He chuckles quietly. "You're right, as always. I'm sorry my dear. It's just… I don't know what to do. How am I supposed to lead anyone in a war? I have no experience for such things!" he bemoans, gently moving her hand from his face to his chest. "My heart has no taste for such vile bloodshed. I am not a warrior… I can barely even lead at all! I'm not a born leader, warrior, public speaker... or anything, really," he finishes, his voice growing even quieter towards the end.

"Well, someone had to step up to the plate," she murmurs in return. "Which makes you brave, if nothing else."

He smiles down at her and leans his forehead against hers. "I love you."

"I love you too," she whispers, leaning in for a kiss.

Just before their lips touch, a feather appears in Zeke's hand in a flash of light. "Ah, saved by the feather," she chuckles before taking a step back.

Sighing, he lifts the feather up to his face. He hesitates. "Kate? What if it's just more bad news?"

"Then we'll deal with it- like we deal with everything," she assures him.

He nods, once again thanking his lucky stars that he had her to help him. "Open message," he murmurs to the feather before holding it to his ear.

Crystal's voice comes through clearly. "Zeke, it's Crystal. The Village needs more strength- as do the Sohos, I hear. Please come and join us in the Village. Bring everyone! We can help protect each other from Patrick's attacks."

Zeke is silent for a moment before looking up at Kate, who smiles encouragingly at him. "Well, there you go," she chuckles. "You got your answer for what to do now."

<<<Nathan>>>

The first thing Nathan hears is voices loudly arguing. They sound muffled by something... probably a door, he slowly realizes. *Why is it so hard to... think?* He groans to himself. *And... move? Why can't I move?! Where...* A loud bang startles him and he's finally able to force his eyes open. His bleary gaze takes in a tall boy about his age as he storms towards him from the stone door that had been thrust open so hard it left a dent in the wooden wall. Letting his eyes explore the room, he finds that the walls are made of both wood and stone, as well as the floor. He's lying on his back on a stone table with his hands tethered to it, as well as his ankles. *No wonder I can't move,* he realizes bitterly.

His inspection of the room is cut short by the boy's face as it takes up most of his view. "Do you know who you are?" he asks.

What a silly question, he chuckles to himself. "Yes."

"What is your name?" he presses.

Frowning, he replies. "Nathan Anderson." The moment the name leaves his lips, the haze in his mind vanishes. He gasps as his memories suddenly come flooding back and strength re-enters his limbs. "Crystal!" he gasps, struggling to sit up. "You... you didn't..."

"No. She's gone," Hunter sighs. Nathan relaxes back onto the cold stone, releasing his pent-up breath.

"Wait... why am I alive?" Nathan realizes. "I was poisoned..."

"Patrick decided you'd be worth more to us alive than dead," he groans, sinking into a chair near Nathan's knees.

"Why?" He dares to inquire.

Another sigh from Hunter. "Because you're the first person to lose their Gifts due to the use of magic," he begins, "And because he wants to use you as a secret weapon against the Dragons."

"Never!" Comes the immediate response.

"Yeah, obviously it won't be a voluntary thing," he smirks, standing. "I'll be back when your arm is healed a bit more," he announces, waving a careless arm in the general direction of Nathan's injury.

The next thing Nathan knows, the crazed Dragon child is gone. Breathing deeply to try and keep himself calm, Nathan begins focusing on wiggling out of his restraints.

<<<Hunter>>>

Hunter stops for a moment outside of the boy's door to collect himself before facing Patrick once more. When he steps forward, he suddenly finds himself face-to-face with a man a little taller than himself. Leaping back, Hunter yelps, "Holy... why, by the Great Eye! You scared the..."

"I am not interested in hearing a description of your surprise," the man interrupts. "I assume you know who I am?"

Hunter nods hastily. "Yes. Of course. My apologies, Dexter," he says, scrambling to bow. "I'll take you to Patrick."

"Good," Dexter replies, his hands behind his back. Hunter's stomach clenches into a knot as he takes in Dexter's intimidating look. Despite being much older than Hunter, he was still quite powerful, and that knowledge and power shone through in his dark grey eyes and stiff, military posture. Gulping, he leads the way down the hall towards the Conference room.

"Patrick?" Hunter calls as he pushes open the door. "Dexter is…"

"On his way, I know," Patrick interrupts, not bothering to turn around. "I'm just quickly bringing Bryce over to join us since obviously that foolish boy, Nathan, disrupted his first portal to get here."

Dexter's dark grey eyebrows raise a little at the news and his thin lips quirk into a small smile, knowing that he had stumbled in upon a bit of information he knew Patrick didn't want him to know. "Why, what's this?" he chuckles in his distinctively low voice. "What have you screwed up *this* time, Patrick?"

Patrick spins around so fast he nearly falls. "Dexter! I… um… I wasn't aware that you had already arrived!"

"Clearly," he laughs. "Maybe you should listen to your next in command before just assuming what he's going to say," he says, winking at Hunter. Warmth blossoms inside of him. No one had ever stuck up for him like that before. "Now then. What's this about a boy named Nathan interrupting Bryce's arrival?"

"Oh, it's nothing, really," Patrick stammers, scrabbling to cover his mistake.

"Obviously not. Unless you want to dig yourself into a deeper hole, Patrick, I suggest you tell me what you're attempting to hide." He orders, eyes set like flint as he folds his arms impatiently.

Patrick flinches. "Well, I'll let Bryce tell you what he knows first… and then I'll tell you what happened from there," he decides with a gulp.

"Fine, fine," Dexter sighs, unfolding his arms. "Get Bryce over here, then."

"Yes, of course," he hurriedly assures, bowing sloppily. "Right away!"

"He grovels far too much, don't you think?" Dexter whispers to Hunter, his eyes glinting with humor. Hunter snickers, quickly warming up to the 'Fearsome' Dexter.

"He certainly tries too hard, I can tell you that," he quietly confides. "Which is usually the reason everything always blows up in his face."

Dexter nods solemnly, his lips twitching as he swallows a smile. "Good to know," he whispers back.

Patrick continues opening the portal, heedless to their words. When he finishes, they all wait expectantly, staring in the direction of the invisible portal. Finally, the shape of a man appears and solidifies into Bryce's strong form. His blue eyes take in Dexter's presence and before anyone can utter a word, he dips into a perfect bow.

"Dexter. How good to see you again. I will admit, your presence here is a surprise to me. To what do we owe the pleasure?"

"Ah, Bryce, always with the gilded tongue," Dexter chuckles. "I'm just here to check up on Patrick's progress- or lack thereof- on Zilferia."

Patrick fidgets uncomfortably. "Yes. Well. ...Bryce, you are to deliver your report to both Dexter and I."

Something flashes across Bryce's face, so fast Hunter almost misses it. Fear, he realizes after a moment. That's what it was. *Interesting. I wonder why he's afraid. Does he have something to hide, perhaps?*

"Very well," Bryce accepts, bowing slightly once more before taking a deep breath and beginning his recap of what had occurred on First Earth.

<<<Nathan>>>

The welts on Nathan's wrists split and begin to bleed before he finally stops trying to yank his hands out of his restraints. Relaxing onto the stone table, he pants from his escape efforts. His wrists burn in protest from their agonizing and pointless ventures, causing his eyes to water. He refuses to cry, however, and instead turns his mind to other things.

Greg! He suddenly realizes. Extending his mind, he searches for his lost Familiar, but he's nowhere nearby. *Oh, Greg. Where are you?* He moans, even as his inactive muscles begin to grow stiff as they cool, his warmth being bled away by the stone.

<<<Greg>>>

Greg stops, cowering, in the cool grass as something, possibly a wildcat, passes over him once again. He continues to quiver even after the figure has gone. He hates being away from his Companion. Without the Bond between them, he felt lost and utterly alone. Standing on his hind legs, he stretches and peers back at Patrick's looming castle. *After I find help, I'll come back for you, Nathan,* he vows, dropping back to all fours and resuming his run through the irritating grass. *I'll never leave you behind.*

<<<Hunter>>>

An aching silence fills the air in the room after both Bryce and Patrick finish their confessions. The stillness is stifling as everyone waits with bated breath for Dexter's reaction. When he does finally break out of his statuesque stance, he surprises everyone by turning to Hunter. "Are *you* holding back secrets that I should know?" Patrick winces at the insinuation that he'd purposely done something to sabotage their mission.

"Um..." he hesitates, then decides to tell him. "Well, I lost the merfolk' Trident," he admits.

Dexter's response is surprise. "Trident?" He turns to face Patrick, exasperation in his voice. "Another rash, power-hungry decision of yours, I assume?" Before he can reply, Dexter just sighs and turns back to Hunter. "My boy, you're perfectly fine. No harm done. In fact, for a boy your age, you've performed admirably. Better than your immediate superiors, even." Bryce looks disgruntled at the remark but doesn't say anything. Dexter pauses, seeming to deliberate over something. Hunter's eyes feel as though they'll pop out of his head. He was pretty sure nothing would surprise him more.

"With Patrick leading these Hunters on Zilferia, almost nothing has gone right. You, however, have excelled at every challenge set before you. I hear you can even twist Gifts to serve you differently than they normally would?"

Growing increasingly confused and anxious, Hunter nods. "Yes, sir," he confirms, voice soft.

"Extraordinary! You are an exemplary servant of Dravyn," Dexter announces proudly.

"...Thank you, sir," Hunter replies, unsure of how to respond.

"And such an extraordinary boy should be allowed to do more than an ordinary soldier would, don't you think?"

Patrick, sensing what's coming, rushes forward. "Of course... but he's so young and inexperienced, of course, and this must be taken into account..."

"Inexperienced?" Dexter mocks. "He's already practically actively leading these people while you passively just sit comfortably in your castle, muttering to yourself about a couple of teenagers! I daresay he has more experience as well as a more realistic outlook than *you*. So, I feel perfectly justified doing this."

Hunter glances at Patrick's horrified face as Dexter pulls off his black gloves, confused about what's going on. His attention jumps back to Dexter as he takes Hunter's unmarked hand in both of his. "Reda elfo eltitu oyevig dnau oyn opur ewop fo eyer ehtonaw otsebi nyvard fo rewop ehtyb." At the end of the incantation, a white-hot burning sensation begins to scald the back of Hunter's hand. Yelping, he yanks his hand from Dexter's grasp. His eyes widen as burning orange lines form an eye identical to the one on his other hand.

"...Ytilibis nopser sihtt pecca I," Hunter murmurs. The eye blinks, then cools to a silvery blue. Both he and Dexter seem to be worn out from their ordeal.

"Congratulations, Hunter," Dexter says, clasping a hand on his shoulder. Turning to Bryce, who had been watching passively, he commands, "Bryce! Come swear fealty to your new commander."

Bryce walks forward with stiff legs before lowering himself into a bow before Hunter's feet. "My lord, I offer up my service and my fealty." Hunter doesn't move a muscle as he stares down at the top of the man's head, unable to wrap his mind around the new developments of the day. *What... what just happened? Did Dexter really just move me up a rank? Just like that? ... Wait, am I on the same level as Patrick now?!*

"Patrick, you too," Dexter adds.

"What?!" Patrick gasps, astonished. "I will not bow to an underling! I raised the boy! I..."

"Yes, and it appears that was the only decent thing you've ever accomplished," Dexter retorts. "However, he is no longer your underling. Rather, you are his. Hunter is now the commander of Zilferia, with you two," he points to Patrick and the still-kneeling Bryce, "as his main officers." When Patrick retains his dissatisfied glare, Dexter presses him. "Will there be a problem?"

Patrick hesitates, then growls, "No."

"Good," Dexter smirks triumphantly. "Now swear fealty to the boy."

With a face that looks like he bit into a lemon, Patrick finally joins Bryce with his knees on the dirty floor and his head bowed submissively. A number of tense moments pass before Patrick finally utters the required words. "My... lord... I offer up my service and my... fealty."

The two men remain motionless as Hunter stares at them, at a loss for what to do. "Bid them rise," Dexter gently directs him.

"Oh, right. Um, rise," Hunter nervously says. Bryce's face is emotionless as he stands, but Patrick's is full of humiliation and frustration. Dexter, however, is beaming with pride.

"Great!" He crows, clapping his hands together with finality. "Now maybe things will finally get moving around here! No offense," he adds to Patrick, his face revealing that he meant what he said and offense was indeed meant to be given. "Now then," he adds, turning back to Hunter. "What's the first thing you're going to do as the leader of the Dragon Hunters?"

Hunter snaps out of his stupor at the question. This was something he was used to- being asked to do things. "Well, I had an idea for what to do with Nathan Anderson," he proudly informs him.

"Fantastic! Now what is this plan of yours?"

<<<Nathan>>>

Nathan's tears are nearly beyond the point of his capability to hold back at this point. Having thrown himself at his restraints with ever more vigor, he got past the point of simple chafing and had managed to wrench his back. Lightning-like pain lances up and down his spine, mostly originating from the base of his neck. His breaths come in short, fast, measured pants as he tries to diminish or at least regulate the pain and his hands are clenched into fists.

When the door to the room opens once more, he stiffens his resolve. He *would not* cry in front of his captors. He just needed to separate himself from his body. He notices that four people enter the room this time. Hunter leads them, with a tall man with dark grey hair just behind him. Trailing behind those two are Bryce and a devastated looking Patrick.

"This is the boy causing all this trouble?" the grey-haired man asks curiously, peering down at Nathan.

"In part," Hunter confirms, walking up to the table to stand beside him. "Crystal's been doing the most damage. The Village Council hasn't helped anything either, of course."

"Council? That's new. Who's on this council of theirs?"

"The King and Queen, their advisors, some of the elders that…"

"Advisors?" The man looks thoughtful. "Who are they?"

Hunter looks a little on-edge thanks to all the unexpected questioning, but he obliges him. "Um, Vladimir, Zelda and Y'vette—although we are holding those two here—and Thaddeus."

"Ah. Thaddeus. That figures," the taller man sighs.

"Dexter, do you know him personally?" Hunter asks curiously.

He chuckles darkly. "You could say that. We have quite the history together. Who were you meaning this boy to target when you send him in as your secret weapon? Obviously he can only get to one person before he's restrained, so who would you choose for him to attack?"

Hunter hesitates as if it's a test. "Well, the Queen seems to be a pretty minor threat, so we were going to send him to kill the King…"

"Of course not," Dexter scoffs, immediately discarding the proposal. "This Giftless boy? Taking on someone with *four* Gifts and who will undoubtedly be on his guard thanks to Patrick's most recent kidnapping of his daughter? We'd be wasting this opportunity! No, you need to target someone more vulnerable."

"Who would you suggest?" Hunter asks timidly.

"Thaddeus," comes the prompt reply.

"Thaddeus?" Hunter repeats, a little surprised. It's clear to Nathan that Hunter had never thought about him. He continues to bite his tongue, knowing that if he speaks up, he'd lose his fragile self-control.

"Yes, of course," Dexter states, as if that was obvious. "He won't be suspecting it, plus the girl, Crystal, looks to him, does she not?"

"You wouldn't dare!" Nathan spits out, anger and fear for Crystal over-riding his own concerns and restraint.

The man just chuckles. "I'll take that as a yes. Why, I'm surprised you've only just spoken up, boy!" His eyes fall on his bleeding wrists. "Ah, I see. You didn't want to show weakness. Admirable."

"You won't be able to get me to hurt anyone!" Nathan declares, figuring it was high time for him to fight back, regardless of the pain.

Dexter chuckles. "Oh, my boy, for you to resist Hunter's Gifts… well, that would make you quite extraordinary, to be sure. And from what I hear, while you are a bother to us, you are *not* that special. Now then," he continues, turning back to Hunter. "Shall we begin?"

He nods, then faces Nathan, narrowing his eyes as he concentrates. A calming voice sounds in his mind, and he finds that he's powerless to resist its call to sleep.

<<<Greg>>>

The Sohos are closer to Patrick's castle than the Villagers, Greg thinks, *but I swear they were closer than this!* He sighs, cursing his small, slow body. *Nathan needs help* now! He then stops suddenly, ears twitching. Were those voices ahead? He stands on his hind legs, peering through the still night air.

The sound of wingbeats overhead causes him to immediately fall back onto all fours, but he realizes it's too late as talons wrap around his torso. With an abrupt yank, Greg finds himself hanging in the empty air. His tail reflexively curls into an anxious knot. Panicking, he sends his thoughts to the bird. *My name is Greg, and I'm a Familiar! Please, there must be some mistake! Let me go!*

His pleadings go unheard, and he realizes that he just so happened to have been kidnapped by the only bird too dumb to communicate with its mind. *No! No way can this be happening right now! Nathan* needs *me! Help! Somebody, anybody, please help me!* He calls, sending out his cry as far as he can with magic.

After a few more seconds of breathless terror, one of the Soho's river birds flies up and begins pummeling the Magpie. The bird's deadly talons spring open, and suddenly Greg finds himself in free-fall, hurtling at terrifying speed toward the hard ground. He squeaks in terror as he falls. The river bird dives to catch him, but its talons snap shut just above his back. One talon scrapes across his skin, but all it does is cut him and spin him around so he's facing the sky as he plummets. Above him, he can see the blue-green bird diving for him once more, although they both know it's too late.

When Greg's small body hits the ground, he feels a brief flash of intense pain, then a merciful numbness. His vision flickers and goes dark.

<<<Zeke>>>

When the river bird returns, Zeke steps away from the group of marching

Sohos. "I'll be right back," he murmurs to Kate before slipping away. *Ty,* he addresses the bird, *What happened? With the Familiar that was in trouble?*

The blue-green bird rustles his feathers anxiously from its perch on a tree branch about the level of Zeke's head. *The Familiar had been snatched by a large Magpie. He fell... I wasn't fast enough to catch him. He's... he's gone.*

Zeke frowns. "Where is he?" Ty wings away in response, and Zeke races after him. They slide to a stop beside the crumpled body of a rat. Stooping, Zeke carefully draws the familiar into his hands. "Crystal may know who this Familiar's companion is. It's only right that we let them know what happened," he sighs before quickly walking back to join his people as they travel through the forest.

<<<Nathan>>>

When Nathan wakes up, he half expects to have thoughts in his head that weren't there before—thoughts or desires to kill Thaddeus, primarily. To his pleasant surprise, he finds no thoughts in his head beside his own. Breathing a sigh of relief, he also notices that his wrists and back feel a little better. *Are they healing me? Why bother when Hunter obviously wasn't able to brainwash me?*

His musings are interrupted when Hunter comes into his room once more. "Ah, you're awake. How are you feeling?"

Nathan chuckles a little. "Well, it doesn't seem like your mind tricks worked on me—so sorry you won't be using me to further your twisted agenda," he mocks.

"We shall see," Hunter replies with a small smile. "Now then. Would you like some food?" he asks, holding up the plate in his hand.

"You're offering me food?" Nathan scoffs. "As if I even have a choice."

"Oh, you certainly have a choice. You can choose to do everything I say or become a simple lab rat for my scientists and sorcerers to study... or should I say dissect? It's entirely up to you."

Nathan hesitates. "How do I know you aren't trying to poison me?"

He just smiles in response, leaning forward to unbuckle the restraints on his arms. "If I were going to kill you, I would have already done so." When Nathan's arms are released, he slowly sits up, wincing at the sharp pain scraping at his spine.

Hunter hands him a plate with a drumstick, a roll, and some strange, colorful glop. "It's called pluva," Hunter explains at his questioning glance. "It's a jelly from Zelon. Don't ask where it comes from- you don't want to know," he chuckles. "But it tastes surprisingly good plus is highly nutritious. Eat it or not, I don't particularly care," he declares before reclining into the chair beside the table.

Feeling Hunter's observant eyes on him, Nathan picks apart the roll, eating the chunks slowly. His self-control wears thin as he bites into the meat, however, and he soon devours it, digging with his teeth at the last bits as they cling to the bone. Having no utensils, he scoops a little of the pluva into his mouth with his fingers. It's about the consistency of Jell-O and is a mix of shades of purple. It tastes like strawberries, grapes, and cucumbers, as well as something else with a bit of kick that he'd never tasted before. Although the pluva was odd, Nathan quickly finishes it off as well, licking his fingers clean.

Hunter leans forward, curiosity on his face as he watches him. "When did you last eat?" he asks.

Nathan pauses as he tries to remember. "Lunch, before I broke in here and busted Crystal out. Why?"

"Ah, then you've only missed one meal," Hunter surmises.

"Really?" Nathan says, surprised. He felt as though he hadn't eaten for at least an entire day. He turns to look out a window to determine what time it was and discovers that in his earlier examinations of the room he had neglected to notice the lack of sunlight- and windows.

"Yes, it's only about six in the morning," Hunter informs him. "The sun's not quite up yet."

Nathan wordlessly hands him the plate as he mulls this over in his mind. "So, what now?"

"Now you rest up a little. When you're recovered from both your cut and your self-inflicted wounds, we'll study you to see how that sorcerer blocked your Gifts and see what other things we can try to turn you into our secret weapon," Hunter evenly informs him as he straps him onto the table once again before standing and walking away, leaving Nathan with only his thoughts.

Nathan doses off and on throughout the day, and by the time Hunter visits him with his dinner, he feels much better. Whatever they gave him to help him heal sure did a good job. After he eats, Hunter releases the restraints from his ankles as well, allowing him to wander around the room and stretch his stiff muscles. He almost laughs with relief when the movement causes him only dull pain- in contrast to the sharp, electrifying pain that he had endured earlier.

"Good. You're doing much better," Hunter observes, watching him closely. "Now we can move on."

"Move on?" Nathan repeats. *That sure doesn't sound good.*

"Yes. Since it's taking a while to get into contact with the man who Fixed you, we'll just have another group of sorcerers examine you with magic and try to discover just what he did to block your Gifts so we can replicate it," Hunter explains, opening the door to the room. Although Nathan had long-awaited the time when it would open and he'd be free to walk out, he now hesitates. *Would I be able to fight Hunter off and escape the castle if I just ran through the door right now?* Another Dragon Hunter appears at the door as if summoned by Nathan's plans of escape. *No. It's not possible to do that right now. But maybe later...*

"Come on," Hunter commands, striding out in front and leading the way down the hall. Nathan walks freely behind him, although the guard follows so closely behind, he knows there's no chance of slipping past either of them. Resigning himself to playing along with Hunter's commands, for now, Nathan quietly trots along behind him, showing no outward resistance.

When they reach the designated room, he enters without complaint, although he stiffens when he sees the fifteen Dragon Hunters standing impatiently throughout the room, surrounding the lone chair as it cowers in the center of the suffocating animosity. The guard behind him shoves him into the room so he can close the door behind them. As the door closes, a panic similar to what he figures Crystal must feel whenever she thinks about this castle rises in his chest, flooding his body with ice. He remains frozen in place and hardly hears a woman speaking to him until she finally suggests the others leave and come back should she call for them. "Besides," she adds, "Who says this job even needs all of us anyway? We might get more from him if he's more relaxed. Too many people is stressing him out. I'll call you all back in if I need." After a few disgruntled murmurs, they all leave.

Hunter is the last to go. "Don't forget to report to me when you're finished," he commands her. "Also, when you're done, lock him up with Zelda, Y'vette, and Chet."

She looks startled at this unexpected change in plans. "All three of them?"

"Well, don't shove them all in the same cell," Hunter sighs, exasperated at having to explain himself. "Just put him in the same area as the rest."

"Ah. Right. Of course, my lord," she accepts, bowing a little. With a satisfied nod, Hunter leaves, shutting the door softly behind him.

The girl turns to Nathan. She seems to be about his age, yet filled with a surprising amount of self-confidence. "Nathan Anderson, is it?"

"Yes," Nathan answers shortly, watching her closely.

She laughs softly. "Nathan, I am not your enemy. There's no need for such discord between us. I would like us to be friends."

"Friends?" he scoffs. "With a Dragon Hunter? Sorry, lady, but you're barking up the wrong tree."

She smiles kindly at him, then leans closer, lowering her voice. "Could you be friends with a spy who's actually working for the King and Queen?" Her light green eyes twinkle at the surprise on his face. Extending a hand, she formally introduces herself. "My name's Alyssa Greenston, and it's a real pleasure to meet you," she says.

After hesitating a few more seconds and scanning her face for traces of deception, Nathan finally accepts the extended hand. "And the same for you. ...So are you going to break me out of this place?"

She laughs. "You sure don't waste a second. I'm afraid I can't do anything immediately, but when I take you to join the other three, I'll be sure to leave the keys in an accessible place for you to break yourself out. Just a word of advice, though," she adds when she catches sight of the elation on his face, "don't try and break out immediately. Wait for about an hour and a half. Most everyone will be asleep by then, including the guards. They've only just returned from their fruitless trek into the mountains and are exhausted. I bet you anything all of them will be dozing off, despite the new threat of Hunter and Dexter."

"Hunter and Dexter? You mean that grey-haired guy I saw yesterday? Why are they so scary? I thought Patrick was the fear-inducing one."

"Oh, he was at one point," she confirms. "But now that Hunter's the leader..."

"Wait, what?" Nathan interrupts, shocked. "Hunter's the Dragon Hunter's leader now? Why? What happened?"

"I heard Dexter was just sick of Patrick's failings," Alyssa shrugs. "Anyway, he's kind of helping Hunter out as he gets used to taking over, but he's pretty much got it down already. Dexter will probably be leaving in the next day or so. ...Oh, and he's kind of the guy over Hunter."

"So, Hunter's *not* the leader?"

She grimaces. "It's a little more complicated than that," she admits. She's about to continue when the door opens and the guard who followed Nathan to the room peeks his head in.

"Any progress yet?"

"Not yet," Alyssa responds cheerily. "But I'm sure it will just take a little time. Just give me a few more minutes, then we can take him to join the others." He nods in acceptance and closes the door once more. "Well, it seems we are out of time to talk," Alyssa pouts a little, turning back to Nathan.

"That's alright," he sighs. "So you're going to help me break out?"

"I'm going to help you help yourself," she smiles. "Just grab the keys from where I leave them. In fact, you could break out the other three while you're in there. Just be careful- the more people you take with you, the more likely you are to get caught."

"Okay," Nathan nods.

"Good. Let's go, then," she says with a wink before pulling open the door. The guard follows the two through the halls into the dark dungeon, grabbing a torch at the top of the stairwell. The flickering firelight helps a little to see the stone steps as they descend, but for the most part, the light is hardly strong enough to see anything very well, for which Nathan is suddenly grateful. He has a feeling the dungeon is quite filthy, judging from the smell cloying the dank air.

"Alrighty, here we are," Alyssa announces energetically. "Your new home sweet home!" She unlocks the cell door with keys from her belt and ushers Nathan into the small room. There's a small, simple cot in the corner and a bucket in the other corner, which Nathan realizes with queasiness must be the 'toilet.' There are no lights except the light given by the torch still clenched in the guard's hand, and that diminishes as he starts walking away. Alyssa stoops closer and whispers quickly to Nathan. "I'm leaving the keys by the door. If anyone asks what happened to them, I'll say I dropped them.

I'll see if I can get the torch to stay down here so you can see. Good luck, Nathan."

After they both leave, a faint, tired voice pipes up as Nathan scrabbles to find the keys. The torchlight doesn't penetrate the darkness deep enough into the cells to illuminate who's speaking, but Nathan recognizes the voice. "Nathan? Nathan Anderson?"

"Zelda?"

"Nathan's here now too?" This time it's Y'vette speaking.

"Come to join the party?" Chet chuckles. Nathan's alarmed to hear wet coughing following the short laugh.

"Chet? Are you okay?"

"I've been tortured off and on by Patrick for weeks. How do you think I'm doing?" he growls.

"Don't mind Chet," Zelda sighs. "He's just had a harder time than Y'vette and I. In fact, Patrick seems to have been not doing much with us at all."

Nathan frowns. "Huh. I wonder why."

"Who cares?" Chet sighs. "You're the lucky ones. I'm not sure how much more of this I can take before I crack and tell Patrick everything I know and pledge myself to him once more."

"It doesn't matter," Nathan quickly assures him. "Because we're getting out of here. Tonight," he murmurs, holding up the four keys. They glint in the torchlight, igniting a flame inside of Nathan. *No one can hold me back.*

Waiting the appointed hour and a half was torturous, but eventually, the time comes for their escape. Now came the hard part- unlocking his own cell. Crawling over to the door, he reaches up and feels for the keyhole with his fingertips. Finally finding it, he fits his other arm all the way through the bars as far as he can before bending it back. Grunting, he maneuvers the key into the lock. It takes a surprising amount of effort to twist the key, but he manages it. As he does so, his back spasms and sends him to the floor. The world around him spins as he pants, struggling to contain the sharp pain running up and down his spine.

"Nathan? What happened?" Zelda whispers.

"Nothing," he grunts, forcing himself back to his knees and retrieving the other keys. Scrambling to his feet, he staggers across the small hallway to

Zelda's cell. Fishing out a key, he tries it in the lock. His trembling fingers drop the key, and taking a steadying breath, he stoops and picks it back up. Tears spring to his eyes as his back screams in protest. Not making a sound of complaint, he fits the key into the lock before slipping it into his back pocket. Zelda slowly creeps out and into the faint torchlight. Her eyes are hollow and she seemed pale and tired, but otherwise seemed to be untouched. She narrows her eyes at him.

"Nathan, what happened to you? Are you alright?"

"I'm fine," he grunts, shuffling to the cell beside hers. Y'vette seems to be in much the same state as Zelda. Chet, however, seemed to be rather harshly beat up. One of his eyes was black, and there was dried blood from his nose and mouth caked on his face, as well as from a cut on his cheekbone.

He lowers his eyes, not wanting to see Nathan's response to his state. "Let's go," he mutters. "Assuming you're fit to lead us out of here, that is."

"I told you, I'm fine," Nathan asserts.

"Alright. Let's go, then."

Nodding, Nathan starts toward the stairs leading upwards; toward freedom. When he passes the torch from its spot on the wall, he tells Y'vette to carry it. She walks behind him with Zelda and Chet following closely. He stops at the wooden door at the top and listens carefully. When there's no sound, he cracks the door open and peeks out. When he sees that there's no one near, he nods to the others behind him. Y'vette places the torch where the guard first grabbed it, by the door. Nathan, wincing a little at the pain, steps out into the hall.

As the others blink rapidly to adjust to the brighter light, Nathan addresses them quietly. "Everyone should be asleep. Be quick and quiet, and we'll get out of here without a problem." The others nod, then wait for him to lead the way out of the castle.

There's a guard at the door that leads outside, but he's asleep, just as Alyssa promised. They sneak past him and emerge bright-eyed into the wind-swept terrain. "I can't believe it," Chet murmurs. "I've been there for so long, and you've been here hardly longer than twenty-four hours and you got us all out. Just like that." Nathan's unsure if it's disdain or awe that echoes in his voice.

"Well, I had inside help," he admits. "That girl that brought me down left the keys for the cells and told me how long to wait until everyone would be asleep."

"You found a sympathizer that fast? Incredible," Y'vette comments.

Another spasm of pain wracks Nathan's body and he grimaces. "Let's just get out of here, okay? We're not home-free yet." They nod in confirmation and follow him through the woods. Although it takes the injured group a while, they finally emerge into the Village.

"It's deserted," Zelda observes worriedly.

"What has happened while we were gone?" Y'vette asks concernedly.

"I don't know," Nathan admits. "Let's continue on. There must be someone still here... somewhere." The rest agree and cautiously follow him deeper into the Village, looking around in the pre-dawn air for signs of other Villagers.

Nathan jumps when an arrow suddenly clatters to a stop by his feet. As he does so, a fresh wave of agony washes over him, sending him tumbling to the ground. "Nathan!" Zelda and Y'vette cry, falling to their knees beside him. "Were... were you shot?" Zelda's hands race over his body, searching for a wound.

"No... I was... hurt before," he admits, his muscles tense as he fights his body's urging to scream with everything he has.

"Oh, Dragonfire!" A young man scrambles forward from behind an overturned wagon. He drops his bow and quiver of arrows as he hurries over. "Did I hit him? I...I'm sorry, I thought he was..."

"Jared!" The owner of the scolding voice strides up from behind a nearby house. His bearing is the opposite of the young man's. Whereas Jared seemed to be a kind and lighthearted man, the newcomer was harsh and weathered, as though he had seen the darker parts of life too regularly. "Did you just shoot at these Villagers? What have I been telling you, over and over again?"

"Identify friend from foe before you shoot," Jared mutters, looking at the ground as he scuffs his boot against the stones.

"Exactly. Now—"

"Excuse me, sir," Nathan interrupts as he forces himself back to his feet. Tears pool in his eyes, and it's all he can do to forcibly keep them from falling. "Jared here is just fine. Don't yell at him or blame him or anything. He didn't even hit me. Just startled me a little."

The older man's hard eyes look him over. "I suppose not, but that's only because he's a bad shot. ...You're obviously in pain for some reason or another, as is that boy," he adds, gesturing to Chet. "Jared," he snaps, returning his attention to the young man, "to make up for your idiotic mistake, escort this group to the hospital. If you come back before the end of the day, you'll get five lashings at the Post! Attend to their every need."

"Oh no, you don't have to…"

The military man waves a dismissive hand, cutting Zelda off. "No, no, I insist. It'll do the boy good anyway." With that, he nods farewell and strides away, his hand ever gripping the sword buckled to his side.

Jared glances up at them through his brown hair as it hangs at the level of his eyes, a bashful smile on his face. "Sorry about that arrow. I'm not exactly used to being a soldier yet."

Nathan frowns at him. "You don't look the type to be a soldier," he observes. "Why did you join?"

"Well, the King ordered every able-bodied man to join his army," he states, as though everyone knew it. *And maybe everyone does. Everyone but us, that is,* Nathan sighs to himself.

"He ordered it?" Y'vette looks like she had just been slapped.

Jared glances over at her bashfully. "Well, yeah, he was really… distraught. I like to think he politely asked us, though," he adds with a small smile. Everyone shifts where they stand uncomfortably until Nathan finally speaks up.

"Well, I'm sure that we can catch up on everything later. How about we all head up to the hospital now?"

Chet nods. "Yeah, we're wasting time just standing here." Nathan resists wincing when he watches him speak. He had already looked bad in the dungeon, but in the light from the rising sun, he looked horrific. His face and arms were covered in bruises, some of them beginning to fade and some of them very fresh. He had numerous cuts and welts as well- and not just on his face, either.

Jared snaps to attention at this. "Of course! My apologies," he quickly says before turning towards the hospital. "Follow me."

Nathan isn't surprised when the hospital staff recognizes him, but he is surprised to be so relaxed as they usher him to a bed. He used to feel smothered here thanks to all the time he was forced to be still and not move. As he lies on the mattress with nurses swarming around him, Jared comes up and stands beside him, looking concerned. "Is there anything you need? Anything you want me to do?" he anxiously asks.

"Yes, actually," he replies. "Go tell Crystal and Thaddeus that I'm here and that I need to talk to them."

Jared looks relieved to have a task to do. "Of course! Right away, sir!" He then spins on his heel and marches out the door.

Satisfied, Nathan leans back onto the bed and closes his eyes. Despite the nurses bustling loudly around him, he quickly fades to sleep, thoroughly exhausted.

22

"Crystal! It's not that hard! Just focus!" The exasperated voice belongs to the gorgeous brunette who sits beside me on my bed, her perfect legs crossed. The jeans were from my closet and were meant for me, although whereas they'd do no favors for my figure, they make Angela's legs look so feminine I was more jealous than I should be. The dark fabric clung to her skin, sleek all the way down where they disappear into her boots- which were actually also mine. Those black, high-heeled wonders didn't trip Angela up at all the way they would me, and she walked like a model in them. Her shirt was a blue silky thing that made her eyes even more beautiful.

The more time I spend with her, the more I hate her.

"Crystal! Are you even listening to me?" She demands, staring at me in dismay.

I sigh. "Yes! Maybe magic just isn't as easy for me as it is for you, okay? Maybe you just need to realize that even though *you're* a shining star at everything you do, not everyone can catch onto something so... *strange* so quickly! So just stop yelling at me!" My rant puts surprise and dismay onto her face.

"I... I'm sorry, Princess, I just... I wasn't thinking. I'm sorry, I shouldn't be so impatient... it's just... Nathan..."

The instant she says his name, I stop listening. Somehow whenever her perfect red lips form the syllables of his name, I feel like she's punching me in the gut. His name sounds all wrong when she says it. I don't know how she messes it up so much, but she does. I feel like she douses it in honey, trying to make it sweeter, when really she just doesn't know that it's amazing the way it is.

Or maybe I'm just jealous.

"Angela, it's fine. Stop apologizing," I sigh, interrupting her ramblings. "I want to bust Nathan out too. That's why I'm mad at you… because really, I'm just frustrated with myself. It took me too long to 'get in touch with my magic,' as you put it, and the longer Nathan's stuck in there with Patrick, the more likely it is that…" I stop and take a steadying breath. "I've been in his shoes. Twice now, actually. I know what they've done to me could be nothing compared to what they're doing to him, and I just…" I break off, refusing to break down and cry in front of her.

Her face softens in sympathy, and she reaches out and takes one of my hands. "I know. It's heartbreaking… which is why we need to do everything we can-" The words die in her mouth as she stands abruptly. "Oh my…! I can't believe I forgot! You have a Familiar, don't you? For Familiars, using magic is second nature… maybe your bird can help you better than I can!"

I feel a pang of guilt. I had forgotten about Nora. Sure, I was distressed and pre-occupied, but that was no excuse. I had forgotten about my friend, who was injured when Hunter took me. "Oh my goodness! Nora! Last I saw, she was hurt. Angela, we have to find her!" I rise as I speak, standing beside her.

She looks at me with sadness in her pretty eyes. "You know you aren't allowed out of your room," she gently reminds me. "But I can, and will, go look for her. I promise." She heads toward the door, then pauses and glances back at me. "Please practice while I'm gone," she pleads before unlocking the door with magic and stepping out.

An idea forms in my head when I hear it click back into place from the other side. *Sure, Angela, I'll practice,* I think with a smile as I slowly walk toward the door. *If magic is the only way out of this prison, then magic is what I'll use as my key to freedom. I'm sure I can figure it out.*

Placing my hand over the lock, I close my eyes and concentrate, pulling energy from the air around me as Angela had directed, filling myself with it. As I'm filled with the buzz of magic, I turn my attention to the small piece of metal that stands between me and my breath of fresh air.

<<<Angela>>>

Angela waves to the cook, Matilda, as she heads out the door, though once outside, her sense of discomfort skyrockets. She doesn't know these people, and they don't know her. Every suspicious gaze that falls on her makes her stiffen a little more. She had to get away from all the scrutiny, and quickly. Spotting a young man in a shoddy, home-made uniform hurrying toward the castle, she quickly stops him. "Have you seen a red-tailed hawk?" At his surprised look, she feels compelled to explain herself. "I know, it's an odd question, but…"

"You're looking for the Familiar Nora?" the man asks. Angela's shocked look must have answered for her, because he nods and continues. "I found her, broken, on the ground near the palace," he explains. "I took her home and have been helping her heal. Am I in some kind of trouble or something?"

"No," she gasps, relieved and surprised that she had already located the Princess's Familiar. "No, you're fine but that bird actually belongs to the Princess, so—"

"Oh! Of course! If I had known I would have returned her to the palace immediately," he assures her. "I was actually on my way to talk to the King and Queen, but I would be happy to return Nora to her rightful companion at the same time. I have a message for her regardless," he admits.

"Alright, let's go to your house and retrieve Nora then," Angela declares, her shoulders relaxing a little.

"Of course, ma'am," he agrees before turning and leading the way through the Village. After a couple of minutes, Angela speaks up again.

"So, what's your name, soldier?"

"Jared," he replies with a cute, shy little smile. "And I'm not exactly a soldier yet. I'm still in training."

"Ah, of course," she nods. "And what is that like?"

Jared gives her a slightly startled look, nearly tripping over an uneven cobblestone. "No one's ever asked me that before."

"What? Really? Why not?"

He gives a tiny shrug and returns his attention to their surroundings. "I don't know. I guess no one really cares to know what it's like for me."

Compassion and sadness well up in Angela's chest. "I'm sorry to hear that."

He shrugs again. "It's alright. It's not like I talk to a lot of people anyway."

"Really?" Surprised once again, Angela examines the young man closer. He looked to be about nineteen or twenty with a five o'clock shadow outlining his well-shaped face. His eyes, she notices as they dart nervously about, were bright blue with a surprising addition of a little green that accented them beautifully. She could sense that he was a very kind-hearted guy and was confused as to why he wouldn't have many friends. So, she asks him. "You really don't seem the type to not have any friends. If I had to guess, I'd say that you were the most well-liked guy in the Village!"

He stops dead in his tracks at this and turns to stare at her. "You really mean that?"

"Of... of course," she stammers, surprised at the intense look he was giving her.

Tears pool in his bright eyes, then he reaches out and pulls her into a tight hug. "Thank you," he says.

"For what?" she mumbles through his shoulder, which her face had ended up being pressed against.

"For thinking so highly of me," he explains, releasing her but taking only a small step back. "No one ever thought I could do- or be- much of anything before. I'm either invisible or the butt of everyone's jokes," he sighs, blushing slightly. "Sorry," he adds after a second. "That was rash of me to hug you..."

She smiles and gives him another hug, wrapping her arms around his neck. "It's fine," she murmurs. "I don't get many hugs."

His arms wrap around her and hold her close. She notices that he smells slightly of pine and apples. "Thank you," he whispers.

"No problem," she says, stepping out of the hug and smiling brightly at him. As they resume walking, she quietly adds, "Also, you can count on me to be your friend." His responding smile is so big it nearly breaks Angela's heart.

"Thank you."

<<<Crystal>>>

"I can't do this!" I shout to myself, dropping my hand from the doorknob. Despite numerous attempts, I just couldn't get the magic to do what I desired. It was like trying to hold water in a funnel. No matter what I did, the water just drained out the bottom, slipping away. "Why can't I use magic? According to Angela, anyone can do it. So why can't I? What's wrong with me? ...Maybe there's another way. A different way than what Angela knows," I think, walking over and plopping down in a chair by the table in my room. After sitting there thinking for a few moments, I sit bolt upright as a new thought comes to me, electrifying me. "The Sohos... they have *dragon* magic! Dragons have magic... and I'm part dragon! Kind of. Maybe if I get in touch with that part of me..."

Rushing back to the door, I rest my hand on the lock once more. Closing my eyes, I summon forth my dragon eyes, which is harder to do than it used to be, but I manage it on the first try. From there, I do as Angela instructed, pulling in energy around me. A word leaps, unbidden, into my mind. "Kcol-nu," I murmur. My eyes open wide when I hear a faint *click* from the lock. "I did it!" I quietly cheer to myself.

Before I leave, I hurry to put on my Glaoud skin outfit, so I can sneak through the palace and the Village without getting caught. I hold my breath as I slip out the door, softly shutting it behind me. I then quickly and quietly race down the stairs and bolt out the door when no one's around. Finally, I'm outside. I pause for a moment to revel in my freedom before turning and heading down the streets of the Village, wandering aimlessly. I don't know where I'm going, I'm just glad to be out of my room.

After a few minutes, I notice Angela walking towards me with a guy- who happened to be cradling Nora in his hands. "Nora!" I gasp quietly. I rush over to them, throwing off my hood. The guy looks like he about has a heart attack at my sudden appearance, but my attention is focused on Nora.

"Nora! There you are! Are you okay?! Oh, I'm so sorry I didn't come find you the instant I was back..."

"Princess, stop," she says, her tail feathers twitching a bit in amusement. *"You haven't been back long, and I hear from Angela that you've been locked up since then regardless. How could I hold you responsible for something you couldn't control?"*

I smile. *"Oh, Nora, I missed you."*

"And I you, Princess."

"Crystal, how did you get out?" Angela hisses, her eyes darting about anxiously.

"Magic," I proudly announce.

Her eyes widen in surprise. "Magic? You did it?"

"Well, I didn't light the candle like you asked, but yes," I chuckle, then turn to the young man still holding Nora. "I take it you were taking care of Nora for me while I was away?"

"Oh, um, yes," he confirms, carefully transferring Nora's small, healing body to me. "My name's Jared, by the way."

"It's a pleasure to meet you," I smile.

He smiles back, then seems to remember something. "Oh, and I had a message for both you and Thaddeus... could you possibly direct me to him?"

"Oh! Well, certainly," I agree, surprised. Who would have a message for Thaddeus and me? I ponder this all the way to Thaddeus's house, but bite my tongue to keep from asking. He clearly wanted to give us both the message at the same time, so I'll be patient and allow him to do so. Angela knocks on the door when we finally get there.

"Why hello, Angela," he says with a smile as he opens the door. "To what do I owe the... Crystal? What are you doing outside of the palace?" He exclaims in alarm. Glancing about, he quickly waves us inside. "Come in, come in, all of you." That seems to be when he notices Jared. "Why, who are you?" He inquires. Growing tired of holding Nora in my hands, I transfer her to the table.

"My name is Jared, sir," he replies with a small bow. "I have a message for you and the princess."

"Oh?" He raises an eyebrow curiously. "From whom?"

"Nathan Anderson. He says..."

"Nathan?!" Angela and I squeal at the same time. "He... he's alive? How is he? Where is he? How did you find him?" The questions pour from our mouths, causing the poor soldier to look quite alarmed.

"Well, he... I mean, he..."

Thaddeus intervenes in behalf of the poor man. "Girls, girls, just let him speak. All things in time," he assures us, although I can see he's almost as anxious as we are to hear Jared's news. "Come, sit down and tell us what you know," he invites, leading him over to his only couch.

He sits down gratefully. "Thank you." Taking a deep breath, he turns back to me. "I found Nathan this morning. I was guarding the perimeter of the Village, and he arrived with three others. The boy was really bloodied up, and the other two were women who didn't seem too bad off," he recalls.

"That must be Zelda, Y'vette, and Chet," Thaddeus figures.

"Well, I took the group to the hospital. Nathan asked me to come find you two," he says as he points to Thaddeus and me, "and tell you that he's back and that he needs to talk to you."

Angela looks taken aback. "He didn't say anything about me?"

"I'm afraid not," Jared says with a small, apologetic shake of his head.

Unlike Angela, I'm ecstatic. "Nathan... is back?! I have to go see him!" I exclaim. "Right now!" I race to the door.

Thaddeus calls after me as I speed out the door. "I'll catch up in a while! I'm not quite as fast as I used to be!" I don't bother to respond as I turn towards the hospital and put my little-used legs to use as I sprint towards the building. I barely notice that Angela runs right behind me, just as anxious to reach Nathan as I am.

He's asleep when I finally arrive, breathing hard. I stop at the doorway and look in on him, sleeping peacefully on the bed. He seems okay, and I sag against the doorway in relief. I sit in the chair beside his bed, earning a glare from Angela as she leaves to get another one so she can join me at his bedside. I reach out and wrap one of his hands in mine, finding comfort in the firm warmth. The sheets on the bed shift as I do so, uncovering his wrapped wrists. The bandages are red over his swollen wrists, and I gasp in concern. What happened to him? His hands were practically destroyed!

He stirs and mumbles my name as his eyes flicker open. "Crystal?"

"Nathan! Nathan, I'm here!" I assure him, leaning forward anxiously and looking into his face.

A faint smile lifts his face. "You're okay," he murmurs.

Tears form in my eyes and I smile and laugh a little. "Of course I am. And you're okay too, right?"

"Oh, I'm fantastic," he chuckles as he sits up a little. I notice that he winces in pain as he does so.

"Are you sure?" I worry. "I mean, you *are* in the hospital, again," I point out.

He smiles. "I'm fine, don't worry. I just hurt myself a little as I was escaping," he assures me. "Hey, do you know where Thaddeus is? I kind of need to talk to him."

"He wasn't far behind me. He's coming, don't worry."

Angela then arrives with another chair, which she drops at the door when she sees that Nathan's awake. "Nathan!" She's at his other side in the blink of an eye, grasping his other hand. I drop the hand that I've been holding and back up a respectful distance. I didn't really feel like watching them being all affectionate with each other. When I hear them kiss, I shudder and bolt out of the room. Walking just out of the hospital, I catch sight of Thaddeus finally wandering up, with Jared following behind.

"Thaddeus!" I call, walking forward to meet him. "Nathan's alright!"

"Oh, good," he sighs, releasing some tension from his muscles at the news. "I was so worried about him," he confides as he follows me back to the hospital. "You're sure he's alright?"

"Yeah his wrists are hurt pretty badly, but he seems to be okay overall," I say, leading the way to his room. I pause at the door, praying that they're done with their displays of affection, then open the door. Luckily there's a healthy amount of space between them.

"Nathan, you're back," Thaddeus says as way of greeting, his cane aiding his slow journey to his side.

He smiles in return and sits up all the way. "Indeed I am."

"How did you get out?"

He hesitates. "There was a spy among them. She left me the keys, so I busted Chet, Zelda, and Y'vette out with me while everyone was sleeping."

Thaddeus waits for more. "That's it?"

"Yeah, the escape went pretty smoothly."

"And the rest of your… stay there? What happened?"

This time Nathan hesitates even longer. I sit down next to him again and take his hand in mine, offering him comfort. "You don't have to tell us everything if you don't want to, I understand that… well, the things Patrick can do sometimes…"

He smiles at me and shakes his head. "No, it's alright…" He pauses and takes a steadying breath. "I passed out from the knife wound not long after you guys left, and probably also not long before Hunter and Patrick found me. I guess they decided to keep me alive. I woke up tied to a table by my ankles and wrists. I tried to get out but they were too tight—hence the wounds there—and I also wrenched my back, I guess. Although the doctor says that I popped my shoulder and a rib out of place." He gives a small shrug with his right shoulder, which must be the uninjured one. "Anyway, eventually Hunter comes in and he says that he's going to use me as a secret weapon or something."

"But he didn't?" I ask, looking him over. "You fought through his mind-control thing?"

"I guess so. It's not like I want to go around killing anyone," he points out. "Anyway, after that he decided he'd just have his sorcerers studying me to find out what the sorcerer who took my Gifts did, and…"

"Did they discover anything?" Thaddeus inquires.

"No, that's when I met the spy. She locked me up as Hunter told her to, and left me the keys."

"Hunter told her to lock you up?" Angela repeats in surprise. "Not Patrick?"

"Yeah. Oh, so apparently this Dexter guy showed up," Thaddeus turns pale at the name, "And he made Hunter the leader of the Dragon Hunters instead of Patrick."

"Hunter is leading the Dragon Hunters now?!" I gasp.

"Yes," he sighs. "Anyway, so Chet was in pretty bad shape when we got out, but Zelda and Y'vette seemed alright. We got to the Village outskirts, and there was nobody there, but then Jared here shot an arrow at me—he missed, don't worry—which made me jump and so I hurt my back more. He then accompanied us to the hospital, which is when I sent him to find you and Thaddeus," he says, looking only at me.

Thaddeus seems to be the most stunned by the news. "Dexter made Hunter the leader of the Dragon Hunters… who knows what this means for the rest of us?" He turns to me. "Did you contact the Sohos?"

"Yeah, they should be getting here around lunchtime," I estimate.

Glancing at his watch, he nods satisfactorily. "Good. That gives us a couple of hours."

Nathan turns and swings his legs out of bed on Angela's side. She supports him when he stands, although he seems fine to me. "Alright, well let's head back to the palace then and strategize or something," he says, bending to put his shoes back on.

"Are you sure you should be leaving the hospital so soon?" Thaddeus worries. "I mean, just look at your wrists and ankles!"

He shakes his head stubbornly. "No, I don't want to stay here. They're making me wait until they heal on their own anyway. They say the more we use the quick-healing stuff, the less effective it is. Our bodies build up an immunity to it, or something. So I might as well wait for them to heal naturally somewhere else."

"Makes sense to me," Angela pipes up, her arm still around him. "Besides, I don't want to let him out of my sight! He tends to get into a lot of trouble, I've noticed," she adds, playfully poking his nose.

Ignoring that, I chuckle a little at her comment. "Him and me both." He sends me a wink at that, which makes me smile like I haven't smiled in weeks.

"Yes, well, we should head back to the palace regardless," Thaddeus says, opening the door. "Since the Princess is supposed to be under lock and key."

Nathan pulls away from Angela as we leave the hospital, which makes a small pout appear on her face. I can't help but feel a little triumphant at that. "You're supposed to be locked up? In your own house? Why is that?"

I sigh and shake my head. "Dad's gone a little crazy. He seems to feel that the only way to protect my life is to take it away. ...Does that even make any sense?"

"What you're saying, yes. Why he's doing it, no," he murmurs, concern lines appearing between his eyebrows and on his forehead. "How can he not see that he's doing the same thing to you as Patrick did?"

"Exactly!" I exclaim, flooded with relief that *someone* understood. "I can't stand being cooped up like that! Luckily, Angela's started teaching me magic," I add, which I immediately regret when he turns to Angela with an admiring look on his face. "You're teaching her how to use magic?"

"Well, I'm trying," she says with a fake pout, glee in her eyes. "She's not learning very fast. I wanted her to be useful when we came to rescue you."

"No," he growls, suddenly angry at her. "You never endanger Crystal like that. I don't care what you think you're teaching her. Don't put her into harm's way to save *me,* when all I wanted to do was save *her.* Okay?"

She looks startled at his sudden animosity. "Okay. Sorry." She looks like she's about to cry.

Sighing, Nathan takes her into his arms to comfort her. "Hey, I'm sorry. I didn't mean to snap like that."

She shakes her head. "No, you're right. It was foolish of me to endanger Zilferia's heir, even for you... I just couldn't bear the thought of you in there with those horrible people..."

He strokes her hair softly. I feel a pang of envy as I watch them, which I angrily shove down. What was wrong with me? "Hey, it's alright."

"You forgive me?"

"I forgive you," he whispers.

Having had my fill of listening to their sappiness, I walk faster to catch up to Jared. "Oh, my goodness, Nora!" I exclaim as I catch sight of her in his hands once again. "I... I forgot again... I'm so sorry I left you behind..." Before she can reply, a thought pops into my head. I gasp. "Oh my gosh! Greg! I forgot to ask Nathan what happened to him! I'm so sorry, I'll be right back," I say to both her and Jared.

"*No problem. Go do what you must,*" Nora assures me. Nodding, I fall back a few steps to rejoin the happy couple.

"Nathan, you never told us—what happened to Greg?"

Concern flattens his features as he regards me. "What do you mean? He's not here with you guys?"

Dread hits my stomach like acid. "Oh no... something terrible has happened to him, hasn't it?!"

He frowns. "...We don't know that yet. He could have just gotten side-tracked on his way to the Village," he rationalizes.

"But how do you know that?" I cry. "We have to find him!"

Conflict darkens his eyes. "We don't know that he's in any danger," he slowly says. "...So I think we should stay here and decide what to do about the Dragon Hunters at this point."

"I do believe that Nathan has the right idea here," Thaddeus concedes from behind us, "Although I hate to abandon a Familiar. We just have to trust that Greg can take care of himself."

Everyone nods in response to this, and I grudgingly agree as well, although the pit in my stomach continues to tell me that something terrible had definitely happened to Greg.

<<<Zeke>>>

Zeke calls for the Sohos to stop before leaving the trees. They were about five minutes from the Village, but he wanted his men rested in case there was any conflict. They unpack food and quickly settle down to eat. Everyone was weary, although new hope also lit their features.

Zeke just hoped it wasn't in vain.

"Zeke, dear, please come eat," Kate invites, holding up a sandwich from her spot on the grass. Sighing, he gives in and does as she requests, sitting next to her on the ground. He accepts the food from her and rests his forearms on his knees and stares at the sandwich in his hand. After a few seconds, he takes a bite. Fresh lettuce crunches between his teeth and the meat is tender and perfect. This time, however, his favorite sandwich does little to quell his anxiety. He hardly tastes the food as he finishes and helps Kate pack up the rest.

Then comes the time for the final plunge. Gathering up his people once more, he turns his sight to the Village. As they walk, the abandoned buildings grow clearer. He frowns as a sense of uneasiness settles over him. Were the people just hiding? Or had the Dragon Hunters already wiped them out? Regardless, he approaches with caution.

Just outside of the Village, he calls the group to a halt. "I'll go on alone from here," he shouts to them. "I'll return when I have secured us a place to stay." With a bit of murmuring, his people accept this and settle down onto the ground to wait.

Kate stops Zeke before he walks into the Village. "Wait," she says, pulling him down for a quick kiss. "I'm not letting you go in there alone."

"Well I'm not letting you come with me. What if they take us for enemies and try and shoot and they hit you? I'd never be able to forgive myself."

"They won't," she quietly assures him. "They are honorable people, even in times of war, and they wouldn't shoot at a woman, especially not without provocation. They'll speak with us first."

Zeke can't find fault in her logic, so he eventually just nods, accepting her plan. "Fine. But stay close to me."

"Not a problem," she replies, reaching out and gripping his hand tightly. With a small smile to her, he leads them into the Village. He stays on edge as their footsteps fall quietly upon the cobblestone streets and stops dead in his tracks when he hears a voice addressing them.

"State your name and your reason for coming here," the voice commands.

Kate lifts her chin to hide the nervous trembling. "We are the Sohos, and we have come to aid the King's army. My name is Kate. I used to be the King and Queen's doctor and friend."

A pause comes before a man who looked to be in his fifties steps out from behind a nearby house. "Kate?" he chokes, walking towards them. "Is it... is it really you?"

Tears pool in her eyes as she recognizes him. "Daddy!" she cries, releasing Zeke's hand and darting forward, running into her father's arms. Zeke watches awkwardly, his hands in his pockets.

"Oh, my darling girl! The King told me after you were taken… what happened. I hadn't dared to hope… that you were even…" He can't muster the energy to continue.

"I'm home, dad," she cries as his hand rests on the back of her head, holding her close. After a few more seconds, Zeke clears his throat, reminding them both of his presence, although he felt bad to break up the happy reunion. "Oh, sorry Zeke," Kate says, pulling back from her father and wiping the tears off of her cheeks. "Dad, this is Zeke, the leader of the Sohos. Zeke, this is my father, Adam Kingston."

"It's a pleasure to meet you, sir," he says with a smile, extending his hand.

Adam shakes it firmly. "And it's a pleasure to meet you. I'm glad my daughter is dating a respectable man," he adds with a wink to her.

She groans good-naturedly. "Dad!"

He laughs, then returns to the business at hand. "So, you're here with your band of followers to aid the King? I admit, I've never heard of a group out there besides the Dragon Hunters. It's good to know there are a few more good guys to join us on this side of the war."

"Yes, sir," Zeke agrees. "Our group is actually made up of mostly those who have left the Dragon Hunters and those that we've rescued from them- like Kate. A few we've saved from the werewolves. …The dragons gifted us with magic stronger than an ordinary human's," he adds.

Adam's eyebrows rise in surprise at the news. "Is that so? Well, I daresay the King will be more than happy to have your assistance," he chuckles. "Where are the rest of this group of people you spoke of?"

"Waiting just outside the Village," he replies. "We didn't want to be seen as hostile."

"Good thinking!" Adam laughs. "Well, you can go ahead and retrieve them now. I promise we won't shoot. I'll go tell everyone of your arrival immediately."

Zeke nods. "We'll be right back with the others, then."

Kate slips her hand back into Zeke's. "See you in a few minutes, dad," she says with a brave smile. He smiles in return, then returns behind the house he first emerged from. As they walk back to the Sohos, Kate gushes to

Zeke, her excitement overflowing. "Oh my goodness! My dad is still alive! He used to live on the outskirts of the Village… I was always so worried that Patrick had gotten to him…"

"Well luckily he seems to be perfectly fine," Zeke points out just before they get back to the Sohos.

"Zeke! What's the news?" an anxious youth asks, scrambling to his feet as he notices his leader's return.

"They said they will allow us to join them!" he informs the crowd. They smile and cheer in relief. Zeke turns to Kate, lowering his voice. "Maybe now things will be easier," he murmurs hopefully.

<<<Crystal>>>

My dad reacts about how I expected him to when he learns that I snuck out. "You did *what?!*" he bellows. Mom tries to interrupt, but he ignores her, continuing his angry tirade. "Don't you realize how dangerous that is? You could have been taken again! Heck, you could have been *killed!* Do you not understand that I'm just trying to keep you safe? Why do you insist on endangering yourself?"

"Dad! I can't live my life in a box! That's no life! What you're trying to do to me is just as bad as what Patrick does whenever he takes me away from here! You're just as bad as he is!" Everyone in the room gapes at me in shock, but I don't care. I'm about to continue when there's a knock on the door.

"I'll get it," Jared immediately volunteers, jumping up and hurrying to the door. We all watch silently as he talks with the other soldier who had just arrived on our doorstep. After a few seconds, he nods and shuts the door before walking back into the room where the rest of us wait impatiently for his news. "The Sohos are here," he announces.

"Good!" I cry, standing. "I'm going to go welcome them and find them a place to stay," I declare. "And there's nothing *any* of you can do about it!" With that, I turn and stomp out the door. No one stops me, and no one joins me either. I'm a little disappointed that Nathan didn't follow me out, but then I realize that he's probably in more pain than he's letting on. So, I set off to greet the Sohos alone. I aim towards the side of the Village closest to where the Sohos used to reside, figuring they would probably be there. I'm right.

"Crystal!" Zeke and Kate call happily when they see me. They both surprise me with a hug. "Thank you," Zeke says when they're finished.

"For what?" I ask.

"For helping us out," Kate explains. "Zeke was really getting worried and we were running out of options, and people." He nods in confirmation at her words.

I shake my head with a smile. "No, don't worry about it. We needed help and more people as well," I insist. "Patrick's really been doing a number on us- and on you as well, I see," I add, noting how few people there are here with us.

Zeke's face suddenly saddens at this. "That reminds me... Jacob!" A young boy races up at his call.

"Yes, sir?"

"Where is the Familiar?"

"With my bags, sir."

"Go get him." The boy hurries away.

"Familiar?" I gasp, dread casting a grey tint onto everything I see. I have a bad feeling that I know who this Familiar used to be a companion to, as well as what happened to him.

"Yes, we found him just after he died," Zeke cautiously informs me. "I was wondering if you or your Familiar knew him or his companion."

"Yes, I imagine I do," I choke out. "Although I desperately hope that I'm wrong about who this Familiar is." When the boy returns with the broken body of a rat in his hands, I nearly break down. "Oh, Greg..." I reach out with trembling hands, but pull back before I touch him. "What am I going to tell Nathan?"

<<<Nathan>>>

"Thaddeus, can I talk with you alone for a minute?" Nathan asks.

He looks surprised at the request, then nods. "Of course." He struggles to his feet with the aid of his cane, then nods for Nathan to lead the way. Jared watches with concern from the couch, as does Angela. Neither of them protest as the two walk away, but their eyes follow them closely.

"What did you want to talk to me about, Nathan?" he asks as they slowly start up the stairs leading to Crystal's room.

"I wanted to talk about Dexter," he begins, watching Thaddeus closely.

A shadow of unease crosses his weary face at the name. "What about him?"

"How you know him."

"I don't…"

"I see your reaction every time I say his name," Nathan interrupts. "So, what's the big secret?"

Thaddeus looks down at his feet, buying time. Before he can respond, Nathan suddenly rips the cane from his hands and drives the metal end into Thaddeus's leg. With a yelp of pain and surprise, he falls back down the stairs, landing heavily at the bottom of the staircase. Nathan stands frozen on the stairs for a moment, the cane clenched in his hands. He had blacked out for a few seconds. When he returned to his surroundings, Thaddeus was on his way down the stairs.

"Thaddeus!" he cries, finally snapping out of his stupor. Dropping the cane, he races towards the fallen man. As he does so, the cane slides beneath his foot. His weight splinters the wood as he falls. His back hits the stairs hard and he cries out at the unexpected and sudden pain, paralyzed by it.

"Nathan!" Angela's face appears before his eyes as he blinks them open.

"Angela?" he murmurs, disoriented. "What…"

"You got knocked out," she explains. "So was Thaddeus, although he's in worse shape than you…" She stops for a moment, biting her lower lip. "They… they say that there's a serious wound on his leg. Which could only be caused by his own cane. They say… that you had to have been the one that stabbed him in the leg with it. …Intentionally." She stops talking and watches Nathan with wide, watery eyes, waiting for his response to this accusation.

He squeezes his own eyes shut, unable to meet her gaze. He hadn't been in control of himself when it happened, but Thaddeus had also clearly nearly died at *his* hands. He doesn't respond to Angela's implied question.

She gasps in shock when he says nothing, and he opens his eyes to see that one of her hands was clamped over her mouth. She lifts it enough to get out a muffled, "Oh… oh my…" she can't finish as she then bursts into tears.

"Angela, let me explain!" he pleads, reaching out and taking her other hand in his. She flinches at his touch but doesn't pull away. "Hunter must have somehow used me to hurt Thaddeus. I would never do such a thing.

Come on, Angela, you know me!" he cries desperately, his eyes searching hers.

After a brief hesitation, she nods. "But Nathan, if Hunter can control you without your even realizing it, how will we know if he's going to make you do anything else or not?"

Nathan groans as he realizes what must have happened. "Hunter put me to sleep before he tried to use his mind control on me. When I woke up, it seemed like everything was normal, so I thought he failed. He must have used his stolen Gifts to not only tell me what to do, but to not remember it when I woke up!"

Angela looks concerned. "Do you think he would have told you to do anything else?"

Thinking carefully, he reflects on his time there. "No... they wanted to use me as a secret weapon, but I'm pretty sure they meant it as a one-time kamikaze attack on Thaddeus."

She nods, then looks down at their joined hands before slowly pulling away. "I'm going to go check in on Chet," she says before walking out the door. Nathan watches her abrupt departure sadly. *Oh, Hunter,* he mourns. *How many ways can you screw up our lives?*

<<<Crystal>>>

I have the Soho boy follow me with Greg, since I can't bring myself to touch his poor, broken, lifeless body. As we head back towards the castle, Jared intercepts us from the direction of the hospital. "Crystal!" he calls. "Good, I found you," he pants.

"What's wrong?"

"It's Nathan."

"What? What happened?" I gasp.

"It seems that Hunter was able to control your friend after all," he says grimly in way of response.

A sickening feeling lurches in my gut at the news. "What happened?" I repeat as he leads us back to the hospital.

"He attacked Thaddeus, but he claims he wasn't in control of his actions at the time," he explains.

"If he says he wasn't in control, then of course he wasn't!" I quickly defend. "...Is Thaddeus okay?"

"It was a close call, but he's alive," Jared responds. "And as for Nathan, see for yourself," he says, pushing the door open to Nathan's room. I'm relieved to find that he's alone in the room. No Angela to be seen.

"Crystal," he says, sounding relieved to see me. "I have to... is that Greg?" His face pales as the Soho boy follows me into the room.

"Zeke says he found him like that," I explain, my voice wavering.

Nathan sits up all the way, staring in disbelief at his dead Familiar. The boy brings him forward and transfers him into Nathan's hands. Tremors wrack his body as he stares down at his dead friend. Suddenly he starts sobbing.

Turning to Jared and the Soho boy, I tell them they can go. After the door swings shut behind them, I walk back to Nathan and sit beside him on the bed. There's barely enough room for both of us. I put my arms around him as he cries, clutching Greg to his chest.

I don't know how long we stay like that, but my muscles are stiff by the time his tears abate. Sniffling, he murmurs, "I just can't believe he's really gone..."

"I know," I quietly sympathize, cursing the empty words. "...I know."

<<<Patrick>>>

Patrick glowers across the table laden with food at Hunter as he discusses something with Dexter. The disbelief and shock he had felt when Dexter had swapped the offices of himself and the boy had long since boiled itself into resentment and loathing. He had *raised* the boy. Taught him everything he knew! Dexter had no right to lift the untried boy higher than himself, and especially not to demote *him* with no reason besides to praise a boy who just happened to have an extraordinarily large amount of luck!

Dexter laughs at something Hunter says, causing Patrick's hand to promptly tighten around a berry he'd been holding. Purple juice drips between his clenched fingers, landing on his steak. Dexter glances up and notices this. "Why, that's a splendid idea, adding more flavor with the Dournberries!" he says, piling more onto his plate, moving them onto his steak before smashing them with his fork. "There are, however, cleaner ways to do so," he adds in a condescending tone, which Hunter chuckles at. Their attitudes towards him so remind Patrick of his lonely school days that for a moment it seemed like he was back there all over again.

The laughter of the other boys echoes mockingly throughout the courtyard behind the school, causing the small, dirty boy who was the target of their scorn to cringe. "Stop it," he quietly protests. The others ignore him.

"He can't even fly!" They chortle amongst themselves. "How can he not have *any* Gifts?"

Tears form in the young boy's eyes and one of the boys finally notices. "Aww, look, the little baby's going to cry!" he calls, bringing the attention of the others to the small, distraught face. "Hey, I know! How would you like to learn how to fly, Patrick?"

Young Patrick peers up at him with glittering eyes and wet cheeks, sniffling. "You would do that for me?" The hope he shows on his face causes a pang of regret in the boy for what he's about to do. But when the other boys flash him knowing smiles, he decides he must continue or risk being persecuted as well.

"Absolutely!" he confirms, helping the younger boy up from the ground. "I want to help you. It must be awful to not have a single Gift."

Patrick follows trustingly as the boy leads the way up a nearby tree. "Now what?" he asks, clinging nervously to the trunk.

"Now you need to give me your belt."

"My belt?" Patrick repeats incredulously. "Why?"

"You'll see," the boy promises. After a pause, Patrick removes his belt and hands it to him. "Now crawl out on the branch," he orders. "Don't worry, I'll be right behind you."

As he slowly crawls down the branch, the wood bends and sways in the wind, causing Patrick to stiffen in panic. "You... you're not going to push me off, are you?"

"No. I'll make sure you don't fall," the boy assures him. "Okay, stop there. Now lie flat on your stomach and hold still." As Patrick consents to the orders and does so, the other boy cinches the belt around his chest and arms, pinning him to the branch. Then he shimmies back up the branch towards the safety of the trunk.

"Wait!" Patrick calls frantically. "Where are you going? What do I do now?"

"Now you bob there in the wind like the loser you are," he says, loud enough that the boys waiting at the base of the tree could hear.

A group of three girls passes below, pausing to witness the spectacle. One of them laughs. "Patrick, you silly boy! Don't you know there are better ways to fly?"

Patrick blinks, disoriented, as he returns to the present, drawn back by a familiar voice. "...Patrick never let me do anything like that! That sounds amazing!"

Dexter chuckles. "I doubt he's ever even done it himself."

"Done what?" Patrick asks, confused.

"Oh, nothing," Dexter sighs impatiently, dismissing his question with a flick of his hand. Patrick just grunts in reply to the action, feeling too down to argue or fight back, bogged as he is with his unhappy memory.

After dinner, Dexter addresses both of them as they walk towards their quarters in the castle. "Well, it seems that things are in order here," he begins. "So I'll be on my way."

"What? You're leaving Hunter in charge of everyone without any training?" Patrick rages.

Dexter lightly raises one of his dark grey eyebrows. "I'm sorry, I thought you already trained your next in line so he could take over when you were unfit to lead. Or did you not have the foresight to do so?" he insinuates with a barbed look.

"Well... of course I did, but—"

"Great! I'm sure he'll be fine, then," Dexter declares, clapping his hands together with finality. "Hunter, you know how to contact me should you need anything, correct?"

"Yes, sir," he replies with a sharp salute.

Dexter laughs and pats him on the head affectionately. "That's a good boy. Try and keep Patrick out of trouble!"

"Of course, sir," Hunter replies, trying hard to swallow his grin. With one last smile at the new leader, Dexter turns and waves his hand through the air, opening a portal without even voicing a spell. Without a backward glance, he then steps forward and disappears.

<<<Crystal>>>

"Crystal?" Kate steps cautiously into the room. Nathan and I look up at her approach, but neither of us says anything. "The Sohos and the Villagers are about to have a meeting... we figure you should be there," she informs me.

I hesitate, but Nathan squeezes my hand reassuringly. "I'll be fine," he murmurs. "Go. They need you."

"...Alright," I sigh, instinctively giving him a light kiss on the forehead before standing and walking towards the door. "I'll be back soon, though. I promise." He gives me a tight smile and nods. As much as I don't want to leave him in his grief, I know that I should also start stepping up and accepting my leadership role in Zilferia, and going to meetings is just one of the things that I'll need to start doing.

Kate leads me back to the Dragon castle, where we find the Village Council and a few of the Sohos gathered around a large table. Susan and Reed are there as well, and they stand to either side of the only empty chair once Kate sits next to Zeke. Sighing, I squeeze past Reed into the seat.

"Alright, it looks like everyone's here," Vlad says. "Since Thaddeus is unable to come at this time, I'll be leading this meeting in his stead. Let's move to the first item of business. Zeke, we have decided that your people can stay in the houses that we had set aside for the contestants of the Games. There should be enough room for you there. You and Kate are invited to stay here, in the Dragons' home."

"We would be honored," Zeke accepts, lowering his head into a slight bow.

Vlad returns the gesture. "Wonderful. Next; Crystal Dragon."

I glance up from the table, which I realize I had been glaring at. "What?"

He smiles kindly at me before continuing. "Since the Princess can and obviously will do as she pleases, I suggest that we don't try and control her so much. Although we may not wish it, we need her in this war. All in favor?"

"Agreed," comes the response after some hesitation. I glance over at dad, who hadn't said anything, although mom had consented to it. Alexander's face droops with sorrow as he holds me in his gaze. "...Agreed," he finally acquiesces, moving his stare to his hands.

"Wonderful. On that note, Crystal, is there anything you'd like to say?" Vlad invites.

I start at the unexpected invitation to speak. "Um... sure, I guess." I clear my throat, buying a little time to get my thoughts together. "...Life as we've all known it is over. There is no going back. Not until the Dragon Hunters are stopped- for good. They've had the advantage so far in this war, but that does *not* mean that we can't turn the tables on them." I reach into my pocket and pull out the diagram of the Dragon Slayer machines that I had been studying. I continue as I unfold the paper and show it to everyone there. "This is a diagram of the machine they built to destroy the dragons. The dragons cannot destroy them due to their ability to resist fire and brute strength. However, as I have been studying this, I have found a way that *we* can break them down- from the inside."

Lying the paper flat on the table, I trace with my finger as I explain. "The *outside* of the machine is the fireproof part, but the inside is completely vulnerable." I point to the chair and the controls that rest inside of the machine. "They are controlled from the inside by a Dragon Hunter, but if we could sneak someone inside of one of the machines, replacing some of their men with ours, we could even use those machines to break down the others. That's the good part about them being powerful enough to take down drag- ons- they should be able to take down the other machines as well," I proudly announce.

No one responds, sitting there in astounded silence until Susan leans forward and looks at the picture as well. "It could work," she murmurs. "There are also some weak links on the outside that although are too small for the dragons to utilize, we could get at with our swords and knives, which would weaken the machines- hopefully enough that the dragons could then crush them."

I nod, verifying her words. "These machines *are not* invincible. We just need to rely on each other to crack them open, and then press on and use our combined strength to defeat the Dragon Hunters. It's not as impossible as it seems," I finally declare, leaning back into my seat proudly.

Zeke is the first to speak up. "I don't know about the rest of you, but I say we go with Crystal's plan."

"Agreed!" The others pipe in. Even dad accepts this, his smile beaming with pride. I smile back at him, happy that I finally did something right in his eyes.

"Wonderful," Vlad grins. "Well, I do believe that's all we had to discuss at this time. Therefore, this meeting is dismissed," he finishes, standing. The others follow suit. After retrieving the paper with the Dragon Slayer designs on it, I race back towards the hospital before anyone can stop me.

"Nathan," I gasp when I open the door to his room. "I'm back."

He smiles at me, tears still fresh on his cheeks. "I'm glad. ...It's good to have someone here with me right now."

I frown a little as I sit in front of him on the bed. "What do you mean? Hasn't Angela been visiting you?"

He grimaces a little. "No, not for a while. She said she would check in on Chet, and she hasn't come back yet."

"Chet?"

"Yeah. I got him and Zelda and Y'vette out at the same time."

I pause, torn between staying with Nathan and seeing if the real Chet is alright. I decide to stay for now. Nathan needs me more. "Why hasn't she come back?"

He shrugs a little. "I guess she just doesn't want to see me right now."

"Because of Thaddeus?" I guess. He gives me a slight nod, his head lowered so I can't see his face. "But... that's ridiculous! She's not blaming *you*, is she?"

"I... well, I'm not really sure," he admits, pain in his voice. I feel a pang in my heart at his tone. I'm going to kill that girl for hurting him.

"Well then that's her loss," I decide. "If she can't trust you, then I guess that's that. She's obviously just too blind to see the real you."

Nathan then lifts his head up and meets my gaze again. He smiles for the first time that I've seen in a very long time. "You have no idea how much I missed you." He then leans forward and wraps his arms around me in an unexpected hug.

I hug him back just as fiercely. "I missed you too."

"Let's never go so long without seeing each other again, agreed?" he laughs, pulling back.

I smile at him. "Agreed."

After that, we talk for hours and eat the dinner that the hospital provides for us. The longer we talk, the more he seems to heal- both mentally and emotionally. He doesn't cry anymore, although sadness lingers in his voice and he avoids looking at Greg's broken body. He says he wants to remember him how he was when he was alive. I understand that.

Talking about what happened on First Earth and at Patrick's castle seems to help him put the events behind him as well, which I'm glad about. I do the same, and don't shirk telling him how I felt about Chet, since I now know that it was just Hunter's mind tricks anyway.

We both seem to heal as we catch up, although our talk goes late into the night. We both fade off to sleep at about the same time. I didn't mind the hardness of the chair, much preferring to stay by Nathan's side and be there for him in case he needed me.

Honestly, I slept better that night than I had in months.

23

Nathan stirs as he feels the warmth of sunlight on his face. Opening his eyes, the first thing he sees is Crystal, sitting in the chair with her face on his bed. She's still fast asleep. A small smile tugs at his lips as he watches her sleep. It had been a long time since he had been able to do so, and he's surprised to find how much he missed simply seeing her at peace.

"Nathan?" A soft voice at the door causes him to turn faster than he meant to.

"Angela?"

She gives him a small smile as she steps into the room. "Hey. How are you feeling?"

"I'm… I'm fine," he replies, watching as she comes to stand by the side of his bed. "What are you doing here? I thought…"

She shakes her head before he can continue. "I know. But I didn't mean it. I know that my reaction yesterday was a little out of hand… you would never voluntarily do that to Thaddeus. I'm sorry."

He smiles up at her, glad he had her back. "It's alright. How is Chet doing?"

She shrugs a little and sits down by his legs on the bed. "He's doing a little better. I convinced the doctors to give him some of that quick-healing stuff, so he should be good as new in a few days."

"That's good." As he says this, Crystal stirs.

"Angela?" she murmurs, blinking open her eyes. She covers her mouth as she yawns, sitting up. "How is Chet doing?"

"He's doing fine, Crystal," she responds with a smile. "He says he'd like to see you, though."

"Me? Why does he want to see me?" she asks. Nathan's gut tightens a little as he notices a slight blush creeping onto her cheeks. Does she... like him? From what she told him, her feelings for Hunter/Chet were because of Hunter's Gifts manipulating her... but did it possibly run deeper than that?

Angela shrugs. "I'm not sure, but I told him I'd send you in."

"Oh... okay," Crystal accepts, standing and running her hands through her hair to straighten it. "I'll be back soon, Nathan," she assures him. He just smiles at her and nods, watching her leave with a frown. Every time he had to say goodbye to her it got harder and harder to do.

Looking into Angela's pretty eyes, though, he scolds himself. He had a gorgeous girl with him right now. He had no reason to feel so sad about Crystal stepping out for a few minutes.

<<<Crystal>>>

I stop outside of Chet's room, calming my pounding heart. I had nothing to be nervous about. This was the *real* Chet I was going to talk with... there was absolutely nothing to worry about. "Chet?" I crack open the door and look inside.

"Crystal!" He quickly sits up on his bed and waves me inside. "Please, come in."

"Alright," I accept, walking cautiously into the room. I sit in the chair beside the bed and keep my head lowered shyly. I'm not sure how to act around him anymore. I can't stop thinking about what I had felt for him when I thought Hunter was Chet.

When he doesn't say anything, I look up to find him watching me with his pretty green eyes. He gives me a small smile. "How are you doing?" he finally asks.

"Me?" The question surprises me. "I'm more worried about you," I chuckle.

He shakes his head. "That's not what I mean. I know you're fine physically. But I also know that you've been through a lot, and you may not have many people to talk to about it. I just want to make sure you're alright on the inside."

I stare at him in surprise. Not many people really cared about how I felt about what was going on. No one besides Nathan, actually. Warmth blossoms inside of me and tears rush to my eyes. "You... you actually care about how I feel?"

"Of course." He takes one of my hands in his and looks me in the eye. "Crystal, if anyone deserves to be happy, it's you. It's not fair that you have to go through as much as you do—especially with little or no credit or relief. Just know that I'm here to talk to, alright? About anything."

When he says that, the tears fall from my eyes. Laughing a little at myself, I self-consciously wipe them away and smile at him. "Thank you."

The next person I go to visit is Thaddeus. I haven't seen him since he fell down the stairs, and I want to make sure he's really doing alright. To my surprise, he already has visitors when I get there. "Angela? Nathan? What are you doing here?"

Angela starts to explain, but Nathan cuts her off. "I needed to apologize to Thaddeus in person."

"But... you should probably still be in bed!" I reply. "Plus, what if Hunter's mind control hasn't worn off? What if you still try and kill him again?"

"That's why I'm here," Angela responds. "Besides, Nathan is feeling much better already."

"It's alright," Thaddeus pipes up. "Although I'm touched by your concern."

I walk up to the other side of his bed, opposite Nathan and Angela. "How are you doing, Thaddeus?"

He takes a moment to respond. "Well, I've certainly been better," he sighs. "My leg is broken, and I cracked a few ribs. I'll be fine in a few weeks, though."

"They're giving you the fast-healing stuff?"

He nods. "It doesn't work on me as well as it used to, however. I used it a little too much in the past."

"Which is why the doctors are making me heal at a normal rate," Nathan comments. "So when I really need to heal quickly, I can still do so."

"Makes sense," I murmur.

Nathan picks up a needle laying on a tray next to Thaddeus's bed. "What's this?" he asks, fingering the sharp tip.

"Painkillers," Thaddeus chuckles.

"Huh." He's just putting the needle back when he suddenly lunges for Thaddeus's neck.

"Nathan!" I gasp, just as Angela grabs him and pulls him back. "Thaddeus—"

"I'm fine," he assures me, his hand over his heart.

Nathan turns white as a ghost as he realizes what happened and drops the needle instantly. He then turns and races out of the room. Angela follows on his heels. I just stand here, shocked at what I had seen, before collapsing into the chair beside Thaddeus. How was I going to help Nathan fight through Hunter's mind control?

After discussing the issue with Thaddeus, the solution becomes obvious and I wonder why I hadn't thought of it before. Hurrying back to Nathan's hospital room, I rush to tell him my idea before he can say anything. "That golden liquid that you gave me... do you still have it?"

After a few seconds of staring at me in confusion, he gasps. "Of course! Why didn't I think of that?" He then reaches into his pocket and pulls out the syringe.

"How is that still intact?" Angela gasps.

Nathan shrugs, then rolls up one of his sleeves. He holds the syringe over his arm. I notice his shaking increase. That's when I realize—he has a fear of needles. "Wait," I interrupt. They both look at me curiously. "Let me," I continue, gently taking it from his trembling hand.

"Thanks," he smiles gratefully.

"My pleasure," I respond, concentrating on slipping the needle into his arm. I then release the remaining serum into his vein, unsure of how much he really needs. A golden haze settles over his body before fading away. "I take it that means it worked?"

Angela frowns a little. "Well, there's no way to know for sure unless he tries to attack Thaddeus again."

"No." Nathan immediately rejects the idea. "I can't endanger him like that- not again."

"Maybe you won't have to," I murmur thoughtfully.

"What do you mean? How else could we tell?" Angela demands.

"The merfolk. The King's Trident, specifically," I explain. "He should be able to find out if it worked or not."

"Brilliant!" Nathan praises, grinning at me. "Let's go, then." He starts walking towards the door, then realizes that Angela wasn't following him. "Hey, you coming?"

She shakes her head sadly. "How could I? Unlike you and Crystal, I can't breathe underwater," she points out.

"Oh. Right. Well, what are you going to do here, then?" he asks.

"Angela, could you keep an eye on Nora for me?" I ask.

She shrugs carelessly. "Sure."

"Thanks!"

"We'll be back soon," Nathan promises, giving her a light kiss on her forehead. She just nods in response, obviously downcast because she can't come with us. I, however, am elated to find that, at last, it can be just Nathan and me.

"So... how are we going to get there?" Nathan asks as we walk out of the hospital. "We can't fly. I guess we could use the Lightning shoes, though..."

I laugh. "I was just thinking we find Vlad and ask if he can fly us there with the helicopter thing they picked us up in after the Third Challenge."

"That works too," he laughs. I watch his eyes crinkle as he laughs at himself. It's been quite a while since I had seen him laugh. If... if Angela was the reason he was so happy now, then I guess... I should at least try to not hate her so much. For his sake.

<<<Nathan>>>

Crystal seems strangely withdrawn the rest of the way to Vlad's house, but Nathan doesn't question her about it. He knows that if there's something she wants to talk about, she'll tell him about it. All the same, he finds his happiness slipping away the longer the silence stretches between them. The wound in his heart from the loss of Greg opens wider without her helping to keep the pain at bay. Her very presence helps him almost believe that he has a hope of healing, and it grows when she talks to him, or smiles, or well, does anything, really. He doesn't say anything, though.

He'll be alright; he doesn't want to burden her. She has a lot going on, after all.

Crystal glances at him and gives him a reassuring smile as if she knew what he was thinking before knocking on Vlad's door. It takes him a few seconds before he realizes that the smile was meant to assure him that the meeting with the Mermaid King will go well, not meant to help ease the pain in his heart.

"Crystal? Nathan? To what do I owe the pleasure?" Vlad asks after opening the door.

"I need to go and talk to the Mermaid King," Crystal explains. "Could we perhaps get a ride from that helicopter thing that picked us up from the Third Challenge?"

Vlad looks shocked for a moment. "Oh, that's right, you're friends with those creatures... sorry, for a moment I thought you wanted to go on a suicide run! Of course you can use it. I actually can't fly it, but Nehru can."

"Nehru? The announcer for the Games?" Nathan confirms, surprised.

Vlad chuckles. "Yes. Just let me get my shoes on, and I'll help you find her." He waves them inside before slipping his shoes on. "Alright, off we go!"

<<<Crystal>>>

The ride seems a lot bumpier than I remember. "Nehru," I shout over the howling wind. "Are you sure you can fly this thing?!"

"Well, I admit, it has been quite a while since I last flew," she reveals as we hit more turbulence. I cling to my seat and grit my teeth. My knuckles are white with how hard I hold on, but I don't relinquish my grip. I'll hold on for dear life until we get there, whether I lose a few fingers or not. I glance back to where Nathan's sitting. He winks at me and gives me a thumbs up. I stick my tongue out at him. He had opted for the safer seat, and Nehru had insisted that I sit up front with her. I figured it would be fine.

I don't think I've ever been so wrong in my life.

We finally reach the islands where Nathan and I had started the Third Challenge, then turn and fly south, away from the shore. When we're almost to the point where I believe the Merfolk to live, I have Nehru fly lower and hover just above the water. I then jump out without hesitation.

The cold water is a shock, but I quickly grow used to it. Nathan jumps in after me. We both surface and wave to Nehru as she turns and heads back to the Village. I told her that I'll just have the Mermaid King transport us back.

Now all that remained was to *find* the King.

When Nathan and I dive back under the water, we come face-to-face with a couple of giant jellyfish. I vaguely remember seeing them when we left the Mermaid King the last time. They seemed to be guarding the walls of the city- some unnaturally high growing seaweed served as the city's boundaries. I wonder if they'll attack us.

Deciding to try and talk to them before we get zapped to death, I open my mouth and introduce myself. Before I can get much out, a small merman swims up to us. The jellyfish let him pass. "Dragongirl! You're back! I mean, the King had me on the lookout for you, but I wasn't expecting a visit so soon!" He beams at us, sighing and smiling happily.

Nathan and I glance at each other, wondering what we should do. He gives me a tiny shrug. Sighing, I turn back to the small blue merman. "That's actually why we're here. Can you take us to see the King, please?"

"Oh, yes, of course!" the young scout excitedly affirms. "Those are actually my orders. I'll take you to him immediately!" With that, he spins around to face the wall of seaweed once more. "Follow me!" he cries, reaching out to touch the seaweed. It withdraws at his touch, causing an opening to appear as if he had pulled back some curtains. Nathan and I look at each other once more before following him through the gap. The seaweed closes behind us.

As we swim, the young merman bombards us with questions and unrequested information. "So, humans underwater. That's something I've never heard of before! Is there some kind of magic you use to change and become more like us?" He continues before we can answer. "This is my first assignment! I just enlisted to the army a few days ago."

"Really? How old are you?" Nathan asks curiously.

"I'm thirty moon cycles old," he announces proudly, puffing out his small chest. *Only a little over two years old? I guess merfolk must grow a lot faster than we do.* "I enlisted as soon as I was old enough! Mom doesn't like it, but Pop seemed pretty proud." He pauses at this. "Well, he wasn't angry at me, at least."

"Is he usually angry at you?" I glance at Nathan as he asks this, wondering why he's so curious about the boy.

"Yeah, I guess so," he admits, turning to look back at us with sad orange eyes. "Anyway, so my name is Curzon. Sorry, I meant to tell you that from the start! Guess I got too excited," he happily continues. *Boy, nothing really gets this boy down for long, does it?* I note with a small, amused smile.

Curzon rambles on for a while longer before we reach the King's sunken castle. As soon as we do, our guide falls silent and stops at the doors, trembling. Nathan catches on first. "He's afraid," he murmurs to me. He puts a comforting hand on the boy's shoulder. "Hey, thank you for showing us the way. We can take it from here, okay?"

"Yeah, and we'll be sure to put in a good word for you," I add.

He brightens immediately. "Really?! That would be great! Thank you so much!" With that, he happily swims away. Smiling at Nathan, we both turn and pull the doors to the castle open. The sunken castle is much the same as I remember. The dark stone covered in rich green moss, which seems to absorb the light, making it feel dark inside, despite the numerous underwater torches burning on the walls.

"Dragongirl! Back so soon?" Kaifeng, the Mermaid King, greets, smiling as he swims up to us.

"I'm afraid so," I reply. "I'm hoping there's something you can help us with."

"You know I'll do anything I can to help. What is it you need?"

"My Gifts were taken or blocked, or something," Nathan replies, his voice shaking slightly. "We're also hoping that you can make sure some... mind control has been reversed for me."

Kaifeng laughs and shakes his head. "You two, always getting into trouble." He peers at Nathan seriously. "I'm not sure I can do anything about your Gifts, not if the same thing happened to you as Crystal. The mind control should be easy enough to discover, however. Was it caused by another's Gifts?"

"Yes, actually," Nathan confirms. "But my Gifts—they were blocked by a sorcerer. It's not... it's not what happened to Crystal."

"Hmm. Well, we'll just see what I can do for you, then," he replies before turning and swimming down one of the corridors. With a glance at Nathan, we quickly follow him through the dim hallway. He leads us to a room with nothing but a safe in it. He opens it and pulls out the Trident. It regains its green glow the instant it's in his grip.

"Now then," Kaifeng begins, turning back to us. "Let's see what we can see about that pesky mind control." Nathan nods and takes a steadying breath. "No, place your hand on the Trident." Nathan does as he's told, and suddenly both of them freeze. Tremors run through their bodies and have labored breathing. After what feels to me like hours, Nathan's hand springs open, releasing the gold as he stumbles back a few steps. They're both panting lightly. My eyes dart between them nervously.

"Well? What's the verdict?" I finally demand.

The mermaid King doesn't respond immediately, staring thoughtfully at Nathan. "Whatever you used to cure him certainly worked. So well, in fact, that I doubt mind control of that sort would ever work on him again." Immense relief floods Nathan's face at the news.

"Really?"

Kaifeng smiles at him. "Really." He pauses. "Ready to find what we can do about your Gifts?"

Nathan runs a hand through his hair; a rare nervous habit of his. He nods determinedly. Kaifeng nods back, then lowers the Trident so it's pointed right at Nathan's chest. He then begins chanting the same thing he had when he'd tried to help me with my Gifts. "Heal. Fix all that is hurt, return all that is lost. Return control to whom it belongs..."

This time I can see what happens on the outside during the process. As the Mermaid King's energy depletes, Nathan seems to buzz with excess. As the King lowers the Trident, Nathan suddenly seems to explode with a white light. He then crumples to the ground. I rush to his side, blinking away the afterimage of that bright light. "Nathan?"

He stirs in my arms. When he opens his eyes, they look all black at first, but it quickly recedes into his pupils, returning his eyes to normal. "Crystal?"

"Nathan, are you okay? How do you feel?" I worriedly ask him.

He sits up and grins at me. "I feel fantastic!" He jumps up in one fluid motion, energy seeming to pour out of him. He then promptly turns into a fox, then turns back. "My Gifts are back!" he crows, taking my hands and happily spinning me around. He catches me in his arms and I laugh, dizzy.

"That's amazing," I reply, smiling up at him. Suddenly realizing how close we are, we spring apart. After a few seconds of silently looking at my feet, I look back at him, brimming with curiosity. "So how does it feel?"

"It's... man, it's incredible. You know how there's some energy we get when we grow into our Gifts? It's like that, only about four times better."

"What... what did you... see while he was using the Trident?" I ask, wondering if he figured out a way to do what I could not.

He shrugs. "A dark room. There was this red lockbox, so I pulled out a key and unlocked it. This white light washed over me, and the next thing I know, I'm on the ground."

"Huh."

"What did you say you saw, again?" he asks me.

I give a light sigh. "There were four pools of water on a hill. The water was supposed to flow, I thought, so I started to remove the stuff blocking it from flowing."

"And nothing happened?"

"Well, I didn't get to finish."

"Then that must be why it didn't work! You just needed more time!" He spins back to the mermaid King. "Can you try again? Please?"

He smiles and stands from the chair he'd been resting in. "Of course. I'm not sure how much time I'll be able to give you, though," he warns me.

"It's okay. Thank you for doing this for us."

He offers a soft smile in return. "Anything I can do to help you defeat the Dragon Hunters," he replies before pointing the Trident at me once more. I close my eyes as he does so, tense with anticipation. When I hear him begin his chant, I open then and once again find myself on the starlit hill. Walking forward, I peer into the first pool, staring at my reflection. Could this be it? At long last? Reaching out, I quickly pull more rocks and twigs out, using both hands and tossing them behind me. I'm about two-thirds of the way done when I feel the tug telling me to return. "No!" I gasp, desperately scrabbling at the stones. Too soon, I'm pulled back to the real world.

"No... send me back!" I cry, turning to an exhausted Kaifeng. "I wasn't finished!"

His bloodshot eyes pierce mine. "Crystal. I have no more to give. I'm sorry. That's all I can do for you. I don't even have enough energy left to send you home. I'm sorry, Dragongirl, but I gave you every second I could."

I feel a pang of guilt as I take in his drained state. "Oh... I'm sorry..."

He lifts a hand and waves it off. "It's fine. Besides, I was actually going to send a garrison of my mer-warriors with you."

"Oh, we can make it home alright," Nathan hurriedly assures him. "We don't need guards."

"No, no," he chuckles. "I was sending them to your Village with you. To help you fight those black cloaked... *land dwellers*. No offense to the two of you, of course. We figure that since they're on land, it would be more productive to fight them on land. We can't kill them all just waiting for them to come to us."

"But... can you even do that?" I ask worriedly.

"My warriors know what they're doing and are willing to make the necessary sacrifices," he assures me. "Besides, I can reverse the spell on any full moon."

"So... they just walk up onto land with us and their tails turn into legs?" Nathan asks.

He nods. "I have already placed the spell on them a few days ago, so yes, as soon as they are out of the ocean, they will be given legs." Stifling a yawn, he waves a hand towards the door. "Now go. They will be waiting for you outside."

"Thank you, Kaifeng," I reply, turning to go.

"Wait. How did you know my name? I don't recall telling you what it was."

"Oh. Yeah, my dad told me," I inform him.

"Alexander? Of course. Well, please do not share it with anyone else. Names contain power, you know."

I nod. "Of course."

"Thank you. Until we meet again, Dragongirl."

I smile at the weary merman. "Farewell, oh King."

"Thanks again," Nathan adds. "For everything." Kaifeng smiles in reply and dips his head to us in farewell. We both bow a little in response, then turn and swim out of the door and back into the hallway. As we make our way back to the front door of the castle, I look over at Nathan and find that he's still bubbling with energy. Literally. Tiny bubbles occasionally lift from the surface of his skin.

"Nathan... are you sure you're okay?" I can't help but ask again.

"Of course," he replies with a grin. "Never felt better. It's like... man, I just can't explain it. It's like nothing can get me down... there's nothing I can't do. I've never felt so powerful." I don't reply for a few seconds, staring at his face as he beams proudly at me. Envy suddenly hits me and my chest feels tight. I look away from him and shove it down before he can notice. I don't want to mar his joy.

But even on an energy high, he still seems to know me too well. He reaches out and takes my hand, pulling me to a stop before I open the front doors. "Crystal. I just want you to know that no matter what happens, I'm here to help you. With anything. I won't stop until you get your Gifts back too." I can't stand to look into his hopeful, hazel eyes, so I look away and don't respond. "Crystal," he repeats, his voice insistent. I drag my gaze back to his. "Crystal, I know you don't trust that it can happen. But I *do*. So just... believe in *me*, okay?"

Standing so close to him, I can practically feel the confidence radiating from him along with the energy. The look in his eyes, the intensity I find there, makes it impossible for me to deny him. Taking a steadying breath to help fight back the tears I can feel threatening, I finally just nod and look away again. He gives a small laugh and wraps his arms around me, pulling me into a strong hug. I lay my head on his shoulder and cling to him, silent tears running down my nose. He puts a hand on the back of my head, soothing down my hair as the underwater current twists it into crazy directions. "I will always be here for you, Crystal," he murmurs by my ear. "Always."

<<<Nathan>>>

Nathan watches the group of mermen as they swim ahead of him and Crystal, but his thoughts remain on her. Now that the high of regaining his Gifts was tapering off, he could actually focus on developing a plan to help Crystal get her Gifts back. Obviously swimming through the ocean day by day to get Kaifeng to help them was impractical, especially during a war, but what else could they do? If only she could find a way to visit those... ponds in her mind by herself, it would be relatively easy to get her Gifts back. Well, assuming it would even work. Still, it was a place to start.

The leader of the mer-warriors suddenly stops and turns to Crystal. They've reached a point where the water was only barely above their heads. Nathan can clearly see the twenty-four other merfolk shivering with fear. He feels a pang of sympathy for them. They were about to abandon all they'd ever known. "Dragongirl?" the leader salutes, "Would you do us the honor of leading us onto your land?"

"Of course," she replies, waving for Nathan to follow her as she swims forward. The mer-warriors part for them. Nathan walks up onto the shore, surprised that he isn't tired or feeling heavy like he usually would after getting out of the water, let alone after such a long swim. *I guess the effects of whatever the mermaid King did hasn't totally worn off yet,* he figures. He and Crystal step back to leave room on the sand for the mer-warriors to join them. The leader, Krasnigor, is the first to emerge from the water, a determined look on his face. His light green hair falls to his shoulders, dripping. Once he's out of the water to his chest, he suddenly falls forward onto his hands and newly formed knees. Crystal and Nathan help pull him the rest of the way onto the sand. Krasnigor gasps as his gills close, leaving thin white lines on his neck. Nathan leaves him to figure out what's happening and helps the next mer-warrior to emerge- the second in command, Keyana.

After pulling her beside Krasnigor, she slaps him away, gasping her first lungful of air. "Leave me alone, human," she snarls. "Don't touch me."

Nathan raises his hands up and steps away. "Alright, alright. Just trying to help." He and Crystal manage to get the rest of the merfolk out of the water without too much of a struggle, but teaching them to walk takes longer than they'd like. The sun had set by the time they and their group of twenty-five warriors reach the Village.

"Crap."

"What is it?" Crystal asks.

"I just realized. Where are we going to put them all?" Nathan responds. "The houses are all filled with Villagers and Sohos."

Keyana steps up beside Nathan. "Mer-warriors are trained to sleep under the harshest of conditions. We will sleep outside."

"Are you—"

"We will be fine," she growls, irritated.

"Alright, fine," he replies, done dealing with her. "You and Krasnigor come to the meeting in the morning at the Dragon castle, then."

"We will come," Krasnigor replies with a slight bow. Nathan and Crystal dip their heads in return before turning and trudging through the Village streets to the castle.

"Man, who knew merfolk were so irritating," Nathan murmurs to Crystal as they walk. "I mean I know Keyana just got her legs, but she doesn't have to be so harsh about everything."

Crystal shrugs. "Remember when we were told that merfolk ate people?

I'm pretty sure Kaifeng is unusually even-tempered for his kind. We can't exactly judge all merfolk on just what we know of him."

"Yeah, I guess that's true," Nathan admits. "Still. I wish Keyana would just chill out." Crystal chuckles a little at this. He looks over at her and his heart squeezes. He had missed her so much over the summer, and when he had heard about her, it was only to discover that she had been kidnapped *yet again...* There was no way he could do that again. Every time he wasn't there to protect her, she got hurt. Her dragon part would get locked away, her Gifts stolen, her own *mind* controlled by the Dragon Hunters... there wasn't much left for them to remove. And there was no way he'd ever give them the chance to take anything else from her, nor take her from *him*.

He would protect her. Always. No matter the cost.

<<<Crystal>>>

I wake up early in the morning, surprised at how good I feel. I don't remember why I'm so happy until I look down at the floor beside my bed where Nathan was sleeping. His words from the day before come back to me in a rush. *"I will always be here for you, Crystal. ...Always."* Warmth floods my body as I realize just how much he cares about me. *Maybe... Maybe if Angela wasn't...*

I stop the thought before it can even continue. Nathan may want to protect me, but our relationship would never reach the point that it had with him and Angela. *Besides, he was probably just saying that because he was feeling so powerful he instinctively felt the need to protect and provide. If Angela were there, he'd have said the same thing. Heck, if Sierra were there he would have said it. He's loyal to his friends.*

And that's all I am to him. And all I will ever be. I sigh heavily, my initial good feelings completely evaporated.

I quickly dress, then wake Nathan in time for the meeting. Keyana and Krasnigor are there, staring warily at all the people in the room, one hand on their sword hilts. "Good morning, Krasnigor," I greet, preferring to talk to him rather than his irritable, sunset-haired companion.

"Good morning, Dragongirl."

"How did you sleep?"

He looks surprised at the question. "We slept fine, of course. We can sleep anywhere, given the need. We can even go days without sleep at all if need-ed," he replies.

"Good, good… hey, I need to go talk to my dad. Feel free to sit down," I invite, gesturing to the table.

"We will stand," Keyana replies stiffly. I shrug and don't reply.

"Crystal," Alexander sighs with relief when he sees me. "There you are. Those two over there, with the orange and green hair. They look… like merfolk."

"They are," I reply. "Kaifeng gave them legs so they could help us fight the Dragon Hunters."

"What? Why would you ask him to do such a thing? To a mermaid, their tails are everything!" he gasps.

"I… I didn't ask him to. He was already planning on sending them before I even got there. It was his idea."

His face is blank with shock for a moment before he can manage to speak. "Well. Okay, then." He then looks over at Nathan, who is standing by my chair, waiting for me to join him. "Why is Nathan here? I didn't add him to the council."

"I know. I invited him." I wait for him to protest, but he just sighs.

"Well then I guess now is as good a time to talk as any." He waves Nathan over, who cautiously joins us. "Nathan. Crystal. I'm sure you are aware that Patrick is, as we speak, having people search for Rex, my other son."

"Yes, that's what I discovered on First Earth," Nathan confirms.

"Well, I can't spare many people to do the same, given this war we're in, but…" he hesitates and Pearl finishes for him.

"We need you two to find our son."

"What? *Now?* Are you kidding me?" I gasp. "Bigger picture, here! I can help with the Dragons, the Merfolk, and the Sohos. I can help with the Dragon Slayers. I can't… I can't just *leave!*"

"You can, and you will," Alexander growls. "You want to help? Fine. But I will *not* allow you to be on the front lines in this war. Do you understand me?"

I glower angrily at him as I roll this new development over in my mind. Was I *really* needed here anymore? The Sohos and Merfolk both know my mom and dad. Everyone can get along just fine without me. And without my

Gifts, dragon part, or dependable magic to use, what else would I even be able to help with?

I look up to find Nathan watching me with those sparkling hazel eyes. Once again, his words echo through my mind. *"I will always be here for you, Crystal..."* He was waiting to see what I would say. I realize in that moment that he would follow me anywhere. *He would probably bring Angela along with,* the voice in the back of my mind whispers.

But I would get to see Nathan more often and not miss him as bad as I had over the summer, I argue back. "Fine," I finally say, looking back at the tall form of my father.

He looks surprised by my sudden acceptance. "Thank you, Crystal."

Nathan rubs his hands together, looking excited. "Great! Where do we go first?"

"Quagon," Pearl replies. Nathan looks over at me and grins. I can't help but smile back.

"You leave today," Alexander continues.

"Wait... *what?*"

"There's no time to delay. Unless you think that we can gain more with you just waiting here, where Patrick can come and snatch you again at any time?" he prods.

I groan. "Alright, fine. But, Nora..."

"We'll send Angela with her when she's healed," Pearl assures me.

I sigh and accept this. "So, that's it? Just... drop everything and go?"

Vlad walks up behind me and lays a hand on my shoulder. "I know it's rough. But I've arranged to have a couple of people who live on Quagon to be ready to assist you with anything you need. They'll help you get to know Quagon and get a rough idea of where to look for Rex."

I look at all of their faces. "Wow. That was sudden... can I have just one day?"

"Why?" Pearl asks curiously.

I look down at my feet, embarrassed. "Well... I'd just... like to make sure that Chet will be okay," I mutter, a blush creeping onto my cheeks, which I quickly banish.

Alexander laughs for the first time in a while, and I look up at him cautiously. "Alright. I'm sure Nathan would like to say goodbye to Angela as well before you two leave anyway, am I right?" he adds with a wink at him. Now it's his turn to blush.

"Well, I… I mean…"

He laughs again and gives Nathan a reassuring slap on the back. "Not to worry, not to worry, I've seen it many times in my day. Alright, you two can both spend the day saying your goodbyes. Vladimir here will prepare a portal for you in the morning."

"Wait," Nathan quickly jumps in. "Can you… send us home first, too? Just for a little bit. So we can pack up the things we need and such."

"Ah, yes of course," Alexander agrees. "That's probably a good idea."

Vlad pipes up once more. "You'll also want to say your goodbyes while you're there."

"Wait, what? I thought you could freeze time between the realms while we're gone," I point out.

"Yes, well, that only works between your home realm and Zilferia. With both of you going to Quagon, it would be impossible to freeze the time while you're gone. Especially with Zilferia so out of tune with the other realms."

"What's this about Zilferia being out of tune?" Nathan asks, confused.

"Zilferia is the central realm," he begins. "The only way to travel between the realms is if you go through Zilferia. It's, shall we say, the 'key realm.' It has a connection to each of the other realms. It's through this connection that we are able to create portals. There are fewer and fewer points on each realm where the portals can be placed, and they're not as stable and predictable as they once were, either. The connection Zilferia has to the other realms is weakened due to the Dragon Hunters and the amount of stress that is being put on the land of Zilferia due to the war. Everything is a little out of balance. So I could usually at least slow the time in your realms while you're gone, but with all of this… I'm afraid I won't be able to do so."

"So, we're leaving our families for who knows how long and we're supposed to tell them and just hope that they're okay with it?" Nathan slowly asks incredulously.

"I'm afraid so," Pearl sighs. "There's no other way."

Nathan swallows and glances at me, then nods. "Alright. Whatever I can do to help."

"Thank you," Pearl says with a soft smile. "Ordinarily I wouldn't be asking this, of course, but…"

"We have no other choice," I murmur, once again looking down at my feet. If the Dragon Hunters were hunting down Rex, I *had* to find him first. Given what they had done to me, Nathan, and Hunter… the odds were not in Rex's favor. I had to save everyone I could from them. This had become my mission, for better or for worse.

The rest of the day seems to pass in a blur. I spend most of it with Chet, but I also said my farewells to the Sohos, the merfolk, and a lot of the Villagers. The news of what we were doing seemed to spread like wildfire through the Village, and every person Nathan or I passed would stop us and wish us luck. Many thanked me for all I had done for them, which surprised me. I didn't think anyone really knew what I had done, and I certainly hadn't expected to receive any recognition. Still, it warmed my heart to hear how many people felt more hopeful about the situation with the Dragon Hunters thanks to me, despite what I felt were failures every time I came in contact with the group.

Chet heals quickly, but not quickly enough to get permission to go with Nathan and me to Quagon. He says he wants to come with me and help me however he can, and while I would like that, I actually side with my parents on keeping him in Zilferia. Although it cheers him up a little when I tell him what a great help he'd be to me, with him protecting my parents and the rest of the Council. I can't help but want to take him with me, though. He seems to get snatched by the Dragon Hunters almost as often as I do. I worry about him.

Nathan spends the night on my floor again since there's nowhere else for him to sleep. The hospital doesn't have much room either, and they already told him he's cleared to go anyway. We're both fine with the arrangement. I feel comforted with him sleeping in the same room, and he's fine sleeping on the floor. He falls asleep before I do. Long before I do, in fact. It seemed to have taken the entire day, but the energy spike from getting his Gifts back had finally led to the small crash that eventually follows. I doubt anything could really wake him at this point.

Regardless, I walk to my balcony quietly so I don't run the risk of waking him. Once out in the night, I breathe in the fresh, clean air and lean on the railing, looking out at the land. The terrible wounds ripped into the earth are cloaked in darkness, and for a moment I'm able to convince myself that there is no desperate war raging on Zilferia. I'm able to convince myself that the only thing I need to concern myself with is finding Rex, with Nathan as my partner. Just as we decided all those months ago, standing in this very spot together.

Everything had seemed so much simpler back then. And while maybe things are worse now, there was one spot of light amidst the darkness that surrounded me. One thing that I could hold onto, through all the crap that happened and all the hopelessness that dragged me down.

After all, he promised he would be there for me. Always.

EPILOGUE

A strong wind roars through the forest, tearing past the trees so quickly they don't even make their usual music. Leaves are ripped from the trees and pulled along through the air, trembling with the force of the wind. Their winding path through the trees goes uninterrupted until-

"Gah!" Hunter cries, prying the leaves from his face. "Stupid leaves," he mutters, dropping them to the ground. The wind gusts once more and he pulls his cloak closer, still mumbling to himself.

"Hunter?" The call comes from behind him- from the direction of the castle, which was getting further away with every frustrated step he took. "Hunter?" The call comes again, closer this time. Recognizing the voice, Hunter stops with a sigh. Soon, a blonde-haired girl comes into view.

"Alyssa," Hunter groans, "I want to be alone. You know that."

She comes closer, mischievousness sparkling in her light green eyes. "No one really wants to be alone, silly. Even the fearless new leader of the Dragon Hunters." She comes closer and makes his hood lie flat on his shoulders and back. She leaves her arms there, resting on his shoulders. "Do you *really* want to send me away, my dashing Prince?" she adds flirtatiously.

He laughs, finally relaxing. "You always know just how to soften me up," he smiles. She smiles in return before stretching up to kiss him. Their kiss is interrupted by a crashing sound in the trees nearby. Hunter immediately jumps back from Alyssa, pulling his sword out in the same movement.

Alyssa mirrors his movements. "Stay behind me," he murmurs, quickly and quietly moving towards the source of the noise.

Hunter emerges into a small clearing. Waving for Alyssa to stay among the trees, he slowly creeps into the clearing. Before Hunter can react, a lithe red dragon slithers into the clearing. It growls at Hunter, who growls back. Hunter then charges the beast, which leaps over him. Hunter's sword lightly scrapes the belly as it flies over him, not even drawing blood. Spinning, he catches sight of the dragon's true goal.

"No!" he cries, panic flooding him. He stumbles in his haste to get to them, but he's too late. Alyssa, who had joined him in the clearing, braces herself for the oncoming dragon. She swings her sword as its paw nears her, severing one of its fingers. The dragon knocks the sword out of her hand and grabs her in its giant paw. It picks her up, spins back to Hunter and growls once more before jumping into the air and unfurling its long wings.

Hunter remains frozen, watching the retreating red beast, Alyssa's cries ringing in his ears. After a few moments, he curses himself for his slow thinking. Using his Gift for flying, he takes to the air. He puts all of his energy into following the dragon, but it's too fast for him and is soon completely out of sight. Hunter finally crashes to the ground, landing roughly and falling onto his knees in the dirt amongst the broken branches. Tears fill his vision for the first time in years, and they can't seem to stop coming.

Finally drained, he forces himself back to his feet. What was he doing crying in the forest when he could be assembling his men to go and attack the beast? He was the *leader* of the Dragon Hunters. Patrick wouldn't deny him this time. He couldn't.

"Don't worry, Alyssa," he murmurs to himself, staring into the sky, which remains empty and silent. Only the stars wink back at him. More tears trickle down his cheeks as he stares into the darkness. "I love you, Alyssa. And I'm coming for you. I *will* rescue you," he vows passionately. "Whatever it takes."

Stiffening his resolve and wiping away his tears, Hunter sets his face into a mask of anger and storms back toward the castle.

There was much for him to do.

BOOKS BY KATIE CHERRY

The Crystal Dragon Saga

Rising from Dust: Companion novella
* * *
Crystal Dragon
Crystal Hope
Crystal Lies
Crystal Curse - June 24, 2020
Crystal Allegiance - July 29, 2020
Crystal Fate - August 26, 2020
Crystal War - September 24, 2020
* * *
Crystal Dragon Saga Boxed Set: Books 1-3

The Dragon Blood Trilogy

Dragon Blood
Dragon Soul
Dragon Heart

ABOUT THE AUTHOR

Katie Cherry is an avid reader who has been devouring books since before most kids could read, leading her to her first attempt at writing a novel in eighth grade. So far, she has most of the Crystal Dragon Saga finished, including a companion novella you can get for free when you join her newsletter. She's also completed the Dragon Blood Trilogy. Her dream is to be a full-time mother while also providing for them through her writing.

1. Find her current progress on Facebook at her profile, Author Katie Cherry, or the Facebook page https://www.facebook.com/KatieCherryFantasy/.

2. Follow her on Amazon to get an email ONLY when there's a new release: https://www.amazon.com/-/e/B07H3FXS7D

3. Join her newsletter to hear about free fantasy books Katie finds, sales, writing updates, and exclusive MONTHLY freebies: https://www.subscribepage.com/katiecherrysfantasyemails

4. Support her on Patreon for early releases, cover reveals, weekly sneak peeks, and eventually merchandise and giveaways! https://www.patreon.com/KatieCherry

5. Join her fan group on Facebook, Katie Cherry's Book Wyrms, to participate in weekly live videos and so much more! https://www.facebook.com/groups/1275626482623759/

6. She's also on Instagram @katiecherryfantasy and Twitter @KatieCherry818!

Printed in Great Britain
by Amazon

46536209R00203